BURSTS OF FIRE

ADDICTED TO HEAVEN
BOOK ONE

SUSAN FOREST

LAKSA MEDIA GROUPS INC.
www.laksamedia.com

Bursts of Fire
Addicted to Heaven (Book One)

Laksa Media Groups supports copyright. Copyright fuels creativity, encourages diverse voices, promotes free speech, and creates a vibrant culture. Thank you for buying an authorized edition of this book and for complying with copyright laws by not reproducing, scanning, or distributing any part of it in any form without permission. You are supporting writers and allowing Laksa Media Groups to continue to publish books for every reader.

Library and Archives Canada Cataloguing in Publication

Forest, Susan, author
     Bursts of fire / Susan Forest.

(Addicted to Heaven saga)
Issued in print and electronic formats.
ISBN 978-1-988140-11-7 (hardcover).--ISBN 978-1-988140-10-0 (softcover).--ISBN 978-1-988140-12-4 (PDF).--ISBN 978-1-988140-14-8 (EPUB).--ISBN 978-1-988140-13-1 (Kindle)

     I. Title.

PS8561.O6785B87 2018   C813'.54   C2017-906856-3
                                      C2017-906857-1

LAKSA MEDIA GROUPS INC.
Calgary, Alberta, Canada
www.laksamedia.com
info@laksamedia.com

Cover and Interior Design by Samantha M. Beiko
Map by Holly Totten
Edited by Lucas K. Law and Samantha M. Beiko

FIRST EDITION

SUSAN

BURSTS OF FIRE

ADDICTED TO HEAVEN

BOOKS BY SUSAN FOREST

ADDICTED TO HEAVEN SERIES
Bursts of Fire
Fields of Marigolds (forthcoming)

Immunity to Strange Tales
  (short story collection from Five Rivers Publishing)

BOOKS EDITED BY SUSAN FOREST AND LUCAS K. LAW

LAKSA ANTHOLOGY SERIES: SPECULATIVE FICTION
Strangers Among Us: Tales of the Underdogs and Outcasts
The Sum of Us: Tales of the Bonded and Bound
Shades Within Us: Tales of Migrations and Fractured Borders
Seasons Between Us: Tales of Identities and Memories (forthcoming)

To *Jim, Margy, Kathy,* and *Terry*.
Fighters, all.

PROLOGUE

The door, crafted of Arcan valley oak and inlaid with exotic woods imported from warmer lands—some from as far away as Aadi-of-the-Valley—gleamed in the light of Talanda Falkyn's candle. Though the hour was late, the door was unguarded. After all, these were days of peace and prosperity in the seven realms of Shangril.

Talanda knocked.

A page admitted her into a dimly lit room. She was expected. Taking her candle, the boy departed and closed the door.

Dwyn Gramaret, King of Gramarye, stood at a generous, glass-paned window. The high tower looked out over his castle's courtyard and walls, over the dark streets of his city to the peaks and vales of his country, and beyond, to the Gods' star-spattered heavens.

The king turned and smiled a greeting as she entered. He was a tall man, powerfully built, and he wore a plain robe of fine, Gramarye yak wool. The prayer stone of the Chrysocolla, if he wore it, was not visible.

Yolen Barcley, the only other occupant of the room, rose from his seat before the fireplace. Like Talanda, he wore the simple, unbleached robes of a magiel, and his skin shimmered, a blur of time shifts identifying him as a magic weilder. A scarf was wrapped about his neck, for though it was summer, the high mountains were cold at night and the wind poked chill fingers through chinks in the stone.

"Magiel Falkyn," Barcley acknowledged her. "Please. Come sit by the fire." He gestured to a deep chair padded with fleece cushions. "King Dwyn and I are most curious to learn more about what brings you all the way from Orumon."

"Sieur." She bowed her head in respect and took the seat he'd indicated. Good beeswax candles and crackling spruce firewood scented the air.

"It is not often two magiels of the Great Houses meet face-to-face." Barcley poured each of them a glass of wine. An old red, likely from Arcan. "At dinner, you mentioned your retinue has been on an extensive journey."

King Dwyn took up his goblet. "How can we be of help? I gather you do not merely while away the long summer days?"

Barcley set the wine bottle on the table where it caught the glint of the fire's glow.

"I have a puzzle," Talanda said. "My king sent me to resolve it. It . . . may be nothing."

"Not nothing," King Dwyn reassured her. "Not if it sent you on such a long pilgrimage."

"I've seen an event in my future that disturbs me." She let the fingers of her left hand slip up to her throat, to touch the death token hidden in her neck band. "I've visited all the kingdoms of Shangril, from Teshe to Pagoras. No magiel of any of the Great Houses has seen what I have seen. Though . . . I haven't told King Artem's magiel yet."

King Dwyn peered at her with sharp eyes.

Barcley cradled his goblet in his lap. "Describe what you saw."

"First, I must tell you what I haven't seen." She rubbed at the fabric on the arm of the chair. "I have seen no future beyond . . . I'm guessing, a year, maybe two, from this summer."

The king shot Barcley a troubled look.

The magiel's eyes narrowed. "You suspect your untimely death?"

The words, so plainly spoken, sent a wave of agitation through her stomach. "What I have seen is King Artem's troops outside Castle Archwood's walls. In siege."

King Dwyn set his wineglass down. "How many times have you seen this?"

"Once."

His lips tensed to one side. "The kingdoms of Shangril have been at peace for five hundred years. We are prosperous. There is no reason for King Artem to attack Archwood."

"I cannot explain it."

"You're certain?" Barcley asked. "Glimpses of the future are fleeting, and by their nature difficult to interpret."

She knew he did not mean to insult her. "There's no mistake. The future is the future. I stood on Archwood's battlements watching archers in the king's colors shoot flaming brands at our walls, as my king ordered our own soldiers to return fire. By my estimation, this event will take place soon."

"You cannot tell how long into the future your travels take you," Barcley pointed out.

But in this case, Talanda could. "My king's daughter was present. She was not more than eight years old."

"And how do the other magiels of the Great Houses interpret what you have seen?" the king asked.

"None has seen evidence of war."

"Perhaps your king in Orumon will anger King Artem."

"My king has no cause to provoke Artem. Doubly none, now. In fact, he would make great concessions to avoid trouble." Talanda leaned forward, resting her wineglass on the table. "I have reason to think the conflict I witnessed is not confined to Orumon."

"What proof?" the magiel asked.

"The other magiels I spoke with as I toured Shangril this summer," she said. "Like me, they witness no future beyond a few short seasons." Kraae, her lover, father of her three daughters, had remarked as far back as fifteen years ago that he'd never seen his old age. He'd dismissed the observation at the time, and so had she. Moments of a life lived out of sequence were meaningless . . . until over long life, patterns began to emerge. But when Kraae gave her the seed of her second child, his remark came back to her and, as precaution, she'd altered her second daughter's heredity. She'd used her magical ability to chose certain bits of her unborn daughter's makeup; made her less *magiel* in appearance. Why? She could not have said. A boding. Five hundred years of peace, but . . . talentless worldlings filled Shangril now, in greater numbers.

Magiel Barcley's face grew somber in the candlelight.

"Many magiels of the Great Houses are advanced in age," the king pointed out.

"So . . ." Talanda shook her head in disbelief. "*All* the magiels of the prayer stones will die? Through natural causes? Within the next year?" She held him in her gaze. "Sire, I'm not yet forty years old."

"These are times of peace," the king protested. "What event could be heated enough to throw Shangril into the chaos of war?"

"King Artem Delarcan called upon my services, not four weeks past. Did he not make the same request of each magiel of the Great Houses?"

The two exchanged glances. "No magiel acceded—fully—to his demand."

"But could his unsavory ambition be related to my riddle?" Ambition. Power. Fear of the strength of magiels.

Talanda had pondered her impetuous choice again, long and hard, when Kraae gave her the germ of her third child. This time . . . she removed all hint of the wavering skin that would mark her youngest a magiel. And the babe had emerged, to the gasp and consternation of all her midwives, fully worldling. In appearance.

Talanda turned to Magiel Barcley. "Sieur. You have lived no longer than I. Your health is good. What futures have you seen, beyond this year?"

The magiel licked his lips, his nostrils wide as he drew breath, and the tendons stood out on the side of his neck above the collar that held his death token.

The fire snapped.

"None."

CHAPTER 1

Meg Falkyn never wore silk again.

Never.

She stewed, half-hidden behind a marble pillar, because she'd worn her maroon brocade robe to court twice already. Now Janat, her younger sister, twirled among the glittering dancers on the polished parquet floor in a froth of golden silk, in the fitted and belled style they'd seen in Arcan. Silk, brought by a trader all the way from Aadi-of-the-Valley, a gift from Mama for her fifteenth birthday.

The dance was boring.

The king and queen were deep in conversation with a wealthy merchant and his wife, and old Nanna, their stout, soft nurse, gossiped with a gaggle of servants. Rennika played dolls on the floor with the king's daughter. Embarrassing. She was eleven. But at least she was well to one side of the dancing.

Meg was sending a silent prayer to Kyaju, Goddess of the Devout, for the tedium to be over, when across the room she saw her mother's face tighten.

A disheveled courier in mud-splattered wool and leather stood by her, white-faced. A letter trembled in Mama's hand.

Mama's ivory robes and shifting complexion stood shock-stark against the splintered swirl of dancers. An instant of comprehension—and implication—was etched on her face.

Color and dark. Movement and stillness. Festivity and terror.

The musicians played a flourish and the dancers applauded.

Mama's gaze leapt over the dance floor, searching. Janat was there, clapping delightedly.

Meg took a half-step forward, pulse ticking, afraid to move through the crowd lest she miss unfolding ramifications.

Muted by the din of the rekindled music, Mama spoke insistently to the courier. He shook his head. She questioned him again, sharply, and again the answer was in the negative. She folded the letter and signaled Nanna.

Mama beckoned Rennika, and the little girl ran to her mother's side. Meg shouldered her way through the shifting patterns of dancers, touched Janat on the elbow, and caught her eye. Puzzled, Janat followed.

Mama was bent over, stroking Rennika's hair and holding her close when Meg came to her side. "Rennikala, you must listen to me." Mama kissed her daughter's forehead. "I need you to be very calm."

"No, Mama! You have to come, too."

The panic in Meg's stomach bloomed, prickling her skin from the inside.

"I have duties here. Nanna will be with you." She looked up at Meg and Janat. "And your sisters."

This was it. The thing—the unknown. Mama had told her. But Mama had known so little for sure.

Rennika fastened her hands around Mama's neck, but Mama disengaged her fingers and held them. "You must not make a sound. You must not let *anyone* know you are going." The fear in Mama's eyes stilled the girl's outburst.

Mama kissed her and thrust her to Meg's side, then gave Meg and Janat a kiss on the forehead and a quick embrace. "Nanna."

Nanna nodded and led the way toward the side of the ballroom. Meg guided Rennika, following Nanna through knots of fine ladies and gentlemen gossiping and watching the dance. Behind, she saw Mama speak to the courier. The courier insisted, and Mama, dread and concern in every line of her face, turned and melted into the crowd.

�֎

To begin with, Rennika found the hush and hustle from the ballroom bewildering; but more, the look on Mama's face and her words had lodged a tight ball of dread in Rennika's chest. "Look at me," Mama had whispered. "You're eleven years old. You must be strong."

Rennika's unease only grew as she ran, following her sisters and Nanna down the dimly lit steps, trying to keep her feet beneath her. At the landing, Nanna rushed them down the passageway to the servants' quarters, peering into each dark doorway and cross corridor. Rennika's heart thumped as it did when she narrowly missed being caught in a game of Catch Thief. Something was very wrong. Mama should be coming with them.

One of the kitchen boys—Brin, with the freckles—rounded a corner and stopped in surprise. He stood to one side as they entered Nanna's apartment, but Nanna smacked him upside the head. "You say a word about seeing us here, Boy, and Magiel Falkyn will turn you to stone!" She meant Mama.

A scream from the scullery startled them all. Then a wave of cries and shouts broke the silence, and the boy pelted down the hall.

✼

The rags Nanna dumped at their feet were peasant clothing. Meg could see Janat's bafflement as she stared at them. Rennika poked them distastefully with her foot.

"Get dressed," Nanna commanded, fixing the candle to a holder on the table and rummaging through a drawer.

Meg thought with a strange detachment, *Janat would have obeyed, had she known how.*

Then the moment broke and Meg took her sister by the shoulders and spun her around. Finding the thread that closed the back of her dress, she bit it.

"What are you doing?" Janat cried.

"Hold still." Nanna had a knife in her hand. She slit Meg's robe up the back. Nanna released Meg and turned to Rennika.

Fists pounded on the door and they stilled, staring at the blank wooden panels and the rattling bolt.

Meg's robe collapsed about her feet and she shivered in the chill, staring at the door.

"Shift. Chemise. Everything but your death tokens," Nanna

whispered.

More fists on the door. "Open! In the name of King Artem Delarcan!" Then shouts and running footsteps resounded in the corridor, followed by silence.

"Hurry." Meg threw a robe and tunic and leggings to Janat and pulled out smaller clothing for Rennika. She tied a rope around Rennika's robe, working silently and efficiently.

"Open up!" A man's voice penetrated the door, and terror grew in her stomach. Then, the rhythmic thumping of shoulders broke the spell, and she threw on her own ragged clothes.

The battering stopped, and a chaos of shouts and swords clashing filtered from the room beyond the corridor. Someone—engaged the soldiers in battle? This was it. The thing—the unknown thing Mama had seen.

Nanna grasped Rennika's arm and pushed Janat ahead into a small bedroom. Meg grabbed the candle and flung the door closed behind them.

A thwack, like something heavy striking the door to the outer chamber, split the cacophony.

�֎

Rennika tripped over the clothes Meg had tried to fit to her. The world had gone mad. But the scariest part was the fear on her sisters' faces. Rennika never cried when she scraped a knee or got punched by a royal cousin who didn't get his way. But she wanted to cry, now.

"Who's attacking us?" Janat whispered. "And how did they get past the castle wall? And the city gates?"

Nanna pushed back a drape. Thin starlight spilled over her shoulders. "Soldiers in the garden. In the colors of King Artem."

"Soldiers—fighting King Ean's men?" Janat asked. "But why?"

Nanna tried the window. It wouldn't open. She pulled the drapes back and with a strength Rennika didn't know the old woman had, picked up a chair and smashed it against the small panes. The chair bounced off, and the window remained intact.

"Wait. Let me. It's warded." Meg gave the candle to Janat, then cupped the lock in her hands. Meg was going to cast a spell without ingredients! Not worldling magic—potions anyone could do from a spell book—but real magiel magic, like Mama's.

Shouts and the clash of steel rang out, both behind them and ahead. But the ward was Mama's, and Meg would know its shape. Rennika did.

The sound of the door bursting open exploded in the next room as the window swung wide.

⚜

Flickering red lit the pavement and walls. Meg and her sisters crouched beneath a wagon in the bailey. The smell of smoke from beyond the great hall filled the air—something burned in the city.

None of this could be real. It couldn't.

Soldiers ran across the cobbles and skirmished in small groups. A handful of King Artem's men in uniforms of gold and green braced themselves at the steps before the main hall doors, taking courtiers and ladies prisoner or cutting them down as they fled King Ean's court. The noise, the smell, was sharper, more horrifying than a nightmare. Soldiers lay like black lumps on the pavement. Some moaned or tried to crawl. Some were still. The nauseating stink of excrement and blood reminded Meg of the butcher's shed in the fall.

Something . . . a blur, a mist? . . . seemed to crawl among the dead. Meg squinted, trying to focus. No. Nothing clear. Perhaps a trick of the dark, or of the inconstant torchlight.

A company of Artem's men rounded the corner of the great hall, rushing King Ean's soldiers. "Run!" Nanna hissed.

Meg tugged Rennika's hand and sprinted through the castle gates. Oh, Gods—

The soldiers, busy with their swords, took little heed of them, as if they were no more than fleeing servants.

They bolted onto the wide boulevard that wound its way from the castle toward the main city gate. Two of King Artem's men managed to run from their quarrels to give chase.

Nanna darted into a lane. Janat, panting, followed her.

There was a shout and a thump and the sound of a man stumbling and falling. Someone—an archer?—had felled one of their pursuers.

The second set of footsteps echoed behind them. Meg hurled spell words onto the cobbles, calling for a stone to find a time when it had risen above its mates. The soldier stumbled and fell to the pavement, striking his head.

Nanna plunged to a stop in the side street, leaning against the façade of a grand house, wheezing. Meg released Rennika's hand, letting her slide to the ground. By Kyaju, it had been close.

"That was a lucky spell," Janat said.

Meg leaned on her knees, blowing hard. She couldn't do another one of those. Not without potions.

Footsteps and shouts echoed in the streets. The smell of burning sharpened.

"Nanna," Meg panted, "what did Mama tell you? She had you find us these clothes. Did she—"

"Merchant Cordal," Nanna muttered, holding her side as if she had a stitch.

"Who?" The name had a familiar ring, but Meg couldn't place him.

"In the artisan's quarter," Nanna heaved. "He . . . can get you to safety."

Mama had known what was going to happen. "Where?" Meg pressed. "What did she tell you?"

"I don't know!" Nanna looked sick, as if she hadn't believed Mama. "Tomorrow," she whispered. "I was supposed to take you tomorrow. I was supposed to say we were going on an outing to the market . . ."

"So, we need to get to Merchant Cordal." Janat leapt to something they could do. But— "How will we get a coach?"

"The city's burning!" Meg couldn't believe how stupid Janat could be. "We're not going to get a coach!"

Janat waved at the chaos in the street. "Well, we're not going to make it to the artisan quarter *walking*."

"We have to get out of Archwood." Meg's thoughts plunged ahead. It couldn't be more obvious.

"Leave the city? Have you gone mad?" Janat whispered. "We've no clothes, no servants, no food—"

A horse screamed.

"All right!" Nanna scuttled to the opening of the lane. "We'll try to get out of the city."

"Where's Mama?" Rennika wailed.

"How do we get out?" Janat cried. "The streets are on fire. We have no guards, no coach. And if the main gates are breached —"

"The shrine," Meg said. "The back wall. There's a gate."

⁂

This wasn't right. Rennika had never been in this part of the city before, but they were going farther and farther away from Mama, going through winding narrow streets that all looked the same in the dark. But no one, not even Nanna, was listening to her.

They jogged on, halting at corners to watch before darting across open spaces. Windows showed uncertain light or faces peering into the street. Bands of people clattered in chaotic groups, some heading down toward the main gates, others uphill or across the city. They passed three buildings with flames licking the windows and the air tasted of smoke and ash. Scattered soldiers fought, or ran one direction or another, intent on some mission. Twice Meg cast weak spells of Confusion—without ingredients—on groups of soldiers who looked as though they might try to stop them.

They halted at the end of an alley, below a wall twice as tall as a man. Here, the sounds of fighting in the city echoed distantly. But there was a gate.

"Where are King Ean's guards?" Janat whispered.

"Maybe they went to fight below," Meg suggested. "Maybe Mama prayed for our safe passage."

"Hush," Nanna said. "Talk later." Nanna was moving, tugging Rennika across the open space to the gate.

Rennika looked behind. She saw no movement on the dark cobbles, heard no crunch of footsteps above the wind and distant shouts.

They crowded under the arch of the thick wall, out of sight of the street.

Nanna rattled the iron bars. "Locked. Meghra. Can you open it?"

Her sister touched the iron, felt the clasp. "It's another of Mama's wards. I can, but this one's more complex. It'll take time. I don't have any talisman or charm, and the One Star hasn't risen yet."

"Janatelle? Can you?" Nanna peered from the guard post down the hill toward the city.

"I can!" Rennika was good at wards.

Janat looked afraid, like the lying kind of afraid. "Mama hasn't shown me magiel magic yet."

"Let me! I'll do it!" Why did no one ever listen to her?

"Hush, Rennikala," Janat said. "If Mama hasn't shown me magiel magic yet, she hasn't shown you."

Meg followed Nanna's gaze, and Rennika looked where they stared. Soldiers trotted up the road.

Meg turned to Rennika. "Rennikala. Can you open the gate?"

"Yes! I told you, yes!"

"By Kanden, let her try," Nanna cried. "They're coming."

Meg nodded.

Rennika felt the shape of the lock. It was like lots of Mama's wards, but three of them put together. She willed the metal bar in the middle to remain back in time in its former position and the five tumblers to remember their places when the lock was open.

The lock clicked and the gate swung wide.

"Go!" Nanna pushed them through the opening and closed the gate as the jogging footsteps scattered to a halt on the road just within the wall.

✤

Exhaustion from the running, the vigilance, and the magic crept up Meg's legs and back and arms as she trudged behind Nanna.

Almost as soon as they'd left the city, following the path to the shrine, they'd heard shouts and the jangle of mailed foot soldiers. The noise came from beyond a rib of rock that blocked their view of a broad ridge connecting the main mountain range to the rounded cliffs where Archwood was built. They'd scrambled up a crack in the rock and huddled, rigid with silence, deep into the night. Below, men moved back and forth along the path, carrying bundles from the wide ridge to the rocky meadows above Archwood.

Mama had seen the future. She'd known something was coming. But what?

There were still too many questions. How could an army have

scaled the unscalable ravines to these high meadows? Into the Gods' reserve. Archwood was built on a cliffy outlier of the Orumon Mountains, and the only approach was by the King's Road and the main gate. Invaders were here, *behind* the city. This made no sense to Meg.

When the movement and sounds of men finally stopped, they crept from their precarious perch and fled up the bands of rock and scree into the wilds.

The sky deepened to starry ink as they plodded up gleaming silver and black rock, finally to crawl beneath the sharp branches of a wind-twisted larch to sleep. And after a shivering night filled with nightmares, cold, and wind, Meg woke to the lessening darkness of dawn. Below her, the city crouched in the gray light. Soldiers glinting in King Artem's colors of gold and green surrounded the walls. Within the parapets, red-clad soldiers scuttled like toys on a game board. King Ean's men. All gates, now, were impenetrable.

Rennika clung silently to Meg's knee as Meg and Janat and Nanna tried to come up with explanations. It was hard to understand what had happened — what they had done by escaping. What was to come next. King Artem must have planned a surprise attack. A small cohort, giving King Ean no time to prepare. Only a few candlemarks of panic and chaos, and Mama's foresight and preparation, had allowed them to escape.

Rennika asked for Mama, and when Mama didn't come, she asked again.

Nanna said that Mama had made arrangements, that Mama would meet them. But then, Nanna promised a lot of things.

"Stop."

Rennika bumped into Nanna and the woman's strong hand steadied her shoulder. The gray mountains and the buffeting wind chilled her through her thin rags. Shards of slate beneath their feet tumbled down to Rennika's left, then abruptly disappeared into a distant valley of dark evergreens, threaded by a silvery ribbon of river crested by rocky peaks.

Rennika poked her head around Nanna's arm to see ahead.

They'd traveled south and east of the fortress in hopes of finding a way down to the valley, and thence to the King's Road and back north to Coldridge. Every step they took upward took them closer to the Gods' domain, guarded by monsters and forbidden. But now the ridge they'd been climbing ended precipitously before them.

Janat slumped to her rump on the rocks.

"Another cliff," Meg accused.

Nanna sighed. "Here. Let's rest a moment." She sat beside Janat.

"I'm thirsty," Rennika whispered. Sun played tag with darkening puffs of cloud, and the icy wind slammed her repeatedly. Off beyond the precipice a black speck moved back and forth across the sky.

Meg refused to sit. She scanned the ridge. "This ravine cuts all the way back to the main mountain."

No one replied. Rennika squirmed between Janat and Nanna, leaning her head on Nanna's soft lap. "These boots hurt."

Meg glared at her, but Rennika turned her head. Nanna stroked her hair and she listened to the wind blow, blow, calm, blow.

"When I get down, I'm having the servants bring me a bath with scented soap," Janat said. "A hot one, full to the brim. *And* a mug of wine. Not ale, wine."

"I'm going to find a shrine to thank the Gods we got away," Meg said.

In the sky, the black speck circled far away with a lazy rhythm. Rennika closed her eyes. The rocks dug into her thigh and she sagged uncomfortably against Nanna's hip. She wriggled to straighten herself.

"Stop it!" Janat snapped.

"I'm cold."

"Hush." Nanna's calm voice.

"There's no way down," Meg asserted. "They built Archwood so high above the mines *because* there's no way down. Or up. Only through the front gate of the city."

Rennika pulled on some fragment of cloth on her arm to cover her shoulder.

"Stop pulling my shawl off! Nanna!"

"We're never going to get down to the valley," Meg said.

"Girls."

"Yes, we are, and you're not coming into my room." Janat pulled the bit of warmth off Rennika's shoulder.

Meg stamped on the gravel. "You don't understand, do you? We're stuck up here and we're never getting down, and pretty soon it's going to be night and we have no way to pray to Kyaju."

Janat cried, "I'm not sleeping out in the cold again—"

Nanna's whole form rose and sank with a sigh. "You can't see any way down?" she asked Meg. "Not anywhere along the ridge?"

"No! I told you! There isn't! And if we keep going, we're going to be in the Gods' realm. And it's guarded by orums."

"Then we'll have to go back," Nanna reasoned.

"Finally," Janat said. She climbed to her feet.

"We can't go back there," Meg cried. "The city's surrounded."

"We'll take a look." Nanna's voice was patient. "Maybe the fuss has settled down."

Rennika opened her eyes a slit and watched Janat march down the gravel imprints they'd made climbing the ridge. Nanna heaved beneath her. "Come, little chick."

Her eyes burned and she closed them. She let her head slip onto the rock shards as Nanna slid from beneath her.

Hands tugged on her shoulders. "Come. Stand up."

"My legs are tired."

"Come."

"Oh, she's just useless. Leave her there." Meg's footsteps followed Janat's.

Cold seeped into Rennika from the rough stone and the wind tugged at her clothing, exploring gaps with chilled fingers. She huddled into the scree and cried.

"Come, chick. Come." Nanna's capable hands pulled her to her feet and she clung to Nanna's hand.

She looked back again. The black speck hunted methodically back and forth over the valley as her footsteps jarred, crunching the rock shards. The speck had grown, and Rennika could discern an array of curled limbs on the thing, so it looked like a flying spider. "Nanna."

"Hush, child," Nanna puffed. "This march is too taxing for me to walk and talk, too."

She cast another glance at the creature. It was making its way, unhurriedly, toward them. Four legs, tucked up under it, like a horse. Three heads, four legs, two wings, and a tail. "Nanna. There's a big thing."

As though Rennika's words were an excuse, Nanna stopped and turned. "What big thing?"

Rennika pointed. "It looks like the drawing in my book."

Nanna's eyes widened. "By Kyaju." She touched the death token at her neck and whipped her head to look down the ridge at Meg and Janat who were now walking together, then back at the bird. "Hush." Nanna took her hand and set off at a jog down the mountainside, pulling Rennika along.

Fear flipped in Rennika's chest as she stumbled over the stones, hearing nothing but the crunch and tumble of scree beneath her. It was surprising how quickly they were able to descend what had taken them all day to climb.

"Meghra!" Nanna's voice was a whispered shout.

Meg and Janat continued to march purposefully down the slope.

Nanna didn't call again, but looked over her shoulder, and tugged harder on Rennika's arm, pulling her off balance. Nanna only ran faster.

"Meghra!"

Her sisters were closer now, and this time Janat turned. She looked to the sky behind them and her eyes grew wide.

She grabbed Meg's shoulder, and Meg shrugged her away but looked to where she was pointing. Meg's mouth opened.

Nanna abruptly changed directions, dragging Rennika across the slope rather than down, and Rennika was hardly able to keep pace in the sliding stones. The wind buffeted her face and the cold air seared her throat as she ran.

Meg and Janat were running now, too.

The bird was big. Maybe like an eagle? Or was it bigger? It was too far away to tell.

They reached a formation of rock fingers slicing out of the scree, and Nanna dragged Rennika up the sliding crumbs of slate between the first two rock ribs. Nanna fell to her side on the gravel, pulled Rennika up beside her, and lay on top of her. There was a crunching of footsteps as Meg and Janat fell prone on the rocks, then nothing but the silence of the wind and their ragged breathing as they lay beneath their cloaks, unmoving on the shale.

Nanna's words were the barest hiss in her ear. "If that creature attacks, you put your death token on your tongue. You hear? Your body's nothing, but your spirit *must* cross into Heaven."

A lump of sickness flashed through her chest.

"You hear?" Her nurse's words were faint but intense.

Rennika nodded, once. Heaven.

The shattered rock was cold and Nanna's weight pressed her back onto its unforgiving blades. She could see the blustering clouds racing across the seething sky. The wind roared across the defile. Had they offended the One God? Were they too close to his lands?

Then, overhead. A gush of wind. A dark form the size of a scaly horse, claws outstretched, diving at them. Three long necks with gaping mouths quested blindly, like huge fanged earthworms.

It swooped low.

Then, with a shriek, Nanna leapt into the air—

Immense wings flapped, once, a deafening blast, and the thing wheeled high, gliding over the rock rib. Gone.

Nanna—

Rennika's heart stopped.

Gone.

Vanished.

Nothing above but cold clouds.

Rennika gasped and her heart resumed, thumping like the smith's hammer. How . . .

Someone moved, a scrape of gravel, but Meg shushed and the silence of the blowing wind returned. The thing had *taken* Nanna. Rennika wanted to jump up, run, but Meg—

She gripped herself, pushing back an unreasoned flutter in her stomach. Cold, and the ache of trying to hold her back off the stabbing stones, crept into Rennika's bones.

After a long time, Meg's profile rose against the leaden sky.

Rennika breathed and lifted herself cautiously from the rocks. Meg scanned the heavens, hiccuping sobs.

Nothing. Only clouds heavy with snow. "Meg?" Her own voice sounded small and wavering against the vastness of the wilds.

Janat rose to her knees and shrilled, a high pitched whine that turned into a scream.

Meg blundered to Janat's side, her face red. "Stop it!" She raised a fist, and Rennika thought she was going to hit Janat.

Janat toppled onto her back, silent as suddenly as she had shrieked.

The flutter crawled into Rennika's gut. "Where's Nanna?"

Meg said nothing, glaring down at Janat and breathing heavily through her nose. Janat lay at her feet, panting with fast, ragged breaths.

The whistling wind filled the void of their silence, and the hazy peaks beyond the valley waited patiently as they had done since the beginning of time.

Meg shook her fist at Janat. "Sound carries." Her hiss broke the spell. "Do you want it to come back? Do you want the king's men to come?"

The worm in Rennika's stomach gnawed and grew.

Janat shook her head, mute, and crumpled against the rock with shaking sobs.

Rennika stumbled over the sharp stones to Meg's side and wrapped her arms around her sister, hot salt trickling onto her lips.

The sky was vacant.

"What . . . what . . ." Janat sobbed, and her face was streaked with tears. "What are we going to do?"

Meg shook herself, staring at nothing. She sat on the scree and bundled Rennika into a fierce hug. She held out her arm and Janat scrambled over, and the three of them gripped each other, rocking and weeping.

"I want Mama," Rennika said in a small voice. "I want Nanna."

Meg grabbed Rennika's hands and looked into her eyes, and Meg's face was more scared than Rennika had ever seen it. "Nanna's not coming back, Rennika. Not ever. It's just us, now."

"Mama—"

Meg's grip on her fingers tightened. "We won't see Mama for a long time. Do you understand? It's just you and me and Janatelle."

Rennika could not keep the worm in her stomach down. She buried her head in Meg's warm belly and wept.

"We have to go back to the keep," Janat said.

"We can't—"

"We *have* to go back to the keep," Janat said flatly, and stood. "King Ean's dealt with the brigands. I know he has. We have to go back."

CHAPTER 2

Nothing Meg said could dissuade Janat, who marched off down the slope. Grabbing Rennika's hand, Meg crunched after her. A part of her, a part Meg tried to push down, breathed easier as they descended from the taboo country.

By the time they came to a halt behind a low rock rib above Archwood Castle, evening had crept into the valley.

In the east, the distant peaks glowed pink with reflected sunset. Below their hiding place, King Artem's soldiers ringed the walls of the keep in siege. Stationed on the steep rocky meadows above the city's rear defense, they gathered in small groups around cook fires and tents, just beyond an arrow's flight from the wall. But the soldiers did not look up the mountain in Meg's direction; their attention was on the parapets, patrolled by King Ean's men. A number of the attacking archers stood along the edge of the encampment, arrows nocked, scanning the wall from below, restlessly alert.

"They're still there." Meg lowered herself to the rocks behind the outcrop, her breath faintly visible in the starlight. "I told you," she said to Janat. "There's no way to get back into the fortress."

Rennika hunched beside her, curling up into a ball. Meg covered her with a corner of her robe.

Janat peered over the rocky crest into the deep dusk punctuated by sparks of campfire. "We'll have to give ourselves up to King Artem's soldiers. That's all," she reasoned. "King Artem wouldn't hurt us."

Meg couldn't believe her ears. "Didn't you see what they did? Last night? To the people running out of the great hall?"

"Well, we can't go up the mountain." Janat glared at her, her voice tight and low. "Cliffs and cliffs and more cliffs."

By the Gods, Meg wanted to strangle her sister.

"We can't go down. We can't stay here." Janat slumped to the gravel beside them. "We can't get into the fortress to find that merchant Mama said would help us. Whoever he is."

But—a thought occurred to Meg. "Janat—did Mama tell you anything, predict anything? About . . . this?" Mama saw the future when she did magic.

Janat eyed her, wary.

Meg had been mulling over their circumstances all day. Ever since they fled the castle last night, in fact. Mama had made hints to Meg, and she'd told Nanna something, too. Though Nanna hadn't believed Mama, she'd at least managed to get them out of the castle before the gates were impenetrable. At the time, Meg had been content to let Nanna follow whatever instructions Mama had given her. But now, Nanna was gone. Dead.

"What do you mean?" Janat asked.

"Seven days ago . . ." Was it only then? Meg bit her lip, trying to remember exactly what Mama had said. Trying to piece together in her memory the glimpses of unguarded emotion escaping across Mama's face as she tried to school herself. Meg tried to recall the muted warmth of the fire behind drawn drapes, the marigold scent of incense lingering from Mama's prayers . . .

"What?" Janat's voice was calmer now, quieter.

"Mama knew this attack was coming. Before the messenger told her," Meg said. "She had Nanna prepare."

Meg needed to piece together what Mama knew, what she'd told each of them.

It'd been late when Mama had sent for her. Meg was in her sleeping robes, reading by candlelight. Nanna had stood in the doorway, an inscrutable expression on her face, as Meg followed the page from their apartments. Of course. Because that was what Nanna believed—that the glimpses of the future Mama saw when she used the Amber Prayer Stone, or when she used magiel magic, were only the ravings of a woman in the grip of Heaven's seduction. A madwoman. Nanna was surrounded by magic, yet Nanna didn't believe in it.

Meg had followed the page through the chill corridors of the castle, the light of his candle flickering over gray stone, gilded picture frames and panel moldings, the soft marble of figurines in alcoves. Then the tall, double doors closed behind her, and she was in Mama's outer chamber.

Mama turned from the soft embers on the hearth and rushed to embrace Meg before she even had the chance to curtsey. "Meghra," she whispered into her hair. "Come." She pulled Meg's hands, hastening her to the couch, sitting beside her, still holding her hands, looking deeply into Meg's face.

Unease rose in Meg's throat. This wasn't the soft Mama, the reasoned Mama. This was the strange woman she became after using the Amber. Meg had wanted to pull back against the grip of those hands, make whatever had alarmed Mama go away.

"Meghra, something . . ." Mama shook her head, as though she'd started with a misstep. "I don't know what's going to happen, but—" Mama licked her lips. "I've seen . . . futures, Meghra. Futures I don't trust."

Such talk . . . it made Meg uneasy when Mama talked of her flights to the future.

"The other magiels of the Great Houses, none of them have seen anything of alarm. Perhaps I'm mad."

"No, Mama."

Mama bit her lip. "I can't see you, Meghra. You, or Janatelle, or Rennikala. None of you."

In the future, she meant. Meg's stomach felt uneasy.

"I see . . ." Her eyes drifted. "King Ean, his wife, his daughter, the servants, everyone, starving. Sick. I see . . ." She frowned a little, dredging up her vision. "King Ean says that without substantiation from the other magiels, my vision means nothing."

Why was Mama telling her this? Frightening her?

Mama blinked, as though trying to remember, and spoke almost to herself. "I think . . . I think I've been seeing this for—years, maybe. But I didn't piece it together." Mama closed her eyes with a short nod, her fingers still gripping Meg's. "A week ago, King Ean and I used the Amber to go to Heaven, to petition the Gods for death tokens for the people of Orumon."

This was not news. Mama's place by King Ean's side was to

keep the people of Orumon supplied with the tokens they needed
to travel to Heaven when they died. Each time she went, though,
Mama was exhausted and disoriented, her time stream muddied
by the magic. She slept or tripped through random bits of her life in
a darkened chamber for days.

"But this time?" Meg said slowly. She didn't want to know. But
she had to know.

"The Heavens had been disturbed." Mama's grip on her fingers
eased. "There were ripples in the flow of time. Someone had been
there, praying, probably within the last week. I couldn't tell when."

Again, not unusual. There were seven prayer stones. Seven
magiels of the Great Houses. Seven royals to accompany them to
Heaven, keep them safe. A just distribution of power. "Could you
tell who it was?"

"King Artem. But Kraae was not with him."

"Not with Papa?" The king couldn't use the Ruby without his
magiel.

"He brought a different magiel. One I've never seen before."
Mama's brows drew together. "I think . . . I think I know why I
don't see you or Janatelle or Rennikala in my future."

Coldness crept over Meg's skin.

"I don't care about King Ean's reassurances." Mama's fingers
stretched like claws, then squeezed into fists. "I'm sending you and
your sisters away. As soon as it can be arranged."

A feeling of dread filled Meg's stomach at her mother's words.
"I'm not ready, Mama, I'm not. Janatelle and Rennikala—"

Mama's face drew gaunt. "Neither am I."

Meg blinked, trying to absorb what Mama had said. Send them
away.

"Watch over your sisters." Mama took her hands again.
"Do whatever you must to keep them safe. You have a great
responsibility, you three. To survive, to fight, to restore balance."
Her eyes flashed, then, with thought. "Be careful. Of those who
would use you for their political advantage. Of those who would
use words to convince you down dishonorable paths." She spoke
quickly, as if she suddenly had a lifetime of wisdom to pass on in
only a few minutes. "Beware of glim."

Meg stared at her, trying to follow. "I don't know . . . I've never heard of . . ."

"Glim." Mama shook her head. "You may hear that glim no longer exists. That the spells for finding it have been lost."

"What is it?"

"A seduction, Meghra, a trap. It seems to bring joy, but it only corrupts." She blinked. "You may never need to worry about it. Magiels learned long ago never to write such spells in books where they might be discovered. But still, be wary."

Meg promised.

Mama shook her head and brightened, but her change in mood was brittle, false. "Now. To work."

Work?

"Meghra, I need you to do some magic."

Meg blinked. Mama had begun her instruction in magic when she was Rennika's age, but for the most part she'd learned mostly history and theory. For the past few years, Meg had studied worldling spells, simple things that required only the combination of magical herbs and animal parts in particular order or under particular celestial signs, according to the instructions in a spell book. She'd only done magiel magic a few times. And, of course, Meg would not use the Amber to travel to Heaven until Mama was old and the mantle of bringing death tokens to the people of Orumon fell to her.

"Magiel magic," Mama said, as if reading her thoughts. She reached over to a spindly-legged table next to the couch and picked up a bit of dried, twisted root. She placed it in Meg's lap. "Nothing elaborate. It will be good practice. Find a time when the root was young. If you can, take it back to seed."

Meg was confused, but she obeyed. She closed her eyes to remove distraction and held the root in her hands. She explored its shape, listening, feeling, reaching back into its time stream, searching for its earlier life.

The room seemed warm, yet there was a chill on her skin.

She opened her eyes and saw what her fingertips had already told her. The root—still only a fragment of the full tree—had shrunk, slightly, to a slender, smooth curl, its ends moist with fragrant sap as though the rest of the tree and its lower root hairs had only just been severed from the piece she held. Sweat beaded her brow, and the ruddy light of the fire had almost died. A great wave of fatigue washed over her.

Mama smiled with quiet pride. "Good," she said, taking the root from her and replacing it on the table. "You did very well. This is—what?—the fourth time you've done magic?"

It was.

"Now. You can sleep in my bed tonight. I will sit beside you."

Meg knew what would happen, and it made her uneasy. Using magic disturbed time. Her own time flow was now interrupted. Over the next minutes or candlemarks—even days, she supposed—she would live bits of her life out of order. She would disappear from Mama's bedroom and reappear in another part of her life, a time when she had used magic. Herself from some other part of her life would appear here. No one observing would see the exchange. She would appear not to move from Mama's bed.

But Meg had experienced this disorientation before, when Mama first had her learn magiel magic. The ordeal had been terrifying.

Mama rose, and Meg rose with her. "Why?" she asked.

Mama led her to the bedroom. "Two reasons. First, I'm hoping you will travel to one of your futures rather than to one of your pasts. You've only done magiel magic a few times before, so the chance of you living a piece of your life from the last year or two is not likely. I'm hoping to ask you what your future holds because I can't see it."

Meg nodded. Mama was blind to any future but her own.

Mama pulled back the thick duvet on her bed. "And I must tell your future self something you'll need to know."

"What?" Meg climbed into the bed, her limbs heavy with exhaustion. "Why don't you tell me now?"

Mama's faint smile in the dark was almost invisible, but her voice made an effort to lighten the gravity of her words. "You can't tell a questioner what you don't know."

CHAPTER 3

"A questioner?" To Janat's mind, the words were frightening. The pink light had left the far mountains, and darkness filled the wilds. A spray of stars splashed overhead, deep in the vast heavens. Sashcarnala's single star had not yet risen.

"That's what she said." Meg huddled deeper into her shawl, her breath white. "I don't know what Mama learned from talking to—" She shrugged. "Me, I guess. From my future. And she told me nothing. Just that she would send us away. But I don't think even Mama guessed how soon King Artem would march into Orumon."

Janat drew in a slow breath, trying to fathom what was happening. The chill that touched her had nothing to do with the cold. Gods, she was only fifteen, just dancing at her first ball.

Meg tugged Rennika's shawl higher over her sleeping form. "I think, last night, Mama stayed behind to protect us. I think she wanted the king's men to believe they'd caught everyone inside the castle. To give us time to . . ." She shrugged again. "Escape."

Escape. Did Mama think someone would hurt them, like in the old tales? The days when kings built walls and waged war?

"I saw other parts of my life that night." Meg's words grated on Janat's ears like the croaks of a raven. "From using magic. I've been trying all day to make sense of them. There has to be something, a clue."

If only she'd stop talking. Janat pushed away Meg's words and peeked over the outcrop protecting them from the eyes of those below. The soldiers were still there, patrolling outside the castle, warming themselves at campfires. If only they could sneak past

King Artem's guards. King Ean—Mama, everyone—was safe inside the castle walls. If only they could just get back inside, they'd be safe, too.

"Are you listening?"

Janat huddled against the rock rib. The jagged projections dug into her palms. She felt sick.

"Janatelle. I asked if Mama did the same with you."

"No." But . . . yes. Janat hunched away, disquiet churning inside her. Mama had taken Janat to her room. Made her touch a bit of old root.

"You have to tell me."

It was horrid. She couldn't talk about it. What Mama had said. Couldn't think about it. She had to think of . . .

"Janatelle!"

"Stop!" The words boiled out. "Don't you understand? Mama even *said* King Ean didn't believe her. The other magiels didn't believe her. Can't you see, Meghra? When she talked to you, the madness of using the Amber was on her. *That's* why she told Nanna to get us these stupid rags to wear, *that's* why she told merchant whatever-his-name-was to take us away." She wanted to shake Meg. "Nanna's right. Mama talks nonsense after she's been in the grip of magic."

"It wasn't nonsense." Meg's voice was cold as the stone beneath them.

Janat held the toes of her boots, glaring at the shale, trying to get the words under control. "I wish she'd just stay in her chambers until she's normal." She covered Rennika with her shawl and dragged the little girl onto her lap. Rennika's small body was soft and warm, squirming fitfully in her sleep. Janat scowled at Meg. "Sometimes I hate her."

Meg's face grayed, as if she'd been slapped.

"Why does Mama have to use it?" Janat lashed out. "She sleeps for days, after. She can't stop crying. We never see her."

"You know why she uses the prayer stone." Meg's words smashed against Janat like the bitter wind whipping down from the mountains. "For death tokens. To keep the city safe from orums and other beasts. For prosperity. For health."

"It scares me, Meghra! When she's like that."

Meg seized her hands, held on as if Janat were going to jump up. Bolt. Maybe she was.

"She's not Mama." Janat wept. "She says things that aren't true. *Can't* be true. I don't—"

"What? What did Mama say to you?"

A crushing tension trembled her chin, and she pushed her jaws together to still them. Rennika woke, shivering, and cried.

Meg looked like she wanted to slap her. "What did she say, Janatelle?"

"She said . . . she said the king lost his mind. He's demented."

"Which king?" Meg pressed.

"King Artem. From Arcan."

Meg sat back.

Finally, Janat had shut her up. But still, her eyes drilled into Janat's face. Janat smudged her streaming tears across her cheek with her sleeve. "Then she made me do magic. Meghra, it was awful—" And after, Janat had vanished from Mama's warm room and found herself shivering in falling snow, clinging, terrified, to a rocky ledge.

"What did you see, Janat? After you did magic?"

"Nothing. More of—" She flung an arm out. "This. Crawling on rocks. I don't want to crawl over frozen rocks."

Meg pulled Janat's shawl close around her, almost a businesslike attempt at solace. "We are the magiels of the House of the Amber Prayer Stone." Her words were quiet but strong. "Someday, praying for death tokens for the people of Orumon will be our duty. We have to survive. Whatever Mama saw coming. For our people."

Survive.

Janat covered her ears and hid her face on Rennika's back and Rennika squirmed and whimpered. Night was on them, snow was coming, they had nothing to eat. "I want to go home. I want Nanna. I want my own room and my bed." King Artem's men couldn't mean them harm. They were magiels.

"We all want to be safe in our beds. But we're here." Though Meg's words softened, they brought no comfort.

Weariness washed through Janat and claimed all her bones. "It's not fair."

"No." Meg put an arm around her shoulders, blocking the

persistent wind. "It's not." She looked up at the stars, screwing up her face as if she would cry.

They only knew dresses and dancing. Children's games. The garden in the castle.

A snowflake settled on Meg's shoulder.

Rennika burrowed into Janat's belly. "I'm hungry."

The complaint brought tightness to Janat's own stomach, but she was almost glad.

At Rennika's words, Meg seemed to shake off whatever despair had come over her. Slowly she released them and climbed to her feet. "We're all hungry." She looked down at the walled city again.

The wind calmed, then, but frost filled the air.

"Let's go."

"Where?" Janat lifted Rennika from her lap and helped her up. The girl could barely stand.

"If the king's men found a way up from the valley to attack the back gate, there's got to be a way down."

Janat was doubtful. Such a way would be steep. She looked down at the soldiers and pulled her shawl tighter. Crusts of old snow had slaked their thirst, but not filled their stomachs. Still, they had to leave this ridge. They needed to find a place to sleep.

"We'll go to the saddle that connects Archwood to the main mountain range."

Where they'd tried to go last night after their escape. Where King Artem's soldiers had most likely come up from the valley. "Where the shrine to the Many Gods is."

Meg tugged the mittens more tightly onto Rennika's hands and the girl wept sleepily. Ranuat, the constellation of the seven murderers surrounding the bright merchant star, peaked over the horizon.

"But if that's how the king's soldiers got here . . ." Janat felt compelled to argue, at least a little. "The path will be guarded." Arguing with Meg felt easy, reassuring. The way things were supposed to be between them.

"Likely." Meg looked tired, almost beyond caring.

"We'll be arrested or killed."

Meg nudged Rennika. "Then you can tell them King Artem would not want us harmed," she said, and her voice was wry.

Janat followed Meg down the slope, almost smiling at the jab.

�֎

The wind blew, cold. In the faint light of the pearly river of stars, Meg picked her way across the rock slide.

To their left, the peak they'd clung to since fleeing the city fell away to a wide ridge that led to scree slopes, rising again to lose themselves in a range of the Gods' impenetrable mountains. On either side of the ridge, forests marched down the steep slopes to the valley. They must find a way along the slopes of shale between the mountain's upper cliffs and Carn Archwood's fortress walls to reach the ridge.

Gradually, they made their way across the slopes. The city was unlit except for a few torches scattered at long intervals along the wall. Below its parapets, blurred shadows of men lay or sat around small fires, or patrolled, scanning the fortress.

Their footsteps crunched, loud in Meg's ears. Rennika slipped and cried out, and she and Janat crouched by the little girl's side, still as hares, silent, watching. How could the men not suddenly turn and raise the alarm and loose arrows in their direction?

And yet, there was no change in the darkness below.

Breathing again, Meg nudged Rennika to her feet, and they continued their agonizing journey.

They reached the bottom of the rock rib. The king's men were still in sight, disturbingly close.

They stopped. Only a few feet below, a well-worn path in the scree wandered from the city along the open, windy ridge that linked the peak where Archwood perched to the Orumon mountains. The ridge was wide and exposed to all eyes; the only trees were huddled in a series of gullies dropping away on both sides. The dark would be treacherous on the high path, but right now, it was their only friend.

Beneath the city walls, the soldiers were mostly quiet and still. King Ean's sentinels stood on the walls, and the Delarcan men paced below, each watching the other.

Meg moved forward, crouching, holding Rennika's hand, and Janat followed. It was only a moment before they were on the path, and the ground felt more solid than it had since they'd left the city. Their feet were quieter here than on the sloping scree, yet still perilously loud. As much as she wanted to run, Meg kept to the same quiet creeping as before.

The path along the ridge descended gently, and then climbed, becoming steeper as it did so, leaving the forested gullies behind. When Meg peered back, they had moved behind a shoulder of the mountain and she could no longer see the campfires of the soldiers or the towers of the castle.

By the Gods, they'd done it. Meg's heart raced and her breath came short in silent jubilation. *She'd* done it! Brought her sisters off the mountain, past the soldiers.

But they weren't safe yet. Calming her pulse, she led them ever upward through bitter wind, finally, to a stone wall. The shrine to the Many Gods.

Snow began to fall.

�֎

An orum chased her. Rennika ran from door to door in the great hall, but all were locked. She searched for the shrine, knowing she would be safe there, but the hall was full of snow and no matter how hard she pushed against it, she could make no headway. Then Nanna flew up into the air, and—

She was lying on polished marble. Why had Nanna allowed her to fall asleep in the ballroom, rather than putting her to bed properly? Rennika would have something to say to her about this. The floor was damp and hard, and Rennika still wore her clothes.

Yet, beneath her worries, she was filled with a deep sense of contentment, as though she was in Nanna's arms, and all was well.

Rennika opened her eyes a slit. Gray light and chill air filtered from some open door onto a wide mosaic floor. She smelled snow.

This wasn't the ballroom in King Ean's castle in Archwood.

Rennika sat up. Janat crouched over a small brazier in the center of a low-ceiled, roughly triangular chamber. Curving muralled walls with multiple openings led to small alcoves for personal prayer and reflection. There were no windows. None were needed, for the physical world was irrelevant here. This was a shrine to the

Many Gods.

Rennika crept to the brazier and huddled next to its warmth. Janat gave her a dipper full of sweet, cold water.

"Where's Meghra?" Rennika's small voice echoed from the marble walls.

"Praying." Janat's whisper shushed around them.

Yes. Of course. Rennika prayed every day before she ate. She could feel the holiness of this place.

Through a wider opening in the complex of niches, the far wall was lined with steps to arched doorways. They were on the lowest level of the shrine, the level devoted to the prayer stone of the Amethyst.

"This isn't the shrine in the great hall."

"This is the Holders' shrine." On the mountain. "It's safe." Janat shrugged, to qualify her comment. She held a hand out, and even though Rennika was too big for such comfort, she crept into her sister's arms.

"I want Mama," Rennika said softly. She tried to shut out the image of Nanna's sudden flight in the claws of the orum.

Janat's embrace tightened. "So do I." Then she pressed her lips together and pushed Rennika back, looking at her as though judging her worth. "Mama made you look like a worldling."

"How?" Rennika wasn't sure if Janat was trying to tease her. The comment sounded as though it could be an insult, and yet she'd said it like a fact, with no meanness in her voice.

"Before you were born." Janat pushed Rennika off her lap. "She picked what you would look like. Strong magiels like Mama can do that. Meg's skin blurs time like hers, I'm in the middle, and your skin is easy to see clearly, like a worldling's."

Rennika decided it was an insult. "I'm a magiel. Like you. Like Mama."

"I know." Janat didn't rise to the fight. Her voice was quiet; she seemed—curious. "And you opened that back gate to the carn, with no potions or spell words. And you did it without being taught how." Her sister peered at her as if trying to see inside her head. "That's a lot of power. More than me or Meghra. *But*—she made you look like a worldling. I wonder why."

Rennika couldn't stop the tears. "No, she didn't!"

"There's nothing wrong with having steady skin."
"Yes, there is! Take it back!" She hit her sister.
Janat shrugged and turned back to the fire.

CHAPTER 4

Huwen Delarcan's practice blade punched the padding on Gweddien's chest, and the older boy fell back onto one knee in the dust, parry defeated.

"Got you again!" Huwen stepped back, exhilarated, sweat dripping from his heavy, tousled hair. The late summer sun was hot; though far away, beyond the fields of golden grain, snow laced the mountains. He signaled his squire to unbuckle his thick padding. "Bring water," he told the page.

Gweddien Barcley climbed to his feet, breathing heavily through his nose, using his wooden sword as a crutch. "I was too hot!" he said by way of excuse, sloughing his own soft armor before the second squire could step forward.

"You—" Huwen poked Gweddien's chest with a finger. "—don't spend enough time with your swordmaster." Huwen's heavy quilting came away in the squire's arms and he stretched, enjoying a moment of cool air before his sweat dried. The page filled his mug from a dampened clay pitcher, and Huwen savored the chilled water.

"I have spells to learn. Competing in games is for princes." Gweddien gulped from his mug and poured the remainder of the water over his head. Then he grinned mischievously.

Huwen caught his meaning and grinned back, anticipation crawling pleasurably under his skin. "You have the magic herbs?"

Gweddien cast a surreptitious glance at the swordmaster across the yard consulting the smith. "We can heat a bowl in the back of the armory," he said under his breath. "My tutor was up late. He'll be asleep before I can recite two histories. Can you dodge yours?"

"Eamon has missed two lessons. Our tutor will let me come to the garden to read." He wiggled a brow. "I just won't say where in the garden."

"After lunch, then," the magiel promised.

Huwen tapped his friend on the arm with the flat of his blade. "Mother's probably eating in the garden. Let's see if there are any shaved meats." He tossed the blade to his squire.

Gweddien was taller than Huwen by half a head and, at eighteen, his senior by three years. But with Huwen's older bastard brother gone off with Father last week to investigate a dispute in the hinterlands, and his younger brother Eamon so ill—and his other brother and sister only little—there was no one for the prince to spend time with. The servants' children didn't learn the warriors' arts, knew nothing about the world, and half the time had to scamper off to serve, or run errands. True, there was a gaggle of boys in Holderford of noble birth and time to hunt or game or wager with him, but they were toadies. Gweddien would be the powerful magiel of the Chrysocolla Prayer Stone in Gramarye someday, and more Huwen's equal. He was glad Gweddien had come to Holderford for the summer.

Mother's garden was one of Huwen's favorite spots. Father's castle topped a cliffy promontory overlooking the confluence of the Arcan and Faolan rivers in a wide, fertile valley. Steep approaches, a long view across the plains, and a natural spring bubbling into a deep pond within the castle walls had made the location ideal for the castle's original builders—warlike men who defended keeps from one another's raiding parties all across Shangril.

But from the time the One God gave prayer stones to his six mistresses, peace had reigned in Shangril. Huwen's forefathers had been chosen to bring the people's petitions to the magiels, shimmer-skinned children of the One God and his worldling mistresses, and to protect the magic wielders as they used the prayer stones to travel to the seven Heavens to deliver those prayers to the Many Gods. The castle walls still stood, but for hundreds of years the gates had been open, manned only in ceremony. The life spring of water within the walls nurtured a garden of weeping trees and soft grasses and bright flowers. Wars were not fought in Shangril, and skill with a sword or bow was only celebrated at games, or used to emphasize a point of honor.

Huwen and Gweddien stepped from the stark practice grounds ringed by stables, smithy, and storage sheds onto the grassy path that wound between shady trees and trimmed beds. The light shifted and dappled here, and the air gentled with the scent of ripe fruit and evergreens.

Ahead, through the lace of leaves, his brother Eamon crouched on the edge of the pond.

Odd.

Eamon rarely ventured out of doors anymore. Huwen had given up trying to do things with his younger brother, or even to talk with him about the histories they learned from their tutor. Eamon would look at him with those unsettling eyes, long and deep, and then shake his head as if to say Huwen knew nothing. It was unnatural in a boy of thirteen. Huwen wasn't the only one who'd come to avoid the strange young prince since he'd recovered a few weeks ago—unexpectedly, magically—from his long illness. Father's magiel had disappeared from the castle the next day, to be replaced by a stranger.

But now, as peculiar as Eamon had become in recent days, something about his posture on the bank of the pond made Huwen's pulse speed. Where was their tutor?

Huwen loped toward the boy.

His brother tipped forward, over the water.

"Eamon," he screamed.

The prince slowly, inexorably pivoted, touched, then slid into the dark depths.

Huwen abandoned the winding path and crashed through the bushes. The song of the brook gurgling over stones and the snap of whipping branches smothered all sound.

He reached the bank and plunged into the cool waters. The water was murky, but Eamon's rounded form sank slowly below him, bubbles of air rising from his mouth and clothing.

Huwen stroked, his boots and jerkin heavy, dragging at him.

He wrapped his arms around the still form and immediately it sprang to life, wriggling, fighting.

Huwen held on and kicked toward the surface, his lungs

straining, his boots dragging him down like anchors.

But Eamon struggled harder, twisting from his grasp. Huwen managed to grab him under the armpits, locking his fingers onto his brother's shirt. He kicked again, chest bursting, and his head surfaced with a thrashing splash. Huwen managed to yell for help and take half a breath before Eamon's squirming submerged him again.

A body dove into the water close by, long limbs, blurring skin. Gweddien. He grasped one of Eamon's arms, and he and Huwen stroked for the bank as Eamon's writhing lessened.

They surfaced, panting, and pulled Eamon's face from the water. The boy was pale, his body unresisting.

"Here! Here!" The tutor stood on the bank, bending low.

The boys dragged the prince the short distance through the water to the steep, grassy shelf and pushed his limp weight up toward the man's waiting arms. The tutor pulled him onto the grass and rolled him on his side as Huwen climbed from the pond, exhausted.

A gush of water pumped from Eamon's mouth and he vomited. His eyelids fluttered.

"Run," the tutor said to Gweddien. "Tell the steward. Tell him to send men and a litter."

Gweddien ran.

Huwen stared at his brother. Had he fallen asleep? No . . .

"And you, my young prince," the tutor said severely. "Your brother is not yet healed from his illness. The day is warm, but this pond is over your brother's head. Suppose he'd drowned? Hmm?" The man glared at him. "Who would have put your brother's death token on his tongue?"

"We weren't swimming." How could he think this? Huwen was still wearing his boots and jerkin.

"He could have been denied Heaven! Did you think of that? With no death token?" the tutor went on. "He could have become a ghost wandering this sphere forever!"

"We weren't swimming!"

The tutor rubbed Eamon's back. The boy's eyes were open and he breathed, but he stared at the ground, seeing nothing. "We will discuss this. With the queen," the tutor threatened. "Once your brother is cared for."

"He fell in," Huwen protested. Fell?

The tutor raised a brow.

"And where were you?" Huwen blurted. The tutor straightened, taken aback. "Fetching the servants to bring lunch? Your place is by him."

The man's mouth became a straight line. He turned back to Eamon, pulling a handkerchief from a purse and wiping the boy's lips, pushing the vomit away from his face.

The tutor's brows furrowed.

What?

The tutor lifted the handkerchief and rubbed the mess from something in the silk.

A death token. In Eamon's vomit. Eamon opened his eyes. He stared at the pale flat disk. "Why?" he whispered. "Why did you pull me out?"

There was a way down the ridge below the shrine. Janat hadn't thought there would be, but, to her credit, as the sun rose, Meg found one. Several gullies sloped away from the ridge, all steep, all treed. The one they chose was interrupted with short bands of rubble-covered cliffs, but with care, they were able to scramble down, or sometimes, to find ways around them. Meg didn't think an army could have negotiated its way up to the ridge, but perhaps a few strong men—a trained strike force—could.

They came to a small clearing with the recent remains of a campsite, and Rennika dashed forward, spying bits of gristle with shreds of salt pork clinging to them in the ashes of a cook fire.

"Rennikala! Don't!" Janat, horrified, ran forward to stop her sister from making herself sick on tainted meat.

"I'm hungry!" Rennika cried, turning on her.

Meg hung back in the trees. "We can't stay here. Messengers to the king might come this way."

Janat grabbed Rennika by the arm and dragged her back into the woods. Rennika sat down, refusing to move.

"Rennikala, get up," Meg said crossly.

"No. I'm tired. I'm hungry. I want Nanna."

Though the air was still cold, the sun emerged from the clouds intermittently, and now a shaft of sunlight fell on a branch over Rennika's head.

Berries.

Janat pulled the branch down. Dark purple. Shriveled. A good four weeks past any nutritional value.

"We can rest for a few minutes. But we need to get lower," Meg said. "There are mining villages and farms in the valley. Someone there will have food. And shelter."

Janat fingered the berries.

Then, stepping around Rennika, she brought the woody stems of the bush into her embrace. She closed her eyes, shutting out her sister's complaints, and felt for a time when the bush was younger, just a little—

"Janatelle!" Rennika cried.

Meg's hand touched her shoulder and she opened her eyes. Clusters of fat, ripe berries dripped from the branches. She pulled a handful into her palm and devoured them. Sweet juice flooded her mouth, and the pulp slid effortlessly down her throat.

"I want some!" Rennika squealed, grabbing at the branches.

Meg squeezed past her through the trees and pushed on the long, springy stems, lowering the tops of the branches to where they could all reach. Janat pulled a cluster of berries from their stems and cocooned them in Rennika's hands.

They devoured the fruit, stripping the bush of every berry it had produced.

Another band of cliffs. Janat didn't think she could go a step further.

Meg was at the bottom, holding Rennika's hips as she maneuvered her way down the last few ledges.

Snow had begun to fall, perhaps a candlemark ago, and the rock was slippery. Janat stood on the edge, hunting for the best way down.

And all at once—

She sat by a table in a sunny room, sewing.

—Oh!

By the Gods. Terror spurted through her. The magiel magic she'd used on the berries—

This was—

She looked around.

An attic with a window overlooking a narrow lane. A bread cart. The aroma of the bread . . .

"Janat?"

She turned. Meg stood by the door, dressed in a plain, well-mended robe. She was thin. But she looked well.

Janat was being battered by waves in her time stream. Living part of her life out of sequence. Like Mama told her would happen when she used magic.

This . . . this was a piece of her life, her future?

Then the drape of night cloaked her, and she was—warm.

"Janatelle." Mama's voice.

She was in Mama's bedroom.

A fire danced on the hearth, heating the room, and rugs and tapestries swaddled them against the chill of night. Janat fell to her knees before the flames. Warmth, even for a moment.

"Janatelle!" Mama was on the floor beside her, shaking her shoulders. "We only have a minute. Where are you?"

Where—

"Answer me, Janatelle. Just now. Before you joined me on the carpet here. Where were you?"

The nightmare that had become her life.

Mama shook her shoulders again.

"Climbing down a cliff." She didn't want to let the image in. "It was cold. Snowing."

Mama seemed relieved. "How long since you left the castle?"

How long?

"Janatelle! We only have a few seconds until you go back!"

"Last night . . . two nights ago? Maybe three."

"Listen to me." Mama was in front of her. Mama never came so close. She was angry with her. "Do you believe me? Do you believe I can see the future?"

This was all so bizarre.

"Do you believe—"

"Yes." No. She didn't know.

"*Good. Listen. A year and a half from now. At the spring equinox. You and Meghra and Rennikala must go to a small lake in the mountains south of Postinghouse. It's near Coldridge.*"

Go to a —

"*Say it back to me.*" Mama shook her. "*Say it.*"

"*Meghra and Rennikala and I have to go to a lake south of Coldridge. Near Postinghouse.*" Janat didn't know where Postinghouse was, but Coldridge sounded familiar. Maybe . . . yes, it was one of the cities Mama had taken them to this summer.

"*At the spring equinox. Say it.*"

"*At the spring equinox.*"

"*It's almost autumn, so the spring equinox will be in a year a half.*"

"*A year and a half.*"

"*Good.*" Her mother licked her lips. "*And you —*"

The room disappeared.

Cold stone danced in front of her eyes. The skin ripped from her fingers and she was falling, backward —

Rennika shrieked.

Janat landed on her back on shrubs and rocks, her head snapping back into a bush, its stems scratching her neck and cheek —

"Janatelle!"

She took a gasping breath, a hand under her neck. Above her, trees stretched, straight and dark, into a gray sky swirling with flakes.

Meg's face appeared above her. "Are you hurt, Janat?"

Janat blinked. Rennika came into view, her face pale with fear.

She hurt all over, especially her feet, rubbing against hard leather boots for three days. Her fingers . . . she brought them up. Bleeding. She tried to sit up, against the insubstantial support of the springy bushes that cradled her. The overwhelming need to sleep after her use of magiel magic persisted, but . . . "No. I don't think so."

Relief washed across Meg's face and Rennika rushed to her, holding her fiercely. "Did you fall asleep?" Rennika asked.

Janat shook her head, more to clear it than to respond. "The magic," she whispered. She straightened herself properly and peered at her fingertips. They were bleeding but not badly. "I shouldn't have used magic."

Meg bit her lips but said nothing.

Rennika lifted her head from the embrace. "I love you, Janatelle. Don't die."

Janat couldn't help but smile. She hugged Rennika back. "I won't." She flicked a glance at Meg. "I . . ." She didn't have words to explain. "I wasn't here."

Meg's eyes told her she understood. For once, she had the grace not to rub it in. Meg sat in the snow beside her and spoke quietly. "Did you see anything useful? A future that can help us know what to do?"

A sunny room in springtime. The smell of bread. She shook her head. There wasn't enough of that scrap to mean anything. "Not a future. A . . . past." She gathered the second moment back to her. "Mama. She told me—she said, you and me and Rennikala, we have to go to a lake. A year from this spring."

"A lake?" Confusion wrinkled Meg's brow.

"Let me say it all before I forget. At the spring equinox, a year and a half from now. The lake is near Postinghouse, and Postinghouse is near Coldridge. South of Coldridge."

"A year and a half? Why a year and a half?"

"She didn't say."

"And why do we need to go there?"

The whole episode was taking on a dreamlike quality, its reality fading. "She didn't say."

"And what about—"

"I was only there a minute, Meg," Janat snapped.

"Think! You have to think!"

"That's all." She slumped back against the foot of the cliff. "Meg, find us a place to sleep. I have to sleep."

CHAPTER 5

Huwen Delarcan stood at his window, its glass frames opened to the chill night air. The scent of approaching autumn was in the wind. He couldn't sleep. Rather, he'd slept, but worry had woken him.

The One God, his star outshining the densest clusters in the River, stood constantly in the north. In the distance, snow-covered mountains stood pale against the horizon, while below, shadows striped the hardpack of Holderford Castle's bailey.

He could not shake the incident from his mind. It had happened over a week ago. Yet, no one seemed to think he was old enough to be told what was going on. Mother, who'd fretted for weeks when Eamon was ill, even failing to discipline Jace or sit with little Hada to sew, went back to fretting over him, dismissing the tutor and haunting the boy's footsteps. Eamon disappeared into his suite again, so Huwen saw neither his brother nor Mother at all on most days.

Father had not returned—he and Huwen's bastard brother, Uther, had been gone almost four weeks and Huwen could not fathom why. His tutor, Sieur Daxtonet, had said other kings were jealous of Father's prosperity and had banded together to charge taxes on Arcan's trade goods. But among the aristocratic boys, gossip had arisen that Father was not merely negotiating the unfair trade practices. There was war. That the king of Midell had been capturing Arcan territory, sending thieving parties to raid Arcan towns. Why, after centuries of peace, the borders or trade goods were under dispute made no sense. But the final insult was that

Uncle Avin, a fearsome man ruling in Father's stead, refused to enlighten Huwen.

However, rumor of war on the far borders was only a distant excitement; Father would come home soon and explain the misunderstanding. What troubled Huwen more was his younger brother.

Eamon had placed his death token on his tongue and tipped himself into the water.

Why?

How could a boy, thirteen years old—a child!—want to die? Heaven was beautiful, certainly. It was more real than this world, everyone knew that. But one's life, here on the lowest sphere, was sacred, too. Huwen could not imagine leaving his home, his family, his ambitions, his responsibilities to the people of Shangril. And most of all, his *life*.

But there was more.

Three days ago, Gweddien had become suddenly silent and thoughtful. He, too, refused to admit that anything had changed, and he, too, disappeared into his rooms.

Servants whispered. Huwen's tutor claimed to notice nothing amiss and redirected him to his studies. His swordmaster and his groom did the same.

And why didn't Father come home?

A horse whinnied. Hooves on cobbles.

Huwen leaned deeper out of the window.

A groom led a saddled horse from the stables to the rail near the tradesmen's entrance to the castle grounds.

Stranger and stranger. Who needed a horse in the middle of the night? A courier?

As Huwen watched, the groom returned to the stables and re-emerged, leading a second horse, this one bearing pack boxes.

No courier, then. Someone planning to be gone for some time.

Huwen pulled on his boots and found a soft leather cloak in his wardrobe. He knew better than to ask Sieur Daxtonet what was going on. He would get no answers. He slipped out of his sleeping chamber, past his tutor into the outer chamber, and past the dozing page, to the corridor.

By the time Huwen eased through the castle's kitchen door and crunched as quietly as he could across the bailey, three saddle horses and three pack horses stood at the rail.

The kitchen door behind him opened, and he whirled to see a tall young man and a woman, cloaked for travel, in startled uncertainty.

"Gweddien?" Huwen was as surprised as they were.

The woman—Gweddien's mother, a half-magiel with skin that barely wavered—recovered first. She pushed Gweddien's shoulder, urging him toward the horses. "Your Highness," the mother murmured as they scurried past.

Huwen scrambled to follow. "Where are you going?"

The groom emerged from the stables with a final pack horse. Spotting them, he tightened the cinches on the saddle horses.

Gweddien's mother cast a worried glance over her shoulder at him as they approached their mounts.

Huwen ran and caught Gweddien's arm. "Gweddien! What's going on?"

The groom helped Gweddien mount a gelding, and his mother turned to Huwen, her lips pursed with decision, eyes flitting over Huwen's head to the castle beyond. "Please, Your Highness. If you love your friend, keep our departure in your confidence."

What—

"Lady." The groom brought a second saddle horse forward.

They were running away. The guards—Uncle Avin, Mother— didn't know they were going.

The woman, in riding culottes, mounted.

Had they committed some crime? "Why?"

Gweddien brought his horse around. "It's your father," he whispered savagely.

What?

"Hush," the mother said.

The groom opened the vendors' gate to the city.

"Father isn't even here," Huwen protested.

"Your father attacked Gramarye's capital city—the king's fortress in Highglen." His friend's lip trembled. "Huwen, my father has been imprisoned."

Huwen stared at him. "What?"

"Hush!" Gweddien's mother admonished him.

The groom mounted the third saddle horse and led the string of pack horses toward the gate.

Gweddien tugged his gelding to a halt. "It's no longer safe to be a citizen from Gramarye, in Arcan."

No—this wasn't possible. There was a mistake.

Gweddien's mother brought her horse around and slapped Gweddien's mount on the rear, spurring it forward. "Get!" she said to her son.

Gweddien shot Huwen a contemptuous look and urged his gelding through the gate.

"I beg you," the mother said, "if you have any softness in your heart, let us leave with our lives."

Huwen could do nothing but stare at her madness.

She pressed her lips closed against tears, then hastened her animal beyond the castle wall.

CHAPTER 6

It was the choking cry that made Rennika lift her head.

Through the trees, the flutter of rags that was Janat called out, "There!" Then she fell to her knees at the base of a tree, holding it as if it were Nanna, and weeping on its trunk.

Meg stopped for a moment, so Rennika, too, fell to her knees in the snow. The steep climb down through the woods and cliffs, filling their bellies with nothing more than snow and icy water, sleeping—or merely shivering—under the prickly boughs of giant spruce trees, was now only a jumble of disconnected memories akin to the shards of a nightmare.

The endless walk through the frozen forest, looking, always looking behind for their pursuers, was no better.

Meg mumbled something, reached down and heaved Rennika to her feet. The knife-pain that cut Rennika with every step in her ill-fitting boots pinched again on her bunions, across the backs of her heels, on the knuckles of her toes.

Holding Rennika's hand, Meg stepped over a log, guiding her on painful steps through the close, straight fir trees in the direction of Janat's cry. They stopped when they reached Janat, who pushed her ragged hood back, her face lit with joy.

Ahead, Rennika could make out a lightening of the forest, as though there might be a meadow beyond the trees. Then Meg made the same choking cry as Janat had. "A house!"

A house.

Rennika collapsed by Janat, and Janat held her and rocked her. "We're safe!" she cried to Meg through her tears. "We're safe! The

Gods have saved us!"

Meg grunted. "Stay here. I'll go see." She trudged in the direction of the opening.

"Will there be food?" Rennika asked. When had they eaten last?

"Food. Yes," Janat sang, hugging her. "And a bath, and a bed, and clean clothes."

"Is Mama there?" She couldn't be, but . . .

"No, no," Janat said. "But they'll take us to Mama. They'll take us back to the castle, or somewhere good and safe. We're rescued. Meg will marry Nevin, I'll be betrothed as Mama promised, and everything will go back to the way it's supposed to be."

They waited a long time.

Snow fell, and Rennika shivered in Janat's arms. "I want to go to the house."

"Meg said to stay here."

But the clouds grew darker and the snow swirled about them. "I'm cold," Rennika said.

"All right. We can go a little way. To the edge of the forest."

They took slow, painful steps through the snow and bracken. Halfway across the farmer's field, they spotted two men walking toward them. Janat cried out and ran, stumbling through the drifts.

And then the men were there, and one of them took Rennika's hand. She was tired and cold beyond caring.

✤

Two boys, the older one about Meg's age, were limbing a felled tree beside a thatch-roofed cottage. The younger boy noticed her and nudged the other. "'Allo," the older boy said.

"Please." Meg's word came out a whisper. "Do you have a bit of bread—" Her throat closed on the joy of rescue, and she felt suddenly weak. "My sisters—"

The boys looked at one another, and the older nodded to the younger who hurried into the house.

Meg's feet were numb, her back aching, and icy air poked through her layers of clothing. The boy regarded her soberly but did not appear hostile as much as unsure.

The door to the house opened, welcoming light and warmth

against the fading afternoon shadows. A woman appeared on the step, pulling a thick shawl around her.

The boy nodded toward the house. "Bes' talkta Momma."

"Thank you," Meg managed, and nodding to the boy, stumbled with stiff feet across the yard.

Surprise touched the mother's face, silhouetted against the bright interior.

"Please—" Meg repeated. "Please, I—"

"Ye pur chil', commin fro' the cold." The mother's gaze flicked about the yard and she held the door wide.

Meg faltered into the stone house, into the warmth and light and savory smell of cabbage broth. A fire danced on the hearth beneath a cauldron, and she pulled her scarf from her throat. The hovel, chinked with moss against the wind, was small and simple, a single room with a dirt floor and a loft overlooking a clutter of rag rugs and rough-hewn furniture.

The mother called to her boys and nattered instructions, as Meg struggled with her mittens. The woman closed the door and pulled a chair up to the hearth, then went to work helping Meg remove her snow-crusted boot. "Me boys've gone fer yer kin."

Meg fought to parse the mother's words, but pain shot up from her foot as the boot dropped to the floor and the woman peeled off her sock. Her toes were white, and blisters had broken on the joints and heel. A chill enveloped her, and she began to shiver.

"Ye needta get outta 'ose close." The mother pulled off the second boot and, grimacing at the damage, scurried off.

Meg rubbed her feet, and they felt like smoothed river rocks. Knifing pain shot up from her toes. The woman had spoken to her several times, and Meg was beginning to realize she could understand her odd words. It was normal speech eroded into a vulgar form. Meg spoke as the woman rummaged through a chest. "We won't inconvenience you long."

The mother returned with a homespun robe, a thick shawl, blanket, and slippers. "Now, chil', tell me who y'ar, and wy yer here." She knelt at Meg's feet and rubbed a foul-smelling salve onto her blisters.

"My sisters and I are from Carn Archwood. We're going to Coldridge." Coldridge. Mama's brother was magiel of the

Amethyst. This past summer, Mama had taken them, with a retinue, to Coldridge where they'd met Uncle Chirles and their two cousins. Meg had ridden in a coach and hadn't attended to where they went but she thought Coldridge was at the north end of the Orumon valley. Now that they'd made their way to the valley, someone would help them.

The woman sat back on her heels and studied Meg, her brows lifting in surprise. "Castle Archwood?"

Meg pulled her shawl tighter. "Yes." Why should the name of the fortress cause this woman to look at her so?

The woman broke her stare and bent to cover Meg's feet with thick, warm stockings. Then she helped her strip away her damp rags and hung them on pegs over the fire.

As Meg was pulling on the shawl, the door banged open, and Janat stumbled in with a swirl of snow. The boys followed, and the older one carried Rennika on his back.

"Oh! Thank you!" Janat gushed as she entered, and with an effort, Meg rose from her chair on painful feet.

The mother sat Rennika down and peeled away her boots and bloody stockings, smearing her feet with salve. She wrapped the blisters with rough bandages, and Rennika cried and clung to the chair with the pain of her thawing toes. The mother took Rennika's clothes and gave Meg a coarse linen shirt and boys' leggings to bundle her in. Meg cocooned her sister in a blanket.

"The Gods bless your house!" Janat squealed as the woman brought her clothing. She looked about the room, clutching the clothes to her chest. "Where shall I put them on?"

The mother gave Janat a worried look. Then frowning, she said something sharp to the boys, and they trooped out into the snow.

Janat reddened as she turned in the single room, but saying nothing, she took herself to a corner to puzzle at how to dress herself.

"Na, ye mus' be brekkin bredw'us an' steyn'n ur home," the mother said as she busied herself finding an array of pots and dishes to lay out on the tiny wooden table.

When Janat was dressed, the mother called something to the boys out in the snow, and they trudged in with two stumps from the woodpile. These, they set on the hard-packed dirt floor, then laid a cut board across to serve as a bench at the table. The mother insisted the chair be moved to the head of the table, and she and her boys watched as the three sisters sat.

This was not right. Why were they being treated with these small honors?

The mother nodded to the boys to sit. She ladled a thick, steaming cabbage soup from the cauldron, thickened with barley and lumpy with vegetables, into small bowls, protesting all the time that "it isna gudinuf, it isna gudinuf." She served Meg and her sisters before she served herself and the boys.

"My mother shall be ever so grateful," Janat prattled, looking in her mug of water, then looking about the table. "You know she's—"

Gods! Meg touched Janat's arm and gave her a quick, piercing look. "Yes, good wife. The Many Gods bless you for your kindness."

"What?" Janat rebuked her, washing back a mouthful of boiled barley.

But before Meg could reply, the clatter of a wagon and heavy horses arrested their attention. One of the boys rose but the mother said something to him, and he sat again. Wrapping a heavy shawl around herself, she slipped into the swirling snow. Meg took a breath.

"What?" Janat said angrily to Meg.

But the two young men were still here. They lowered their eyes over their bowls, chopsticks moving steadily, but they would hear anything she said to Janat. She spoke under her breath. "You do as I say."

Janat straightened, eyes wide, unable to speak with shock and anger.

"We're not at—home," Meg said in the same hissed undertone. "This isn't a game."

Janat blinked at Meg and closed her mouth, breathing furiously through her nose.

The boys finished eating, blushing and silent. Janat fumed, and Meg worked away at her meal, trying to think through what she could tell these people.

The door opened and a big man entered with a chill gust and a flurry of flakes, followed by the mother. He closed the door, his wife hanging back by his side. He reminded Meg of the castle's old gardener as he unwrapped layers of snow-crusted garments. But his expression turned from surprise to awe to doubt as his gaze lit on each of them in turn.

When he had hung his garments on a peg, he came forward and knelt before Meg. "Lady," he said. "'Tis an honor t'have ye in me humble home."

Janat smirked.

The mark of respect was gratifying, yet unsettling. "We are in your debt, Sieur." Should she act the aristocrat or the fleeing refugee?

The man came to his feet awkwardly, head lowered, fingers working.

Aristocrat. It felt right. "Please, sit. You must be tired and hungry."

He bobbed his head but did not sit. "W'your Lady's leave, mum," he said by way of preamble to something more.

Meg folded her hands in her lap and faced him. Had she guessed wrong? She'd made her bluff and could see no way forward but to continue.

The man licked his lips. "Mum. Lady, ye canna stay here."

Janat drew in a sharp breath.

The older of the young men lifted his head quickly and the mother opened her mouth as if to speak.

Meg's pulse closed her throat. Was this family in league with King Artem's men? "I see," she said to the man, summoning her courage.

"It's . . . it's . . ."

"The wee chicks'll stay," the mother cried. "Look at them! How can ye—"

"And defy King Artem?" he snapped. "You know his troops came this way."

The mother's words stopped as if cut by a knife.

He turned to his wife and spoke in a soft voice as though he would not have the others overhear him, but his words carried in the silence of the snapping fire. "The miller's story be true. I was in t'village today. Soldiers did more'n pass through last week. They levied—stole—every egg 'n' block of cheese 'n' side of goat t'be had, and they left a dozen men t'hold the village hostage. Everyone was kept indoors for two days."

The whole valley. It made no sense. The world had turned upside down.

"King Artem's men?" the mother said in disbelief. "Why?"

His lips barely moved, yet his words articulated clearly in the small room. "Arcan attacked Carn Archwood."

But it couldn't be. A misunderstanding, a momentary madness.

"Attacked t'carn? Yer daft. T'Gods would never permit it!"

"Why?" It was the older boy who asked.

The father shook his head. "Old Tomwy Yakherd who farms below t'carn sent his son down t'village for food. Soldiers took over the fields of eight farmers for their encampments. His son *saw* flaming balls launched at t'city. Saw smoke and flames behind t'carn walls. 'Em poor buggers. No one's getting out of that fortress 'til King Artem's army says."

Janat stood, her face pale in the light of the single candle.

"The king wouldna attack his own allies," the mother said.

Meg gripped Janat's arm and she slumped slowly into her chair. The woman spoke truly. The Gods could never permit an insanity of this scope.

The man gestured at Meg. "You knae who she is. Who all of 'em are."

The mother's lips remained shut, doubt in her eyes.

"Did ye ask'm why they're here, dressed in rags?"

Meg shifted in her seat, feeling her regal air falter.

The father turned back to Meg. "Yer running f'yer lives, aren't ye? From t'castle."

Meg lowered her eyes.

"By the One God, Pa." The older boy spoke, startling them all. "Give'm to t'king's men! We don't want fireballs here!"

"We will not!" the mother cried. "Young girls? You say they be King Ean's magiels? D'ye want the wrath of all t'Gods to fall on our household, then?"

The father ducked his head to Meg and indecisively dropped to his knee before her again. But his words were not indecisive. "Lady. Sieura."

Meg tried to straighten in her chair but could not school her face.

"As ye can see—" He gestured ineffectually. "—I have a farm. I have a family."

The mother shrank back into the shadows.

He lifted his gaze to Meg's face briefly. "I won't turn ye over to King Artem, I promise ye that. I won't say a word. But—"

Janat bit her lip, tears of rage and disappointment coursing down her cheeks.

His words went relentlessly on. "I hope ye can see we mean ye no harm. Ye can understand . . ."

"Thank you for the food," Meg said. "And the clothing. We'll be gone directly."

CHAPTER 7

The contrary wind was cool, the sun uncooperative. Three days of rain had meant that today was the first possible day to use the sun dial and sextant, and Huwen's tutor was adamant that he mastered the mathematics of astronomy. Huwen's precious paper was covered in tiny triangles and even tinier figures. With Father at war with two rebellious keeps, Huwen could see no point in learning such impractical abstractions.

And how could he concentrate when Jovan, second son of Father's chancellor, had boasted—secretly and smugly—he'd overheard that Arcan had *started* the war. That King Artem's greed had angered the kings of Gramarye, Midell, and Elsen. Huwen immediately challenged Jovan to a duel, of course, and Jovan turned green and took the words back, but the others looked at Huwen aslant, as if his outburst were only a confirmation of Delarcan volatility. Worse, Jovan's apology could not erase what had been said. Of course, people in other countries—foreigners—would tell lies about Father. Kings were appointed by God; they had a huge responsibility to care for their subjects, and they deserved certain privileges. This had always been the way of Shangril.

Huwen should be at his father's side on the borders, like his bastard brother, not wasting his time behind castle walls like a woman. Uther would never be king, but he, not Huwen, had been at Father's side for the past eight weeks since the other countries had risen up. Sieur Daxtonet's mathematics and astronomy were an irritating drone, like the whine of a mosquito.

And, to be fair, the tutor's words also were not half as compelling as the occasional glance from Lady Saffen's youngest handmaid, Anwen. Lady Saffen Brille—Huwen's second cousin—was only thirteen years old, but Anwen, who sewed with the ladies in the garden and ran to do Saffen's fetching, was Huwen's age, almost sixteen: And, like him, she was tall and . . . filled out. He had exchanged smiles with her before, several times, and once, he'd been bold enough to lean over her shoulder as she read on a bench by the roses. He'd breathed in her bewitching perfume, and seen the milky tops of her breasts where they disappeared into her bodice.

"Your Highness?"

Huwen turned his head.

The tutor smiled patiently. "And the hypotenuse is . . .?"

He consulted his drawing.

But before he could respond, a page rushed into the garden. He bowed cursorily. "Your Highness! Lord Uther Tangel has arrived with news from your father! Pagoras has fallen! Prince Avin summons you. Sieur Daxtonet, ladies, please come."

With a flurry of exclamations, Huwen's tutor and the ladies set aside their tasks and hurried off behind the page.

Uther! And news of father—

But . . . Huwen slowed.

Anwen was here, walking beside him. Glancing at him. Now.

Uther would be here for at least a few days, and whatever he reported had already happened. It would not change. The news would be talked about for days or weeks.

But to be alone with Anwen . . .

Huwen touched her arm and adjusted his stride to fall back behind the others.

Anwen caught his smile and they slowed, allowing the ladies to push past them on the path. He grinned, and she grinned back and caught his hand. The touch of her fingers sent thrills of pleasure into his core.

They reached the garden gate.

Across the bailey, courtiers crowded the door of the great hall, a flock of servants at their heels.

—they didn't have to follow. No one would notice.

Huwen bit his lip and she raised a brow. She had thought the same thing. The stables. He cast a glance across the bailey, then tugged on her hand and led her swiftly through the stable door.

The interior was dark and smelled of horse and hay, but the stable boys had followed the others. They were alone. His heart beat pleasurably in his chest, and he pulled Anwen into an empty stall.

Grinning, she sank into the hay, tugging his hand. He followed, delightful anticipation growing. "They'll see the hay on us," he whispered.

"We'll brush it off." She lowered her lashes, demurely. Then, surprising him, she lifted her chin and kissed him softly, tentatively on the lips. An explosion of delight skittered across his skin. He released her to catch his breath, then kissed her back, sweetness multiplying within him.

She pulled him closer, rising to her knees so their bodies touched. He caressed her neck below her death token collar, her shoulders, her skin soft as silk across her collarbone, fire plunging through his groin.

And then she did the most amazing thing. She took his hand and guided it to cup her breast—

A rustle and a gasp—

"Oh! Excuse me, My Lord—Your Highness—" A boy stood behind Anwen, a pitch fork in one hand, a look of dismay on his face.

Anwen turned, squealed, and jumped to her feet. Huwen rose beside her, his face heating.

Anwen bobbed a truncated curtsey and fled.

"I'm sorry—I didn't—"

Huwen straightened his doublet. Speechless, he stalked away, trying his best to maintain his dignity.

But when he reached the courtyard, Anwen was not to be seen. Huwen scanned the empty compound, at once frustrated and angry with the stable boy, ecstatic and floating, and urgently in need of a release.

Something was happening—there was news—in the castle, and perhaps he would find Anwen there, but he would not be able to touch her, to talk to her. To stand at her side, or more likely, to stand across some crowded room trying to catch her eye, could only frustrate him further.

He needed to be alone.

He ducked into the great hall through the kitchen entrance and took the deserted servants' stairs to the royal wing. His suite was empty—everyone was listening to the news—so he bolted the door and flung himself on the bed, stripping out of his Aadian breeches to touch his throbbing penis and release the flood of pleasure pent up there.

Then he lay panting on the bed, exquisite visions of Anwen dancing in his head.

But he could not stay. Soon, the servants would return to their posts and his tutor would notice he was missing. And he was anxious to hear Uther's news. He cast about the room for something with which to clean himself. He found a towel, but his pitcher was missing. By Kanden, what a nuisance.

He didn't want to walk into his tutor's room in nought but a shirt and stockings—the man could be back at any minute. But a door opened to Eamon's adjoining room. Surely, his brother would be listening to whatever news Uther had brought.

But Eamon could never be counted on to go very far from his suite of rooms. Huwen eased the door open and peeked in.

By the Gods.

Eamon stood by the window, shaving knife in one hand, shallowly cutting his bare arm. A flagon of red wine, well drunk, stood beside an empty glass. Blood trickled to his elbow and onto the floor from multiple wounds.

Eamon's head snapped around.

Huwen let the door between them drift open. "Eamon."

"Go away."

The last thing Huwen would do was go away. He stepped into the room, closing the door behind him.

His brother's knife hand lowered, a look of exasperation on his face. "Leave me alone!"

"What are you doing?"

"None of your business!" He nodded at Huwen's groin. "What were you doing?"

"Not trying to kill myself."

Eamon slumped back against the sill of the window. "I'm not trying to kill myself."

"No? If your hand slips you might succeed."

His brother glared at him and then glared at the floor.

Huwen reached out and took the knife from him. He breathed, and rested it on a table. "What are you doing?" he asked softly.

Eamon shook his head. "Nothing."

"Why?" Huwen shook his head. "I don't understand."

He shrugged. "It makes me feel . . ." He shrugged again. "Better."

"Feel better?" Huwen almost shouted. He lowered his voice. "Feel better?"

Eamon's face closed. Huwen sagged back in disbelief.

"Don't tell."

Tell? That's what worried Eamon?

His brother bit his lip. "Don't tell Mother," he said softly. "With Father still away. She doesn't need—" He waved generally at himself and the blood. "—this."

It was true. Mother fretted.

"And if you tell, well, anyone, it'll get back. You know it will." Eamon poured water from the pitcher onto a cloth. Huwen's pitcher.

"How can I not tell Sieur Daxtonet? Or Uncle Avin?"

"Uncle Avin doesn't need to know. It's not his business. I'm not the heir." He began to sponge his elbow and forearm, wincing a little.

"Is that what this is about?"

Eamon turned his too-knowing eyes on Huwen. "No."

Huwen found a second towel and bent down to rub the blood from the stone tiles.

"Sieur Daxtonet . . . he's tired of all this." Eamon found a clean towel and dried his arms.

Huwen scrubbed at the last spot. "How can I not tell? You're my brother. You . . ." He wanted to say, "you might be a pain, but . . ." Instead, he said offhandedly, "I love you."

"I'll stop." Eamon rolled down his sleeves. "I'll take care of it."

Huwen eyed him.

Eamon reached for the wine and smiled brightly, as he hadn't done for as long as Huwen could remember. "I'll stop."

❧

The half-timber house at the edge of the village had a jettied second floor, large enough to block its chicken coop and pig pen from both the stars of Ranuat, and the eyes of passers-by. Meg crawled through the frozen garden, scavenging an occasional pod of woody peas, and digging hopelessly with a stick into icebound earth around the carrot or two that had been missed during harvest. Janat was back in the shrubbery with Rennika, with a stomach that would keep nothing down, a curse upon her from some tainted morsel.

They hadn't gone home. The Gods had not restored the world. Meg hadn't married Nevin, and Janat had not got her bath and bed and silk gown. Instead, they'd found themselves scraping for food, for warmth, for shelter, running from sticks and boots. It was all Meg could do to keep them from freezing and starving.

Meg crept back, and the three of them huddled just within the pig pen, sucking on the half-dozen woody peas Meg found, dozing a little, and watching smoke rise from the chimney.

"I miss Faris." Rennika huddled close to Janat.

King Ean's youngest, three years younger than Rennika.

"Faris." Janat's bitter words came from the dark. "Do you think she's still in the castle with her nurse and sisters? Playing with her dolls, safe and warm?"

Meg was reluctant to answer. But Janat had been wheedling, more and more of late, to give themselves up to the kind protection of King Artem's men. "Or is she dead?" Meg asked. "Everything I hear holds that bearing royal blood is a crime, unless your name is Delarcan."

"You don't know that," Janat accused.

"You don't know it isn't," Meg retorted.

Rennika began to whimper.

Meg pulled her ragged shawl—a stolen blanket—over Rennika, resting her cheek on the girl's dirty, tangled hair. How could she explain to her why Nanna had taken them away from all that was safe and good, why couldn't they look for clemency from the king— especially when Janat kept insisting they could?

"I miss Cook." Janat's voice was quiet in the dark.

Faint candlelight glowed behind the waxed linen coverings on the house's windholes.

"I wish we had a real shrine where we could pray." Meg needed hope and strength more than she needed food. "Remember the shrine at King Artem's castle in Holderford?" As simple an act as naming the Gods in their Heavens gave her solace. "I think that was the most beautiful shrine I ever prayed at. The candlelight on all those gold and amber panels. And King Larin had the best seamstresses. Remember the honey cakes—"

"Don't talk of food," Janat said softly.

Meg acquiesced. But she could not surrender the comfort of her memories. "The best shrine was the old one off the road from Silvermeadow to Zellora," Meg said. "You could feel the holiness in every stone."

And, she had been infused with a feeling of peace in the shrine when they escaped, where they paused for only a few candlemarks before their flight down the terrifying cliffs below the ridge. That sensation of contentment had borne her a long way on their journey.

A bitter breeze nibbled at them from the north.

Presently, Meg clucked at her sisters. The windows in the house had become dark.

They crawled across the pig pen.

The pigs were well-fed and sleepy, snuffling and snorting a little as the three made their way to the trough. There were still good-sized lumps of turnip and something slimy that tasted of meat, laced with crunchy bits that might've been carrots. Meg shoved as much of the cold slop into her mouth as she could, Janat elbowing her into Rennika to snatch a few chunks, despite her uneasy stomach. The pigs snorted.

The door to the house slammed open, and a brilliant candle lantern swung into view. "Here! You!" a voice cried.

They ducked and scrambled back from the light.

The man shouted and his hard boots clattered on stone. The light flickered wildly. Moving lumps beneath their feet squealed in terror and bucked out of their way. Meg pushed Rennika over the wall where Janat had heaved herself, and the three of them plowed through the snow on numb feet toward the woods.

But this time, luck was not with them. A handful of growling dogs sprang up from nowhere and chased them down a lane, back toward the village. They rounded a corner into an alley and a form loomed up out of the dark.

Meg skidded to a halt and, grabbing Rennika's hand, scrambled a quick retreat to the lane. But the way was blocked by the semi-circle of growling dogs. She dropped Rennika's hand and pushed her behind her skirts.

Janat screamed.

Meg turned.

The dark shape was a man, and Janat was caught in his arms. She shrieked and struggled, her hood fallen back from her face. Her shifting magiel skin—

But it was night and Janat's skin was not very capricious, and she and the man who held her were in shadow. "Hold on, now," he said.

Meg pulled a stick from the nearest shanty and whipped it over her head, one eye on the dogs, and Rennika scrambled to a crouch behind a frozen rain barrel. The shanty collapsed against the side of the wagon that formed one of its walls. "Hey!" cried a voice within.

The man held Janat by her upper arm. His body was hard like an ironmonger's, like the apprentice who pushed the bellows for King Ean's smith. "Hunter. Down," the man commanded one of the dogs. The beasts cringed, snarling. "What do you run from?"

Meg rushed forward with her stick, but the strong man ducked back and Janat wound up between them.

The second man extracted himself from the remains of the shanty. His nose was crooked above a straggle of beard. He was young and slighter than the other man, not yet fully muscled, but he bore himself with ease and confidence.

The house owner wheezed up the lane behind them and seized Janat's other arm in pudgy hands. "Young Finn Kichman," he said to the strapping man who'd spoken to the dogs. "I thank you. These thieves were in my garden," the house owner accused, his accent thick but his words recognizable. "In my pig pen!"

"Refugees from the fighting, I've no doubt." The man who'd crawled from the shanty appraised them with a look, then turned to reconstruct his tent. "Let them eat with your pigs, old man."

Meg backed off, the stick ready, eyeing all three men and the dogs. Not promising.

"Thieves?" the house owner cried. "It's not your place—Lad—to tell me how to deal with thieves."

With a crank of his wrist, the wagon man surprised Meg and wrested the stick from her, nodding politely. "Be thankful you're not turned out of your home in this weather, Sieur. Suppose soldiers took your house?" He waved the stick at Janat. "This might be your daughter. Have pity on them."

Janat looked exhausted by her struggle and unsettled stomach. Could she run?

"I have no wife, nor daughter," the house owner spat.

The wagon man shook his head and repaired his shanty.

"Are you Sulwyn Cordal?" Finn, the strong one, turned to the shanty man with respect. "From up valley, near Archwood?"

Cordal. Meg had heard the name. Somewhere. She peered at him in the dark. He'd been unwavering in demanding his stick back, but he'd spoken with kindness.

The wagon man looked up from his work. "That's me, yes."

"Oh!" Finn dropped Janat's arm. "Your cousin's been expecting you. Colm told me what you've done." He regarded the young man with admiration.

They could escape. Meg nodded at Rennika and tried to catch Janat's eye.

"Colm!" Sulwyn Cordal gave his shanty a disgusted shake of the head and abandoned the task. "I was about to look for him."

But Janat was by the glazier's shop, leaning on the wall as if she would be sick.

"I was headed for the tavern, but I'll take you to him," Finn offered. "What about them?" He nodded at Janat.

"Give'm to me." The house owner snatched Janat's arm again.

Rennika slipped to Meg's side. Ready. The girl knew.

"Please, Sieur," Janat squeaked, using the low accent they had been practicing. She swallowed, and Meg wondered if she would vomit. "I'm a refugee, turned out by the king's men, just as he said." She nodded at the shanty man.

The three men halted at Janat's words and stared at her.

"Colm's with some others," Finn said slowly to Sulwyn, "by a cook fire in the square."

Sulwyn looked at Janat curiously. He removed the farmer's hand from Janat's arm and took her, himself. "Good, then. We'll sort it out there."

"Please," Janat said again. "Just let us go."

But the man, Sulwyn Cordal, guided her with a quiet authority toward the village square. Meg, loath to remove her hood from her face, stumped after them, holding Rennika at her side. The house owner, suddenly quiet, followed.

CHAPTER 8

A cook fire in a square where three roads met had melted a patch of snow, exposing the cobbles. Some scary men sat on stumps or stood warming their hands and holding mugs. The smell of roast goose tormented Rennika's stomach so she wanted to cry, but Meg stopped her beyond the reach of the fire's light.

"Sulwyn!" One of the men came forward, arms outstretched, his hood falling to his shoulders.

Sulwyn Cordal—the nice one, who'd built a shanty next to his wagon—clapped this new man on the hand. "Colm. Good to see you. It's been a long time."

Colm gestured to the stumps. "Sorry for the rough welcome, and no place to stay. I'm sleeping on the tavern floor, myself."

Would he give them food?

Sulwyn accepted a mug from one of the men, and Colm nodded to the others around the fire. Sulwyn wasn't as old as the others, but still they looked at him like he was.

"These are all reliable men," his cousin Colm said. Everyone they'd met in the last weeks seemed to be someone's cousin or brother-in-law or aunt.

Finn, the one who'd grabbed Janat, pulled a spit from the heat. He sliced Sulwyn a portion of dripping goose meat, and it was all Rennika could do to keep from rushing forward.

"Who's them?" A man jerked his head in their direction.

"Thieves," the house owner said, giving Janat a shove into the firelight. Janat had her hood up again.

"Spruce Falls has no thieves," the man said, biting into his dripping meat.

"No? What of the man who was robbed of two hens just last week?" the house owner said.

"Stolen by a fox, old man." Finn laughed at him. Good.

"I tell you," the house owner with the pigs warned. "Orumon isn't as safe as it was last summer."

Sulwyn took a barley dumpling from a pot beside the hearth. He spoke to Meg but held the dumpling out to Rennika. "Come, girl. For the child. Tell us your story so we can decide what to do with you."

Rennika was a bit insulted to be called a child, but she looked to Meg for consent, then darted into the warmth and snatched the dumpling, cramming the sticky lump into her mouth, barely chewing.

Janat slumped onto a stump by the flames, holding her stomach. Rennika huddled close by her, licking the oil from her palms. Meg came forward and reached for the offered food.

"Wait."

Rennika stilled, watchful, holding Janat's fingers. What did Colm want?

Colm's hand clapped on Meg's exposed arm. The men eyed her hand, their meal in abeyance. Colm tugged Meg's hood from her head. He pushed Janat's hood back as well. "Magiels." He pulled Rennika's hood back, too.

He said it like it was bad.

"Just village magiels, Sieur," Meg said, and Rennika knew she was trying to speak the way the others spoke, but not very well. "Only refugees turned out when our home was burned."

Colm held out the pot of barley dumplings to Meg but peered at her closely. "You talk odd, for a village magiel from these parts."

Meg shrugged and lowered her eyes, taking a dumpling.

The tightness in Janat's hand told Rennika running would come soon and suddenly.

The nice one, Sulwyn, narrowed his eyes and studied them more closely in the firelight. "Three sisters."

"Gah! What are you after?" Colm said, giving the nice man a mug of beer. "A magiel and a half-magiel. The young one's a worldling."

Sulwyn waited as though his words were a question.

"No, sir," Meg mumbled after a moment. "What he said." She nodded at Colm.

"You all have a semblance." Sulwyn considered them carefully. "Narrow faces. Oval eyes."

Meg said nothing but looked down. Rennika watched the men's expressions for a sign she'd be sprinting again.

"High-talking magiels," Finn said, putting a stick on the fire and giving it a stir so the flames leapt up, making light. "Probably servants for a lord."

Janat lifted her face. "Yes, sieur. That's it."

"So are you village magiels, or aren't you?" Colm pressed.

Janat stopped chewing. Rennika couldn't understand why they talked as if being magiels was a bad thing, but she ate a dumpling and got ready to bolt.

"Where are you from?" Sulwyn asked Meg, and his voice was nice.

"Up valley," Meg replied. She looked at him as though she thought he was familiar but couldn't remember.

"Where, up valley?"

She hesitated.

"Archwood?"

"Archwood's under siege," Finn said, nudging Sulwyn's arm, filling the wagon man's cup. "No one's getting out of Archwood."

"Where are you going?" Sulwyn persisted, still scrutinizing Meg.

She shrugged. "Down valley."

"Just what we need," Colm said, but his voice wasn't as nice. "Hey, Sulwyn. Couldn't we avoid the king's men better with a little magiel magic?"

Sulwyn drank deep and pulled a stump closer to the fire. "Leave them be, Colm. Let them eat a little and go." He eyed the man with the pigs. "You want to take these girls to the reeve? Hmm? I wouldn't want to anger a magiel."

The man's eyes darted from Meg to Janat and back. "No. By the Many Gods, no." He bowed to them uncertainly and backed away, picking up his pace as he left. Rennika stared. How odd, the way the house owner listened, even though he looked old enough to be Sulwyn's father.

Sulwyn found a second cup and poured a splash of water

into it as they watched the farmer go. "So," he said to the others. "Business?"

Colm shot Sulwyn a look of shock.

"They're only refugee magiels." Sulwyn turned back to them. "You're not going to tell King Artem what we say." He gave Janat the water. "Are you?"

Janat shook her head sharply.

"There." Sulwyn smiled at Janat.

"So?" Finn asked Sulwyn under his breath, his voice eager. "Rumors are that everyone in the valley is ready to fight. Is it true?"

"Aye. Most." Sulwyn refilled his own mug. "Some are afraid, keeping out of trouble, and some . . . it's hard to tell. But most." His voice, too, was quiet, almost masked by the crackle of the fire. "The men of my village, and those in Larch Meadow and Storm River and Fisk support King Ean of Orumon. We have some wealthy and influential traders and guildsmen, and we look to band with others. Send a delegation to King Artem. Get our country back. Get our capital out of siege."

"A delegation?" Finn spluttered. "Traders and guildsmen? Artem came here with an *army*."

"We don't want war," Sulwyn said.

War . . .

"We've *got* war," Finn shot back.

Colm glanced at Meg and spoke so quietly Rennika could barely hear him. "As near as we can see, King Artem, with all respect, is mad. Madmen don't listen to argument. We're with the men who sent you, Sulwyn, but we can't be naive. Even our reeve is on board, though he makes a show of cooperating with the king's men." He shook his head. "He has no choice."

"If it comes to fighting, it comes to fighting," Sulwyn whispered. "But if we can make the king listen without bloodshed, we will. Send one of your number to Black Earth Creek by midwinter. There'll be a council of commoners."

Rennika squinted at Janat. *What's a council of commoners?* She shrugged. But Janat frowned in annoyance, not understanding.

Finn whistled. "Commoners."

"Yes." Sulwyn nodded significantly. "No matter how strong or respected a king might be, he can't just take away his allies' freedoms. Trample their fields, steal their food, hunt their rightful king."

"A king can do as he pleases," Colm said. "He's appointed by the Gods."

"He can't," Sulwyn repeated. "It's wrong."

"Well, make your delegation," Finn said. "But men will rise up. The people will overthrow him."

"Yes, but how?" Colm argued. "How do we organize? Where do we get weapons? How can we possibly succeed if we oppose the will of the Gods? Men won't rise up for that." He shook his head. "People won't risk their lives and their families. They'll grumble and live with what Artem Delarcan gives them."

"Then we need to find men willing to fight." Finn's words were soft, but they rang with conviction. "I'm a smith. I'll make swords. Armor. Arrow tips. Whatever we need."

"In secret," Colm finished for him. "With no money and no iron. When your master's looking the other way."

"We don't have answers yet," Sulwyn reminded him, draining his mug. "That's why we're having a council."

"All right, fight. Fine. And then what?" Colm said. "Taking this matter—the governance of a country, for the sake of the Gods!— into the hands of men?" He scoffed. "Men? It's blasphemy, and we'll pay for it." He looked at Meg, as if to invite her opinion. But Rennika didn't think he believed what he said so much as he wanted Sulwyn to correct him.

Meg said nothing.

"Our cause is moral and right, and the Gods are on our side," Sulwyn said quietly. "The Gods will right this wrong. But they'll do it through the actions of men."

Janat's fingers tightened in Rennika's.

"I'm going to Coldridge to see if we can find allies there," Sulwyn said.

Coldridge—where Uncle Chirles lived.

"Coldridge? In Teshe? You're leaving the country?" Finn leaned forward and whistled with appreciation.

Rennika looked at Janat's face, stiff with tension in the firelight. Ready to run? Or ready to vomit again, more like.

Footsteps crunched in the snow behind them.

"Cover their faces." Sulwyn's voice, and a hand pushed Rennika's hood down.

"Colm Cordal." A man spoke.

Janat kept her head bowed. The man sounded annoyed, though not, she noted hopefully, angry.

"I told you before, there's too many of you here. Go to your homes."

"Sorry, Sieur." Colm Cordal. Sulwyn's cousin.

From beneath her hood, Janat saw the feet of the men around the fire shuffle as they rose to comply. She nudged Rennika.

"There's more here now than there were before." The man's legs appeared before them, barring the way. "Here. Show yourself, woman."

Janat raised her eyes in question but said nothing. None of the men in the ring spoke.

"Yes, you," he barked. "And the little one."

These were King Artem's men. She'd met King Artem. He was a kind man. He would never hurt them. All she needed was a bed. But once they saw who she was—Meg was wrong—they'd take the three of them to safety.

One of the soldiers came forward and took Janat's chin and held it up in the firelight.

She froze, shocked at the unwanted touch. Men did not touch women this way. And certainly not magiels.

"Pretty." Then the man's hand dropped as if he had contacted something hot. "Your face has some blur to it." He blustered. "Did your mother lie with a magiel, girl?"

Janat felt herself blush, but she didn't speak.

"Get away, you." The lieutenant slapped his man's hand. "Stand back there, girl, until I tell you different." The leader nodded at Meg. "And this one?"

"Lieutenant." Finn interposed himself between Meg and the soldier, his voice sweet as honey. He pushed a cup into the captain's hand. "This is the third time today you've inspected us."

"I know. Listen, I have orders." The one who spoke, the one with the metal pin on his neckband and the mug in his hand, looked doubtfully at Finn. Three men stood behind him, all wearing cloaks of green. He scrutinized Meg, still seated and clutching her stomach as if she were ill, her head bowed beneath her hood.

Finn produced a wineskin, adjusting his posture to direct the soldier toward the fire. "Sieur, these young girls just brought us food and drink," he soothed. "Come, eat something with us, and we'll be finding our beds."

Colm Cordal pulled the last spit from the fire and cut meat for the soldiers. "These men harm no one. The winter stores in their villages have gone to support the king's troops and they've been displaced, looking for charity. The butcher gave us a goose." He held a savory chunk of meat on the point of his knife for the lieutenant.

Janat backed toward Meg, clutching Rennika. They hadn't recognized her. Hadn't offered them help. But the lieutenant had seen she was a magiel, and it made him afraid.

If only she could lie down. Sleep.

"There's a new decree," the lieutenant said. "Magiels aren't to mix with worldlings. You shouldn't be eating from the same stew pot." But he took the hot meat and juggled it between his fingers.

Finn poured mead into the lieutenant's cup. "Sulwyn, why don't you take your *cousins* home?"

"Your . . . 'cousins.'" The lieutenant shook his head at the deception. "Listen, if it were up to me, we wouldn't be here. I've a wife and three daughters in Arcan."

"So, why are you?" The young man, Sulwyn, put an arm around Janat's shoulder. His sudden closeness was unnerving and somehow pleasing at the same time, though she didn't have the energy to resist. By Ranuat's murderers, what role was she to play in this charade? Nothing made sense.

"Common knowledge soon enough. I may as well tell you." The lieutenant tore a chunk of meat with his teeth. "Worship of the Many Gods has been outlawed."

What?

There was an audible gasp among the men.

"Outlawed?" Finn blurted.

The lieutenant drank his mead. "All but the One God."

The men stared at him. Finn stiffened as if he held himself back from striking out.

Rennika hugged Janat's arm to her chest.

The world had turned into a mad house. Janat tried to glance at Meg, but Meg sat, unmoving, her head down, feigning illness. Too dangerous to run, even if they wanted to, with all these soldiers, and her stomach roiling. And Sulwyn's arm still draped across her shoulders.

"Don't blame me." The lieutenant shoved the last of his meat into his mouth. "But the prayer stones have been destroyed, so there's no way for a magiel to deliver your prayers to any God but the One. All the prayer stones, but the Ruby, of course. Well, and the Amber, but it'll be captured when Archwood falls. Maybe ten days, at most."

Mama's Amber.

"That's—that's—" Finn sputtered. "Outrageous! The king—"

"By the Gods, why?" Colm asked.

The soldier who'd touched Janat took a threatening step forward. "We don't question King Artem Delarcan."

Sulwyn Cordal released her, and interposed himself between Colm and the soldier.

They had to leave. Oh, Gods, they had to get home.

"Sergeant!" the lieutenant snapped.

The soldier stepped back insolently.

The lieutenant washed his meat down with wine. "Just let the others know," he said to Finn. "Times have changed. Don't look to King Ean for help. Or the Gods."

"But the king's authority comes from the Gods!" Finn purpled. "Artem can't—"

"It comes from the One God." The lieutenant shoved his cup into Finn's hand. "King Artem can. And he has."

Colm glowered at the ground, his fists balled.

Janat looked to Meg, but Meg's face was covered by her hood. Gods, why wouldn't she look at her? They had to *do* something. Step across the circle and align themselves with King Artem's men, perhaps?

"Men can only pray to the One God." The lieutenant's gaze swept over each man in the circle. "And *only* through the Ruby. The sooner everyone understands that, the better off we'll all be."

King Artem Delarcan had the Ruby.

The lieutenant stepped away from the fire. "Oh." He turned back, looking at Janat curiously. "By the way. There's a rumor in the valley. That a magiel escaped from Archwood. We have orders to bring him to Holder's Crossing."

It was all she could do not to lock eyes with the lieutenant, signal, show him again her likeness.

"Him?" Sulwyn asked.

"Or her." The lieutenant wiped his fingers on his pants, his gaze lingering on Janat for a moment before dismissing her.

He thought she had only half blood. Thought she wasn't the magiel from Archwood. Nausea rose up again in her stomach.

The lieutenant stepped away from the fire. "When I return, you'd all best be gone."

CHAPTER 9

"Blasphemy," Colm said in a low voice. "The prayer stones. Smashed."

Meg listened for all she was worth.

"And bloody dangerous. Hunting magiels. Destroying prayer stones." Sulwyn Cordal poured the last of the wine into his mug and kicked snow into the fire. It sizzled and smoked.

The others gathered their things and began to disperse. Snow began to fall again.

The Amber. The lieutenant said King Artem would have it in a few days. That meant he expected the walls of Archwood to fail.

"By the Many, where will our death tokens come from now?" Finn asked. "Does the king want his people cursed to wander as homeless spirits once they die? Deny them access to Heaven?"

"Merchants and petty lords have become too rich," Colm said. "Too powerful. The people have come to expect certain rights." He eyed Sulwyn. "They think they can force their will on a king. This is punishment."

"The king would say he's protecting royal authority," Finn said. "But he's grabbing power."

And Mama. When—if—the city fell, the castle fell . . .

For some unfathomable reason, Janat was looking daggers at her. She frowned back. *What?*

Colm pulled Meg's hood back and eyed her like King Ean's Master of Horse sizing up a colt for sale. "So. Are you the magiel the lieutenant spoke of, from Archwood?" he asked. "Or are you just a village magiel with high-born speech?"

Meg's throat constricted. He knew. They all knew. But what would they do?

Keep her and her sisters. Mama had said, *Be careful. Of those would use you for their political advantage.*

Coldridge, capital of Teshe. They had to survive until they could get to Coldridge. Mama had a brother there, a magiel, Uncle Chirles. Meg had met him last summer when Mama took them on the endless journey across Shangril's seven countries. And—King Larin of Teshe would surely help them.

"Speak, girl!"

"I'm no one, Sieur." Meg mumbled, trying her best to copy the vulgar accent. She lowered her gaze.

"Lying, to save yourself." Colm fastened his fingers around Meg's wrist. "Bargaining advantage," he said to the others.

Meg jerked back, but Colm's hold was solid.

"What are you doing?" Sulwyn Cordal asked.

"Why not?" Colm replied. "She's valuable. We could get this valley back."

We. Who were these men, who talked about councils of commoners and bargaining with King Artem, and fighting?

She and her sisters could not outrun these men.

"You think we're in a position to bargain with a *king*?" Finn asked. "He'd just send a dozen men to take what he wants. We need to raise a fighting force first."

We.

"Save her, then," Colm shot back. But the others eyed him with doubt, and his voice became less certain. "Bargain when we're ready."

"Let her go."

Colm eyed Sulwyn and dropped Meg's arm.

Finn picked up the mugs and skewers, and then emptied the wine skin's remains into Sulwyn's outstretched mug. "Listen, we have to get out of here before the lieutenant comes back," he said. "Talk about this later." He took off at a jog, following the others through thickening flakes of snow.

"So? What do we do with the magiel?" Colm asked. "We have to put her somewhere. Until we decide."

These men . . . they were organizing. Creating a force *outside* the armies of the kings.

Sulwyn Cordal shook his head in disgust. "They're free to go."

"But—"

"We think, first. Then act." This man. Not tall or broad. Not wise with age. But people did what he said.

Colm shrugged. "All right." He snorted a rueful laugh. "I guess we're not quite ready to keep prisoners. No place to keep them."

Sulwyn smiled at the quip, and Colm shrugged off down a lane leading deeper into the village. Sulwyn turned to look at them— Meg and her sisters huddled together in the snow next to the remains of the fire. "Do you have a place to stay?"

"No," Janat said sullenly. Meg could not fathom why she was angry. But this man had nothing to offer them.

Rennika lifted her head. The little thing. She was faint with cold and exhaustion. They all were.

"I have a shanty. It's not much, but if you want to share it, I'll sleep in my wagon."

There was no longer any use disguising her accent. "We've no reason to trust you, either."

"You're free to go." Sulwyn opened his hands wide, indicating the road from town. "It's late. It's cold." He nodded at Janat. "She's ill."

Meg chewed her lip. He was right.

Sulwyn held a hand out, indicating the way they'd go.

"And tomorrow?" Janat asked. But they were already moving down the lane toward the shanty.

"I don't know," he said. "If you want . . ." He shrugged. "Leave before dawn. I shan't help anyone, king or commoner, to stop you."

King or commoner. These men were . . . different. More than just gossiping farmers. *Becoming* something more than just gossiping farmers.

They turned the corner and Meg peered through the swirling ice crystals at the half-constructed shelter. She had to keep her sisters alive. If they fled, would King Artem's men come for them in the middle of the night? Or would they die of cold in the woods? By the Gods, she wished these decisions didn't fall on her shoulders. "Thank you," she said, finally giving in. "We'll use the shanty." She eyed him dubiously. "Will you have enough . . . blankets?"

He shrugged amiably and lifted his mug, his face flushed and his collar open. "I have a bottle of mead to keep me warm." He repositioned the poles, straightening the cases and blankets that formed its roof and walls, dividing his supply of bedding between the shanty and the wagon.

Janat plucked at Meg's sleeve. "I don't trust those men," she said under her voice.

"You want to take the road? With wolves and orums?" Meg whispered back. "You're too sick to walk all night, and Rennikala certainly can't. We'll freeze in the snow."

"Then why don't we just turn ourselves over to the king's men? By the Gods, Meghra, they'll take care of us. We can live in Holderford Castle with our cousins." She fought to keep back tears of frustration. "I don't think I can take any more of this. We weren't meant to sleep in the snow and eat garbage. We weren't."

"Haven't you heard a thing anyone's said?" Meg hissed.

"I've heard it all," said Janat. "But it isn't true. It can't be true."

The simple fact was that Meg didn't understand. Janat *had* been listening to the men, not just tonight, but whenever men talked big about fighting and getting back their—what? Common men didn't have lands or rights or freedoms. So Janat had no idea what it was they were trying to get back. She suspected they didn't, either.

But Meg was just a bully. She thought Janat couldn't have a brain in her head. Meg couldn't see that the men were divided among themselves. They had no plans, no leader to bring them together, no weapons. And certainly, no hope against an army.

Meg said she was taking them to Coldridge, to Mama's brother, but that had been weeks ago, and they were still high in the Orumon valley, with no way of knowing how far it was to Coldridge, or how to get there. They were starving, and their desperation was pointless.

Besides, Janat had met King Artem. He could seem stern, sitting with King Ean at the head of the table, but she'd heard him laugh. He had a deep, infectious laugh.

Janat eased herself out of the shanty without waking Meg or

Rennika.

In the back of the cart, the long, blanketed lump that was Sulwyn snored softly in the silence of falling flakes. Snow in the air all around shimmered in the dark, settling gently on the drifts.

The hamlet of Spruce Falls could not have consisted of more than fifty shops and homes, most of which were laid out along the road that had brought them from Carn Archwood, and along a scatter of winding lanes. It would not be difficult to find King Artem's men.

Shivering, Janat pulled her rags more tightly about her and followed the road uphill toward the center of the village. Since she'd emptied her stomach, she felt better, if exhausted. She passed the place where the rebels had discussed their plans earlier. A smudge of charcoal stained the snow. The village square was deserted now, though light and music seeped from the tavern windows.

Further on, up the hill, a spark of firelight lit the road and reflected off the buildings nearby. A sentinel stood guard before the reeve's house.

"Who's there?" The sentinel drew his sword, scanning the terrain in their immediate vicinity. He wore Arcan colors.

"Friend," Janat called, halting well away from the light of the fire.

"Identify yourself."

"Janatelle Falkyn, daughter of Talanda Falkyn, of Orumon." Meg would be mad, but Janat would send for her and Rennika once she was safe.

The man straightened. "Magiel," he muttered. He sheathed his sword. "Welcome, Janatelle Falkyn," he called, but there was a squeak in his voice, and she wondered how old he was. "It is an honor to serve you."

She hesitated. The fire crackled merrily, and the soldier was welcoming and subservient—as so he should be. But— "Where are the rest of the soldiers?"

"My captain is at the tavern just now, but I can help you. He will wish to greet you as soon as I inform him you are here."

Soft beds. Food. A place in the court of Holderford.

"Janatelle!"

Janat turned.

Down the road, slipping on the icy cobbles, Meg ran, scowling with fury. "What are you doing?"

"What we should've done weeks ago." Janat turned and hurried toward the sentinel.

"Janatelle!" Meg screeched.

In that instant, Janat reached him and his fingers fastened about her wrist. Startled, she pulled back. But the firm grip held her.

"Let go of her!" Meg ran up behind Janat as the sentinel drew his sword again.

His grip slipped momentarily and he cried out as Janat yanked back. Meg was biting his wrist.

Janat squirmed, shock and fear exploding in her heart. "That's not how you treat a magiel!"

He walloped her across the cheek.

Pain erupted from her mouth, flashing across her jaw and head and she stumbled, almost blinded.

No! This man would not do this to her.

He shoved Meg back and there was an instant of confusion. The sentinel seemed unprepared to use the awkwardly long weapon on her.

What could she—magic.

His foot. She grasped his arm, felt the shape of his body from within, found a time when his foot was in a different position. Moved it to that time—

Footsteps resounded on the cobbles behind her. Another soldier?

Her attacker's foot slipped and he toppled—she intensified the speed of his fall and he cracked his head. His sword clattered to the ground. She whirled to face whoever—

Sulwyn Cordal.

He kicked the sentinel's sword away, knelt and took his dirk. He cast a quick glance around the street. Empty. "The captain is in his cups, and his men not much better. We have a bit of time. But—" He shook his head. "—how in the Gods' names are we going to explain this?"

Janat sank back, her chest tightening, a pain in the back of her throat.

Meg chewed her lip. "A spell of forgetting?"

But she had no ingredients. "Do you know the cast?" Janat whispered.

"There's one in my book." Meg shrugged. "I read it once."

Her book. In Castle Archwood.

"I . . . could . . ." Sulwyn looked down at the soldier's dirk in his hand. "I could . . . cut his throat." His face was pale and sick in the dark. "And we could leave tonight."

Meg drilled him with shocked eyes.

Dread sank through Janat's stomach. Her folly might cost this soldier—boy—his life.

"They'd hunt for us anyway," Meg said.

Janat couldn't implicate this stranger, Sulwyn. She shouldn't have drawn in Meg. Gods, what had she . . .

Sulwyn swallowed and gave a jerk of his head. "Go. Get the cart ready. We'll deal with soldiers when they come."

"No." Janat stilled his hand.

Meg flashed a look of anger at her.

"It's my fault." Her breath became tight, and her words choked. "There was a struggle." She pointed to the prints in the snow. "He was robbed of his purse. He fell, hit his head. He can't speak."

Meg's scowl dissolved.

Janat's mouth dried. "I'll do it."

"What?" Sulwyn asked.

"Dislodge a nerve. In his tongue."

※

Sulwyn's wagon creaked and bumped over the ruts and rocks of the King's Road. They'd thrown everything into the cart and driven through the night. The sun had risen and, so far, there was no sign of pursuit. Finn had offered to mislead the captain, tell him there'd been too many thieves in Orumon since the war displaced people.

Meg held onto Janat for warmth, Rennika between them, asleep. Sulwyn's blankets covered them to the chin. They owed this stranger much, but he'd made light of the difficulties. He was happy to annoy foreign soldiers, he said.

But . . . Cordal. Meg had heard the name before. When?

She shook her head. It would come. She hoped the merchant would be able to untangle the faint path through nameless villages and lonesome farms that made up the King's Road. These past weeks, Meg had been hard pressed to know when she was following a path to the next town, and when she was leading her sisters on a winding game trail with no destination. Last summer, Mama's retinue had brought them all down the valley in a coach, but the trip had been slow and uncomfortable and she'd paid no attention to how their guides distinguished the King's Road from any of the other forest tracks.

She shifted a bit of blanket more firmly under Janat's head against the jolt of the cart. The sound of the running river rushing endlessly on their left had finally soothed her sister to sleep. Janat's weeping and bruises had torn at Meg's heart as much as the girl's foolishness had angered and frightened her.

Fifteen. Too young for the brutality of this world.

Overhead, the inky branches of trees blotted out all but glimpses of the almost-black sky, and the occasional snowflake still drifted down to melt on her cheek. The air tasted cold and sharp. Sulwyn slumped on the front seat, more a reminder to his pony to keep walking than a guide.

Cordal. Nanna had said the name. *That's* where Meg had heard it. When they were fleeing the castle. A merchant, one they were supposed to find in the lower city. One who would bring them to safety.

Meg scrutinized his back in the dark, swaying with the rolling of the wagon. He was from up valley. But from a village, he'd said. Not Archwood. If he'd been in Archwood the night of the attack, he'd still be there, she was sure.

She adjusted her position, settling back against the bump and jolt of the grain sacks. She must learn more about him. What he knew of Mama's plan.

They needed some form of protection. Mama had taught Meg a few spells, using the magical properties of everyday objects like kitten livers, newts' eyes, and snowmelt collected under the stars of Kyaju, as well as rudimentary magiel magic, the manipulation of time. But not enough. And they couldn't depend on strangers, like Sulwyn, rescuing them every time they did something stupid.

Janat's eyes were open.

"You should rest," Meg whispered.

Janat gave her a piercing look, then scrutinized the night around them. "Is this Sieur Cordal's cart?" she whispered through swollen lips.

Meg stared at her. "You know it is. We just ran—"

"Leaving Archwood," Janat murmured. "Heading for Coldridge."

Meg wasn't sure if this was a question or if Janat spoke to herself. "Yes."

"I used magic that night." Janat's attention riveted on her. "I haven't got long. What do you need to know?"

Meg was taken aback. This was not the Janat she knew.

"Listen." Janat nodded to confirm her thought. "I can help you." She spoke clearly through her mangled mouth. "But only for a few minutes."

"Yes. I was just . . ." Meg stared. "I—I need a tutor. In magic."

Instantly, her sister understood. "You won't find one in Coldridge." Janat riveted on her. "Along the road to Silvermeadow. Gweddien's mother. She taught us. Remember that name, Gweddien Barcley."

This Janat had come from someday, elsewhere in her life. From her future.

"You might think Rennika's too young, but teach her, too. Everything you can. You have to be strong, Meg. You have to. For her—and for me. You might not think it, but I'll need you. Do you . . . " Janat's eyes flickered, and she fell silent, staring at the wagon as it bumped its way through the woods.

The moment of time travel had passed. But if she came from the future, she still lived. When? How long in the future?

Meg tucked the blanket under Janat's chin where it had slipped. Janat had been older, that was sure. So there was hope. Wasn't there?

A weight descended on her shoulders. Be strong? Wasn't that what she was doing? By Kyaju—*and Janat ran off to give herself up to the king's guard with some story she's a magiel princess—or near enough—in need of protection? That Artem Delarcan would take her into his care?* How stupid, how utterly—and now it was up to Meg to patch things up. Be strong. Hah!

Janat blinked and shook her head, frowning at the woods in bewilderment. "Why did you wake me?" she whimpered through cracked lips. "I was having the loveliest dream." She thought her travels to other parts of her life had been a sleep fantasy. She was still so young and confused, the tenderness of childhood rounding her cheeks. Starvation had not yet stolen all her softness.

Janat looked away, a thought creasing her brow.

Meg took Janat's hands. "Janat. You can't think of that soldier."

Janat tried to pull away. "He was no older than you, Meg. And I took . . . He'll never talk to anyone again."

"And he would have thrown you into a prison, or worse."

Rennika woke and sat up.

"We have to survive," Meg pressed. "Not run to others for help. Take care of ourselves. Do you understand?"

Janat nodded, but her eyes were unconvinced.

Rennika cocked her head. "What happened?" She'd barely woken last night when they transferred her into the wagon.

"We have to hide who we are."

"How?" Janat asked. "What have we ever been trained to do?"

Meg reflected. "Well. For one thing, we can change our names."

"Change our names?" Rennika perked up, interested.

Meg considered her. Dirty, disheveled and dressed in rags, she hardly looked a princess. The name Rennikala struck Meg suddenly as absurd for this waif. "Aristocrats and magiels usually have long names. What if we call you . . . Rennika? And for a last name . . . Falconer."

"Rennika. Rennikala. Rennika." Rennika savored the word on her tongue. "It sounds funny."

"Janatelle can be Janat," Meg said.

Janat gave a slight shrug. "And Meghra?"

"Just Meg," Meg said, rocking with the heaving of the cart. "And we can learn the commoners' accent. Sieur Cordal can teach us."

"Can we have our names back after we go to the tarn?" asked Rennika.

"Yes." Meg tucked her cloak closer about her shoulders. "And once we've righted the world, you can have whatever you want to eat."

"Raspberries," Rennika said. "Raspberries with yoghurt. And honey."

"And cakes made from wheat flour from Midell," Janat whispered, gazing up the valley toward the mountains. "Apples from Midell, and wine all the way from Arcan. And furs! And a wool robe made in Highglen, so I'm never cold again, dyed with scarletberry and indigo and marigold. And—dresses made of brocade from the looms of Fairdell and silks from the valley of Aadi." She smiled, but her smile was sadder, now, touched with the knowledge that such things would never come to pass. "But the world's changed, hasn't it? We'll never go home."

Meg had no answer to this. Her sisters fell silent, each wrapped in her own thoughts. Feasts and dancing at court. Candelabras lighting the palace like day. The musicians and the parquet floors and the paintings on the walls and the children playing amongst the fountains and gardens. That had been their life. But it was a fantasy now; a fantasy far away. "Tell me your dream, Janat," Meg said softly.

Janat's frown faded into thoughtfulness. "I was with Rennikala."

"Rennika. Remember."

"Rennika," she corrected herself. "Just the two of us. We were in some shabby room, but we'd cooked a chicken for supper and some vegetables I've never seen before." She smiled at Rennika. "You were laughing at something, Rennika. We ate with our fingers, and the meat was juicy and dripping with grease, and, oh, Meghra, so delicious." Janat shrugged, but her cheeks glistened. "That's all."

There was a future, then. And in it, there was food, and there was joy.

CHAPTER 10

In the lower valley, the road to Coldridge cut a wide swath through forest, field, and river flats, its mud rutted by army supply wagons and churned by the hooves of hundreds of King Artem's horses. Had the clay not been frozen, it would have been impassable. As it was, Sulwyn gave his plodding mare slack and she picked her way through the grooves and clumps. Meg trudged from frozen clod to frozen clod when the chill and the jouncing of the cart became too much for her, and rode when her legs were tired of walking. Crystal blue skies ruled the cold, clear days, and stars glittered in the vast firmament at night.

Meg saw an orum from far off, heading south, as they crossed a snow-drifted gravel flat beside the River Archwood. "Rennika! Get in the cart!" She reached over the back of the box and held out her hand.

Rennika ran through the snow. "It's too far away. It won't—"

"Get in!" Meg said impatiently, sitting on a sack of grain. "You don't know what an orum will see or hear. Remember your death token."

Rennika scrambled across Meg's knees as Sulwyn urged the pony forward toward the protection of a copse of spruce trees.

"Halt in the name of King Artem Delarcan!" A voice rose behind them in the distance, barely audible above the clatter of the cart wheels and the rush of the open water. Meg peered out of the back of the jouncing wagon to see two men on horses, some distance back, pursuing them.

Green cloaks.

And beyond, the orum wheeled. It turned toward them. She touched the hard, round coin sewn into the collar at her neck.

"Sieur Cordal!" Janat cried.

Sulwyn turned in his seat.

The men on horseback gained on them. But the orum in the distance drove its wings with terrible power, all three heads trained in their direction.

The pony neighed in terror and plunged into the forest, overturning the cart and jamming it in springy willows, gripping the vehicle fast. Sulwyn leapt out, lifting Rennika to the snow as Meg and Janat scrambled for safety.

Meg ploughed through the willows, trying to keep her feet, trying to keep Rennika upright. Ahead, the pony snorted, struggling against its traces. Sulwyn set it free from the cart. Behind them, the pounding of hooves and terrified neighing told her the soldiers' beasts had scented the orum.

A blast of wind struck Meg's back with a hail of snow, knocking her into the willows. A man yelped behind her. Looking up, she saw the flash of an inky shadow as wings snapped branches on either side of her. From the orum's center mouth, an arm dangled. Then the creature disappeared beyond the treetops.

"Down!" Sulwyn yelled, and Meg yanked Rennika beneath the branches of a spruce tree. A riderless horse shoved past them, stumbling into the woods.

Meg pushed Rennika behind the bole of the tree, shielding her sister with her body, looking back the way they'd come, toward the river. A soldier—the lieutenant who'd questioned them?—leaned over another soldier who lay in the snow. Janat cowered beneath the cart, sobbing. A sword glittered in the snow. Sulwyn darted out and snatched it up.

The orum.

It came in low and landed at a gallop on four horse-like legs, shattering the icy water, charging with open mouths.

One head reared over the lieutenant who drew his sword and slashed at the base of the creature's neck. The center head plunged into the injured soldier's belly, tossing him back and forth like a cat worrying a mouse. The third head snaked lightning-fast toward Sulwyn, who stabbed at the thing with the soldier's weapon.

Meg cringed in the forest as the lieutenant's sword lodged in the creature's neck. The orum cried out like a thousand strident gulls, its neck whipping in a great arc, lifting the man from his feet.

A dagger flung from the cart glinted in the snow. One of Sulwyn's they'd used for cutting food—

Meg untangled herself from the willows to snatch the blade up, dove at a hind leg and slashed the orum's ankle. Sulwyn stabbed wildly into the thick skin of the third neck.

The orum lunged forward, stumbling into the wagon. Sulwyn's blade flung wide, missing Meg, its tip slicing across the center neck. The lieutenant scrambled to his feet, pulling the sword from its first neck with a gout of blood, but the thing's needle teeth tore a chunk from his back. He squealed in pain and dropped his sword.

Now even Janat, with her bruised face, darted forward. Scooping the lieutenant's blade from the snow, she held it in both hands, braced for the orum's attack. The orum screamed and feinted over her, but the lieutenant, unbuckling his ax, buried this new weapon deep in the pit of the monster's throat. The first head flailed into the sky and blood spurted from the wound.

With a predator's sense for weakness, the center head, its neck streaming from a dozen cuts, darted across and bit deeply into the lieutenant's shoulder, gripping like a snake bound on swallowing him whole. Meg rushed forward and stabbed at the center head.

Sulwyn Cordal severed the third head and the orum collapsed to its knees. Panting and smeared with crimson, he lifted a weary arm and shoved his blade deep into the throat of the center neck.

Meg stumbled backward in the snow as the thing collapsed, twitching. Janat dropped the lieutenant's sword and, stepping back, wrapped her arms around Meg. The two sisters rejoiced with hysterical tears.

Rennika crept cautiously out from behind the tree.

Sulwyn knelt by the king's lieutenant. The man shivered, his mouth opening as if he would speak, wild fright in his eyes. With bloody hands, Sulwyn Cordal tore away the man's neckband and, finding his death token, placed it on the man's tongue. "Find your Heaven," he murmured. The lieutenant closed his lips, coughed, and sank into Sulwyn's arms.

Rennika clung to Janat who held her close. They stared at the still-twitching creature in the snow.

Sulwyn staggered to his feet. He swayed, looking down at the vanquished orum. "We killed . . ." He turned, a look of incredulous, joyful horror on his face. "We killed . . ." He paled to the color of porcelain, and fainted.

✤

Rennika tried to blink away the images that crowded in on her: of blind teeth snatching the soldier's arm, of blood spurting over Sulwyn's shoulder, of Meg running out before the thing and snatching up the knife, of Janat with her sword at the ready. All mixed with remembrances of Nanna on the mountainside. Nanna, who dried her tears when Faris wouldn't play, who sang to her at bedtime, who taught her letters.

And the blurry thing. Or things. Shimmers like the warp of water that flicked in and out at the edges of the battle. Nothing she could see clearly.

One of the soldiers' horses had broken a leg in its terrified plunge through the dense woods and had to be put down; the second could not be found. But Sulwyn returned late that afternoon, leading his mountain pony from some isolated mountain vale.

Rennika and her sisters spent the day cleaning themselves up the best they could, bandaging their cuts and sprains and bruises— nothing worse, by the grace of Kyaju—and burying the two men in rocks pried from the river edge, what they could manage on frozen ground. Sulwyn repaired the wagon.

As she worked, tears and terrors shook Rennika at odd moments, and Meg or Janat would comfort her, but they couldn't erase the pictures in her mind.

Sulwyn could say nothing all through this work but, "We killed it. We killed an orum. Only four of us! And two—women!" He shook his head and chuckled, then covered his face as though he would faint again.

✤

Meg was famished when they sat on stumps in the snow to feast on horse flesh that night. She and Janat had cooked it on a spit over a small fire, chancing there would be no more soldiers nearby to be drawn by the light and smoke.

"I think we need something a wee bit stronger than ale tonight." Sulwyn produced a bottle of amber-colored liquor—nothing Meg had ever seen in King Ean's great hall, and not made in Orumon for market. He poured a parsimonious splash each for Meg and Janat, telling Rennika she would have to wait a few years for hers, and a more generous measure for himself. "Drink it slow," he said, squeezing his watery eyes closed on an ample swallow. He smiled. "Now that's good Teshe barley."

Meg put the mug to her lips. It smelled strongly sweet and nutty, and felt like pins and needles on her tongue. The drop she sipped tasted bad, and it burned and choked her. She made a face and set her mug aside. "Why do you drink it?" She ladled boiled barley into their bowls.

"Ah, why, indeed?" Sulwyn raised his mug into the firelight. "Aqua vita. Water of life. Nectar of the Gods."

"King Ean serves nothing stronger than mead." Meg sliced horsemeat onto the barley and passed out the bowls. "And that, only for important occasions. Otherwise, his court drinks only beer or ale."

"A drop of whiskey never hurt anyone," Sulwyn asserted, and already he looked more relaxed. "It soothes the nerves, brings laughter to the lips, and makes for merry talk. It makes men more accomplished—according to the men—and women prettier. And, on days that are particularly trying, it sends flight to the world's demons."

Janat giggled. Her mouth was still bright with bruises, but the swelling had mostly gone down. "There's no demons here."

Sulwyn toasted her. "It works."

Meg bit into the hot meat, dripping with juices, watching Sulwyn across the fire. "You're not—" She hesitated, not sure how to phrase her question.

Sulwyn looked up from his bowl. His eyes flicked to Janat. She'd been watching him since he came back with the pony, and now she smiled and sipped her whiskey.

"You're not a fighter," Meg finished lamely.

Sulwyn grinned and licked his fingers. "No," he said, regarding her cheerily. "I suppose most men of your acquaintance have been trained with a sword." He winked at Janat.

Meg considered. Yes. Weapons training was a part of the life of a highborn man. And soldiers, of course.

"But—don't lowborn men have to be good with a blade to survive?" Janat asked.

Rennika looked up from her meal with interest.

The man's brows shot up. "Lowborn?"

The darkening of Janat's soft, capricious skin was visible even in the flicker of the firelight.

"My father's a merchant," he said instructively, pouring himself more whiskey. "My family owns no land or titles, but we were reasonably well off. Food on the table—good food. I had a tutor as a child. I can read and write."

"Oh." Janat's blush deepened.

A merchant. Merchant Cordal of Archwood had been part of Mama's plan.

"You might not know it, but your King Ean Olivin was a very fair man." Sulwyn offered to pour again into Janat's cup.

"That's right." A memory popped into Meg's head, and she covered her own mug with her hand. "Janat, remember the fuss? King Ean took on three advisors from the guildsmen. And two merchants as well."

Janat shook her head doubtfully.

"My father was one of his advisors." Sulwyn scooped meat and barley with chopsticks from the bowl held close to his mouth.

Merchant Cordal. Then, Mama would have known him. But . . . should Meg say something? She suspected Sulwyn knew who they were; or at least guessed. Had his father—if that was Mama's "Merchant Cordal"—told Sulwyn about their plans for escape? Sulwyn had said nothing.

"A good king recognizes that what a man contributes from the sweat of his labor or the product of his thinking can make a country wealthy. There's value in more than just aristocracy. King Ean was like that." He set down his bowl and scooped a handful of snow from the ground behind the stump he sat on, and wiped the juices from his chin. "Men like him should be emulated. Not besieged."

"Sieur Cordal . . ." Setting her bowl on the ground, Meg lifted a corner of her robe and wiped her mouth.

"Call me Sulwyn. Sieur Cordal is my father." He held his wet hands up to the flames.

She gave him a short nod of acknowledgement. "Do you know who we are?"

"Meg!" Janat's chin shot up.

Meg said nothing to her sister but studied Sulwyn's reaction.

His response was measured. "I think I do."

She waited, while Janat stewed.

"The day before King Artem's forces attacked, my father sent me to Archwood village to purchase this mountain pony and cart, and supplies for a long trip." He nodded to the darkness behind him. "He said we'd be taking three people on a journey, but he didn't say where. He also said that the commission had come up suddenly, that it was secret, and we would leave on the morrow." His gaze flicked down into the fire. "My parents and my sisters are still in Archwood."

And Mama.

Rennika put her plate in the snow and leaned her head against Janat.

"Did you . . . did you want to show me? Who you are?" he asked.

There was a way for a trueborn magiel of the Great Houses, one descended directly from the One God, to reveal him or herself. To let the firmament of the Heavens shine through her skin. But . . . "You may take my word."

He nodded. "I will."

"And you didn't learn where your passengers were to go?" Meg asked.

"No." He gave a quick shrug. "Like you, I'm homeless now. I can't pursue my trade; I have no merchandise to sell. This cart and a few coins are all I have left. There's no way to free my family, other than by doing what I'm doing. Working to get this lunacy undone." He leaned on his knees and took up his empty mug. "I . . . I've heard things. Seen things. Put things together. Were the three of you my father's passengers?"

Janat looked from her to Sulwyn and back, but she said nothing.

"I think so. We weren't given information. We're . . ." She realized.

"We were just cargo. You don't tell cargo where it's going."

"But valuable cargo, I think." Sulwyn's gaze flicked to Janat's apprehensive face. "You're Talanda Falkyn's daughters, are you not? The magiel heirs to the Amber?"

Meg gave a slight nod. "Every time someone finds out who we are, bad things happen. We are either pariahs or bargaining chips."

"And you don't know where my father was supposed to take you?"

"No."

He gave a grim shake of the head. "Given what I've heard—only rumors, mind you—I can't think of anywhere that's safe. If it's true, if worship of the Many Gods is outlawed and the prayer stones are being smashed . . ." He ran his tongue over his teeth. "King Artem can't have anything good for you, if he catches you. And no one who values their own skin would want to be associated with you unless they can sell you."

"Coldridge." Janat had her arm around Rennika's shoulder, and Rennika was all eyes, frightened. "We have an uncle and cousins there. We visited him last summer."

"If Teshe isn't already occupied by foreign forces," Sulwyn said.

Meg shrugged. "We have to go somewhere. If you would take us that far, we would be grateful."

Janat nodded, and she finished the last of her whiskey.

Sulwyn found a stick and stirred the fire, which had burned low. "I will. At the very least, even if your uncle is . . . not available to you," he said carefully, "Coldridge, by all accounts, should be a large enough city to hide in."

"Is that—is that why you're going to Coldridge?" Meg asked. "To get King Larin to help King Ean?" She'd gathered as much from the conversation she'd overheard in Spruce Falls.

"If I can. If not, I'll keep going until I find someone who'll listen. I'm only a journeyman merchant, not even a member of the guild. Nothing says King Larin will heed me. But, by your leave, King Delarcan's gone mad. That has to be evident to everyone. Perhaps, together, king and commoner can make Artem see the folly of attacking Orumon."

Meg sat back on her stump, stomach satisfied for once. Yes. This man, Sulwyn Cordal, this merchant's son. He had the right of it.

Surely, in Coldridge, King Larin would see things this way as well, and end the madness of these past weeks.

CHAPTER 11

They'd worked out the details. At sixteen, Huwen was finally considered ready to accompany his father on his campaigns and, to his irritation, at fourteen, so was Eamon. Why Eamon, who would not rule and hardly had the temperament or the backbone for a battlefield, was to be trained in war and leadership, was beyond Huwen.

Tomorrow, he and his brother would travel with Father's magiel, a thousand replacements, and a supply train to Teshe, a country on the edge of the wilds. A contingent of the soldiers would turn off the road after only a week's travel to deal with a province announcing it had separated from Arcan so it could divorce itself from what it called "the king's war."

It was disgusting. Didn't peasants know kings were God-appointed? How did they expect to govern *themselves*?

Huwen's new status came with a loosening of his leash, at least in terms of pleasures of the flesh. Anwen was not accorded the same liberties, but her family, seeing the girl fancied none less than the king-to-be, turned a blind eye. Huwen lay, now, spent and sleepy, in Anwen's bed in her parents' grand house in the upper city, playing with a curl of her hair. The day had been cold with the promise of coming winter, but the embers in her fireplace pushed back the chill. "I'll miss you," he said, and it was true. He'd miss Anwen very much on the long road, and in the rough tents at the siege of Archwood, beyond Coldridge's last comforts.

"I'll miss you." Her body fit his exactly, made for him. "I hope I get your baby."

He grinned, though she faced away from him, and he knew she couldn't see it in the dark. The thought of Anwen having his baby pleased him. But— "It's best you don't."

She turned in his arms. "You don't want me to bear your child?"

"I didn't say that." He thought she knew. "You deserve better. You are the most amazing woman. I want you to be happy, and proud, and have the best of everything."

"Better than your child? What could be better?"

He hesitated. "I don't want you to be the mother of bastards."

She stilled, silent in the dark.

"I can't marry you."

Still, she said nothing.

"You knew that."

A tiny puff of warm breath touched his chest. "Yes."

He *would* miss her. Not only this winter, as he accompanied Father on his campaign, but forever, when Father arranged a political marriage for him.

"It seems so unfair." Her voice was soft in the dark.

He had to agree. "The commonest man can marry for love. Even a second son, on occasion. But a king must make alliances."

It was a part of his future that had never concerned Huwen until he'd met Anwen. He understood better now, his father's relationship with his mother. Father and Mother did not argue. Each had his and her own sphere of power, of friendships. But it was an ill-kept secret that Father still visited Uther's mother in her chambers.

But Huwen loved Anwen. "I want the best for you."

"I have the best."

He smiled at the top of her head. "For now, perhaps. But I don't want you to be the one who walks through a room leaving a wake of whispers behind." Uther's mother had her own suite in the great hall. But as a one-time servant girl, she had no status at court, and no friends among her own class. She had a garden and a friend to sit with her.

"I . . ."Anwen's words were tentative, a whisper. "I would be your mistress."

"No, Anwen."

"I would!"

But how could he deny her plea? How could he deny his heart?

"You'd only be unhappy. We should vow, here and now, never to see one another again. You should move to another city, find a wealthy land owner like your father. Build a life."

She was silent for a long time, and presently he felt her quake with silent sobs. Pain, such as he had never known, shot through his chest then. He hadn't meant to make her cry. He hadn't meant to hurt her.

"I only want what's best for you," he tried to explain, but his words sounded hollow, even to himself.

"I—know." Her voice hitched, and the words brought forth a torrent of hiccupping sobs.

"Shh, shh," he said. "Don't cry. Please, Anwen, don't cry. I love you."

"I—know." But the sobs would not, could not stop.

He held her, rocking, deep into the night.

�֎

The tutor, soon to be reassigned, opened one eye and mumbled something unintelligible as Huwen, dismissing his guard, crept through the man's room and into his own. Anwen had finally fallen asleep; and well before the winter sun touched the eastern sky, he left her bed. Today, he left his mother, the women and children, and the cloying protection of Uncle Avin, to finally meet with Father and learn what it was to rule. He would ride for Coldridge and then to the siege at Archwood, the last of Shangril's seven countries to reconcile its differences with Arcan.

As he eased the bolt into its place behind him, a gray shape shifted on his bed.

"It's me," the shape said before Huwen could reach for his knife or call out.

He peered between the open bed curtains. Eamon. Fully dressed. Waiting.

"What are you doing here?" Huwen breathed.

Eamon sat up and leaned back against the headboard. "Nothing."

A lie, obviously, but one Huwen knew he would not expose by arguing. He was too exhausted, too drained by excitement and heartbreak. He slipped out of his breeches, stockings, and jerkin, and, nudging his brother aside, slipped under his sheets in his shirt and small clothes.

"Were you with Anwen?" Eamon's words came from the darkness.

"Yes."

"A farewell," he murmured, quietly, almost to himself. "Until you return."

The romance of his younger brother's words rankled. "Not 'until I return,'" Huwen snapped. "Forever. She's only an estate holder's daughter."

"And you hold that against her?"

"No!" Huwen took a calming breath. "I won't be allowed to choose my bride. Be happy if you're able to choose yours."

There was a long silence, and Huwen began to grow sleepy. Just a few candlemarks, and he and Eamon would be called to ready themselves to ride.

"I won't be able to choose my bride," Eamon said softly.

"No?" Huwen left his eyes closed. Eamon was too young to know his heart. "Why not?"

"The one I've chosen won't have me."

This made Huwen open his eyes. "Who?"

Again, there was a long silence, and Huwen began to doubt that Eamon would answer.

Then his brother's voice drifted out of the lessening dark. "She's beautiful. Royal. Of an age. Virtuous."

"Sounds like I should marry her," Huwen mumbled, sleep tripping his words.

Again, no reply.

"I was joking," Huwen said. "You know I love Anwen. How do you know this girl won't have you? Have you asked Uncle Avin to speak to her father?"

"No."

"Then how do you know? What has she said?"

"Nothing."

Huwen was getting tired of the riddles. He was about to send his brother back to his room, when he spoke again.

"I've kept my promise to you, Huwen. I don't cut myself anymore. The thought of her keeps me alive."

Huwen was wide awake, now. "How do you keep such an—intense—love secret?"

This time the silence was filled with waiting. "She doesn't know I've been thinking of her."

"Never—" This was bizarre. Huwen had to clarify. "You mean you love a girl you've never been with? Not even to talk to?"

Eamon's weight lifted from the bed and in the soft light Huwen could make out his shape approach their connecting door. "You're not the only one leaving his love behind."

On the far side of a wide, swift river, Carn Coldridge was visible for some distance, perched on the edge of a sweeping upland. As Sulwyn's pony picked its way down from the ridge on a winding road, Rennika and her sisters crowded forward in the cart for their first glimpse of the city. They were in Teshe now, not Orumon, but Rennika was not sure when they had crossed into the new country.

The city, if she could call it that, was on top of a small, flat hill, its edges disappearing into farmland, so different from Archwood's high walls among the peaks. Squashed mountains fell away north of the carn, disappearing into a band of flat snow clouds. To the east lay an endless land of forests and hills under a morning sky so huge it seemed to Rennika to press down on her like a giant hand. Like Archwood, swathes of trees near the town had been cleared for farmland, and the fields were hidden now under a blanket of white. Huddled against the wind outside a crumbling city wall, a pleasingly careless array of shops and houses stood along crooked streets. On a high point within the city, a second, higher wall surrounded a castle, but the castle seemed plain and stark.

Meg and Janat pulled their hoods over their faces as Sieur Cordal—Sulwyn—guided his pony over the icy wooden bridge, across the fields, and up the hill. Soldiers in King Artem's colors stood at the city gate.

Apprehension crept into Rennika's stomach. Why weren't King Larin's guards here? These men watched carefully as the carts and farmers passed under the gate's open arch but didn't stop them or question them.

They halted on a side street next to a wide square with a boisterous market and Rennika craned to take in everything at once. She was glad she didn't have to cover her face: there was so much to see, and everything was noisy and colorful and fascinating.

She'd been to the market in Archwood only twice in her life, and this market was different—filled with music and smells and noise. On a corner, a pair of wrestlers grappled one another as a frantic crowd waved purses in the air. Further down, a long area had been fenced off for archery competitions. Everywhere, shoppers and dawdlers wound past one another in the crush as traders called out their wares, and an inordinate number of Arcan soldiers kept watch.

Janat huddled, if possible, even more deeply into her corner of the cart, her eyes never leaving Sulwyn, but Meg peered out from under her hood with interest. Even Sulwyn tried to look everywhere, mouth gaping at the strangeness of it. Rennika wondered if even he had never seen a town like this before.

Sulwyn nodded down the main avenue to the town square and castle gate where the soldiers in green and gold patrolled. He ran his hands over his pony's back and legs. "Stay here. I'll ask about King Larin and his magiel." He loosened the pony's harness.

Meg looked curiously into the market. "It's cold enough. I could keep my hood up. I could go with you."

"We should stay here," Janat said.

Sulwyn agreed. "I'll be back soon."

Rennika peered around the back of the cart as Meg slid to the ground. The scent of roasting mutton drifted on the breeze. Janat sidled into a niche between two buildings where she could watch the alley from beneath her hood without being seen.

Rennika took in what she could of the market from the alley. It was confusing and exciting all at once. Farmers with carts of strange vegetables and carrots and sacks of unmilled grain beckoned to passersby. Shop doors stood open, and some vendors even displayed their wares on tables or on blankets over the ice and mud. In the midst of the endless flow of people, groups huddled about braziers, and the smell of soup and spice mingled with scented candles and incense, and the stink of offal and unwashed bodies. Hawkers shouted over the squabbles of hagglers.

Sulwyn was true to his word, returning only a short time later, bearing a loaf of flat bread and a block of cheese, his water skin filled with ale. He broke off chunks of bread for each of them. "Teshe capitulated even before King Artem marched on Orumon." He seemed to be speaking to Meg, but he kept looking at Janat. "King Larin keeps his throne, but the men in King Artem's colors are everywhere, not just about the castle."

Janat's fingers reached for the death token collar at her neck. "King Larin would give us to Artem?"

"Seems likely." Sulwyn shrugged. "Maybe your magiel uncle could still help you."

Rennika stuffed bread and cheese into her mouth, her eye on the crust that Janat didn't seem to want.

Meg slumped against the wall of the building. "We could try another city. Maybe the king of Gramarye will take us in."

King Gramaret. Rennika remembered him from their trip with Mama last summer.

Meg gave Sulwyn a tentative look. "Gramarye—is it—is it far? Or Midell?"

"I don't know." Sulwyn wiped his hands on his pants and passed around the water skin, and then produced blankets and a water jar from his cart. He gave the blankets to Janat.

Janat took the gifts with an air of surprise.

"Well." Sulwyn stood awkwardly in the street holding the jar. "Keep well," he said finally.

"Are you going?" Janat shuffled a little, looking sick with apprehension.

"I have my work." He spoke as though he apologized to Janat. "I have the name of a man to contact."

"Thank you," Meg said. "For all your help."

Janat bit her lip. "I . . . You've been very—good. To all of us. I appreciate it." She lowered her eyes. "We all appreciate it."

Sulwyn bobbed his head, his eyes never leaving Janat's face. "I've seen people here who hail from other cities. Some are hazy-skinned. They could be magiels or at least mixed. With so many displaced, you should be able to find crowds to blend into." He let out a puff of breath and looked around, as though he didn't want to leave. "Well. I better go now."

Janat attempted a smile of thanks. "It's . . ." Janat licked her lips. "It's good work that you do."

Meg shot her a look of surprise.

Sulwyn puffed out another breath of air and glanced at the market. "Yes. Well. Goodbye."

"Goodbye," Janat said.

He hesitated for a moment, then placed the water jar in Meg's hands and climbed into the cart. Taking the reins, he prodded the pony into the street.

Rennika shook her head. That was strange.

CHAPTER 12

For the first few nights in Coldridge, Janat and her sisters shivered in a rickety shanty they built from sticks and the blankets Sulwyn had given them, a shelter which afforded no protection from thieves or worse. But Meg came back from a foray into the streets, saying a group of refugees was squatting in a vacant mill and at least it had a roof. The place was crowded, and some resented the three newcomers who were not family to anyone already there, but most took no notice of them.

A place to stay out of the snow was an immense luxury. But they still needed food. Money.

Now Janat watched, her hood shielding her face, as a woman with skin that rippled faintly in time, sat on a blanket in the market, trading small phials for money. Some patrons gave the woman one, two, even five chetra for a single small container.

Janat could make potions. Of course she could. Even worldlings could make potions, but a magiel could make strong, effective potions. If only she knew the recipes. If only she knew which ingredients to blend, which spell words to chant, which constellation to cast under, which of the Many Gods presided over each prayer. Janat had the ability; she merely lacked the knowledge. This mercurial-skinned woman must have the knowledge.

She needed to approach the woman in private.

After a time, Janat's patience was rewarded. A crone took the woman's place, and the woman left the market. Janat caught up to her as she reached an unobtrusive doorway along a narrow side street. "Excuse me."

The woman turned. She measured Janat in a glance and seemed to find her wanting.

"You're a magiel," Janat said. "You cast for your local village?"

The woman's eyes hooded. "I cast for four villages," she retorted. "And my wares are good enough for the merchants and tradespeople of Coldridge."

Even better.

"I'm a magiel. I'd like to learn some spells."

Distain crept into the corners of the woman's eyes. "You're half-talented at most."

She meant the almost-still cast to Janat's skin. "No, I'm full magiel. My mother conceived me to have steadier skin."

The woman snorted.

"She did."

"Then, why didn't she teach you your spells?"

"She was teaching me." But Janat had lessons in reading and writing, history, politics, and religion. She'd rarely needed to cast spells for every day, useful things, and when she did she could look the procedures up in a book.

The woman turned to enter the house. "I have all the apprentices I need."

"Well, could I just copy out a few spells from your book?"

The woman spun back, a frown of incredulity on her face. "I have no book," she scoffed. "And if I did, I'd hardly give my secrets to some fraud talking like a toff, to steal my customers."

Steal—

The door slammed, and the woman was gone.

"There's going to be an execution!" A girl rushed into the mill where Meg and Janat sat on the mill stone with the women, trying to sew.

Most of the fugitives left the mill during the day and Rennika had gone with them to watch the beggars and pickpurses. Rennika was a little too old to apprentice to begging, but her soft, vulnerable look masked a surprising willingness to hold her own in a tussle, spawning a grudging respect among the children. She was catching on to their accents, and the little beggars had begun to let her follow them and try her hand. She'd already brought in a few chetra, from which Meg was able to buy two steel sewing needles. She owed the sharp-eyed woman beside her for the thread and fabric, though.

"That's not news," one of the refugees remarked.

But all heads lifted at the girl's interruption.

"Come to the square, right now!" She urged. "King Artem's going to destroy the Amethyst!"

"That's lunacy," an old woman cried.

Tasks forgotten, the refugees scrambled to their feet.

"I swear it." The girl ran to the door, shouting over her shoulder. "The crier's announcing it in the street, right now."

Meg hurried with the rest of them down the narrow steps, Janat just behind.

The street was awash in rabble, all heading in the direction of the great square before the castle gate, all talking and shouting at once.

At first, Meg could see nothing over the throng filling the plaza. Soon, though, a military rhythm of boots announced a procession of soldiers. Ahead, a file of steel-helmeted men, apparently on some type of raised platform, formed a line. They knelt, revealing an array of royalty on tiers behind them. And there he stood, behind a line of armed knights. King Artem, in full steel plate armor, staring down his nose at Teshe's people. Behind him, Meg recognized two young men—boys—as the princes, Huwen and Eamon. Taller and older since she'd seen them . . . only last summer?

"Hear ye, citizens of Teshe!" a herald called out from the front edge of the platform, and the talk and rustling of the crowd died.

This was it. Meg had been wracking her brain, trying to think of some way to get into the castle, to let her uncle know they were here.

And, this was a distraction. While everyone was watching the spectacle, Meg could ease her way toward the open gates behind the platform, in case the opportunity presented itself for her to slip inside.

She touched Janat's arm. "I'll see you back at the mill."

Janat frowned but nodded.

If only Meg could find a way to have a moment alone with Uncle Chirles, or even King Larin, she could let him know what'd happened in Orumon. Surely, her uncle could find safety for her and her sisters, if not in Coldridge, then perhaps in one of the king's country houses.

"By order of His High Majesty, King Artem Delarcan," the herald said, his voice carrying over the gathering, "the people of Teshe are hereby informed that the One God is acknowledged as the only and true God of all of Shangril."

There was a hush of indrawn breath through the crowd, as Meg wormed her way toward the back of the platform.

"And, that the worship of any lesser God or Goddess is forbidden."

A murmur of unrest erupted.

Anger boiled around Meg, and the same anger rose in her own chest. It was not up to a man, even a king, to deny his people worship of the Gods.

The herald had to call out for his words to carry. "Such worship is the worship of demons."

The mob shifted forward and Meg was carried momentarily from her path. By Kyaju's devotion, how could King Artem, of his own will, take an entire people's religion from them in a stroke?

"And as a consequence," the herald shouted, his words barely audible over the bleats of the assembly, "the prayer stones to the false demons are hereby abolished."

The mass pressed forward, and Meg was wedged, unable to move, watching the spectacle.

And . . . a blur in the corner of her eye . . .

No. She looked along the platform. Nothing.

Not nothing. There was another. Nothing she could pinpoint, just a place where for an instant, a corner of her vision shifted as though she looked through a glass, or through water, at something distorted. Then the illusion was gone. Was she losing her sight?

Then, Uncle Chirles, in the plain homespun of a magiel, stepped forward, barely visible above the heads of those around her. His two sons, mere children, stood on the platform behind him. His inconstant skin paled as he removed the Amethyst from about his neck and held it up for all to see. The jewel's facets glinted a deep violet in the cold afternoon light, its golden setting gleaming in the slanting sun like a nest of writhing snakes.

Trembling, he laid the jewel on something out of sight beyond the crowd. A slab of granite, no doubt, in the center of the platform. The flickers of distortion around the edges of Meg's vision multiplied.

Meg stilled, her gaze fixed on the drama before her, and her fingers crept to the death token at her neck.

A black-hooded axman stepped forward, this time wielding no ax, but instead, a sledgehammer. He measured his stroke with an eye and then, raising the hammer in a single fluid motion, brought it down with a resounding crunch.

The crowd flinched back as shards flew in every direction, splinters lancing those closest, drawing blood.

A shudder of power reverberated through the square. Meg felt its impact on her skin and in her heart, and she was blown back into the peasants behind her.

No. By the Many Gods, no.

Thunder rumbled in the distance—or perhaps within her skull—despite the wintry weather.

How would murderers and thieves now gain access to the lowest sphere of Heaven and find their forgiveness in death? How would Uncle Chirles and King Larin of Teshe go to the spheres of the Gods to pray for death tokens for their subjects? The prayer stone, and its power, were utterly destroyed.

How could this be?

The grumbling resumed, lashing and furious. Gaps appeared about her, as people exhorted their neighbors. Meg had to move. She wormed her way toward the end of the platform.

Now King Artem, himself, raised his hands and stepped forward. "Hear me, people of Shangril! The old ways are gone. Embrace the new." He stepped back and nodded to his chancellor.

Soldiers grasped Uncle Chirles's two arms. Two others seized his sons. Before the magiel could do more than flinch in surprise, a soldier bound his hands behind his back.

What?

Meg caught a glimpse—

Someone brushed the remaining shards of the Amethyst from the stone slab and placed a block of wood across it. Uncle Chirles was shoved to his knees, his head stretched across the block. Hazy mirages flicked near him, disappeared, and flicked again.

"No! By all that is Holy!" her uncle screamed, writhing. Two soldiers pinned him down, hard. "Not my sons!"

Uncle Chirles—

"In the name of the Many Gods, you cannot—"

The executioner gave his sledgehammer to an assistant and took up the ax.

"This is blasphemy!" Uncle Chirles shouted.

King Artem nodded, and her uncle's face, just visible, paled with shock. The Holder of Histories placed his death token on his tongue.

Again, with the same single fluid stroke, the executioner raised his ax and brought it down—

Meg averted her face. But she could not keep it averted.

Blood spattered those closest, and the severed head fell to the platform with a thump.

Her stomach seized and she gagged. There were executions in Orumon, of course there were. But not many, and she'd never seen one.

This time, a wave of outrage and shouting filled the square. Meg's sight cleared.

A tomato smashed itself against the plate armor of one of the king's guards.

Like a machine, the guards on the periphery of the platform nocked their arrows and raised their bows. Soldiers on the parapets did the same.

Cold skittered over Meg's neck and back. A soldier shoved Uncle Chirles' older son—her cousin—

There would be a moment of chaos. Just as there had been in Archwood. She had to make use of it.

Meg pushed down her nausea, shoved against the milling crowd and freed herself into a gap between the mob and the castle wall. Pressing herself against the stone, she made herself small and wriggled along its rough surface. In a moment, she grasped the edge of the gate.

The crowd went silent and a child's scream was cut short.

A horde of soldiers poured through the opening.

In their wake, she darted into the castle.

Meg knew the layout of Coldridge castle. She'd been here last summer.

But as she darted up the cobbled entryway, Meg realized this knowledge would do her little good. She must still pass through three gates before she could gain the inner courtyard. The Gods were with her. For this brief instant in time, all three gates were open and empty of soldiers.

She didn't fool herself that the murder hole between the second and third gate contained no eyes spying from above or rocks ready to pour down on her. But she had surprise on her side. She scooted past the second gate and, flattening herself against the wall, scuttled through just as the third gate was lowering. She ducked and rolled beneath it, reaching the courtyard before the portcullis spikes found their slots in the cobbles, rocks tumbling through the murder hole behind her.

She scrambled into the stairwell, clambering up its spiral as shouts erupted behind her. She followed a passage she'd discovered while playing Catch Thief with the younger children one afternoon. Images of Uncle Chirles slashed her vision as she ran.

She dashed, finally, into the kitchen. A half dozen surprised faces flicked up from their work, and a scullery maid at her elbow screamed.

Meg grabbed the girl by the shoulders. The name came to her. "Bess," she cried. "It's me! Meghra Falkyn!"

The scullery maid stared at her, speechless with shock. There were four or five others in the small room. Cook, the cinder boy, a few more.

"Bess, I have to talk to King Larin."

Bess continued to stare, her mouth open.

Cook was at her side in a stride. "Meghra Falkyn?"

"Yes. Do you recognize me?'

Cook peered incredulously into her face. "Meghra Falkyn. How . . ."

"Archwood is attacked. It's under siege by King Artem. I have to tell King Larin."

Tell King Larin. Unless his head was next on the block.

"Siege." Cook nodded. "We were attacked and taken. Late summer. No siege. The king capitulated." She spat on the floor. "He can't help you."

Uncle Chirles. The sickening crunch —

Meg shook the thought away. "I have to try. I have to talk to him. Is there any way you can sneak me into his room?"

Cook's brows knit. "Not easily. And, too risky." Then she nodded: a short, decisive nod. "I'll do what I can." She turned and glared at the servants who stared at them in horror. "And not a word from any of you," she bellowed.

The sounds of footsteps and shouting in the corridor gave Cook an instant to react. She snatched a knife from the table at her elbow and an onion from a basket, and shoved them into Meg's hands.

Meg grasped her meaning. She hunkered down by a table, slicing.

Cook flicked her fingers, and the servants returned to their duties. Bess picked up the bucket she'd been carrying and slipped Meg a shy smile before taking it out to the well.

A handful of soldiers poured into the room, spreading out to search, looking beneath tables, in cupboards, behind crates, eyeing each scullery girl, drudge, and apprentice.

"A spy entered the castle." One of the soldiers addressed the room. "Has anyone seen him?"

Cook shrugged. "No, Sir."

Spy. Meg's vision flashed with a picture of her uncle kneeling at the block.

The others murmured in the negative, heads lowered.

Two soldiers continued to inspect the servants. One approached Meg. She put her knife and onion on the table and stood respectfully, hands at her sides, staring at the floor.

He pushed past her, looked under her table, and continued searching.

"You have a magiel?" The soldier who'd spoken seemed to see Meg for the first time.

Cook bobbed her head. "Daughter of a village healer. A half-wit, not fit to apprentice in magic."

Meg wilted a little, in confirmation. By Kyaju, had they seen her skin as she dashed through the gates?

The sickening crunch of the axman's blade echoed in her ears.

The commanding soldier grunted. "If you see anything untoward, report immediately," he said. He nodded and left the room, followed by his men.

CHAPTER 13

Cook commandeered an upstairs maid to take Meg by way of the servants' stairs to the king's keep. Cook found Meg a long-sleeved apron, scrubbed her face and hands and put a cap over her hair, and the girl carried a tray of berries and cream while Meg carried a bottle of whiskey. Cook warned Meg as she wrapped her own shawl over her shoulders, she had no idea how a magiel with capricious skin and no proper livery would convince the guards she was one of the servants, nor how Meg would ever get out. King Artem and his magiel had taken quarters in the keep very close by King Larin's.

But getting away was not top of mind; once Meg was under King Larin's protection, the difficulty would lie in retrieving Janat and Rennika. She could not afford to entertain other possibilities.

Meg followed the girl up the back stairs, seeing but not seeing the flagstones beneath her feet. *If the king would only give her refuge.* The cook's comment about him capitulating with no siege repeated in her mind despite all she could do to shove it aside. Was she walking to her own execution?

Uncle Chirles.

A guard stood back by one of the double doors but scrutinized her closely as she followed the maid into an antechamber. A desk and chair near a glass-paned window, and a narrow servant's bed with attendant wardrobe, table, and chest, occupied the other side of the room. Tapestries covered the walls and narrowed the window, and only a few wavering candles fought back the gloom of the overcast day. A page waited at a large door opposite the double doors to the corridor.

The maid was just approaching the page to be admitted to King Larin's private chamber when a tumult of footsteps preceded a half-dozen men spilling into the room.

King Artem, a powerfully built military man with a full mane of silver-streaked lank hair, strode in at their head, followed by a handful of guards. A tall magiel lined with age, white haired, and wearing unbleached robes scurried at the king's heel, speaking in an insistent but restrained voice. "Sire, magiels do not require prayer stones to see the future."

Meg and the maid, bowing, backed away swiftly, as far as they could toward the wall.

This magiel. Meg remembered. Papa had fled King Artem last summer and was replaced by a new magiel. She'd heard a rumor that Papa was dead.

Where was King Larin?

"By your reasoning we should kill all magiels." The king stopped in the center of the room to glare at him, and the others halted as well.

What?

"Can you come up with no other solutions, Wenid? If restricting them to certain streets, certain markets isn't enough, what about this potion you mentioned? Glim. Use that."

"No."

"No?"

The magiel's voice took on an odd tone, less confident. "That is going too far. I was wrong to mention it."

Meg couldn't help herself. She peered up at the tableau from beneath her bowed head. Wenid. Had she heard the name before? And . . . glim.

"You saw the crowd's reaction to today's events," the king snapped. "Killing magiels only fuels resentment. The message is lost."

"And who rules Shangril?" Wenid's boldness returned, and he spoke as if he addressed merely another man, not a king. "You, or the rabble?"

Shangril. All seven countries? How could—

"I've already decreed death to magiels of the Great Houses," the king said. "I will not condemn every magiel in the empire."

Empire. Meg caught her breath. *Death? All magiels of the Great Houses?*

The House of Amber. Mama.

Janat and Rennika. Her.

"Magiels and Holders are symbols about which the mobs rally," Wenid persisted. "You must end their influence, once and for all."

Artem waved his hand in dismissal. "Magiel magic is weak compared to prayer stone magic. Common village magiels are no threat."

"Common village magiels have decided battles by breaking horses' legs. Even trusted magiels in our own ranks have turned traitors." Wenid took a step toward the king and lowered his voice. "And we can't pray to the One God to intervene in every skirmish. The cost would be too great."

Artem shot him a black look but did not step back.

"We must establish the authority of the One God." The magiel watched the king's face. "And the authority of the one true king. Now, and beyond question."

"The petty nobles have no ability to mount opposition."

"On the contrary. Magiels lead a hidden blasphemy," the shimmering man clipped, his voice still constrained. "As long as every village has a magiel, the people will continue to go to them, at night, in secret, prayer stones or no. The Many Gods will still be worshipped."

The king flicked his finger at the page and the boy opened the door. "I said I would bring these uprisers to heel," he said to the magiel. "And I will. Now, leave it be, Sieur. I would meet with my sons."

Wenid opened his mouth as if he would speak, his dark eyes boring into the king. But he grudgingly bowed his head.

The king swept into the chamber, the page following, closing the door behind.

By Kyaju, all magiels? Killed? It brought bile to the back of Meg's throat.

But this was only Wenid's plan. The king had not yet agreed.

The maid gave her a bewildered, frightened look.

"Leave," one of the soldiers said to them. "The king will send his page if he requires aught."

Yes. Leave. *Now.*

Meg followed the maid to the double doors.

A mailed arm extended a spear between her and the maid. "Stop."

Meg stopped, her heart stopping as well.

The maid made good her exit, casting a quick glance of pity at Meg before she disappeared down the corridor.

"We have no magiels for servants."

Meg felt the eyes of the guards—and the king's magiel—on her. "I—I'm new, Sieur." She prayed to the Many that the accent she'd worked so hard to perfect would not betray her. "In t' kitchen."

Wenid approached, and she lowered her head. "Explain yourself."

The door. Only a few feet from her. With the guard blocking it. Could she use magic? Not against Wenid. Her breath fluttered in her chest and she felt faint.

That was it. What Cook said, about her being dim. She let fear flood her, poke tears to the back of her eyes and allowed her lips to tremble. "I—I—"

Wenid tilted his head back as if the curse of her dull-wittedness was contagious.

She swallowed and licked her lips. "Me Ma's village magiel t'Big Hill," she sniveled, looking from the magiel to the guard and back. "T' village burnt—"

Wenid snorted. "The basement cell will suffice until I can come." He waved a hand at the guard and went into the corridor, muttering. "And the king wants the likes of this in Shangril."

The guard narrowed his eyes at her and she lowered her head again. "Come with me."

She shrank back. "Please, Sieur! Ask Cook!"

❈

There were two guards.

Artem had attacked every country in Shangril.

They manhandled her roughly into a cold and dank room in a small complex of half a dozen cells beneath the guard tower, reached down a short flight of stone steps from the bailey. Coldridge castle wasn't big, and though rebuilding over the centuries had turned parts of it into a warren, this once–cold cellar was uncomplicated, thank the Gods, and located near the main gate. Its locks would be simple to circumvent once the castle slept. If she had that long.

Artem's magiel would have him outlaw—kill—every magiel in Shangril. Gods, there must be thousands. Tens of thousands. More.

One guard released her, standing ready, while the other swiftly manacled her to the wall. Thereafter, they kept their distance. Clearly, they knew better than to let a magiel touch them. Even a simpleton.

Unlike lowborn magiels, Meg was a daughter of one of the Great Houses of magic wielders reaching back to the Goddess Kyaju, and she had some limited ability to throw a spell—to cast with words at a short distance, without ingredients. But, shivering with fright and regret in the cell's manacles, she could see nothing, in the dim light filtering from the waning afternoon, to cast *upon*. Raising a flagstone to trip one of them would get her nowhere but a deeper dungeon.

Smash the Amber. Kill Mama. Deprive the people of their death tokens. Their access to Heaven.

Could she—did she have the stomach—to close the throat of one of them, hold it closed until he died? Open a blood vessel in his brain?

Even if she did, the other would raise the alarm. Her options fled, one after the other.

"What's your name?" The wary one asked. The other lit a handful of candle stubs fixed to a rickety wooden table.

Dull. Common. She must appear a half-wit. She looked from one to the other and let her fright take deeper hold of her. In the dim brilliance and flickering shadows, the questioner produced a thick leather strap. "Meg!" she yelped, cringing.

"Where you from?" He slapped the leather across his gloved palm, the thwack a promise.

"Big Hill!"

"Sieur."

"Sieur! Big Hill, Sieur!"

He slapped the leather again.

A third guard arrived, carrying a small cask, and the second grinned. "Does your thirst never end, Dunn?"

"Could be a long night." Dunn reasoned, and even in this light, Meg could see his complexion was florid. "Could get dry."

Ale? Or—Sulwyn said in Teshe they drank whiskey, and she'd seen how it made Sulwyn, and Janat the one time she tried it, silly and sleepy.

The Gods were with her. Something on which to cast a spell.

※

Meg willed the unfermented barley wort in the whiskey to find a time when it became alcohol. She cast a second, and a third spell to strengthen the brew, every minute apprehensive that one of them would become suspicious of her before the liquor had taken full effect.

But the charm worked. The tipple made the florid guard drowsy and the second stupid. It made the wary guard belligerent, and she felt the sting of his thong across her arms and thighs and face more than once before his arm weakened and he joined the others in incoherence.

By then she'd released the locks on her manacles, and when the cruel guard began to stumble, she darted from his witless attempts to grab her and out of the cell, closing—and locking—the door behind her.

Stars spangled the sky when she emerged from the dungeon.

Every magiel. Dead.

But the king hadn't agreed. He'd argued with Wenid. Told him to use something else. *Glim.*

The main gate. With a colossal effort she found a moment when the portcullis was raised, and stepped through that doorway in time to her freedom.

Her escape was a confession. They would know she'd overheard. Was dangerous.

But she'd barely stumbled across the city square, its bloody platform motionless in the starlight, into a narrow lane, when the world . . . left her.

She sat by a campfire in the snow in watery winter daylight. She was still dirty and hungry, but she wore a warm cloak. Horses were tethered in a rude corral and rough linen tents were scattered in a thick forest. Flakes fell from a dull morning sky. Colm—the same man she'd met in Spruce Falls, but thinner now, with dark rings circling his eyes—sat across from her, and a score of other men slept, talked in hushed tones, or silently polished swords. Curious. But she was grateful: none seemed to take more notice of her, than of one another.

She opened her eyes.

Now, she was warm and lying in a soft bed beneath a velvet canopy. Mama's room. Mama sat by her, waiting. It was the night Mama had made her do magic.

"When are you?" Mama took her hand.

"A dozen weeks . . . I think." Meg wondered at the magic, yet understood her momentary window. "From when we left Archwood."

Mama caressed her cheek. "My poor daughter. Are Janatelle and Rennikala—"

"They're well. Alive, anyway." She sat up and took Mama's two forearms in her hands. "Mama, tell me—"

"I will curse this valley." Mama nodded firmly in the dark. "If Artem takes it, I will curse it. I've been preparing the spells—"

Not madness! Not obsession, by the Gods! "Mama! What do I need to know? What's glim?"

"You can release the curse I set, Meg. Only—"

And she was gone.

Lying awake in a summer field. Alone beneath a cerulean sky on grasses redolent with clover and marigolds, humming with bees. She wondered . . .

She'd stood so close to Wenid. He was the key, whispering in the king's ear. Should she have killed him? Reached out with her magic and pinched a blood vessel in his heart?

Gods, too dangerous.

But did her life matter, really? If she could save the magiels. Mama. Her sisters.

Could she kill?

The thought made her feel weak. No . . . no.

Yet . . .

Killing. Power. Might taking that life, that miserable life, be good?

Gods, no! She shook the thought back and rolled onto her stomach, heaving with nothing to disgorge.

CHAPTER 14

Meg woke like a drunkard in a doorway. Townsfolk bustled in the street. Voices nearby. Angry. Whispering . . .

"He can't take the prayer stones."

"He did. And our magiel." They spoke of Artem.

And considered death to all magiels. She struggled to sit. Coldridge. She was back in Coldridge. Gods. Her stomach heaved. The plague that was High King Artem's madness had taken over the world.

"There're more of us than there is of him. I thought those hotheads were mad, but—"

"Bah, you can't—"

What could Meg do? Nothing. She was one woman, one *girl*, and the high king had *armies*. Only the Gods could rectify this blight.

A clatter of footsteps and the knot of plotters scattered.

Soldiers?

Sunlight was poking fingers between buildings from the east. She had to hide. A hazy-skinned girl covered in bruises, one who'd overheard what she shouldn't have. The king's men—Larin's *and* Artem's—would be hunting.

❀

"Janat." Rennika's whisper was clear against the tiny breaths and snores and mouse skitterings of the mill in the predawn gray.

Rennika hadn't woken her. Janat had barely slept, and when she dozed, she only stood again in the crowd below the king's platform, seeing the prayer stone smashed. Uncle Chirles. Her cousins. Sometimes Meg, or . . . herself. Rennika had whimpered in her arms most of the night. The child had been there too; she had seen what no child should ever see.

Rennika, still cuddled close, turned in her arms, speaking so those on mats or cloaks on the floor near them could not hear. Though, for that matter, many were likely also awake. "Where's Meg?"

Poor thing. First Mama, her home, everything she knew. Then Nanna. Now . . . "I don't know." It was the last thing Janat wanted to tell her. To think, she and Meg squabbled, but she never thought Meg would be *gone*.

"I'm scared." Rennika clung to her.

Abruptly, Janat could no longer lie on this floor. She had to move, to *do* something. "I'm going to look for her." As quietly as she could, she rose and pushed on her boots.

"Me, too." Soundlessly, Rennika readied herself, and a sliver of gladness touched Janat. They crept from the mill.

Janat gripped Rennika's hand and they made their way toward Market Square. Though it was early, people were in the street, but there was a new flavor to their vigilance, to their voices. Energy. Anger.

They approached the square through a narrow lane, empty but for a confusion of footprints in the snow, where a stack of crates had fallen and rats were gnawing on stinking turnips. The passage opened onto a larger road.

King's soldiers.

Janat halted, Rennika bumping her from behind. She turned, covering her face. "Go back."

Rennika shuffled a few steps and they scurried through the snow toward the bend in the lane. *By Ranuat, don't let the soldiers see my wavering skin.*

The crunch of the ax resounded in Janat's ears, and she saw again Uncle Chirles's head arc . . . bounce—the brilliant red spray—

"Meg!" Rennika's fingers slipped from hers.

Janat looked down the lane. Rennika was running toward a figure swathed in rags.

The figure turned, and Rennika threw her arms about it. A cry of happiness, and the figure returned Rennika's embrace.

Janat let out a breath, unaware her lungs had ceased to function. She ran.

Meg blinked, freed a hand from Rennika's grip and pushed it across Janat's cheek as though proving to herself that Janat was there, real. A massive welt purpled her right cheek and her lip was split.

"Meg!" Janat cried in an undertone. "What happened? We were—"

"Let's go." Meg held both of them close, but propelled them down the cobbled street in the direction of the millhouse. She limped, but her expression, the glimpse Janat had seen, was grim.

"We thought the soldiers got you," Rennika said, peeking up from the safety of Meg's arm.

"I'm . . . fine." But she wasn't fine. She was scared.

"Where were you?" Janat insisted.

Meg pushed her to avoid a man moving slowly with a cane. "I got into the castle."

The castle—to get help from Uncle Chirles. But Uncle Chirles was dead.

"King Larin can't help us," Meg said bitterly, still wary, still pushing them toward the mill. "He's saving his own skin by helping King Artem."

They'd come all this way. *All this way.* Janat felt the blow in her stomach. King Larin *had* to help them. "That can't be."

But someone had beaten Meg. The memory of the king's soldier in Spruce Falls returned.

They reached the mill and Meg opened the door. A small group of refugees huddled at the far end in animated discussion. Meg held back from entering. "King Larin would turn us over in an instant. He's given his own suite to Artem. His guards questioned me until the middle of the night. I barely got out."

Janat shook her head slowly. Last summer. King Larin had given them a banquet, invited the titled landowners and richest merchants and tradesmen, slaughtered lambs and geese and partridge . . .

Meg closed the door behind them and spoke very low in the dark. "That could've been us," she whispered. "In front of the crowd yesterday afternoon. Uncle Chirles and us, with our heads cut off."

❈

Meg and her sisters fled Coldridge.

They stayed for some time in a crowded basement with the constant itch of lice, in a town called Grassy Bluff, somewhere in the indeterminate borderlands between Teshe and Midell. Meg listened—hard—to gossip and rumors, waiting for the decree that all those with mercurial skin were to be executed. That it did not come brought her no relief.

Sometime after midwinter there was talk of a council of commoners meeting at Black Earth Creek, and Meg knew Sulwyn must have been there, but she heard nothing firm of its resolves or actions.

She avoided shrines, usually guarded by suspicious soldiers, though she prayed each morning before she rose and each night before sleep. At these times, images flickered through her mind of her ordeal in King Larin's dungeon; of Artem's words, and Wenid's. And when Meg woke in the night, her thoughts were not pious. Her mind turned over fancies of creeping through the corridors of the great hall at Holderford and the vengeance she would wreak on King Artem.

More and more frequently, Meg saw a faint blurring at the edge of her vision, and Sieura Barcley, a refugee and magiel fleeing some unnamed nightmare with her near-to-grown son, tilted her head to one side when Meg confessed she saw them. "Ghosts," the older magiel murmured.

Meg's spread hands, holding a skein of wool, lost their rhythm.

"Spirits of those who died with no death token." A frown of grief touched Sieura Barcley's eyes. "They're drawn to death. Hungering to see if the mortal's shadow will rise to one of the Heavens, in that final moment." She stared past Meg, her own fingers stopped on the wool she balled. "Or linger here, on this lowest sphere, stretching thinner and thinner, hopeless. In pain and agony. Forever." Her hands resumed. "We can see them. Worldings can't."

Meg touched the woman's wrist, wondering who she'd seen perish, deprived of their death token. Then the moment passed and the woman smiled, and they finished spooling the skein.

As Sulwyn predicted, though, Meg and her sisters were able to melt into the masses of the dispossessed. They gained occasional work in sculleries or mills or farms—enough to fend off starvation. With her fine, fair hair and trusting brown eyes, Rennika made an excellent beggar and sometime thief.

But one day as the winter sunlight was growing stronger, an arrow shot from a rooftop killed King Artem's general as he led replacements for the siege at Archwood. The shantytown and attics and basements were combed and any whose aspect met with a soldier's displeasure was executed. The three of them, along with half the refugees in Grassy Bluff, fled to the countryside.

The King's Road was no more than a mud track sparsely dotted with frightened villages. In none of these did the wanderers find welcome, work, or tolerance. Artem and Wenid had seen to that.

Wenid pulled the shawl closer around his shoulders. The wind, constant on the exposed ridge below Archwood's wall, was not strong by mountain standards, though it was touched with glacier ice. The hollow on the lee of the ridge overlooking a wide valley captured warm winter sunshine, and his seat among the lichen-covered stones was softened by blankets. For once, the king's magiel did not chafe at sitting; indeed, he had slept much of the morning. Along with a dozen soldiers, he'd been cursed by some foul meat or tidbit in last night's supper and spent the early candlemarks vomiting. A healer had been called up from King Artem's larger encampment in the valley but not yet arrived.

Gravel crunched and Wenid turned to see Artem making his way down from the ridge. The king sat on a slab of stone. "I followed your advice," he preempted. "Magiels are being arrested on small pretexts, and what magiels are not filling my prisons, have vanished. Hiding."

Wenid's relationship with the king had never been friendly,

possibly because Wenid did not grovel. But Wenid liked to believe their understanding was stronger for it; that Artem knew he would get an honest opinion from his magiel. At the same time, though, Wenid knew he could be condemned for any advice he gave that missed its mark. Now appeared to be one of those times.

The king eyed him. "We barely arrive at the siege and you become ill. Are you like to die? One of my men who was cursed by the food is dead, and another's on death's door."

Wenid returned his king's sour look. "I will survive."

"This time."

Wenid squinted in the sunshine. He did not have the energy to parse out his king's political machinations. "What concerns you, Your Majesty?"

"Only the power of my rule," Artem said mildly. "The Ruby is no more than a bit of glass without a magiel to wield it."

Wenid thrust his tongue into his cheek. "I am not about to die."

"But you will someday."

"Not today."

"—and when you do, there is not a magiel of any of the Great Houses to pray with the Ruby." The king snorted with derision. "They resent the destruction of their own prayer stones. And— surprise—their persecution."

"Which you knew when you took me on," Wenid shot back. "At the time, you felt the cost to be worth it." Wenid let out a breath. By the One, he detested the fawning this obstinate king expected, the placating. But challenging Artem Delarcan directly only raised voices and tempers, and entrenched the king in his bullheaded position.

No, a softer tactic was best. "In any case, you would not want such a magiel."

"No?" Artem's brows shot up. "The Great Houses are not good enough?"

Wenid breathed to calm the rush of temper that bloomed in his chest. "And when you accompany a magiel to Heaven, Your Majesty," he asked reasonably, "can you control his petition?"

The king's nostrils flared.

"Even direct him to supplicate himself before the One God, rather than before one of the demons? Hmm?" Wenid asked. "I think not, or you would not have needed me."

Artem leaned his elbows on his knees, breathing like a bull preparing to charge.

"I see your point, Sire." Again, Wenid was more than reasonable. "I have no children. We need to plan my succession."

The king nodded abruptly, as though he had reached a decision, and straightened. "It's settled, then." He stood. "Once you are well, you will return to Coldridge to view the magiels imprisoned there. Or Highglen, or Cataract Crag if you prefer, though Coldridge is the closest. Pick a likely one to train." He turned to crunch back up to the camp.

"I think not."

The king stopped, his air of satisfaction replaced by surprise. "No?"

"The same argument applies." Wenid wondered where he had come by the energy to be articulate. "Some village magiel might protest he will carry out your wishes. But do you trust that he will erase a lifetime of beliefs in demon Gods once he is surrounded by the glory of Heaven?"

Doubt touched the king's cheeks.

Wenid pressed on. "Do you trust that half-borns and bastard lines have the power to reach the highest sphere of Heaven where the One God resides?"

Artem thrust his jaw to one side. "Your policy of killing magiels—"

"Is sound," Wenid said sharply.

"—will cripple us. Possibly sooner than later. And I see you offering no solution."

"I will study on it." The energy imparted by his anger had burned out, and immense fatigue rolled over Wenid like a wave.

"You are saying we need a full-blood magiel we can educate from birth," Artem summarized.

Wenid closed his eyes and opened them again. "That . . . yes, that would work."

"Then, you," the king said, looming over him as he shifted his weight in preparation for leaving. "Will beget a child."

CHAPTER 15

"Rennika!" Meg's voice drifted on the breeze.

Rennika sprang to her feet and peered over the tall brush. The evening wind felt silken over the low hill on which she stood, easing her sunburned cheeks. Below, a stream wandered through a meadow dotted with a few thickets. Rennika didn't know where they were. Some of their party said they were in Teshe, or Midell, or Gramarye. Some said they were in the vague borderlands somewhere between. Some towns they'd visited claimed to have no king at all, gone outlaw and paying no tribute. But just now, the sun shone and spring had already come to these lower, *softer* lands. The view the Many Gods had laid out before her would've been perfect if it weren't for the lingering stink of blood and the bodies lying in scattered heaps among its grasses.

"Is Janat with you?" Meg called as she marched up the hill from the collection of makeshift tents beside the brook, well upwind of the battlefield.

In their camp, a haunch, marinated and roasted all day in a pit, was being unearthed, and the aroma of the tender meat made Rennika instantly hungry. "Yes! We're with Gweddien!"

Meg shaded her eyes against the westering sun. "Tell them your lesson's done for today. We're about to eat." She turned and sauntered back to the gathering band.

Rennika crouched by the young magiel and touched the velvety plant in his hand. Like her and her sisters, Gweddien was born of one of the Great Houses and had lost his home. Unlike them, Gramarye had given up the Chrysocolla with little fight, though his father had died in prison. Gweddien and his mother had run from the executioner's ax. He knew King Artem and his children, as Rennika and her sisters had, but here, in this foreign land, and within these camps, they never talked of those days.

"We heard," Janat said. "What else can feverfew do?" she asked the gangly boy.

Gweddien stripped the leaves from the stalk. "Well, it eases pain in old folks' knees and hips. And you can put it on insect bites. It works especially well for sufferers whose Tarot signifier is in the House of Cups." He picked up the sack of herbs he'd collected and made his way down the hill toward the encampment, Janat following.

Janat sniffed the leaf she carried. "Smells bitter."

Rennika trotted behind her.

"It's a good plant, though," the young man advised. "When we get to a big enough town, I'm going to make feverfew potions and sell them for money. Spells by worldlings never work."

"Yes, they do. For an candlemark or two." Rennika had learned a few things, traveling with the refugees. Meg had asked Gweddien's mother to teach her.

"Mine will last for weeks, if I infuse them with magiel magic," Gweddien boasted.

"Good idea," Janat said, but Rennika knew Janat wouldn't do it. She hated using magic.

The day had been remarkably good. Only this morning, they'd found a horse on a battlefield below their encampment that was still feebly kicking, and tonight their little band would feast. And, there would be enough meat to dry over low fires—if the weather stayed fair—to last them for weeks.

They'd found all sorts of knives and bits of armor. Saddles. Small personal effects like bronze mirrors and razors. As much as they could carry. Even a cask of some kind of Midellian licorice liqueur. Tonore Warrick's mother had found a metal cooking pot and Tonore helped his uncle repair a light cart they could fill with salable goods and push to the next town. They'd been wealthy land owners at one time.

Meg came out the richest, with three chetra from a dead soldier's purse, and Janat got a good linen shirt with no holes, that would almost be a robe for Rennika. Meg was able to wash the blood out in the cold brook, so there'd be hardly a stain. And, here on the hillside, Gweddien had found the feverfew.

They were singing, and the men—and some of the women—were dancing a Teshian jig around the fire, and Janat was giggling so hard she almost fell over and spilled her licorice drink, when Tonore caught sight of movement down the valley. He nudged his mother and pointed.

The singing scattered to a halt and the dancers, sweating and breathing hard, turned.

A lone figure, hood thrown back, came slowly up the road from the battlefield.

The smiles faded. The men reached for sticks and stones and Rennika tensed to run. There were people so hungry, they would kill for food. She knew.

But no others appeared on the road; the traveler was alone. If there was trouble, their numbers would protect them.

Whoever it was stopped as though seeing them for the first time, then turned and hurried back toward the battlefield.

"Hold," Sieura Warrick said to the others. "It's a woman. Another refugee."

Rennika squinted into the fading twilight.

Sieura Warrick stood and flung back the cloak she'd worn against the annoyance of mosquitoes. "Wait!" she called out.

The woman on the road faltered to a stop. She turned uncertainly.

"We mean you no harm!" Tonore's mother cried.

The woman hesitated. Frightened? Or wary?

Janat nudged Meg. "We don't know anything about her."

Rennika reached for the reassurance of Meg's sleeve.

"Come!" Sieura Warrick detached herself from the group and walked a short way down the hill. "We have food."

All watched as Tonore's mother made her way toward the woman. No one let go of their sticks.

The woman eyed her doubtfully for a moment then, catlike, crouched, a glint of blade in her hand.

Rennika squirmed behind Meg. *Please, Gods, don't let this be another time to run.*

Sieura Warrick stopped in the path, hands open and out to her sides. She spoke to the woman, though the two were too far away for Rennika to make out her words.

The woman swayed where she stood, confused or weary.

Tonore's mother spoke again, approaching slowly.

The woman's knife faltered. Then she lurched forward and almost fell into Sieura Warrick's arms. Supporting the woman, Tonore's mother brought her, stumbling, up the hill.

Rennika retreated behind Meg, watching the strange woman.

Blodwyn—who wouldn't tell her last name—was a bundle of sticks, even more emaciated than the rest of them. She tore ravenously at the band's communal food bowl, eating uncleanly with both hands, not heeding Sieura Barcley's admonishment not to make herself sick, and Rennika was at once frightened and sorry for her.

Blodwyn watched them as she ate, her gaze roving from face to face, lingering fearfully on the three men. The bruises she wore were beginning to heal but her clothes were shreds, and her feet—when her shoes could be eased from them—were a mess of festering blisters and half-healed cuts. Meg helped Sieura Barcley apply soothing herbs and bandage them with linen torn from the shirts of dead soldiers.

When they were done, night had deepened. Blodwyn gathered her shoes in her arms and crept to the edge of the firelight. She turned and, eyeing them suspiciously from beneath wild tangles, pulled her dirk from her purse. "Now," she whispered through broken teeth. "What payment do you take for your food?"

The others lifted their heads.

"No payment," Tonore's other uncle said.

"There's always payment!" The woman's voice was low and hoarse.

"We've had good fortune today," Sieura Warrick said. "We share."

"You think I'm stupid?" the woman croaked.

There was a stunned silence. The fire snapped.

"You'll come to me in the night! You think I don't know it?"

Rennika looked to Meg for explanation, but her sister's face reflected the same bewilderment Rennika felt.

"No—" Sieur Warrick said.

Blodwyn turned her knife to him. "You'll be the first! You and these other two!" She nodded toward Tonore's uncles.

"Payment. Yes, you're right," Meg said.

"Aha!"

"But we don't need the kind of payment you suggest."

Blodwyn snorted her disbelief.

"You see." Meg gestured. "There are plenty of women here."

Blodwyn hugged her shoes more closely. "You'll rob me, then!"

Meg gave her a slight shake of the head. "We have boots. A battlefield full. You have nothing for us to take."

"What, then?"

Yes, Rennika wondered. What?

Meg rested her hands in her lap. "You can pay us with news. We're making our way to Theurgy, in Midell."

Yes, news! How clever of Meg. Some said King Artem had taken Midell. Others said Midell was still a free country. She knew Meg worried that the king of Midell would decree death to magiels if Artem took his lands.

"Theurgy." Blodwyn drew into the shadows, her eyes glittering in reflected firelight. "You can't go there."

"Why not?" Sieura Barcley asked. "Do you come from there?"

"Haven't you heard?" the woman screeched. "The city's been under siege all winter."

Rennika's heart sank.

"I knew it," Sieur Warrick muttered.

"Where can we go?" Meg asked.

"Castle Theurgy's fallen." Blodwyn hugged her knife and shoes as one who clung to her last remaining comfort. "Three—no. Four days ago?" Her brows knit in confusion. "Perhaps longer."

"Did you live in Theurgy?" Sieura Barcley asked gently.

"We hid in the cellars." Blodwyn stared at some figment in the flames. "For weeks. My sisters. Their children. The baker's nieces and nephews. The king didn't have food for us. Curses rained over the walls from catapults. Curses that made us burn with fever. Curses that made us vomit and die. My brother," she wept. "My mama . . . my husband—" Blodwyn collapsed on her bundle.

Tonore's mother crept toward her. "Hush—"

The woman sprang to life and waved her knife, and the others jerked back.

"The payment," Meg insisted. "Tell us. What have you seen?"

Blodwyn's eyes flicked back and forth. "The king was beheaded." She laughed. "The Citrine Prayer Stone was smashed."

"Oh . . ." Sieur Warrick slumped. "No."

Janat stared at Blodwyn. "The king . . ."

Rennika wasn't sure she remembered the king of Midell, but it might have been his daughters who plaited her hair into long braids one day. And the next day, her hair was all curly.

"His magiel? His family?" Meg asked.

"The ax." Blodwyn grinned, though her eyes shone with a sickly, wild look. "It was a holiday. There were banners. Food. In the square before the castle. Each of them. One at a time. Death tokens on their tongues, then chop. Chop. Chop. Chop."

Janat drew back, her fingers on her own death token.

"Who—who's the new king of Midell?" Meg asked.

"Prince Eamon Delarcan."

"He's not more than fourteen years old!" Sieur Warrick said.

"And Jace Delarcan rules Pagoras, and Hada Delarcan rules Gramarye," Blodwyn sang.

"That makes no sense." Janat shook her head. "King Artem's *children*?"

King Artem and his family had come to Archwood for a winter celebration . . . when? Rennika and Jace had built towers from blocks of firewood, falling on each other and giggling when the pieces toppled to the flagstones. Huwen and Eamon had raced around the bailey through the snow with mock swords, much to Meg's disgust, until their tutor took them for an outing. And Hada was just a chubby little baby, crying until her mother nursed her.

"Can the king's madness be worse?" Tonore's father spluttered. "I supposed he's left Crown Prince Huwen governing Arcan as he goes about his campaign?"

"Regents," Sieura Warrick reasoned. "Of course the king's taken the land for himself and his family. The dukes' estates will go to his cronies. That's why he's waging this war. Greed."

Sieur Warrick's brows narrowed. "Woman," he said to Blodwyn. "Is this true? Or are you the one who's mad?"

Blodwyn spat in the dirt. "You call me a liar?"

"Where did you hear this, about the child princes ruling the carns?" Tonore's father challenged. "Did Artem announce it when he beheaded the king of Midell?"

"I heard it from them as know." She hugged her shoes and gripped her knife.

"Who?"

"Talkers. In the tavern. In Seedmarket."

"Gossip." Sieur Warrick dismissed her words.

"It's true!" Blodwyn flared.

Sieur Warrick shook his head.

"They were plotting." Blodwyn rose to her knees in the firelight. "They're going to get their own king, and their own army, and they're going to fight King Artem."

Meg lifted a brow. "Uprisers?"

Janat's soothing hand on Rennika's back stilled.

"Who?" Meg asked. "Who was talking? What were their names?"

Blodwyn looked at Meg as though she were mad and sat back in the darkness.

"Was one of them Sulwyn Cordal?" Meg persisted.

"Meg!" Janat admonished.

Meg fastened her eyes on Blodwyn, ignoring Janat.

Blodwyn shrugged. "I don't know."

Meg sighed and slumped back.

Rennika wanted to see Sulwyn again. He'd been good to them.

Blodwyn lifted her head with sudden memory. "Might have been. The one with the broken nose. In the corner. Someone might have called him Sieur Cordal. Sulwyn. Yes."

Meg exchanged looks with Janat. "Aye, his nose was crooked."

"Yes." Blodwyn nodded with conviction. "Sulwyn Cordal. He was the one. The one the king's men were hunting. Didn't talk much, though." She shook her head ruefully.

"What?" Meg probed. "Why?"

"Cut up in the battle," Blodwyn said. "A curse in the wound bloated his leg. Deluded with fever." She sheathed her knife. "He's probably dead by now."

The hillside above the battlefield was dusty and dry where Janat and Meg picked feverfew. The sun beating on her back was the first real heat Janat could remember since summer. Their way from Coldridge had taken them down into the high hills, where spring came earlier than Janat had ever seen it.

She straightened, stretching her muscles. She could see far out over the battlefield to farmland beyond the river, and hazy treed hillsides in the distance. There was a smudge on the horizon that looked to Janat ominously like smoke. The world seemed vast and trackless. "What's *wrong* with going to Seedmarket?" She challenged Meg. She knew her voice sounded peevish, but she persisted anyway. She'd woken with a headache, probably from the licorice drink from last night. But also, Meg was being bullheaded for no reason. Like always.

"It's not up to me." Meg stripped leaves and stuffed them into her bag. "Rennika, get up and help."

Rennika lay in the low scrub, almost asleep.

"We always follow the other refugees," Janat insisted. "Why can't you suggest we go to Seedmarket?"

"It might be dangerous." Meg turned back to the bushes before her. "Blodwyn said there was fighting there, not three days ago. A band of locals declared the town under the rule of a council of commoners. Rennika!"

Rennika dragged herself into a sitting position, but Janat pushed past her. "We have to go somewhere to sell our spoil. Blodwyn says Seedmarket's not far."

"It's not up to me. Rennika, pick up your bag."

"Besides. We don't *have* to go with the others," Janat pointed out, stuffing feverfew into her sack. "We could go on our own."

Meg stared at her. "With soldiers and bands of thieves roaming the countryside? Not to mention wolves, cougars, and bears? And not knowing the way? Make sense."

Janat hesitated, hearing her own words for the first time. "Well." She picked at the bushes furiously. "If you won't ask the others, I will."

Rennika began to pick leaves. "You think they'll listen to you?"

"I'll be sixteen, my next birthday," Janat shot at her. She turned to Meg. "Old enough to be mistress of my own house. Besides." She bent closer to Meg and whispered, "Don't you want to see Sulwyn again?"

Meg pursed her lips, holding back a reply.

Janat sighed in exasperation. "Well, I do. I'm going to ask them." She marched down the hill.

CHAPTER 16

Sulwyn wasn't in Seedmarket. Though she didn't say anything, Meg could see Janat was vexed.

Blodwyn had flown into a rage at the suggestion the band go to that village, and in the end, fled westward alone rather than accompany them.

The village of Seedmarket bore the scars of recent fighting: scorch marks and burnt thatch, broken fences, and trampled fields and gardens. Only a handful of villagers remained, toiling to repair the damage. The town had no food to share, no coin to purchase the refugees' booty and no pay to hire their labor. Many of their number had left, refugees themselves. Sulwyn might—or might not—have been among them. When the small band stayed the night, the exhausted townspeople didn't even compel the magiels to camp separately.

In the morning, they pushed their cart down the road to the next town. And the next, and the next.

When they reached Silvermeadow, a remote village untouched by war in what might have been the kingdom of Gramarye, Tonore's father got work cutting trees. Meg and Janat built a shanty, and helped Sieura Barcley and Gweddien work spells into sachets of feverfew, while Rennika explored the streets, begging.

❧

Cursed cough. The warming days of spring were no time to be shuffling from one room to another in the great hall, wearing a shawl, trying to avoid that daft healer and his potions.

Wenid Col allowed his man to help him into a formal—if plain—surcoat, and give him his cane. Ten days ago, he'd slipped on the marble stairs and twisted his knee. Blasted nuisance.

He approached the king's chambers and the guard admitted him immediately. Artem had come to Coldridge from the ongoing Orumon campaign for a council with his dukes' emissaries. Rebels had begun attacking forts and lesser strongholds in a random patchwork campaign, and from Meadowhill to Three Rivers to Seedmarket, partisan attacks had left swathes of the country in chaos. The generals needed their king. He would ride out again within the week, but Wenid would be in no shape to accompany him.

Artem—lean and grizzled and somehow out of place in his fine brocade doublet surrounded by embroidered draperies and richly dyed wool carpets, small touches Wenid had imported to the stark castle—sat on a spindly-legged chair, leaning forward with his elbows on his knees, deep in conversation with a young soldier.

Uther Tangel.

The boy seemed to have filled out in the past year. Well, he was no boy, now. A courier, by his dress.

Wenid hesitated in the doorway. "I apologize, Your Majesty. I was told you wanted to see me?"

Father and son stood.

"I should go," Uther said. "We returned late last night. I have not yet even seen the barber." He bowed to both of them and took his leave.

The king sat once more, tea and fruit tarts on a low table before him. He waved at the buffet, and Wenid perused the dainties with disdain.

"I see you're not getting any healthier."

"Your point?" Wenid poured himself a cup of herb tea, his hand shaking and spilling half. Where was the maid servant?

"When we spoke at the camp at Archwood, you were to select a magiel woman to mother a child." Artem leaned back in his chair. "What progress?"

Wenid was not one to sidestep difficult issues, but this one gave him pause. His king—his life's work, his God—hung by his petition to have magiels hunted. He fumbled for a napkin and mopped up the spilled tea as best he could, spreading the mess. "Several attempts were made," he said as matter-of-factly as he could, blotting at the stain. His throat was dry, tight. "None . . ." He groped for words. "None was successful."

Artem's lips twisted in a suppressed smile.

"The women were unsuitable." No. This was what Wenid had told the women. It was not the truth. He put his napkin on the table but could not meet Artem's gaze. "I . . . was unsuitable."

Artem rubbed his thumb along the arm of his chair. He did not speak for a long moment. "Then, we are left with a problem that is unsolved. A serious problem."

Wenid extended his hand to select a biscuit. It fell back into his lap.

"A male magiel," the king concluded.

To perform what Wenid Col could not. Obviously. The logical inference.

"Of one of the Great Houses, plainly," Artem said quietly.

Of course.

As if the Great Houses had not been accounted for. The magiels of the Emerald and the Azurite were women, and neither had sons. The magiel of the Amethyst and his sons had been put to the executioner in Coldridge. The magiel of the Citrine and his family had committed suicide before the fall of Midell. Kraae Elder, Wenid's predecessor, had been hunted down and killed in a remote valley, and his children belonged to the magiel of the Amber, Talanda Falkyn, who hid in Archwood; they had only daughters. The magiel of the Chrysocolla had died of a curse in prison but his son—a boy, but old enough—had left Holderford in the middle of the night last fall and disappeared into the masses of refugees roaming in displaced bands across the countryside.

"And, there is the issue of compliance," Artem continued. "With two unwilling participants, getting your successor becomes more and more difficult."

A male heir to one of the great magiel houses. There was only one.

"You said once you had a spell that could compel any magiel. I suggest you use it."

Son of the magiel of the Chrysocolla in Gramarye. Still alive? Unless he had met with accident or disease. Somewhere in Shangril. Likely posing as a village magiel or half-born.

"Wenid."

Wenid reached for a biscuit. The prisoners. One would know him, or would know someone who knew him. What was the boy's name?

"Wenid."

Wenid had a weakness for jam. He spread a thick glob on his biscuit, and the name came to him. "Gweddien Barcley." Wenid's biscuit paused before reaching his lips. If the boy hadn't changed it. He bit into his biscuit. It was worth a try.

"Who?"

"Give me four weeks." Wenid smiled to himself and added honey to his tea. "I may be able to find such a magiel."

"Gweddien Barcley," Artem Delarcan mused. "Of the Chrysocolla?"

"The same." Wenid sipped his tea.

"You know where he is?"

"No. But I think I can find him. I'll want spies and money for bribes." His mind worked. How best to winnow out information from unsuspecting dupes. The challenge piqued his interest.

"Very well." Artem rose. "Keep me informed."

Wenid rose as well. "One last thing, Sire. I've been meaning to bring this up."

"Yes?"

"With the term, 'magiel' out of favor, you might wish to change my title."

Artem hesitated. "Oh? To what?"

Wenid shrugged. "Chancellor."

"Ah." The ghost of a cynical smile touched the king's lips. "The ascetic exemplar desires something worldly. We shall discuss it. When you present me with your child."

CHAPTER 17

The candle guttered, and Wenid lit a new taper from the flame, pressing its butt into the soft wax. A dozen other candles stood at various stages of depletion, dripping wax around the perimeter of the large oak table. Once polished smooth, the surface was now a map of nicks and spilled ink tracing the work of decades—possibly centuries—of scholars and magiels. Dusty scrolls and thick bound books lined the shelves and filled the bins and chests, and now, lay scattered on the table. Wenid had taken to war at his king's side immediately upon assuming Kraae Elder's position as magiel of the Ruby, and it was only now, half a year later, he'd ridden to Holderford and begun to explore this chaos that was his predecessor's library.

He'd sent his spies out, hunting, listening, tracking down rumors of magiels. Half-borns and magiels of lesser ability he'd found and sequestered, but the Barcleys of the Chrysocolla still eluded him. The attack on Gramarye had been botched from the beginning. Gramarye's king had escaped, though not the prince; while his magiel had been imprisoned early in the war and was now dead, the magiel's wife and son had disappeared from their summer sojourn in Holderford immediately thereafter.

But, Artem's men would track down rumors of a shifting-skinned man of nineteen years with a talent for spells.

In the interim, Wenid need a charm. There was only one certain to compel a magiel. Glim. Wenid pushed his tongue over his mouth in distaste.

Of course, it was possible that subterfuge would suffice; that imprisoning the Barcley heir with a woman and leaving them alone—perhaps with some threat of a short life, to speed things up—nature would take its course, and Wenid would only have to harvest the child. The boy was nineteen, after all.

But Wenid's plans were larger than this; he wanted not one child, but a selection. Life, especially in times of war, as Artem had pointed out, was too precarious to depend on a single successor. And, Wenid did not trust the women he had selected—particularly those he had attempted to impregnate himself—not to be uncooperative, guessing his plan. They might poison Gweddien against the thought of fathering a child. And he did not want to enchant the woman in case taint spread to the child in her body. No, just a spell for Barcley. In case nature did not take its course.

And so, he hunted. The library at Holderford was extensive.

His search had, finally, borne fruit. A scroll locked in a box ensorcelled with invisibility.

Down of a snowcock, plucked under Ranuat's apogee. He could send a soldier to comb the mountains above Fairdell and shoot one; Ranuat would reach her apex in a week; the scroll said nothing about the feathers being fresh, though Wenid could make them so.

Beetle wings dried in Black Willow smoke. Easily done. There were large, iridescent beetles in the mud near the river with strong magical properties that would do very well.

Three drops of ice melt. At this time of year, he'd have to send a man to the mountains. Winter marigold root and bud. A pestle of eagle bone for the grinding and mixing. Yes, all of this was doable. The spell words, the time bending. Wenid nodded.

A spell to make the glim visible. Then, the finding.

He would need to travel, himself, to the mountains to harvest the delicate, rare plant. Only a magiel, with the help of the finding spell, could see the glim. With his increasingly fragile bones and wasted muscle, that would prove the challenge. He could send no one in his stead.

※

The woman with the burn scar on the left side of her face must be an upriser, Rennika decided. Almost every day—often several times a day—the woman came to the only tavern with an inn for travelers in Silvermeadow. She idled in the street or near the bridge over the steep gorge, scanning those who approached the tavern, passing subtle signals to some with her eyes. But the woman turned away or averted her gaze whenever a soldier in green and gold appeared. Rennika told Meg her suspicions, and Meg said the woman was probably a strumpet.

But Rennika didn't think so. Strumpets liked soldiers. Besides, once, she overheard the woman's speech. It was as though—like Gweddien and Janat and Meg—she copied the coarse accent but didn't always remember to use it.

Of late, one particular soldier had taken to watching this woman, and Rennika wondered how long it would be before there was a confrontation.

Rennika sat on a stump, her back propped against the tavern's clay daub wall one evening after sunset, weighing the three coins in her purse and watching spears of rain pock the dirt. The tavern, Gweddien had pointed out, was the best place in Silvermeadow to beg, and with her unagitated skin she could linger there without being chased off. Rennika pulled her hood over her head. She hadn't seen Gweddien for three days. She wished he'd come back from wherever it was that he'd gone so they could gather live spider legs like he'd promised. Besides, his mother was sick to distraction, hunting furtively for him.

Rennika tried to shake the worry away.

Twilight succumbed to an approaching squall. Beyond the candlelight that leaked, along with raucous singing, through the public house's windows, the street was dark. Would the soaking she'd get by loitering be worth the chetram or two she might earn—candlemarks from now—from tipplers leaving the tavern? Those who drank spirits, Rennika found, were usually more generous or more careless with money. If they weren't too drunk.

Wind gusted along the deserted street, slapping her with a handful of cold spring rain.

The three chetra she'd already earned telling Tarots would be enough. She'd go back to the shanty before the storm. Still she sat, shivering in her thin cloak, too cold to move. Anyway, the shanty would be wet, too.

There was a movement on the road on the far side of the bridge. A traveler. No, two.

Very well. With an effort, Rennika pulled herself to her feet. A glance told her these two would not give her money. The man was already drunk enough to stumble, and the woman staggered under his weight. But Rennika would try to beg a chetram off them, then make her way home.

As the two crossed the bridge, Rennika recognized the woman with the scarred face, so perhaps she was a strumpet, after all. At that moment, the suspicious soldier emerged from a side street.

The woman and her burdensome companion saw the soldier, but could neither retreat nor pass before the king's man accosted them. Over the rush of the river and the patter of the rain, Rennika could not hear what the soldier said, but—

The man.

It was—

"Sulwyn!" Rennika leapt to her feet and dashed through the rain, onto the bridge to fling her arms about his waist, almost knocking him off balance. He gasped and looked down at her, his face invisible in the shadow of his hood.

The soldier grunted.

The scarred woman had abandoned Sulwyn, who now steadied himself against the railing of the bridge. The woman seemed to hug the soldier to her as he made choking noises and grasped her shoulders. They danced for a moment, teetering on the slippery boards of the bridge until, like a felled tree, the soldier toppled over the railing and into the canyon, almost pulling the woman with him.

"Are you all right?" Sulwyn's croak was nearly overwhelmed by the rain.

"Ranuat." The woman's voice shook as she peered over the edge of the bridge. "He's—" She held something dark in one hand, a knife—

"Go!" Sulwyn rasped. But with his free hand, he gripped Rennika's shoulder as though she were a charm that decided life and death.

"Sulwyn?" It was him, wasn't it? His voice had changed and his features were indistinct in the dark, yet Rennika was sure she'd recognized his form, despite his gait.

The woman tore her gaze from the black depths and, propping herself beneath the man's armpit, continued their interrupted journey toward the inn. Rennika clung to Sulwyn—if it was him—and he gripped Rennika's shoulder painfully.

Sulwyn leaned against the jamb, wheezing, as the woman opened the door. The three of them staggered in from the rain to light and warmth. Someone near the door sprang from his chair and accepted—Sulwyn's—weight.

Rennika peered up, under the man's hood. He was more than thin. Gaunt. His face sprouted a straggle of beard, and his eyes were dark with liquid pain.

He looked down and smiled at her.

Sulwyn. She grinned back.

The patrons parted in faltering silence as the woman and the second man, the father of a boy Rennika played with, bore Sulwyn unsteadily to the kitchen. Then the music recovered with a lively jig as though the musicians had only forgotten their role momentarily, but now resumed a sham meant to swallow Sulwyn's passage, as though he'd never been amongst them.

Sulwyn's fellows eased him down a steep, narrow stairs, and another man accompanied them with a candle. Rennika followed. The flicker of light illuminated barrels along one wall of the cellar, and a rack of wine bottles against another. Between these and the shelves of root vegetables, a pallet lay on the floor, and the woman and man eased Sulwyn onto it. The tavern patron set his candle on the hardpack beside Sulwyn, his breath visible in its glow, and Rennika squirrelled herself into a corner, out of the way.

"Will he live?" The woman loosened Sulwyn's cloak and pushed his hood back.

Something in Rennika's chest flipped. Sulwyn could die? She flattened herself into the shadows to give the woman room to kneel by his side. That was why he couldn't walk—he wasn't drunk—

The man who'd borne him down the stairs loosened Sulwyn's boots. "This is the one the king's men hunt?"

Sulwyn's body shook with cold. The woman covered him with a blanket. "He needs warmth. We need a brazier."

"He needs to be hidden," the man with the candle corrected.

Rennika's friend's father. Fearghus, she thought his name was, a hawklike man who'd always frightened her. "And medicine."

Meg. The feverfew.

"He needs a magiel," the woman rebuked.

"I'm a magiel," Rennika blurted, disobeying Meg's warning.

The man with the candle startled, seeing her for the first time. "How did she get in here?" He whipped his head angrily to the woman. "Nia?"

Nia—the strumpet with the scarred face—shot a frightened look at Rennika. "She knows Sulwyn."

The candle man, Fearghus, leaned his fist on his thigh. "That's no—"

"She helped us," Nia stopped him. "I don't know how she knew—"

"Get her out of here!" the candle man said.

"She's a magiel," Sulwyn whispered.

The others turned to him.

"Listen to him, Fearghus," the man holding Sulwyn's boots said.

"Her skin's as still as mine," Fearghus growled. "This is no place for children."

With an effort, Sulwyn turned his head and opened his eyes a slit. "Your sisters are here?" His voice was papery and weak. "Janat? She's—"

Rennika wished she could reach out and touch his forehead. "We have a shanty," she said helpfully.

Nia crouched across the pallet from Fearghus. "This little girl distracted Artem's soldier. She gave me the chance to gut him and drop him in the river." The scarred lady held her bloody hands up in the light.

Fearghus frowned at Rennika in surprise.

"My sisters are magiels, too." Rennika edged into the ring of light. "They have healing herbs."

"Bring them." Sulwyn's teeth chattered with cold, his eyes pressed tightly in pain.

Fearghus closed his mouth and sat back. "Beorn." He spoke to the boot man, his voice softer. "Bring the healing women here."

Beorn rose. "Will there be time?"

"Not if you stand there, gawking," Fearghus snapped, and Beorn rose to leave. "Shantytown. Meg."

"Can I—" Rennika reached out a tentative hand. "Can I touch him?"

The others stilled in silent assent. Nia gave her a small nod and a smile.

Rennika laid her hand on Sulwyn's forehead, which was uncomfortably hot. She didn't know why she wanted to touch him, or what she hoped to do. Something about the way he felt was wrong, though. She closed her eyes. But the hurt did not come from Sulwyn's head.

Nia breathed audibly, and Rennika opened her eyes. The grimace of pain had left Sulwyn's features.

"Where is he hurt?" Rennika asked.

"His leg." Nia turned to Fearghus. "The man who brought him from Theurgy was only candlemarks ahead of a troop of Artem's men, them mounted, and him with a cart. He had to press on. He barely stopped to let Sulwyn off."

Rennika lifted the blanket from his leg and pulled the cuff of his breeches up. She felt the flesh above Sulwyn's knee.

"Led them away. Good thinking," Fearghus approved. "The king's men followed him?"

Sulwyn's leg was bloated and spongy, and the skin was hot.

Nia nodded. "Yes. But I had to get Sulwyn away from the road. There was no time to send for help. So I brought him here from the rendezvous myself."

At Rennika's touch, Sulwyn flinched and drew a sharp breath. A rope of hard skin wound across his leg. The wound was not fresh, but it had closed without healing. A heavy curse lay in the wound.

She closed her eyes and felt back in time, searching for a moment when his flesh was whole and healthy. There. Days ago. Weeks, maybe. She pulled bits of clean muscle and unknotted skin forward, tugged it into the present. But the cut was large and the curse within had spread through his body, too diffuse for her to track down. At least, not without potions.

She opened her eyes. Beneath her cloak, her robe was drenched in sweat and she shivered, chilled, and tired. The injury on Sulwyn's leg still felt swollen and scarred, but its heat was less, and his face was peaceful now. He had drifted into sleep.

The woman with the scar, Nia, placed a hand on her arm. "Thank you," she said softly.

But Sulwyn was not healed. "He needs my sisters' herbs and spells," Rennika said, suddenly very weary. They weren't here yet. Hadn't Beorn gone to get them?

"Come." Fearghus touched her shoulder, and she saw that he wasn't as frightening as she'd once thought. "I'll take you home."

The squall had subsided to a steady rain, and Rennika shook with cold as she walked in silence by Fearghus's side. The streets were empty and dark, and her feet were numb with the chill of splashing in icy puddles—

And then she lay on dewy grass on a warm night. Black trees, rattling with restless twigs, blotted out a lightless sky.

Where—

—was the street? Fearghus?

She reached out and ran her fingers through the grass. She was—here. Wherever "here" was. Delicate perfumes of poplar and spruce, frost and glacier, wafted on the air. She sat up. The last embers of a cook fire had died some time ago. Dark forms slept just beyond its ashes. Silvery dew etched each branch and unfurled bud on aspens rising out of a predawn mist.

This couldn't be real. How could she walk and dream at the same time? And . . . she touched the grass, smelled the sweet air, listened to the chirp of morning birds—

But she had known something like this before, a sudden daydream, intensely real. She'd had them all her life.

Then—

She was in a dark lane, faintly visible in the gray of approaching dawn. Snow, hard and trampled to ice, dirty with frozen offal, lay underfoot. She leaned against a stone wall and her body was cold, shivering, her feet bare and lacerated. She wore an elegant robe . . . silky on her skin, beneath a good woolen cloak, but something was wrong with it . . . torn. The front of her dress was open to her waist, and she held the cloak tightly closed over breasts as large as Meg's.

And blood. On her nose and chin, on her hands. Her nose was broken, her body bruised.

Another dream.

But—

Meg held a wrinkled robe up to the fading afternoon light at a window closed in by panes of glass. A new time, a new place.

Rennika knew this room. The nursery in Archwood Castle, as real as she remembered it. Rennika sat on a cushion on the floor. She looked around the room. Nanna sewed the seams of Janat's bodice. Her new, yellow silk gown, the day she turned fifteen. The day King Artem's army attacked.

Nanna! Though she knew it was a dream and not real, Rennika ran to Nanna's side and gripped her. She wanted to be held in Nanna's arms, hold her close.

Meg went back to her room. "Not until you're dressed, and that's after I'm dressed!" *She poked her head through the doorway. She put her tongue out at Janat.*

"The king's army is going to attack us!" *Rennika cried. If this was real, if she could choose to run to Nanna, perhaps she could make things that were going to happen—not happen.*

"Turn," *Nanna told Janat.* "Rennikala, go sit on your cushion."

Janat did as she was bid and bumped into Rennika. "Rennikala! Go sit down!"

"Nanna!" *Rennika held her harder.*

"Are there really going to be oranges at court tonight?" *Janat asked.*

"That's what Cook said." *Nanna snipped her thread, tolerant of Rennika's desperate hug.*

"Children aren't going to get any," *Meg called from the other room.* "The fruit are small and there aren't many—"

—Rennika stumbled. Rain poured down her neck in the inky night, and Fearghus grabbed her elbow so she didn't fall.

She was surrounded by shanties. "Which is yours?" Fearghus asked.

Which? She stared at him, tears welling from her eyes. Where was Archwood? The nursery—Nanna—

"Rennika?" Fearghus held her upper arms, bearing her weight.

Gone. Nanna was gone. Taken by an orum. Rennika crumpled into the man.

"Hush, child," he murmured, pulling her gently from him. "Which is your home?"

Home. She wiped her nose on her sleeve and turned in the dark.

"There." She pointed at the shanty.

Those minutes—seconds—she'd spent in the meadow—the nursery—were real. Real.

"Rennika?" It was Beorn. "Which shack is yours? I've been hunting and calling."

"Fool," Fearghus muttered.

Shaking, she led the way to her . . . home. "Janat?" she called, and heard the tremble in her own voice. A hardness rose in her throat. Squatting in the mud, she lifted the flap and entered. She needed Janat to hold her.

Nanna was gone.

There was a movement in the familiar darkness. A head lifted from a pallet. "Rennika?" Janat whispered. "We were worried about you—"

Rennika buried her head in Janat's shoulder and clung to her, felt the solidity of her flesh.

"What happened?" Janat asked in alarm.

How could Rennika explain?

"Child?" Fearghus called from outside the shanty.

"It's Sulwyn." Rennika lifted her head, joy mixing with fear and grief. "Sulwyn Cordal, Janat!"

Janat sat upright, and Meg raised her head. "Sulwyn?" Meg pulled her blanket around her shoulders and crawled to Rennika.

"Where?" Janat pushed Rennika back to see her better in the dark.

"He's sick. A cursed wound," Rennika told her. "At the tavern. He needs medicine."

"You've seen him?" Meg cried.

Janat scrambled to her knees, hunting for her shawl, and Rennika was suddenly bereft. She didn't know what had happened to her while walking back from the tavern. But . . .

Was this madness? Mama had sometimes talked strangely, looked at them, at their rooms, like she hadn't seen them for a long time. People whispered that magiels went mad. When they used magic. Rennika . . . had used magic. Was she mad?

She'd seen Nanna. Been with Nanna. Touched Nanna. It had been real.

She'd lived a moment of her life *before* it had changed.

She could go back to that moment. But . . . how?

But Janat plucked a sack from a nail in the wattle of the building that formed one wall of the shanty, and flung on her robe. "Let's go."

CHAPTER 18

Meg dashed through the tavern door, pausing for only a moment as her eyes adjusted from the brightness of the lane. But the innkeeper's wife put a hand on Meg's arm, beckoning with a nod.

Meg followed her to the side of the room, frowning in puzzlement.

"Dwyn Gramaret arrived last night," the innkeeper's wife said in a low voice.

"The king of Gramarye." Meg was impressed. "What's he doing here?" Rumor had it that, within a week of receiving King Artem's proclamation, Gramarye had capitulated and given up its prayer stone. The Chrysocolla was publicly smashed and King Gramaret disappeared—fled in cowardice from the chopping block. His wife had been killed and his crippled son had been captured. His home was given to King Artem's young daughter, Hada, only nine years old, to be ruled by a regent until she came of age.

The innkeeper's wife shrugged. "I don't know. But he had news." She touched Meg gently on the shoulder. "Here. Sit."

Bad news.

Meg sat at a table next to a sunny window and the woman sat beside her.

"Meg. King Artem has decreed death to all magiels."

So. Here it was. Though she'd known it was coming, it still took her by surprise. "Did . . . something happen?"

The woman shrugged. "His armies tried to use magiel magic in his unholy war. One of his magiels waited until a critical moment, then cast a spell that helped the uprisers he was fighting. He lost in a rout."

The self-proclaimed high king of all of Shangril. Against peasants. A warm pleasure touched Meg's chest.

"All magiels are to be hunted and arrested, or killed."

The pleasure evaporated. Death. Real. King Artem's magiel, Wenid, had urged him to do it, back in Coldridge, back in the winter. And now, he'd done it.

The woman licked her lips. "Meg, if you're going to come here to visit Sulwyn, you have to come in by the back door."

Meg's attention whipped up. Separation of magiel and worldlings. Like she'd seen in Teshe and Midell. Now, here, in Silvermeadow. Next would come the beatings.

"You know my husband and I support the men. Support you."

"Oh?" The word, the fury, the rage, came out as a tiny choking sound.

"But if our inn is sacked by soldiers looking for magiels, think what they might find."

Too much. Sulwyn. A nest of uprisers.

Meg bit down on her wrath, schooled her breathing. The innkeeper's wife spoke true.

Meg surveyed the tavern. She knew most of the scatter of patrons by name and face, but not all. She'd become complacent. "And Janat?"

The woman shrugged. "She's not that wavering. But, yes, maybe her, too. For everyone's safety."

Fury threatened again to spill out.

The woman looked uncomfortable, and Meg knew the grim set of her mouth had betrayed her rage.

"Best use Rennika for your messages," the woman said. "Only come if you must."

The back way.

Meg swallowed her bile and lifted her brows in a shrug of reluctant agreement. The woman was right.

The wife nodded in relief as Meg raised her hood and left the inn.

She made her way cautiously through the village, working her way back through the inn's stable and chicken yard, to the kitchen door. She slipped in, then, and as quickly as dark stairs and sick-chamber silence allowed, hurried to the cellar.

Sulwyn was alone, reading by candlelight, and Meg found herself pleased that Janat, ever ministering to him, was not there. He lifted his head when she entered. "Meg." He smiled the smile she had come to love.

"How do you feel today?"

"Better and better." He set his book aside and, shifting his blanket, used both hands to lift his leg, resting his foot on the floor beside his pallet.

In the dim light, the redness and swelling seemed to have all but disappeared. She touched the thick, jagged scar that bisected the muscles of his thigh. "How's your walking?" She sat back and emptied a small pouch of spelled herbs into the mug of water by his side. "And the pain?"

"Six steps from the stairs to the shelf, and six steps back," he reported. "The pain's bearable." He nodded to the bottle of rice wine on the floor by his pallet.

She gave him a mock frown and placed her hands on the muscles above his knee as he swallowed the herbs, and waited for his blood to bring the medicinal spells to the injured site. "I'm almost finished the book of poetry you lent me." She treasured the rare moments she had with him, talking about books.

A ghost of a smile touched his eyes, and he leaned back on his pillow. "Eric Stewart. His works were banned in Pagoras, Midell, and Arcan. Have you read 'What Man Would Not Wear a King's Circlet'? That was the first poem my father gave me to read." His father, who'd advised King Ean on his council of commoners.

She felt herself blush a little. "Yes, I read that one. And 'Good For All.'" A warmth spread into his muscles beneath her palms as she pulled the magic of the healing potion forward. "I'd never read poetry like it before." She tilted her head. "The things those poems talk about. Freedom from want, freedom from fear. Freedom from . . . coercion. Do people believe such things are possible?"

"In King Ean's court, there were some who did. Your king read that book, you know."

She gave him a sharp look. "A king? Would read about . . . sharing power?"

"When his council was finished its business, my father said, they would discuss such ideas." He smiled. "Apparently, the debates were lively."

"Do you believe in . . . rule of men?"

"How much rule?" he countered.

"'The fish school, leaderless, in harmonious direction'?" she quoted.

Sulwyn snorted a small laugh. "No, of course not. The One God gave us our kings. But kings can listen to their subjects. I believe in that."

She massaged his knee, the magic coming easily, pulling healthy blood from before Sulwyn's injury into the damaged tissues, though she would need rest and solitude later. The book had made her think. Freedom to choose was not only freedom to search for joy, but also freedom to fail. Freedom from want might be bought at the cost of freedom of speech.

Sulwyn leaned back on an elbow. "Do you believe in shared rule?"

"Me?" She darted a glance at him and laughed.

"Why do you laugh? Commoners can clamor as much as they want for recognition, but nothing will happen until people like you, Meg—the magiels and the kings—give such ideas support."

"Magiels live in service to their people," she shot back. "Mama's *life* was devoted to bringing them their death tokens. You don't know the price she paid—"

"Shush!" He leaned forward in pain and stopped her fingers on his knee. "A magiel may serve the people's spiritual needs and yet be unaware of the pain in their bellies."

She peered at him in the dim candlelight. He was close to her, his expression at once intense and gentle, and she was suddenly confused about whether the thumping in her heart was from anger or the touch of his hands on hers.

He released her fingers and slowly leaned back against his cushion. "It is a provocative book. I'm sorry if lending it to you was . . . offensive."

She looked back down at her hands and eased the pressure on his leg. The healing of the herbs was almost complete. She allowed the strength of the magic to subside. "No," she murmured. "The book was interesting. I have a lot to think about." She let her hands slide from his knee and covered his leg with the blanket.

Footsteps on the stairs. Meg turned.

Janat brought a bowl of red rice and lentil soup and set it on the floor by Sulwyn's mattress, eclipsing the light from the candle. "I have a message from King Gramaret. He says to call him Dwyn. He can meet with you, Fearghus, and Beorn at supper."

Politics. Meg wondered if Dwyn Gramaret had read Eric Stewart.

"And Nia? I want her there, too." Sulwyn tasted the soup and grinned his pleasure at Janat.

"He didn't mention her." She blushed at his smile, then raised her head. "Oh, he brought word of Gweddien. Tonore Warrick—do you know him?—reported a rumor that Gweddien was seen in the company of Arcan soldiers. On the road to Coldridge."

"Oh, no."

Gweddien, arrested? His mother would be inconsolable.

The fatigue from using the healing magic crept into Meg's bones. It was time to go before she found herself stumbling and incoherent. She rose and climbed the stairs.

Janat chattered by Sulwyn's side as he ate his soup, gazing into her eyes with . . . unsettling . . . affection.

❈

"Have you eaten?" Sulwyn asked Janat when Meg had slipped up the stairs.

She hadn't.

With a wicked grin Janat didn't understand, Sulwyn gave her a cushion to ward away the chill of the earthen floor and sat on the edge of his mattress, sore leg extended, placing the bowl between them.

She sat cross-legged on the cushion in the wavering candlelight. "There's only enough soup for you." Mama would've been shocked if she could've seen Janat here, alone, with a man. Nanna, too.

In reply, he lifted the spoon to her lips, his other hand beneath it in case of spills.

She leaned forward a little and opened her mouth, the bowl of the spoon touching her lightly, and swallowed. A chill of unexpected pleasure shivered inside her as she lifted her eyes to look into his.

His finger grazed her lip, lifting a drop of liquid away, and heat—

and something else, something wonderful—coursed through her.

He lowered the spoon, the roguishness in his eyes replaced with . . . what? Intensity. "Is the door bolted?" he whispered.

He always kept the door bolted against— "No. Meg couldn't have—"

He gave a slight nod, and she scrambled to her feet, her breath coming short in anticipation and curiosity. She ran up the narrow stairs and feeling the bolt in the dark, slid it closed.

When she returned, Sulwyn had uncorked his bottle of rice wine. Sulwyn, the one the rebels looked up to, the one the conspirators in Spruce Falls respected, with his crooked nose and shock of thick hair, and . . .

He filled his mug with the sweetly sharp-smelling drink. He tasted it, and his jaw tightened imperceptibly in the candlelight. He offered her the mug.

Exquisite expectancy suffused her, just to be alone in his company. Part of his adventure. One of them. She was sixteen, now, and old enough.

She took the cup and tasted the cool liquid. It was astringent, yet faintly sweet, prickling her throat as she swallowed, its heat dissipating in her in a pleasant relaxation.

His eyes never leaving hers, he touched her hairline, gently raking his fingers into her thick waves, tracing the line of her jaw. Astonishment tingled every part of her body, her nipples startling with wonder, her groin heating with pleasure.

Sulwyn drank back the remainder of the wine and poured more for her.

Gods, she had been a child, before. Older girls, not Meg, but some of the others in Archwood, had giggled with secrets they refused to share, looking over their paper fans at some of the young courtiers. They knew.

She had known nothing until now.

She took a long swallow and set the mug aside, giving in to its relaxation and bliss.

Sulwyn's amazing hand slipped behind her neck, flooding her with delight as his lips closed on hers. His tongue touched hers, exploding tingles of desire into every part of her body. His strong arms slid her onto the mattress and he was over her, his face half-lit by the candle, his hips sliding over hers, his hand slipping down her neck to her collar bone, the soft rounding of her breast . . .

She had known nothing, nothing in her life, until this moment.

❈

The cell below the castle in Coldridge was chill, winter or summer. Wenid, dressed in layers of wool, wore a fur cloak. He'd had a comfortable chair brought down for his vigil, and there was a table with a dozen candles on it, scrolls to read, two goblets and a bottle of wine. He really didn't know how long he would be here.

He removed a pouch from his robes. Glim.

The potion Wenid had created from the instructions in Kraae's library was a paste which, once he climbed—slowly and painfully, and with much help—to the rocky ridges east of Holderford, he smeared on his eyelids. The potion made the glim visible, flecking the mosses that grew on the rocks among the winter marigolds, glimmering in a dissonance out of step with time. He'd gathered the tiny plants, dried them, and now poured a little of the powder into the bottom of one of the goblets, invisible in the dark. The scroll had been vague about how much to use. He hoped an excess would not be dangerous, though the flick of smudged edges in his vision suggested ghosts were gathering.

Presently, the guards arrived with their prisoner. The man—boy—was capricious-skinned and tall, though not as tall as Wenid. He was undernourished and not yet fully filled out, dressed in patched but serviceable clothing. The prisoner looked nervously about the small dim room, eyeing the fur-covered pallet on the floor. He shot a fearful glance at Wenid.

He'd been given a week with the women, both in their joint prison where Wenid hoped dark and fear would drive couples together, and individually in comfortable rooms, but Wenid's spies told him nature had not taken its course. It was regrettable, for the boy, but time pressed. Wenid had already decided on a name for his project. The loveliest of the winter blossoms. Marigolds.

"Bar the door and wait within," Wenid ordered the men. "Remove his manacles." When this was done, he nodded to the frightened young man. "You may call me Wenid." He wanted to relax the—prisoner. It was best not to think of him as an innocent.

The lad's head bobbed and he looked at his feet.

Wenid had been reassured that this was Gweddien Barcley. In the end, his heritage was perhaps no matter; by his skin he was clearly a magiel. If he was not of the House of the Chrysocolla, he would still sire more magiels.

Wenid hesitated, then splashed wine into both goblets. He could not have compunction in this business. The boy did not matter, only his child.

He handed the goblet with the glim to the boy.

The boy lowered the cup suspiciously, his eyes unable to keep from flicking toward the pallet. "What do you intend to do to me?"

Wenid snorted in disgust. "Not what you think," he said acidly. "If I wanted to lie with you, I'd have taken you to a warmer room." He looked pointedly at the boy's goblet. "And if you suspect me of lacing your wine, be assured." He drank from his own cup. The wine was astringent, choking. "There. See? Nothing to worry about." He sat in his own comfortable seat and nodded to a plain chair. "Please, sit."

But the boy had used a low accent. Had Wenid's spies been misled?

The lad perched gingerly on the wooden chair. A blanket had been draped across it, and he tugged at its edges, pulled it up around his knees. Wenid hadn't been prepared for the boy's youth. Naiveté.

"You are a magiel." Wenid said the words he'd rehearsed. "A difficult heritage, since the king's decree that magic wielders are forbidden."

The boy held his goblet stiffly in one hand, clutching the blanket around him with the other. If only he didn't look so frightened.

Wenid forced himself to go on. There was no room for second thoughts. "I am in a position to give you, and your mother if you wish, a comfortable life in Holderford." This was all true. "Pleasant apartments. Food, clothing. The company of women." That would make up, a little, for what he was about to do.

The boy's form became rigid. He'd schooled his expression, but Wenid could see derision and disbelief there. "In exchange for what?"

"Your help in ending these unfortunate uprisings." He took a small sip of his wine, a nudge. "Speak with those you know who would oppose King Artem's rightful rule. Help them to understand the glory of the One God, and the dangers of demon worship. Together, we might save much bloodshed." It was nonsense, but the boy must relax . . . swallow the potion. Then, what followed would be out of Wenid's hands.

"And if I did, would Artem return the lands usurped from the kings who stood up for their people?" The boy was challenging him. "The lands Artem gave to his sycophants?"

"What's done is done." This boy might use a low accent but he didn't question why he'd been asked to be a spokesperson. He spoke directly and clearly. He was no peasant. "Those kings had the opportunity to swear allegiance to King Artem and the One God when they were first asked. And some did."

"So, *no*, then." In the dim flicker of the candlelight, the boy's face darkened in anger. An idealist, a fighter. That would soon be gone.

If only the boy would calm himself, he might drink. There were other, uglier ways to get the glim into him. Wenid hoped it would not come to that. "You are only a village magiel, I think. Who owns the lands you live on hardly makes any difference."

The boy straightened. "I am the son of Yolen Barcley, magiel of the House of the Chrysocolla, in Highglen, whom you left to die of a curse in prison," he said, and his voice modulated, a flawless highborn accent. "King Gramaret lost his castle and all his lands when King Artem stole the Chrysocolla and destroyed it."

"Of course, I need proof you are who you say you are."

"I speak the truth and have no proof beyond my word. However, it is nought to me, if you believe me or not."

"If you are truly a magiel of one of the Great Houses, descended from The One God, himself, you can show it."

The boy tilted his head slightly. "Very well." He lifted the blanket over his head, shielding him from the candlelight. It took a moment for the boy's unmasking, but his skin glittered in the lightless space like an inky night sky, filled with infinitesimally tiny sparks of light. The universe of the Gods, the Heavens visible through his skin. The miracle was breathtaking.

"Are you satisfied?" Gweddien lowered the blanket.

Wenid took a breath and topped up the wine in his goblet. "I am." He reached over to refill Gweddien's untouched cup.

Confirmation. It was a relief, and at the same time, a niggle. Their backgrounds were not dissimilar. Yet, didn't Wenid understand the pain the boy would live? In service to the One God? It was his own pain.

The boy drank.

Wenid watched, a sickness turning in his stomach. He looked away and finished his goblet.

"We had a peaceful country," the boy was arguing. "Men could become wealthy through their own labor. Men could become learned. Men had hopes of raising their station."

All of this, true. But a wealthy country put greed above worship. An educated country questioned the divine right to rule. A country where men changed their stations became unstable. None of this would happen; not while Wenid had the king's ear. "Thank you," he whispered. "Your thoughts on these matters are helpful."

The boy did not hear him. He listened but listened to some sensation deep within himself.

"Would you like to lie down?" And now, the bliss would begin. Wenid knew it. Envied him. Wept for him.

The boy frowned. "The wine . . . is strong."

Wenid nodded to the guards who helped the boy to the pallet and covered him with furs. "You may leave, now," he said softly when they were done. "He will be no trouble."

Meg woke, chilled, with spruce needles trickling down the neck of her robe and the roar of the river in her ears. The afternoon was waning to twilight, and the early summer heat beginning to abate, though it was cool beneath the low spreading branches of the spruce tree.

A man's voice was audible over the water. "The stones were chinked with moss, and the wind came right through. I visited it once."

Meg sat up to dig the twigs from her robe and knocked the branch above her, precipitating another shower of needles into her hair and clothing.

"When did your father come to Archwood?" A different voice, pitched higher, muffled by the rushing water.

"As a boy." Sulwyn? "My grandfather had earned enough to buy his contract by trading wines. Ever since I was a boy, we always had the best wines in our home."

The space beneath the spruce tree was dim. Dusk had crept along the river when Meg wasn't looking. She'd wriggled under the ground-sweeping lower branches of the spruce to recover from the morning's healing, away from Janat and Rennika and the squalor of the shanty town, and to escape the heat. Just to close her eyes in the cool, summer-scented echoes of the river. She'd fallen asleep.

"So that's how your father became a trader." The girl's voice was only audible above the sound of the river because she sat so close to Meg's tree. Who was Sulwyn with? Nia?

"Yes. Hard work, of course." Yes, that was Sulwyn. "But it couldn't have happened if King Ean hadn't seen the value of letting men have rising hopes." Meg peered through the thick branches. Pants and stockings and boots. He sat almost close enough to touch. "Dwyn is a lot like King Ean," he went on. "The people of Gramarye love him. But we need to build a following in Midell and Pagoras, and especially in Arcan. Dwyn and the rest of us have worked out a plan. We leave soon."

Leave?

"King Gramaret?" The woman—girl?—he was with, sounded impressed. If he was seducing her, it couldn't be Nia. Nia liked women. "What's your work?"

—the voice. Was Janat's.

Meg felt a stab of guilt.

"Emissary. Raising support. Meeting and talking to men of substance."

Negotiating with men of power? A thrill of fear and adventure coursed through Meg.

"You don't have to go." Yes, Janat. Unmistakably.

But Meg couldn't stop listening. Sulwyn, meeting men who'd lost everything. Angry men. Or—perhaps, men who still clung to their money, afraid. Fearful men were dangerous. Covert talks, hidden in alleys and basements. King Gramaret had to remain concealed, protected; his emissaries did not. Could not.

Perilous.

"We have a moment of time, Janat. Only a moment in which to act. Everything's turned upside down. People are angry. They're confused. Artem is distracted. This is our opportunity to put the rule of law ahead of the whim of the king. And the Amber might be the only prayer stone other than his own that Artem hasn't smashed. We *must* preserve the Amber. When Dwyn leaves, I'm going west."

"But you could be hurt again."

Why were Sulwyn and Janat sitting on the riverbank, alone? Janat wasn't even interested in politics, not like Meg.

"Why does it have to be you? To do this work?" Janat's words were almost drowned by the rush of the river. Was she crying? Trying to stop him? Meg listened as hard as she could above the roar.

"King Ean, Janat." Sulwyn spoke with quiet passion. "Under his rule, my grandfather earned enough to buy his serfdom from his master. My father became a trader. I had a *future*. Do you know what that meant to me?"

Meg would have gone on such a quest in a trice.

"I could have been someone of influence. One day, I might even have held property, or perhaps my sons, or my sons' sons. Do you know? Some of the guildsmen in Archwood *owned* their own shops."

Kyaju. He was right.

"If Artem's Ruby becomes the only prayer stone left, will his magiel bring death tokens back from Heaven for everyone? Hmm?" Sulwyn asked. "Or *only* for his highborn allies? Will he condemn anyone who thinks differently from him—to wander for eternity when they die?"

"I know," Janat conceded. "This fight is . . . who you are."

Meg itched to *do* something. But she was a woman, stuck here, taking care of Janat and Rennika. Hiding out in a village in the middle of nowhere. Hiding the dissonance of her skin.

Sulwyn's tone altered. "Do you know how long you and your sisters will stay here?"

"No."

"It would be wise for you not to stay in one place for too long," Sulwyn advised.

Of course! Meg had been saying that since they arrived. But Janat wanted to stay—with Sulwyn.

These words. They were private.

Something had changed.

When had Sulwyn and Janat started excluding her?

"The people of Silvermeadow have been good to us," Janat hedged.

Kyaju. A sour taste filled Meg's mouth and she was suddenly hot. Janat was just turned sixteen. And what about Sulwyn? Twenty? Twenty-two?

Sulwyn's voice kept on, melodic tones over the shush of the river. "There are rumors that Talanda's daughters escaped Archwood. It's only a matter of time until King Artem finds out who you all are."

Meg wanted to be anywhere but where she was.

Sulwyn spoke again. "Dwyn says Elsen is far from Artem's war. It fell early in the war and is at peace, now."

Maybe if she crept out the other side of the tree? But she'd rustle the bracken and they'd hear her.

"Would you . . . would you consider . . . coming with me?"

Go? With Sulwyn? A sting bloomed in Meg chest.

"With you?"

The words made Meg's face burn, made her want to be anywhere but here.

"I thought I could take you somewhere safe, maybe a small village in Elsen, and I would come to you when I could. I know it's a lot to ask—"

"Yes!"

The river sounds rushed on, and Meg could hear nothing. She shifted. From her place she could see Sulwyn's legs and a bit of Janat's robe. If she stayed quiet long enough, they'd leave. *Please, Gods, let them leave.*

Neither of them spoke. No sound, only the boom of the river. Janat's skirt stirred.

Meg could not help herself. She moved a branch to look.

Sulwyn held Janat close to him, indecently close. Her arms

were about his neck, his face bent over hers, eyes closed, their lips fastened.

Meg's stomach punched, her hand frozen to the branch, eyes unable to turn away. Janat—dear Janat—was only sixteen—

And Sulwyn. Meg had thought him better than that. To kiss a child—

Their lips parted. Janat looked deeply into the man's face for a long time, her cheeks pink, contentment on her face. Sulwyn laid her on the grass on her back and leaning over her, traced the finger of his free hand along the edge of her cheek. He touched his nose to hers.

Meg drew back into the dusk beneath the spruce tree. This was wrong.

But . . . Janat and Sulwyn looked . . .

Happy.

The sound of the river would mask Meg's leaving. She crept to the far side of the bole and out from beneath its branches, and made her way by a long and circuitous route through the woods, back to the town, thinking long and hard as she did so.

Sulwyn . . . loved Janat.

CHAPTER 19

The summer air—even at night—had taken on a softness Rennika had never felt when she lived in the mountains. As the strawberries faded, the raspberries grew heavy on their canes. When she wasn't begging or running messages, Rennika helped Sieura Barcley find herbs under auspicious celestial signs, and the magiel, still grieving her son's disappearance, instructed Rennika in magic.

But now as summer mellowed, Sulwyn had told them he was leaving. And Meg and Janat talked of going somewhere, too, which Rennika couldn't fathom. They had friends in Silvermeadow. Her sisters had found enough work to live and they weren't beaten often, as long as they stayed out of the way. Rennika didn't want to go back to wandering.

But the morning came when Sulwyn packed his cart, Janat had scrubbed his clothes and hung them to dry, then later, folded them and brought them to him. Meg and Rennika went to the tavern stable to say goodbye.

Janat was sitting on the stone wall that divided the yak pen from the horse stalls as Sulwyn brushed the mare Sieur Dwyn had procured for him. "If there are no buildings there, you'll have a lot of work before winter," she was saying.

He stroked the tolerant mountain pony with a wide brush. "No merchant is a stranger to work," he said as Rennika and Meg slipped through the barn door.

Rennika ran to him and wrapped her arms around him. "Don't go!"

"I have to go." Sulwyn hugged her back. "I have to work."

"Get someone else to do it." She climbed onto the stone wall beside Janat.

"That's part of my work," he said, pulling the bridle from its hook and sliding it over the mare's head. "Showing others why they should join us."

The door opened and a tall man peered in. "Ah. Sulwyn." It was the man who was once king of Gramarye, and didn't want his title used, so they all called him Dwyn. He eased himself through the door and closed it behind him. He had a head of thick dark hair with bits of gray that fell to his shoulders, now tied back but for a few strands. His clothing was good but used, and he covered it with a ragged woollen cloak. His boots, though, had not yet worn out.

Sulwyn led the pony to her place before the cart. He nodded at Dwyn, which was completely wrong to Rennika, though Meg had explained why it must be so. "Sieur. I thank you again for your generosity." He gestured to the horse and cart.

Dwyn's nod was graceful and kingly. Like the other refugees, he struggled to copy the low accent. "You're working for Shangril," he said. "You need tools to accomplish your undertaking." He swept a glance over Rennika and her sisters. "What of the magiels?"

Rennika startled. He knew?

Sulwyn took the harness down from its peg. "They've been discussing staying in Silvermeadow for the winter."

"Out of the question. Too many people here suspect who they are."

"They do not!" Janat cried, but the king silenced her with a glance.

Meg lifted her head. "Sieur—"

"Silvermeadow is on the King's Road," Dwyn said in a tone that permitted no debate. Meg looked as though she wanted to argue, but for once she didn't.

Rennika looked to Janat for support, but her sister only stared at Sulwyn, sudden fear on her face.

Sulwyn draped the harness over the mare's body. "My father had a friend, a trade partner, actually, with cousins in Wildbrook."

"Where is Wildbrook?" Meg asked.

"The country of Elsen. North and west of here. Some distance."

The deposed king placed his hands behind his back, head lowered, centering on Sulwyn's words. "The King's Road will take them through Midell."

"Beorn is going to Pagoras. He could see them safely past Midell." Sulwyn's fingers stilled on the buckle and he gave Janat a reassuring look.

"How long a journey?" Meg looked from one man to the other.

Sulwyn limped to the other side of the mare to adjust the straps on the harness. "Two weeks, depending on the weather."

"They can't all go," Dwyn said.

Rennika gripped Janat's hand.

"Why not?" Meg demanded.

With a look, Dwyn deflected the question to Sulwyn.

Sulwyn's fingers fell from their work and he turned to Meg. "Three of you together. Your accents. Your ages. One scintilating, one variable, one steady."

"Be plain."

He shrugged apologetically at Janat. "It's clear who you are to anyone who knows what to look for." He flicked his gaze to the king.

"There are rumors Talanda's daughters escaped Archwood the night of the attack."

Janat hung her head.

"No one has substantiated them," Sulwyn interjected, finding his mug. "So far, the civil war has thrown the country in chaos. No one knows—for sure—who's been killed, who's in exile . . ."

"Nevertheless," Dwyn said. "The king's men will be watching for three young girls. Just as Sulwyn described."

Janat's grip on Rennika's hand tightened. "You can't separate us."

The king looked at Janat. "You may not wish to live, but as magiels of a great house, your place in this war is of far greater importance than your personal desires."

"But there are lots of displaced magiels, lots—"

"What about Spruce Falls, Janat?" Meg asked in a low voice. "And Grassy Bluff? It took no time for people to start suspecting who we were. And that farmer's house when we first found our way out the wilds? Women—children—" She looked at Rennika.

" —don't travel. Especially not alone."

"We're refugees," Janat countered. "Things have changed!"

"But as the countryside settles. As King Artem imposes law. As people begin to live their lives again," Dwyn said, "it becomes more and more dangerous for the three of you to be seen together."

Janat's grip on Rennika's hand was hard. She wouldn't let the men split them. Meg wouldn't—

Dwyn took a deep breath. "Perhaps the two. Meg and Janat can go together. For now, until we can come up with a plan."

Janat released Rennika's hand and threw her arm protectively around her shoulder. "You won't take Rennika from us!"

"A servant of mine—a good man," the king said. "He's taken a small yak holding above Highglen." He nodded at Rennika. "He could take the young one. Make a story about a niece whose parents were caught in the fighting." He peered thoughtfully at Rennika. "You look worldling enough."

"I'm not a worldling!" Rennika's heart began to pound. She shrank into Janat's protection.

"I'll provide a small stipend for her keep, and she can learn to help out with the holding," the king offered kindly. "It won't be easy, but she'll be out of harm's way."

"No!" Rennika cried.

"Send Janat with her," Meg said reasonably. "I don't mind traveling with Sulwyn alone."

Janat shot her a sudden dark look.

Sulwyn drank from his mug. "I won't be going to Wildbrook. I head west. I would only give you a letter of introduction."

"The young one has a convincing accent. My man can explain her." Dwyn nodded at Janat. "You, girl, lovely as you are, must keep the role of a refugee for now."

Sulwyn set his mug down and hobbled to Janat. "He's right. And it's a generous offer." He took Janat's free hand and looked into her eyes. "Rennika will be sheltered and cared for. Fearghus can take Rennika to Gramarye before he goes to Arcan. She'll be all right."

Sulwyn couldn't do this. Rennika had *helped* him. When he was ill. And now—

Janat's arm on her shoulder loosened as she looked into Sulwyn's face.

A hardness gripped Rennika's throat and tears sprang to her eyes.

"And in Gramarye—and I think in Orumon—children do as they are told," the king said.

Rennika looked to Meg, but Meg was biting her lip, looking down. "Meg," she whispered.

Meg looked away for a moment, as though she couldn't meet Rennika's plea. "It's safer for all of us," she said at last. "And it'll only be for a little while. Until Sulwyn and Dwyn can restore Shangril."

"Until the day comes," Sulwyn said to her, "when we need a magiel again."

Kandenton was a pretty little village clinging to the side of a ravine above the rushing Kandon River—more of a creek, really—surrounded by thick, dark forest. Dwyn Gramaret had suggested, and Janat and Meg had agreed, that they leave Silvermeadow early and keep up a steady pace that they might reach the hamlet by nightfall. Rennika had been hard pressed to keep up, but she'd walked all day without complaining, and Janat had come to realize that her younger sister, now just turned twelve years old, was getting taller. A hint of curve promised to sprout beneath her lean figure.

Janat was tired when they trudged beneath the eaves of the cantilevered buildings lining the King's Road. The village had a shrine, smithy, tavern, mill, and a scatter of houses, everything to supply the community for miles around. There were no soldiers, and children in the streets seemed friendly enough, as though war had not yet touched this corner of . . . she thought they might now be in the country of Gramarye. Meg, of course, had dropped her sack and gone first to pray at the shrine in thanks for their uneventful day, and to ask for continued good weather and safe travels on their way to Zellora.

Zellora was where Fearghus would turn south to take Rennika to Highglen, and Janat and Meg would go north with Beorn. Then later, if they could find the way alone, to a small village in Elsen, called Wildbrook.

Beorn stepped out of the tavern to where they waited in the warmth of the summer evening. "The taverner welcomes magiels. He has a stable out back, and his mare is about to give birth. Her nipples began waxing three days ago. For a spell to ensure the foal's safe birth, he'll put us all up for the night, with supper and breakfast. He says there's an apothecary down the street who owes him a favor, if you need herbs or animal parts."

Janat flicked a glance at the narrow strip of sky above the street. The day had been warm and clear, and the evening promised to be cloudless. Tonight, Kyaju's arrow would high and bright, near the One God's star, an auspicious time to cast a birthing charm.

"Oh, Meg! A baby foal!" Rennika perked up, the day's despondency sloughing from her shoulders. "Can I do it? Can I cast the spell? Remember, I helped Sieura Barcley ease that woman's birth on the road from Fairdell when she was going to give breech? I remember the spell."

Janat couldn't suppress her grin at her sister's eagerness. "Yes, let her."

Meg smiled her assent, and Rennika ran to the apothecary.

The tavern was crowded with locals and ringing with choruses held together by tin whistles and spoons and a lute. Rennika rejoined them just as the wench brought small bowls of steaming rice and yak dumplings to their table. Beorn and Fearghus stayed in the lively room after the girls left, drinking rice beer and listening to bawdy songs and talk of the political situation in the south.

But Janat knew the stable was where Rennika had been itching to go all through the generous meal. Once they could eat no more, they followed the taverner out to the quiet, rich-smelling stall where his fine mare paced and pawed. The taverner brought them an armload of towels and fixed three candles to niches in the stable walls, then left them to their work. Janat soothed the sweet creature, offering bits of apple, as Meg cut a single hair from the mare's tail and Rennika laid out her ingredients.

The charm was a simple one: a worldling spell. Janat knew how to cast it, as did Meg, and it was usually cast without magiel magic. The herbs it required, and the binding words and the celestial arrangements that maximized its effectiveness were sufficient. But

Rennika wanted to practice her magiel magic. She would get no teaching in Highglen.

"You'll have time rebounds," Meg warned. "And we have a long way to walk tomorrow. And the next day, and the next."

"I'll just do a little," Rennika begged. "The apothecary had a kitten's heart, but it was harvested two days ago. It'll work so much better, fresh. And we can use less poppy if I age and concentrate it."

"A mare doesn't need poppy."

"If she visits her future, we might learn something," Janat pointed out. "This is a safe place to use magic. We have beds for the night." She worked her way along the mare's side and felt the beast's swollen belly. "She's pretty heavy. The foal may come sooner than the taverner thought."

Meg knelt in the straw and pulled a bowl from her sack. "All right." She smiled.

Rennika squealed with pleasure and set about combining her herbs and other ingredients, bringing each to its most fecund time, chanting the spell words under Sashcarnala's solitary star, and painting the final paste on the mare's belly. Then she tied the single plucked hair from the mare's tail into a long loop and embedded it in the potion on the horse's skin.

The mare calmed, once the potion was applied, and it became clear to Janat that the spell was strong. The foal would be born this night.

At midnight, after endless pacing and nipping at her belly, and a handful of grunts, the mare dropped the colt with ease in a gush of birthing fluid onto the straw of the stall.

Janat squeezed Rennika's hand. Then the three of them helped the little thing struggle from its sack. It blinked and shook its head, surrounded by a scatter of legs, as the sticky waters dripped away. The mother turned and sniffed her newborn, nudging it with her nose and licking it clean.

"Oh," Rennika murmured, tears streaking her face. "It's so delicate."

"No," Meg said. "See?" She put a blessing on the colt's naval and checked the afterbirth.

Within minutes, the spindly horse gathered its legs beneath it, and came to a wobbly stand. Janat held back her giggles, but she couldn't hold back her smiles. She led the colt to its mother's teats, and it began to suckle.

She almost missed Rennika's stillness and the age and worldliness that crept into her eyes. Meg touched her arm.

"Rennika?" Janat whispered.

Rennika gave her a single knowing nod.

"When are you from?" Janat asked quietly.

A tiny frown creased the child's brow, as if she weighed her words. "You're strong," she said at last in satisfaction. "Remember. You're sisters. Hold on to that."

That wasn't much help.

"What do we need to know?" Janat persisted.

The girl took a long look around the stable: the foal nuzzling its mother, the candlelight, the mellow smell of straw and horse. "Remember tonight." Her words were passionate, and Janat wondered if she might cry. "Remember Kandenton." She nodded and took a deep breath, and smiled. "Remember this gift."

"But Rennika!" Meg rose to her knees.

And then Rennika blinked and the eloquence left her eyes. She gasped a little to see them both staring at her.

"When were you?" Meg asked again.

Rennika stared at them for a moment, reassembling her memories. "In a shrine, high on a hill. An ancient one—its walls had mostly collapsed. But it was a holy place. I could feel it."

Janat sat back. "Was there anything? Any clue?"

Again, her sister thought. "It was night, and I was alone. All my ingredients were laid out." She shook her head. "It wasn't a time in my past."

Meg sighed. "Nothing."

A sorrow descended on them, then; each, separately.

But Kandenton was a jewel. As Rennika had said: it was a glittering moment of happiness.

Janat touched Rennika's fingers and reached out a palm to take Meg's. It was impossible to know if they would ever be united again.

❖

Carn Highglen, for all it had at one time been a seat of great power, was a small, almost deserted city tucked high in the mountains of Gramarye. It perched on the edge of a hanging valley behind an impressive outer wall very much like Archwood. It took Rennika and Fearghus three days of steady trudging to reach it.

Within its walls, destitution was evident. Though the city had fallen to King Artem less than a year earlier, many had abandoned it. Seeing the destruction of their prayer stone, they fled to neighboring countries—Midell, Teshe, even Arcan—seeking a land where they could pray to their Gods. Disillusioned, some had returned, but not enough for the city to thrive. Shops stood empty, and doorways and alcoves sheltered rag-wrapped vagrants. Of magiels, they found none. Under the regent King Artem had put in place to rule until Princess Hada came of age, magic wielders were not welcome.

The sun was brilliant and the morning air crisp when Fearghus took her through the city to the meadows beyond, where drovers kept their yak herds. Beyond the city walls, trees grew only in stunted clusters around meadows of tall grass. The wind blew cold from high glaciers, numbing Rennika's fingers and face, so like Orumon that she could have cried. High above the city, they found a moss-chinked stone hut with a shed for the milk yak, and a barn with chickens and a pig.

Colin Cutter, Carn Highglen's one-time master of livestock, was an old man whose two sons had left for the promises of rebel uprisings, and whose wife had died in the spring. He had little to spare, but for a girl to cook and mend and heal while he watched his herds, he would share his yak milk and fire.

He sat at the table, silent, as Rennika stood by the door the next day, forsaken, watching as her rebel protector bundled himself up in his threadbare cloak and trudged into the rain.

CHAPTER 20

The smithy stood below the road on the edge of the village of Farfalls, between a willow-banked stream and a farmer's field. Beyond the water, autumn's frost had gilded the poplars, and thickets of them blazed in the last of the season's heat between stands of stately dark spruce and fir. Sulwyn limped down the gravel path from tavern, the only place in the village where a traveler could spend the night.

Weeks, he'd been gone from Silvermeadow, but the thought of Janat never ceased to make him smile. Janat, laughing too hard to run from his playful chase. Janat, singing as she scrubbed her chemises by the river. Janat, lying abed, sleepy after lovemaking.

The clang of hammer blows rang out from the smithy, and smoke rose from its chimney. One last stop, and then . . . he would go to Wildbrook. He prayed to Ranuat that the sisters had found their way there without incident.

Bleating sheep scattered before him as Sulwyn made his way around a post and wattle house with a thatched roof to the smithy. Below, a field of heavy oats stretched all the way to the rustling trees by the river.

He peered into the dark interior of the smithy. A fire burned fiercely, and an apprentice pumped the bellows. A rotund man Sulwyn didn't know examined a cast iron cylinder in the sunlight at the far end, near the horse stalls. Working over a chipped slab of granite, Finn Kichman held a horseshoe with long tongs in one hand and an impressive hammer in the other.

Sulwyn smiled. The country's upheaval hadn't touched Finn. He was the same strapping young man he'd met in Spruce Falls almost a year ago.

Finn caught his eye, struck the horseshoe twice more, and then plunged it into a bucket of water. He dropped his tools and wiped the sweat from his brow. "Can I help you?" He slurped a dipperful of clean water.

"Finn. It's me, Sulwyn. Cordal."

Surprise gave way to joy on Finn's face. "Sulwyn!" The smith tossed his dipper into a bucket and grabbed both his shoulders, pushing him out to arms' length. "I didn't recognize you."

Sulwyn grinned. "This is what the better part of a year on the road can do to a man."

"You need a barber, a tailor, and a cook. And a bath."

"This?" Sulwyn teased. "From a man with no shirt and sweating like a pig?"

Finn guffawed and perched on the edge of a crate, pulling on a grimy shirt. "Here, sit down." He pushed his hammer and tongs from the granite slab to make a place for Sulwyn. "You," he shouted over his shoulder. "Donnell. Leave off those bellows." He tossed the apprentice a chetram. "Run to the baker's and come back with a loaf."

The boy nodded and strode away. "And ale from the brewer's!" Finn called in afterthought.

Sulwyn surveyed the smithy. "When Dwyn told me a man named Finn Kichman was working with us, I knew I had to come. I'd no idea you'd left Orumon."

Finn shrugged, muscles rolling under his skin. "There's nothing in Orumon but a chewed-up road and soldiers. Besides, I wanted to see foreign parts. When Colm left, I came with him as far as Coldridge. Then I came here, to Farfalls."

"Colm's a good man."

"I'm glad you're here." Finn stood. "I've made over forty blades. Swords and dirks, mostly." He put a hand on the ladder to the loft.

Sulwyn straightened in surprise. "Weapons?" He cast a glance at the stranger by the horse stalls.

Finn followed his gaze. "Oh, you don't need to worry about Orville. He knows." He climbed the ladder and, reaching into the loft, pulled out a sleek broadsword.

"We're planning a negotiated settlement. Not war." Sulwyn spoke in a low voice, still eyeing the stranger. Dwyn wanted to use peaceful means to regain their lost lands and freedoms.

"We pray to Ranuat weapons won't be needed." Finn descended with the blade. "But Artem may have some say in the matter."

It was a complaint many—particularly the younger, or the disfavored—had made. Some of those Sulwyn approached accused Dwyn of naiveté or cowardice, or worse, complicity with Artem, even called for a different leader—usually a local petty lord. More and more asked for weapons. More and more had initiated bloodshed. And received it, in return.

"Has anyone even spoken to Artem?" Finn gave him the sword to inspect.

"We're still trying to unite the voices of those who would oppose him." Distractedly, Sulwyn admired the craftsmanship.

"I've heard the high king's returned to the siege of Archwood, and his younger brother in Holderford has no authority to seal an agreement." Finn took the weapon and held it up in both hands in the sunshine.

"It's impressive, Finn. I know nothing of weapons, but you appear to know your craft." Sulwyn had no stomach for war. "But forty blades—and no training or armor—is enough to get forty men killed."

"This is just one smithy," Finn responded. He nodded to the crates. "And, we've pilfered more." He laid the blade carefully on the marble. "Armor will come. So will training. That's up to Dwyn to organize."

Sulwyn noticed with a start that the stranger was watching their conversation.

"Here." Finn waved the other man over. "I want you to meet Orville Haye."

Sulwyn pushed himself to his feet and the pudgy man ambled over and shook his hand. "Sieur," Sulwyn said. Orville was a name he'd never heard before.

Sieur Haye nodded a smile. "Welcome." His clothes were nondescript, neither rich nor ragged; his face was round and curls black. Nothing about him stood out, and yet . . . Sulwyn couldn't place his accent. Neither aristocratic, nor Northern, nor Gramaryan. And Sulwyn knew most.

"Orville's from Aadi."

Aadi? Sulwyn stared. Was that possible?

But, yes . . . perhaps that was the difference. His lips were just a little wider than most men's, his eyes a shade smaller. "How did you even *get* here from Aadi? The cliffs at Cataract Crag are unscalable."

"And yet," Finn pointed out, "Shangril trades with Aadi. *Someone* scaled those cliffs."

But, *this* man? This . . . wedge of cheese?

"Sieur," Orville said. "People journey—of—Aadi. Hard. Rare. Is done."

By Kanden, the man could hardly speak the language.

"He came up the pulleys," Finn grinned. "Like a side of pork."

"They're for cargo, not people."

Orville spread his hands. Clearly, he was here.

"I'm sorry, Sieur," Sulwyn insisted, "but what interest would a man from Aadi have in the affairs of Shangril?"

"Oh, he lives here now," Finn interrupted.

Stranger and stranger.

"These pieces?" Finn indicated a series of cylinders and odd-shaped cast iron parts on a bench. "We're creating a machine of war."

A machine . . . of war? "That's pretty vague."

"Your country different—of—mine," Orville Haye said. "We have—thing—you do not."

"Be specific."

The Aadian put his back to the crate and folded his hands across his belly. "We have—" He gestured. "Machine. Made of better—" He looked at Sulwyn and pointed to a sword.

"Steel."

"Steel. Thank you. I give one—small one—toy—to pulley man. Paying for journey."

"Toy?"

"Very *good* toy. You not have." Orville Haye looked helplessly at him.

The man's language made him seem simple, but Sulwyn suspected he was not. A toy that could bribe the pulley man to bring him up the unscalable cliffs made no sense, but Sulwyn didn't press the point. "But what interest do you have in our politics?"

"Nothing." The fat man tilted his head. "And all thing."

Sulwyn watched him struggle for words, wondering if he was going to continue.

"I not go back to Aadi. Finn say, I am stay. I work with you—give my knowing." He leaned over and whispered. "You is—are—good. Shangril king not good."

Donnell rounded the corner of the smithy carrying two sloshing tankards, with a fragrant loaf under one arm.

"Ah. Food," Orville observed. The Aadian broke the loaf in half and appropriated a tankard, leaving the rest on the granite slab beside Sulwyn. "Donnell and me. Go to creek. You—" He indicated to Sulwyn and Finn. "Talk." He nodded reassuringly to Sulwyn and went with the apprentice down the hill.

"What are you and Orville Haye up to?" Sulwyn whispered, taking the tankard Finn offered him.

"I told you. A war machine, like they have in Aadi. It's like a battering ram, only better. Orville made the plans and he's showing me how to build it."

Finn dropped a heavy purse beside Sulwyn and, tearing off a hunk of bread, sat on the crate.

Sulwyn opened the purse strings and poured coins into his palm. "Gold?" The coins were like none he had ever seen before. "This is a fortune."

"Traders in Pagoras don't want to see trade with Aadi hurt by the unrest caused by King Artem's politics." Finn washed the bread back with ale. "Shangril has things—gems, yak wool, furs—things people can't get in the valley of Aadi because it's too hot. And they'll pay for them, but not if war interrupts the flow of goods. Trade is good. War is bad."

Sulwyn held up the purse questioningly.

"They collected money to help us resolve the situation. Just be careful. Bands of ruffians on the roads will kill you just for food these days."

Sulwyn took the remaining heel of bread. "Dwyn can use it. King Artem is taxing any petty aristocrat, any guildsman, any merchant who opposes him, just to be sure they have no funds to raise an army."

"And is that working for him?" Finn smirked.

"The opposite. It makes them angrier." Sulwyn washed down the last of the bread. "Though after the king of Midell was beheaded this spring, and with the uncertain outcome in Orumon, they're nervous." He shrugged. "Plenty of them are betting on the Delarcan army. They won't commit."

"There's still plenty as would fight for us." Finn finished the ale.

Sulwyn shook his head. "We're better off using peaceful means."

"One swift blow, Sulwyn. Then, peace. The kings have their countries back. The people have their Gods. The merchants have their trade."

"And Artem?"

"King of Arcan, like he was before. Or, better, lop off his head and let the Gods choose a successor."

"Lop off his head? How? He's crushed the prayer stones and killed the magiels of all the Great Houses. No one's strong enough to oppose him. The Ruby would defeat us at every turn."

"Artem won't take the Ruby or his magiel from the siege at Archwood. He needs them there or Talanda Falkyn will use the Amber to break the siege. His hands are tied. If we take Holderford — or any city — while Artem's busy, we'd be fighting a battle with no prayer stone on either side," Finn reasoned. "Sulwyn, you have to convince those men, the ones who are holding back. Talk and diplomacy are getting us nowhere. We have weapons. We need to fight."

Sulwyn shook his head. "Dwyn's our king."

"Then tell him. And tell him we need a magiel. Magic on our side will be indispensable."

"Indispensible? Magiels don't have that kind of power."

"Talanda Falkyn's daughters would." Finn rolled his eyes at his surprise. "Come on, Sulwyn. You know we met them in Spruce Falls. Colm wanted to keep them, but you spirited them away in your cart after that fuss with the guard who lost his tongue."

Sulwyn's pulse sped. "What makes you think they were Talanda's daughters?"

"Colm figured it out. They are, aren't they?"

Sulwyn brought his breath under control, but he spoke in a tight voice. "Who else knows?"

"No one. Colm only suspected, and I didn't know for sure."

"They're marked, Finn. Artem would have them hunted down. Don't you dare breathe this to a soul."

"Sure." He shrugged. But he returned Sulwyn's stare with one of his own. "You still know where they are, though," he alleged. "They're too valuable to us—and to Artem—for you to have just lost track of them."

"No."

"Sulwyn?"

"I said, no. We're not putting them on the front lines of any battle."

Finn whistled. "That's pretty strong. Are there personal feelings—"

"No!" Sulwyn shot him a look.

Finn angered. "Are you having a love affair?"

Sulwyn clapped the tankard on the crate and rose to his feet.

"I've guessed it, haven't I? Two for two." He placed his foot on the crate Sulwyn had vacated, cutting off his exit. "Listen, Sulwyn, this war is bigger than your—"

"They are too young."

"But not too young for you to bed? Which one, Sulwyn?"

Anger surged up his neck, and it was all Sulwyn could do to breathe. Hold himself rigid.

Finn stood as well. "I like you. I do. But the needs of the people of this country are more important than the lives of three girls."

Sulwyn chewed on nothing, inarticulate.

"Magiels of the House of the Amber," he went on. "Now that Kraae is dead, the most powerful magiels in Shangril. Even with no prayer stone, think of what those three can do."

"Untrained. Untested. Artem will eat them for breakfast."

"Sulwyn." Finn lowered his voice. "It's not up to you. To say yes, or no. It's up to Dwyn."

Sulwyn caught his eye. "No, Finn." His head shook slowly from side to side. "It's up to them."

CHAPTER 21

The day was utterly calm, and the shutters on both sides of the garret stood open to a mild blue sky. Beneath the pleasant warmth, a tang of autumn's chill sharpened the air as Meg sewed, and enticing aromas rose from the bakery below. In Elsen, bread was leavened with yeast and it smelled, and tasted, like food for the Gods.

Meg liked this airy attic. Kyaju had blessed them here. But, so had they put down roots in Silvermeadow and Grassy Bluff. There was no telling when they'd be forced from this snug home, only that they would be. And, though the village of Wildbrook was quiet enough, its people tended to be royalists, supporters of Artem, whom they called the High King of Shangril. Their friendliness barely veiled a suspicion of anyone from "away" and Meg knew their flight would come immediately if a careless word were dropped in the wrong conversation. Some villagers crossed the street to avoid their erratic complexions, and Meg did not go out unhooded. She hoped they could last the winter.

Janat put the broom in its place and slid onto the chair across the table from her. "Read to me?" She held their book up invitingly.

"Who'll finish this chemise for the glass blower's daughter?"

"I will." Janat held her hand out.

Meg let out a breath of mock exasperation and gave her the sewing. "Very well. But I've read the first chapter so many times, I can recite it." The only other book they owned was one they'd made themselves, writing out the more complex spells they'd learned.

"The part when the One God blesses the first king, then." Janat said, looking out the open window to the street below.

Meg observed that her sister looked more and more frequently for his return. She scanned the pages.

"Wait—no! Before that. When the One God meets his second mortal mistress." She smiled at the thought as she poked her needle into the chemise. "Rennika always liked that story."

Gods. It had been high summer when they'd last seen her. Meg wondered what Rennika's home was like, how she was doing. Fall came earlier to Gramarye than it did here in the valley.

Janat reached a hand across the table and took hers. "Meg, I miss her."

Meg missed her, too. For a moment, there was no sound but the chatter of the women at the well, down the road, and in the distance, the clop of hooves.

Meg released Janat's hands and found the place in the book. "The One God came upon a maiden at the well," she began. "The worldling's name was Kyaju, and she—"

"Meg." Janat sprang up on her chair, leaning out the window, eyes bright with delight. "Sulwyn!" She leaned further out. "Yes! Sulwyn's here!"

Sulwyn—

"Look at this place!" Janat cried. "Meg, the sewing! I'll—" She cast around, scooping a scatter of blankets onto the pallets.

Meg shoved the book into the trunk and gathered the fabric and thread.

"Cut the rind from the cheese and slice it onto a plate. He'll be hungry." Janat patted her hair into place and went to the window, again, her cheeks pink. Her face fell. "Oh."

Meg peered over her shoulder. Below, by the curve in the road, Sulwyn hobbled up the street, deep in conversation with three men. One was Colm, Sulwyn's cousin, another she recognized as the smith they'd met so long ago in Spruce Falls, and the third one Meg didn't know, but he was an odd-looking man. Fat around the middle, with a pudgy face. Meg wouldn't have been able to avert her eyes from staring at the stranger, if Sulwyn hadn't been in the group.

Janat's eyes brightened, the way a jay's eyes did, brisk and brittle. "He's brought company. We'll cut some sausage. I'll have to find a chetram to take to the baker." She bustled to the sideboard.

"I wonder if they'll stay over." She laughed nervously. "Of course they'll stay over."

A wave of anger unexpectedly washed through Meg at Janat's nervousness, and all at once she wanted to be anywhere but this small attic when Sulwyn came through the door. "Give me your chetram," she said to Janat as evenly as she could. "I'll go to the baker's."

�֍

The sausage turned out to be unnecessary, as one of the men carried a joint of salt pork, which set Meg's mouth watering. One of the others brought a small keg of beer. When the men, laughing and joking, climbed the stairs to the garret, Meg looked away as Sulwyn gave Janat a big grin and an even bigger kiss. Janat seemed at once pleased and embarrassed, and pulled away, scolding him for the traveler's stains on his clothes. Appropriating the pork, she sent the men to put their feet up and stay out of her way as she rummaged for carrots and butter and crocks of pickled beets.

Meg went to the baker's, then flitted about the table, laying forks and filling the men's mugs with beer. Then she filled her own mug with beer and, scurrying out to the woodpile, brought in a stump to sit at the edge of the men's conversation. Finn brought out a bottle of thick clear liquid, the licorice liqueur that Meg and Janat had once tasted in Midell, saying it was time for the evening to start. Meg preferred the beer, but Janat took a small quantity, sitting by Sulwyn's side among the men. The men made faces when they tried it, but by the end of the evening, the bottle was empty.

Dinner was hearty—richer and more generous than many Meg could remember—and the drink and conversation lasted well into the night. Mostly it was the men who talked, their voices growing louder as the evening wore on. Some petition with a royal clerk had been surprisingly successful, Meg gathered, and the men replayed each part many times, with great animation, changing the particulars as they reminded one another of the details.

Meg joined in the debate, asking about King Artem's siege at Archwood and whether this realm or that one sided with Artem or with the uprisers. She argued, establishing and defending her position. Sometimes the men—usually Sulwyn—conceded a point, but more often they argued back or pointed out a complexity or contradiction that Meg had missed. Usually, they laughed or dismissed her, but Meg only argued harder.

And Meg noticed that as Sulwyn leaned forward, Janat sat back, watching and listening, silent, rising to refill portions on the large central platter or refill her glass of beer. Her sister's eyes grew blacker as the evening wore on, but Sulwyn did not notice, or take her part, as he did Meg's. But that was none of Meg's business. Sulwyn laughed and argued with her and the men as though Janat was not at the table. As though she was the servant she pretended to be.

"And, we finally have support from Storm River," Sulwyn repeated, pushing his fork back. He hunkered down into his chair, his lame leg extended, a mug of beer in his lap. "They'll uphold a cessation of violence if we call one."

"That sounds like good news," Janat put in uncertainly.

"Why?" Meg asked, and Janat shot her a look of contempt. "Why call a truce?"

"And Zellora and Ubica," Finn said loudly, the beer getting the better of him. "Dwyn convinced the petty lords and guildsmen of both towns to throw in with us."

"We've been petitioning King Artem." Sulwyn turned to Meg. "Beorn and a dozen others met with his chancellor, and they've negotiated an *audience* between Dwyn and Artem. If we can vouch for all the uprising factions."

"On neutral ground," Colm added.

"And can you?" she asked. "Vouch for all of them?"

"If the high king meets our six stipulations." Finn grinned, his face flushed. "We'll work like dogs getting a letter from every militia and activist this war has spawned." He raised his glass and with a ring of cheers, the men toasted.

Janat cleared the platter from the table. "What's to stop Artem's men from dishonoring the rules of parley?"

Like the trap Janat had walked into in Spruce Falls.

"We'll have men there." Finn walked a trifle unsteadily to the cask and refilled his tankard. "We have weapons. Our troops have been training."

Janat eyed him and returned to the sideboard with the forks and napery.

"'The spirit does not die with the man,'" Meg quoted.

Colm shot her a look of respect. "Eric Stewart," he murmured, taking the last morsel of bread. "I didn't know you read banned works of political philosophy."

Sulwyn gave her a lopsided smile and she warmed. "A book Sulwyn lent me."

Janat stoked the fire. "But 'the man' is still dead."

"Also, now that Colm is with us, Orville and I want to show you something." Finn gestured broadly to the quiet, odd-looking man. "Orville?"

Orville, the round fellow with small, twinkling eyes, gave a short nod. He beckoned Meg. "Bring water. Hot." His words sounded strange, like the first time she'd heard the low speech, but different.

Curious, she brought him a dipperful of water from the cauldron and found he'd placed a tiny machine on the table between the pickles and the butter where all the men could see. He filled the machine's copper vessel with the water, and brought glowing coals from the fire to burn in a box at the bottom.

At first, nothing happened. The copper vessel began to hum and shiver, and steam rose from its spout, nothing Meg hadn't seen daily in the kettle. Then, a delicate upper structure began to turn. A tiny hammer struck little bells, chiming a short, exotic tune.

The machine was a wonder. A miracle.

"This is what he paid the pulley man. One like it," Finn said, swigging his beer, "for bringing him up the cliffs from Aadi."

Colm whistled. "Pulley man probably sold it for a small fortune."

"It's a marvel," Sulwyn said, lowering his mug, "but it's not a weapon."

"Not this one." Finn pushed his empty plate aside. "But Orville has the plans. And, we've made a test explosive. It works."

The fat man nodded. "You see, now? Is easier to show than to tell. But principle is same." He struggled for a moment with words. "People of Aadi trade fruit, music, spice, silk," Sieur Haye said. "Never secret." He nodded at the toy. "Steam. Has power."

With such machines, would people still need magic?

The stream of vapor slowed and the music stopped. The stranger then pointed to various parts of the machine, explaining what each part did. Meg—and, she suspected, the others—didn't follow most of what he said.

"Do it again," Meg said.

"This weapon you've built . . ." Colm put his beer mug down. "How powerful is it?"

"Put it in the middle of an army on a battlefield. It could wound a third of them," Finn boasted.

Sulwyn whistled.

"Wound?" Colm asked.

"Meets two objectives." Finn said sloppily. "We have no desire— no desire—to kill our countrymen. Not even Artem's soldiers. Most are conscripts. And, wounded men need support." He looked around the table, hands spread to show off his reasoning. "Ties up men Artem could use."

Sulwyn looked the men around the table in the eye. "No one must tell anyone about this." He turned to Janat and Meg.

Janat gave him a quizzical look.

He held out his mug and Colm lifted his to touch it. Finn and the foreigner joined their tankards to the group.

"Promise."

"I promise," Meg said, adding her cup to the cluster.

"I promise," Janat repeated, joining.

✤

Meg woke much later in need of the chamber pot and a drink of water. The rumble of men's voices had been replaced by snores and the rustle of leaves beyond the windows. The sinking star of Sashcarnala shone through the open shutters, and yellow candlelight flickered from somewhere in the room. She lazed in her blankets, drowsy and unwilling to venture into the chill of the night.

"But why so soon?" Janat's voice, hushed, floated from the far side of the room. The sound of bowls and wash water accompanied it. She must be tidying up. "Wait, Sulwyn. Stay here with me. Please. Until we can follow Mama's bidding—"

"King Artem will never give up that siege until Archwood falls and everyone in it is dead." The whisper, fierce and suppressed, was Sulwyn's, clumsy with drink. "Not unless we give him a reason. A peace he can live with. *And* a peace the people can live with."

"You know what King Artem wants? You read his mind?"

Meg peered across the room at them. Janat stood by the side board, washing dishes, sleeves rolled, hair in faint disarray.

"And what do you think you're going to find at that tarn? Hmm?" Sulwyn leaned in, close to Janat, his hair wild, his linen shirt open at the neck, a ruddy flush in his cheeks. "The Amber? A prince? Nothing short of both is going to change anything."

Janat glared at him. "You talk as though what we see and hear in this world is real," she said in a low voice. "It's not. Only the Heavens are real. Faith is believing, even when there's no evidence we can touch. You know that. One day we'll be returned to our rightful place."

"You fill your head with dreams." Sulwyn pushed frustrated hands through his hair. "What service do you do yourself when those dreams of turning back time to some . . . romantic . . . era have no hope of fulfillment?"

"No hope? Of course there's hope! More than hope," Janat whispered. "It will happen, Sulwyn."

"Your mother may have set some events in motion, but she can't know how they'll play out."

"Stop. Wait." Janat put down her dish towel. "*You* tell me, now. What would *you* do with us, you and that band of ruffians you travel with, stirring up trouble wherever you go?" Janat leaned back against the sideboard and tossed back the dregs of her beer. "Use us? Magiels of the House of the Amber. Your political pawns? Is that your interest in us? Don't tell me you haven't thought of it."

"What? Janat!" But the color of his already flushed cheeks deepened.

Help the rebels. Meg almost sat up.

Janat set the mug on the sideboard, and lifting her wash basin, tossed the gray water out the window. "You think you're going to *talk* the king into giving up power?" She put the wash basin back. "Into sharing his Gods-given right to rule, with a bunch of . . . of *commoners*?" She said the word with disgust.

Of course not. Without Meg or Janat—or Rennika, whom Dwyn

had hidden away — and the Amber, the uprisers would never coerce Artem into sharing power.

"Common. That's what you think of me, isn't it?"

"Don't put words in my mouth."

Unless the foreigner's steam machine was more powerful than magic.

"We're not talking about making things the way they were." Sulwyn's voice lowered, tight and slow, as if he explained something to a child. "A different system of governing. Different. One that's never been done before."

Even without the Amber, magiel magic had been helping upriser plans. But if they had a magiel whose direct lineage could be traced to the One God . . .

"I think beer fills *your* head with dreams," Janat countered. "Revolution. Maybe war. Killing." She wiped the sideboard. "Dying."

"It's better than a privileged few living off the work of the poor."

Janat whirled. She launched herself at him, fingers clawed.

"Hey!" He grasped her forearms before she could harm him, and they tussled silently. "I meant nothing!"

"You're as bad as the others!"

"Janat—"

"Big upriser leader! You think only of your own glory—"

Privileged few. That had been Meg. And Mama, and Janat, and King Ean . . .

"Hush, Janat. Hush." He engulfed her in his arms, and Meg wondered if he was going to cry. "I think of your welfare. I do."

Janat tried to pull away, searing him with a look.

But Sulwyn was right.

And the Gods were not coming to their aid.

"I'm sorry. I'm so, so sorry," he said. Janat's arms wilted and he gathered her, unwillingly, to him. "It's me, Janat," he said softly. "You know I care for you. I don't want to see you or your sisters hurt."

But over her shoulder, he grimaced. A lie. He'd just . . .

What? Betrayed?

Who? Himself? The uprisers?

Gods. She saw it, now. They'd wanted him to give them a magiel.

And he hadn't.

Then Janat collapsed, weeping, into his embrace.

A magiel, working with the uprisers. In the service of a new . . . world.

Sulwyn wrapped his arms around Janat, shushed soothingly into her hair, and rocked her until her sobs faded. He quenched the candle and led her to the nest of pallets.

Meg closed her eyes, but she did not sleep for a long time.

CHAPTER 22

"You like him!" Rennika shrieked with laughter, dodging pedlars, craftsmen, and pickpurses as she chased Ide across the stone-arched bridge. Autumn in Gramarye was brief, but today was like summer, and good weather brought the farmers and tradespeople and thieves to market.

Ide threw her arm onto the bridge's broad marble balustrade, braking herself to a spinning halt. "I do not!"

Rennika plunged to a stop beside her, leaning her upper arms on the polished stone to capture a waft of cool spray rising from the glacial river below. Colin sent her to Highglen by herself once a week or so with a goatskin full of milk, to do small trades for things they needed, and to watch out for items brought up from the lower valleys that might only be occasionally available. He did the big trading himself—huge bundles of raw yak wool and, later in the fall, live yearlings for slaughter. He said the sharp wool traders would cheat Rennika. She didn't mind not going to Highglen. When she stayed in Highglen with Ide's family, she could spend some of her time picking up her own coins, as she'd learned to do in Coldridge.

"Oh, Tonore!" Rennika mimicked. "You're so strong!"

"I never said that!" Ide protested. "I said he was pretty strong if he could hammer a sword blade flat. And I never said it *to* him." She draped herself over the balustrade and stared into the flickering depths of the rushing water. "Besides, you like him, too."

Rennika leaned on the railing beside her. "What if I did?" Rennika had been surprised when Tonore and his mother—his father was killed—appeared in Highglen in the early fall. They hadn't spoken of her secret, her magiel sisters and talent with cures, and she knew he wouldn't. "He doesn't notice. *Either* of us." She lazed there, the late afternoon sun on her shoulders, breathing in the smell of the river and the sounds of Princess Hada's city. This would be a good place to live for the rest of her life. Here, or perhaps in that wonderful village where she and her sisters had once helped an innkeeper's mare birth her colt. Kandenton.

"He likes you better," Ide said. "You don't have pox scars on your face. And he thinks I'm just a child."

"Tonore doesn't care about your scars. He's got an ear lobe missing."

A dozen soldiers in cloaks of green passed them, keeping an eye on vagrants.

Ide grinned at her sidelong. "You think?"

Rennika bumped her with her shoulder. "Yes."

"Tomorrow, let's watch Tonore make horseshoes." Ide kicked a pebble between the balusters and watched it fall into the cold, foaming current below.

"We did that today."

"So?" Ide giggled. On the river, the dippers flicked in and out of the froth.

Rennika had three chetra in the purse tucked under her robe, and in her stomach she had a stolen cheese dumpling. The begging today had been profitable. "All right. But not until afternoon. There are good patrons by the shrine in the morning."

Ide shrugged. "Fine. Hey!" She pointed. "Who's down there?" On the opposite shore, a jumble of shops and houses crowded one upon the other: the district of artisans and refugees and paupers. A tumble of children spilled from the streets and down the bank toward the river in a game of Siege Breaker. "Let's go!"

Ide and Rennika ran down the arch of the bridge and onto the stony shore.

"Ha! Rennika! You're with me," cried a long-legged boy a year or two older than her.

She dashed to his team and Ide ran to the other to play with them as the afternoon lengthened. Back and forth, their ragged lines moved upriver and down.

A girl tried to dart between two boys and was caught. "Prisoner! Prisoner!" cried one of the boys, who took the girl under the bridge.

"Look." A boy of perhaps five or six with a smear of dirt across his face pointed to where the bridge met the bank.

A man with a black beard and unkempt hair huddled in the shadows with a child of about three tucked under his arm, watching them.

Rennika peered at the pair.

"What are you staring at?" the boy who'd invited Rennika into the game yelled belligerently at the man. He picked up a rock with his good hand.

Alerted, the others turned.

"It's a magiel," Ide sneered.

The little boy with the dirty face picked up two or three rocks.

It was, indeed, a magiel. Even in the dark beneath the bridge Rennika could see his skin shifting like Meg's, as did the boy's. Not a high magiel of the Houses of any of the prayer stones. A low magiel, likely a part-blood.

The magiel held his son closer. They were only children, but he was afraid.

"Get out of here!" the boy who'd captured the girl "prisoner" yelled.

"Demon!" one of them cried.

Someone threw a stone. "Cradle robber!"

"Disease bringer!"

"Child snatcher!"

The children moved closer. Stones thwacked the rocky shore near—but not too near—the magiel. A smudge flickered on the edge of Rennika's sight. A ghost.

The girl who'd played the role of prisoner picked up a handful of stones. She frowned curiously at Rennika.

Gods. She'd always let on she was a worldling. Rennika picked up a rock and followed the others.

"Magiel!" Ide yelled.

One of the stones hit the magiel on the thigh.

Rennika hung back, words caught in her throat. She could not say them, could not call out. Yet, neither did she call out against her friends.

The rock was heavy, leaden in her hands. A momentary blur, closer to the magiel this time. More ghosts.

With a skitter of tumbling gravel, a half-dozen soldiers in gold and green ran down to the rocky shore. "You urchins get out of—"

"Magiels!" Ide interrupted.

Rennika's breath stopped. Words choked her. She stared, helpless, as the pageant played in front of her.

The soldiers turned to look where Ide pointed. They halted, facing the fugitive. One man unslung his bow from his back.

No—

The magiel scrambled to his feet, gaping at the soldier with the bow. He backed away, shoving the boy behind him.

Meg had put herself in front of Rennika, how many times—

The soldier pulled an arrow from his quiver. He nocked it. They were not arresting the man. This would be murder.

The boy clinging to his father's legs began to whimper. The children stood in silence, watching.

The magiel held his son, eyes tracking the men's every movement. The archer stretched his bowstring back, and his knuckles hovered by his right ear.

With a tiny plucking sound, barely audible above the evening birdcall and the rush of the river, the arrow took flight, whistling as it cut the air.

The distance was short, the target unmoving. The arrow buried itself between the man's ribs.

Rennika felt the blow in her throat.

The magiel fell back, a dark patch blossoming on his stained and ragged shirt. The little boy fell beside him, screaming in grief. A flicker, like she was seeing the magiel and his boy under water for a brief instant. The ghosts were waiting.

The soldier drew a second arrow and, nocking it, stepped forward a pace.

The child stood, uncertain, drawn to his father, knowing he should run.

Run! Rennika willed. *Run!* But where could they run?

The soldier let the second arrow fly.

On impulse, Rennika found a gust of air that had been under the bridge only moments before and brought it forward in time. It knocked the arrow false.

Still, the man and his son did not move. The man panted, eyes fixed to the archer. His fingers scrabbled at the band on his throat. He had a death token. Thank the Gods.

She could do it again. And again. And what would be the result? Fear. Blame on the magiel. Greater oppression.

Before the man had a chance to pull his death token from his collar, a third arrow pierced his neck and his head pitched backward into the gravel, eyes rolling back, glassy.

The shifting-skinned boy sprinted, but two thwacks broke the silence and feathers bloomed in his back. He fell on the gravel beneath the bridge.

Ice filled Rennika's veins. He had no death token.

The soldiers approached the man and his twitching son. "You, children, go home now," the captain said to the rest of them. The children scattered.

Rennika's rock slipped from her fingers. She ran into the street.

❀

Rennika excused herself early from Ide's mother's table saying she was sleepy from rising early, which was true, though Ide was disappointed they weren't going to whisper on their pallets until her mother threatened to turn them outside to sleep. Still, Rennika lay for such a long time on the sweet-smelling straw in the lingering twilight of autumn that she wondered if her life was not going to jump. She'd done such a small magic. A puff of wind. And the consequences of her interference had changed nothing. She wondered if the ripples of her life would be so brief as to be undetectable. That had happened before.

But in the silence of the children's loft, wedged between the wall and Ide and her three brothers, she rolled over to discover herself *standing in a much smaller body in bright summer sunshine, in the garden of Archwood. Mama, holding her hands, was seated on a stone bench in the dappled shade of a fragrant willow. Nanna was just jumping up to chase someone—maybe Faris or one of her younger brothers. There were shouts of play behind her.*

Mama's head snapped up, startled. "When are you?" she asked.

It took Rennika a minute to understand the question.
"How old are you?" Mama clarified.
"Twelve."
Mama's eyes seemed to calculate. "You're not in Archwood."
"No . . ."
"Have you been to the tarn? Did you get the Amber?"
The question made no sense.
"Are Meghra and —"
Then.

She was walking through spring sunshine, in a trackless forest, following a tiny brook. A cool wind ruffled her cloak, which was too thin for the crisp weather. She was taller now, and she held a little girl's fingers. The little girl let go of her hand and, giggling, ran ahead, stretching her legs to clamber over fallen trees that Rennika could step over easily. "South, up, upturned cup, bare a dead man's shoulder," the child sang.

Down up, Down down up. It was Mama's nursery rhyme. Seven falls the soldier.

The men left Meg and Janat's attic before dawn the next day, and Sulwyn did not return for three weeks. When he did come back, he found work in the tannery and for a time it seemed it would be a golden winter. There was food on the table, a fire on the hearth, and the tensions of war were only rumored, far away beyond distant roads.

But peace was an illusion. Meg began to ache for something she could not define. To move beyond the garret where her sister slept behind a curtain with the man who'd saved them. To leave a village where she must hide her skin, guard her words. To see more of Shangril, to see the pledges of fiery men kept, to fill her promised role of intermediary between the people and their Gods. To find a worth in herself that others could see.

As Sulwyn's tightly suppressed excitement ripened into curbed restlessness, Janat became snappish and teary. She was drawn to the window, where she watched swirling flakes, the lowering of gray skies, and one day at dusk, the approach of a traveler.

When the knock came, Meg's hands stilled on her sewing, a thrill of anticipation awakening in her skin as Janat opened the door, her arm extended across the frame, forbidding entrance. "Hello, Colm."

He had changed. One arm hung from his shoulder, limp. His clothes and beard were ragged, and shadows circled his eyes. He was thinner. But his expression was bright, taut.

"Sulwyn's not here." Janat's voice was as cold as the snow falling in the hills.

"I saw him at the tannery. He'll be along soon." Colm's gaze took in the room, flitting over the accoutrements of well-being, and landed on Meg. Did she see a hint of satisfaction in his eyes at finding her? He unslung a sack from his shoulder. "He said I should stay the night."

There was only the slightest hesitation, then Janat took a step back, the posture of impeccable servitude infusing her whole body. It made Meg angry, but the promise of news, of movement, kept her still.

Colm shuffled in and, making himself scarce behind the curtain, fell asleep on Janat's pallet.

When Sulwyn breezed through the door, flushed with beer and filling the room with the familiar stink of the tannery, Colm's snores were deep and musical. Janat stood at the sideboard chopping potatoes. He faltered for a moment, watching her back, letting his sack slide to the floor. She said nothing but stiffened when Sulwyn placed a hand on her waist. Meg let her embroidery slide to her lap, waiting without speaking, ready to spring up at the hint of bidding.

Sulwyn saw this, and letting his hand drop, filled a mug with ale from the pitcher and strode over to sit on the floor by Meg. He leaned in to her. "Have you prayed today?"

His animation filled her with excitement. "Of course."

The sound of chopping clacked from across the room.

"To which Goddess?"

"Kyaju." There was news. Colm had brought it. Why would Sulwyn say nothing?

"Ah." He nodded. "For shelter in a storm?"

Appropriate shelter, she wanted to correct him, but a feeling warned her that now was not the time. "Yes."

He nudged her shoulder with his. "Good. Kyaju keeps you safe here, in Wildbrook, far from the storms of war." He curled his feet under him, cross-legged. "Would you pray for me?"

"What for?"

"I may need shelter from a storm." He smiled wistfully up at Janat.

Janat swept the potatoes into a pot.

※

Janat sat up. Something was different.

She gathered her blankets to her chin and in the dim light, frowned at the place where Sulwyn's pallet should've been. She jerked awake, staring stupidly at the empty spot on the floor. He was gone. Of course, he was gone. He'd left with Colm.

"Meg!"

Her voice fell dead. She climbed to her feet, wrapping her blanket about her shoulders and stumbling to the window. It was late, past dawn, but the street was still empty. Cheery sunshine burst over the hills and stabbed her eyes.

She checked the sideboard. The new loaf was gone, and the round of cheese. Meg's cloak was missing from its peg.

Meg's pallet, too, was missing.

Janat tried to generate explanations. An early walk. A trip to the bakery or chandlery before their masters were awake. An illness.

No.

She pulled herself a mug of beer from the keg, a sudden need to fog the swirling thoughts in her head.

Moisture dampened Janat's cheeks, filled her nose.

Meg and Sulwyn. Sulwyn and Meg.

CHAPTER 23

The party of uprisers reached the top of the ridge where the trees opened out to a rocky promontory. Below, the Orumon River meandered out of the mountains across a broad valley over wide gravel flats. Beneath a dark overcast, a wind blustered down from the distant peaks burdened with stinging ice crystals. At Sulwyn's signal the column disbanded and he divested himself of his pack, unhooking his wine skin. Finn, Orville, and their crew began unpacking the machine. So far, there was no sign of Dwyn and his escort, or Fearghus and the promised rebel delegates from Storm River, Zellora, and Ubica, but all should be here within the day.

Colm lowered his sack, one-armed, to the ground. His injured arm had recuperated somewhat, but Sulwyn worried that some muscle or fiber had been severed that would never fully recover.

Sulwyn drank deeply and surveyed the stony expanse stretching on either side of the river. He noted the treed hillsides above the open space. Archers—from both sides—could provide protection should the need arise, equalizing the power differential between the self-proclaimed high king of seven countries and Gramarye's king-in-exile.

Colm rested his foot on a stump. "When I was a boy, my tutor showed me maps of the seven kingdoms. Where the best ceramics came from, the softest woolens, the sweetest fruit."

Sulwyn's father had done the same.

"A guildsman could own his own shop," Colm said. "Afford baubles for his wife." He shook his head. "How can one man rob so many of their future in a stroke?"

Sulwyn understood. "Tomorrow." He smiled. "It all changes tomorrow."

Colm looked over his shoulder to where groups of uprisers talked quietly among themselves. "Gods willing."

Sulwyn followed his gaze. Finn was there, and his odd friend from Aadi, with their crates of machine parts. "We can only pray the work of our delegations won't be for naught. Artem will be reasonable. We won't need to test that . . . engine."

Meg emerged from behind a group of pack horses and sat on a log near where Orville and Finn shared a morsel of hard biscuit. She often listened to—and intruded on—men's conversations.

"You wish we didn't have her along," Colm observed.

Sulwyn sat on a rock and corked his wine skin. He'd promised Finn he would ask Janat and Meg if they would help the uprisers, but he hadn't been able to bring himself to do it. Janat was too precious. But Meg had taken matters into her own hands. "You know my opinion. She shouldn't be here."

"This is exactly where a magiel should be."

There was no point in arguing.

"She's safe enough." Colm ate a handful of nuts. "You watch her as if an orum's going to swoop down and carry her off any minute."

A Falkyn. One of three magiels of the House of the Amber. It was madness having her anywhere but hidden as far from the king and his emissaries as possible.

"You know we need a magiel," Colm persisted.

Not her.

Colm offered him some nuts. "And, she doesn't have a bad head for tactics, actually."

"We have no shortage of would-be tacticians." Sulwyn took the bag.

Colm drank from his water skin. "Meg's committed, Sulwyn. To our cause."

Sulwyn shrugged and ate, looking out over the valley.

"I don't think you see it," Colm persisted. "Who, more than Meg and her sisters, has a greater reason to see Artem brought to heel? She wouldn't object to seeing his head on a spike."

"None of us would." Sulwyn rose and tied his wine skin to his sack.

"She wants to see Shangril regain the kind of shared power the people had when there were seven connections to the Heavens." Colm argued as if he had put up an objection. "And you know Dwyn will need a royal magiel."

The thought of Meg becoming Dwyn's magiel rankled. She was too young. Too . . . unschooled in the realities of politics, for all her romantic philosophies.

"Stop worrying."

Sulwyn loosened his mare's cinch and untied his pallet.

"She's strong, Sulwyn. Stronger than you think." Colm nodded toward the valley. "I don't think you—or she—have any idea of what she's capable."

"The strength of her magic, you mean?"

"No." Colm stood and swung his sack over his shoulder. "The strength of her will."

The promised snow had not fallen, and sun flirted with cloud the next morning as Sulwyn and Colm sat astride good horses a few paces behind King Gramaret's swift gelding, awaiting the arrival of King Artem. Beorn and Fearghus were positioned ahead of the exiled king, and an array of guildsmen and commoners, all mounted, spread out in a semicircle behind. All were dressed in clean plain clothes, and the Gramarye standard snapped from a half dozen staves.

Invisible in the woods on the hillsides, their archers—and Sulwyn had no doubt in his mind that Artem's archers as well—ensured compliance with the truce, for what that was worth. On the ridge, Orville's mysterious weapon had been uncrated and assembled. Sulwyn had no idea whether Orville's extravagant promises could be kept. Meg had armed Dwyn with a spell of personal protection, which gave Sulwyn more confidence, and given four vials containing curses to their forward foot soldiers.

As the sun approached the zenith, a bit of color appeared far up the valley where the road to Orumon emerged from the forest.

Banners.

This was it. This was what they had worked for, sacrificed for,

for over a year.

King Artem's guard approached at a steady walk, giving plenty of time to intimidate them with the size of his party, their fine garments and bright swords. At length, the delegation came to a halt a half-dozen yards away. Artem sat tall and assured on a long-legged black, his heir behind, and a score of courtiers in fine accoutrements. His magiel and second son were absent; no doubt ensuring the siege at Archwood remained intact.

Artem would undoubtedly have magical protection, though, and likely, magical weapons at his command.

A dozen Arcan banners flew in the stiff breeze, and beyond these, the standards of the other six nations of Shangril, including Gramarye—and Orumon. Sulwyn's stomach turned to stone. Such insults were intended to enrage. This did not bode well.

A captain brought his mount forward. He raised his voice over the rush of wind and river. "My Lord Majesty, King Artem of Arcan and High King of all nations of Shangril, is benevolent to his subjects, and has come from his business in the south of his realm to hear your petition. I caution you to be brief and clear in your supplication."

No. Artem had no intention of meeting the delegation, even part way.

Still, Beorn urged his mare ahead. "King Dwyn Gramaret, unjustly plundered of his rightful lands and subjects after five centuries of peace beneath the caring watch of the seven Gods, represents the voice of those whose homes and livelihoods have been destroyed by the unlawful and unprovoked attacks of Arcan's monarch. King Gramaret, and those he represents, demands the return of all appropriated lands, reinstatement of the independence and governance of each kingdom to its rightful monarch, and further, that the King of Arcan sign the charter made jointly by all nations, to be ruled upon six conditions which bind him subject to law."

"High King Artem," the captain replied in a tone reserved for servants, "and his beloved kings in Midell, Pagoras, Teshe, Gramarye, and Elsen, agree that each kingdom be ruled by its own monarch subject to the guidance of its High King in Arcan. The former king of Gramarye needs only to swear devotion to the One true God, forsaking all others as demons, and peace shall return to Shangril."

No mention of the restoration of lands. No agreement to be bound by law. No freedom of worship, of speech, of self-mastery. None of the tenets of the charter. Sulwyn flicked a glance at Dwyn. His countenance was grim, his eyes stony.

"The position outlined by King Artem's servant," Beorn announced, "meets none of the conditions necessary for a return to peace. Nor do these statements suggest hope for—"

Sulwyn saw no signal. Only shields raised in unison over Artem and his party, as a volley of shafts appeared, whistling through the air from all sides. The uprisers' horses screamed and scattered, their riders flinching, some falling to feathered arrows. Colm took an arrow to his thigh, and Sulwyn wheeled his mount, spurring it after Dwyn's fleeing gelding.

At the same instant, a dozen of Artem's courtiers, cloaks flying to reveal armor beneath, spurred forward, sprinting to surround the party.

The rules of truce, betrayed.

Sulwyn urged his horse on, his lame thigh screaming. He raced Dwyn's galloping roan, a half dozen of their own in pursuit.

A shriek whistled above.

Sulwyn urged his mount faster, gaining on Dwyn's flank. Something—more massive than a mere arrow—arced overhead.

An explosion—the ball vanished in a spray of flying shards.

A cloud sprang up from the ground behind him and a handful of men and horses leapt incongruously into the air. A thump of heat knocked Sulwyn and thunder blasted his ears.

His horse screamed and went down, bashing Sulwyn to the stones.

A scalding rain and spears of iron showered down, piercing his armor.

And then—in barely a moment—the destruction was over.

A thousand superficial cuts pierced the side of Sulwyn's face, his thigh and arm. The blast's echo rang in his ears. Dust obscured the gravel flats. His horse scrambled to her feet and bolted.

Coughing, Sulwyn picked himself up and turned to see the chaos.

Dwyn, holding his horse's halter, stumbled from the cloud of settling debris. He choked on dust but was remarkably untouched. In a moment, Colm followed, limping.

Men lay everywhere, some still, some moaning and stumbling to their feet. Splinters of iron were driven into the ground. A scatter of uprisers staggered in disarray. Across the gravel flats, what remained of Artem's party, similarly, floundered to catch mad horses and flee.

❈

They marched all night. They were not followed. Two of the wounded died before Dwyn called a halt, just before dawn.

Meg allowed herself two candlemarks' sleep in the shelter of a spruce tree until the tents were pitched, then, with the help of three of the less injured, went to work attending to the wounded. Of the thirty men who'd ridden to the parley, only half returned, and all—but Dwyn, whom she'd been able to protect with a spell—had suffered a range of burns or been pierced by at least a dozen shards from the *bomb* lofted by Orville's machine. Beorn was not among the men who had returned.

Late in the afternoon, Fearghus came to the healing tent to summon Meg to report to Dwyn. Tired beyond sleep, she gave instructions to her assistant and then went to the king's tent.

Sulwyn and Colm sat alone with the king at a camp table littered with tankards and maps. Other than Fearghus, no guards or servants remained within. Dwyn gestured for her to draw up a chair. "Rest, Meg, and eat," he said gently as servants brought bowls of vegetables and skewers of freshly hunted venison. "You have proven your worth on this day."

She sank into the rough folding chair, its canvas a greater luxury than she could imagine. She'd used magic in today's healing and she knew her next candlemarks would not be restful. But the warmth of the king's words suffused her with a mixture of happiness and pride, assuaging for a moment the deep melancholy welling up in her, now that the distraction of work was gone.

Sulwyn's gaze fixed on the king, objection unspoken, as Fearghus let the tent flap fall closed behind him and returned to his place at the table.

The king leaned forward and spoke in a voice that would carry no further than their immediate circle. "Meghra Falkyn of the House of the Amber," he said to Sulwyn. "One of the few magiels of any of the Great Houses still alive. You've certainly dragged your feet about bringing her to me."

Meg hated being talked about as if she were not there. But it was not her place to interrupt a king.

"She is eighteen and untried," Sulwyn said in an equally low voice. He addressed the king as an equal, as if the beer, or perhaps whiskey, had erased any sense he might have had of his station.

"And we are now at war," Dwyn responded. "Should we obtain the Amber—or the Ruby—she will become my magiel of the prayer stone." The king pinned her with his eyes, confirming the appointment.

Magiel of the Amber? With Dwyn. A peer to the king. An unbidden thrill flashed through her, followed by a flick of guilt and fear.

If Mama died.

"Do you accept?" Dwyn asked.

She hesitated, then nodded. "I will, My Lord."

"It is done." Dwyn lifted his fork, ending the debate. "You will attend council at my will." He eyed Sulwyn.

"Yes, Sire." Gods. It was everything she'd wanted.

—not everything. Not the post of people's magiel. But still.

Sulwyn sat back, his countenance haggard and unsatisfied.

"Now." Dwyn turned to Fearghus. "Bring the foreigner."

Bowing, Fearghus rose from his meal and left the tent.

"Your duties will continue as they have been for Sulwyn. Spells and potions when we require them. Healing. Once we have the prayer stone, then of course, you will be praying in Heaven for the needs of our people."

Death tokens. More. The Gods' favor in war. Protection against orums. Against the curse of disease. For prosperity. The list went on. Mama's work.

Mama's burden. The cost to her body. Her spirit.

But this was the life Meg had been born to. This had always been her future.

She would have been elated, had she had the energy.

The tent flap parted. "Sire." It was Fearghus.

"Come."

Fearghus stood aside and Orville stepped into the candlelight. He spotted the king and nodded in a perfunctory bow.

Dwyn swiped his plate with the last of his steamed bun and pushed the dish aside. "Finn Kichman told me you had a weapon never seen before in Shangril. One that could cut down a large swath of Arcan forces if Artem betrayed the rules of parley. He did not say that your weapon would cut down our own men as well."

Meg filled her plate with steaming beets and a few chunks of venison, then found she was too tired—and too overwhelmed by her new appointment—to eat.

Again, the round man bowed briefly, as if the action were distasteful to him. "My Lord, I admit the machine fail." Though his accent was heavy, Meg marveled at how well he'd learned Shangril's common tongue. "The *bomb* should explode hitting the ground, not in the air."

"And our own men were wounded. The need to care for wounded can cripple an army more than losses through death. Whose side are you on?"

The small-eyed man pierced him with his stare.

"Do you work for Artem?"

Meg stared at the little man. A spy?

"No!"

"Then explain yourself," Sulwyn said out of turn.

Orville glared at him.

"King Gramaret is waiting," Sulwyn said testily.

"There's nothing for explain," Orville said. "I have no love for kings. Artem, Prime Minister of Aadi—who is in real, a dictator—or any other."

"Or King Dwyn. Is that what you imply?" Sulwyn pressed. Colm put a hand on his arm, and Sulwyn pulled it away. Sulwyn did not usually let drink get the better of him, and Meg wondered what made today different.

"I have been filled of rich men, call themselves kings, steal from the poor and make life hard for people they should rule," Orville said in disgust. "You cannot pay me to work for a king. Any king." He turned to Dwyn. "I hear you are different. You hold up independent people who rule themself."

"Then why are you blowing up my men?" The king sat back in his camp chair.

"The thinking, the numbers, on the steam catapult is wrong. What happen yesterday is a mistake. It can be more correct. More Arcan soldier was killed or hurt than uprisers. Artem runs."

"Not thanks to you," Sulwyn pushed, and Meg wished he would return to his tent to sleep.

Orville raised a brow. "Yes. Thanks to me. Listen. You know nothing. This is small, little country—"

"Where you choose to live," Sulwyn blustered. He refilled his tankard.

"It suit me, yes. Now."

The king scrutinized him. His eyes narrowed. "You're a fugitive."

The quick turn of Orville's head. The king's words had landed true.

"They're looking for you in Aadi?" Sulwyn cried.

The fat man's eyes shifted from one to the other.

"What did you do?" Sulwyn crowed. "Murder?"

"Murder? No!" A small smile crept over Orville's lips. "Theft."

Everyone at the table stared.

"Money. Five very small steam toys, and molds to make steam engine parts." He shook his head wryly. "It was toys, put me into the most big trouble."

Gold, Meg could understand, but—

"Toys?" Dwyn asked.

Orville gave him a patronizing look. "There are more countries, not only Aadi, down there. Below your cliff, Sieur. Many want beauty of steam. Power of steam."

The king's voice took on a dangerous tone. "Explain what this *rube* doesn't understand."

Orville let out a breath. "I am engineer. With things in my head and some small example, I am . . ." He shrugged. "Sell secrets to enemies of Aadi."

"You're . . . a spy?" Sulwyn spluttered. Meg couldn't think of a more unlikely man. "But not for Artem."

"And?" Dwyn pressed.

The pudgy man shifted from one foot to the other. "I am almost caught."

"Almost?"

"Well, I come here. No one expect that. Run from civilize. Me, who never live, but a city."

From civilization? Shangril was uncultured? Backward?

"The gold you brought with you," Dwyn said. "Where is it now?"

"Spend on your war, *My Lord*. To keep Finn and me alive while I teach him how to make steam engine. Some I give to this one—" he nodded at Sulwyn "—for your war."

"That was *your* money?" Sulwyn asked.

"Why did you need Finn?" the king asked.

"I am not smith. I have molds and knowing of steam ideas, but I need someone who can work with iron." Orville smiled at Dwyn. "Gold can be spend. But business, a new thing that everyone, *everyone*, Sieur Gramaret, want? That is a more, *more* money idea. I have show steam power and people talk for years. And soon or later, someone with heads—and someone with money to pay—will see. My idea can work here, just like where I come from."

Meg digested this.

"My Lord," Orville said, this time without sarcasm. "You do not know. You have, here. Steam is big idea. It works. If you go to Aadi, you see it. And more. Black powder." He gave the king a conspiratorial smile. "Wait. Watch what *cannon* do to your enemies."

Dwyn looked at him intently, but did not interrupt.

"My machine is to make me rich, rich man." He nodded significantly. "Me and Finn. And, make you and your war—"

A clatter of boots and shouts beyond the walls of the tent interrupted the man's words. Fearghus leapt to his feet and flung back the tent flap.

"Sire," a voice shouted.

The king, followed by the others, emerged into the crisp chill. Meg wormed her way around the men to where she could see a handful of scouts. Every able-bodied man in the camp was running toward the king's tent.

The scout lifted a man's severed head by the hair for King Gramaret to see.

Shock squeezed Meg's heart. Beorn.

"Two horsemen charged past our guard and threw this on the ground before riding off," the scout cried, breathless. "Our men have given chase."

"On foot?" Fearghus asked.

"Some. Others are saddling horses."

King Gramaret's face was unreadable in the dark, but his voice was thick. "Beorn Ygrelle will not die unremembered."

The men surrounding him growled their agreement.

He took the grisly prize and raised it over his head. "To war!" he cried.

The men shouted. "To war!"

CHAPTER 24

A movement at the bend in the road distracted Janat from her sewing.

She breathed. No threat. Dogs barking at travelers.

No—

The limp. "Sulwyn!" Janat's needlework tumbled to the ground, pins scattering, as she leapt from her chair and opened the attic window.

Two figures in the snow. Not one.

Meg.

She waited, her breath coming in shallow gasps, as Sulwyn and Meg plodded up the hill, dogged by a scrabble of welcoming children.

They disappeared below her window and she turned to the door.

The door opened. *Sulwyn*. Real. Here.

By Ranuat's murderers, he looked worn out. A growth of stubble, and thin, too thin. But his eyes were bright and alive.

Then Sulwyn was across the room, wrapping cold arms around her and kissing her as though Meg was not standing in the doorway grinning.

Janat held out her arm to Meg, and when Meg joined the embrace, Janat held her close and looked into her face and held her again.

Sulwyn and Meg sank onto the chairs at the table, full of chatter and questions, shattering the silence and solitude of the last weeks.

Janat squandered logs on the fire and added salt mutton to the gruel. She made the portions generous and opened a whiskey bottle in celebration, but she had no appetite. To have Sulwyn back, here—to be inches from him, where she could reach out and touch his hand, laughing and joking and well—was hard to fathom. How many times had she seen him in her dreams at night or in her thoughts during the day, laying in some trackless forest or a back alley or dungeon, hurt or worse? That he was here seemed almost less solid than her fears.

And Meg was back, too. Healthy and whole, though dirty and, like Sulwyn, too thin. Quieter than before, Janat thought, and sometimes . . . did Meg's gaze linger—on Sulwyn? As though she knew something now that she hadn't before.

It was as though they all pretended everything was fine. And she poured another dram.

"Tell me all your adventures!" Janat tried to be bright and sparkling. She ignored her food, eyes flicking from Sulwyn to Meg. "Where did you go?"

Sulwyn's face had a merry glow. "I can't tell you that—"

But Meg knew.

"—but I will tell you that wherever we went, people flocked to us. Everywhere in Shangril, the people want their freedom of worship back."

"Was it dangerous?" Janat knew both Sulwyn and Meg would minimize the risks they'd faced, but she had to ask. "Was there fighting?"

Sulwyn swallowed a spoonful of porridge and tilted his head. "There was some fighting. A lot of marching."

"Was anyone killed?"

He quaffed his beer. "Some. We had—what?" he queried Meg. "Three at Cascade Creek?"

"Four, with twelve injured. Seven are still with us but five went home. Two with amputations."

"That's right." Sulwyn squeezed Janat's hand, then released it. "I knew Meg would remember exactly."

"I had to do the amputations."

They had shared . . .

Meg reached out a hand and put it on Janat's wrist. "But, Janat, I have to tell you my real news."

Janat was not certain she wanted to learn Meg's real news.

"Dwyn Gramaret. The king!"

Janat knew who Dwyn Gramaret was.

Meg's eyes shone. "He asked me to be the royal magiel of Gramarye-in-exile."

Royal magiel. Like Mama.

"Mostly my duties are no different from what I've done the whole time for the uprisers, spells of protection and healing and such. But he found me a horse to ride, almost at his side, and I'm part of his council."

"Oh." Janat was uncertain how to take this news. "That's wonderful."

"So I'm only here for a short time."

"You're not staying?"

"Neither of us can stay," Sulwyn said between mouthfuls.

Janat thought . . . she assumed . . .

"I've mostly just come back to copy the spells in our book," Meg explained. "I need my own book of spells. And to see if you have any herbs or spider legs or other ingredients I can take." She grinned at Sulwyn. "Maybe a little Elsen ganja."

"Oh." Janat was still trying to adjust to this rush of new information. Sulwyn was leaving. "Of course. I have a . . . dried salamander liver. Some yarrow and snake root." Gods, such common things. For birthing and crop health.

Meg nodded.

They were leaving. As soon as Meg copied out the book. Returning to Dwyn. And now, war.

There was a strained silence. Sulwyn poured them all another nip. "To a bloodless coup," he toasted, and they all raised their glasses.

"How . . . how did you find Sulwyn?" With an effort, Janat wrenched herself from the slippery slope of self-pity. "After he and Colm left here?"

Meg's gaze flicked briefly to Sulwyn's face.

He smiled indulgently. "It's all right."

Meg spooned her gruel. "They'd just gone down the road and camped. I followed the path all night and caught up to them as they were having breakfast."

"Why didn't Sulwyn send you back?"

She shrugged, a small smile touching her lips. "He tried, but I just kept following."

"Didn't he get mad?" Janat cocked her head and looked at Sulwyn with open curiosity and, she hoped, not accusation.

"Yes," he answered for Meg, "but she didn't care."

Disappointment. That was what Janat was feeling. But why? She'd stayed at home by choice. The last thing she ever wanted was to follow Sulwyn into his work. Into danger. She never wanted to be a royal magiel. "So, how did you get to stay?" She pushed on, unable to stop herself.

"Well, others joined us." Meg forged ahead with spirit, as if she, too, worked to keep the mood light. "The uprisers were talking about how they wanted to stop the king's troops from crossing the bridge over the Farfalls River without a fight. So I said, why didn't they curse the horses?"

"Ah," Janat said.

Meg warmed to the story. Yet, the more animated Meg became, the flatter Janat felt. "Some of the rebels wouldn't listen to a woman, but Colm said it might work."

"Colm? I thought he didn't like you." The name popped from Janat's mouth on its own accord, and the acidic words followed.

"He's all right," Meg said guardedly.

"Then, what curse did you use?"

"I didn't have any ingredients, did I?" Meg said. "So first I had to collect herbs—"

"There are sleep-drop mushrooms in the forest," Janat interrupted.

"I know. I found them."

Janat could have made the spell. "So you drew the curse by the light of Ranuat's constellation?"

Meg grinned at Sulwyn, and he grinned back, and an unexplained ache wrapped Janat's heart. "Ranuat's stars had set, but Sashcarnala was bright, and it worked anyway. The stars had good alignment. And the uprisers let me stay." Meg broke a hunk of bread from the loaf. "They grumbled and ignored me and treated me like a servant—"

"Hey!" Sulwyn objected.

"*And* I had to walk at the back." Meg's eyes sparkled.

"We used your potions. More than once," Sulwyn defended himself good-naturedly. "You weren't *just* put out to spy."

Janat's eyes prickled and her chest felt heavy. She watched as Sulwyn gave Meg a lopsided smile. Meg lifted a brow, her eyes never leaving his.

"Actually," Sulwyn said to Janat, "Meg's use of magic saved us more than once. It turned out to be a good thing she was there."

There was no air in the room. Janat couldn't breathe.

Meg blushed and lowered her eyes.

"Excuse me." Janat stood, and the two looked up at her in surprise. "I need—I just need a bit of air. It's hot. The fire's too hot." She left the room, closing the door behind her and leaning on it.

There was no sound from the room at her back. By Ranuat, what had she done? Left for no reason. Erratic. Childish. What would Sulwyn think, that she was angry? Weak?

The tears leaked onto her face. She couldn't stay in that room.

※

Sulwyn found her. Of course he found her. She'd slumped to the ground in the snowy alley behind the house, her back against the rough wooden walls, beside a discarded barrel the landlord used for refuse. The tears and moans, streaming from her, were gone now, and she was empty.

"Hey." He stood before her and she ducked her head, ashamed to be seen. Her eyes were swollen and her hair was bedraggled and she wanted him to go away and never come back. And she wanted him to engulf her and hold her and make everything all right.

He sat beside her against the wall and put his arm around her shoulder, his breath sweet with whiskey.

She didn't move. Didn't pull away. Didn't draw closer.

"What's wrong?"

How could she reply? What could she say?

"I thought you'd be happy to see me. See us."

"I am." The words were small, squeezed.

"Then why the tears?"

How could she explain? It was all . . . so complicated . . .

He waited, but the more she struggled with how to respond, the more confused she became. She was useless. She was too young for him — everyone said so — too timid, too . . .

"I . . ." His utterance trailed away, as though he, too, could not put his thoughts into words. "I thought I might tell Colm, tell the others. I thought I might take some time away from the cause. Stay here." She sensed he looked at her sideways, gauging her response.

"Stay here. With me and Meg." The bitter words snapped out.

"Meg?"

There. It was said.

The closeness of his arm on her shoulder loosened. "She's Dwyn's magiel."

What *was* she hoping to hear? The vision of Meg in his arms burst into her mind then fled as quickly.

"I never had anything to do with Meg." The words were low, defensive. "I never looked at her."

No? Not tonight, at the dinner table?

He gently removed his arm from her shoulder, and loneliness engulfed her.

The silence between them stretched.

"If that's what you . . ." His sentence trailed off. ". . . you think . . ."

Hurt? Him? Sulwyn wasn't the wounded party.

"I can find some place to stay."

No. She didn't want him to leave. She wanted him to stay, to hold her, to make everything right.

Hesitantly, he climbed to his feet.

She hugged her legs and buried her face in her knees.

After a time, his footsteps echoed quietly in the alley.

✤

It wasn't until Janat opened the door to their room that she saw the flicker of candlelight. Blast. She'd come home too soon. Someone was awake.

"Come in." Meg's voice. A command, not an invitation, albeit a gentle one.

Janat entered, shivering. She closed the door and leaned against it, hoping the signs of her tears weren't visible in the faint light. The fire had died to dull coals.

Meg sat at the table swathed in a blanket. A quill, paper, and their shared book of spells lay open in the glow of a candle. The rest of the room was in shadow, but Sulwyn didn't seem to be there.

"Sulwyn's gone." Meg's voice was low, uninflected. "He came to get his things."

Janat had nothing to say. She tried to smother her shivers.

"I think he's gone to the tavern for the night."

Janat gave a small nod. All she wanted was to slide under her blankets and turn away from the light.

"What did you say to him?"

That was none of Meg's business.

"Whatever you said, you hurt him—"

Hurt *him*? "Are you in love with him?"

Meg's eyes flashed up, then. "What?"

But Meg had heard her. "Does he love you, too?"

"What are you talking about?" Defensive. Guilty.

Meg had always been jealous of her, of what she and Sulwyn had. "How did you do it? Did you use a love potion?"

"No!" And then, quickly, as though she realized too late the trap she'd fallen into, she went on. "His work for the uprisers is important. I help him with his work. And now—"

"And you've forgotten Mama's plan? The meeting at the tarn."

"I haven't forgotten anything. That's weeks away."

"You never talk about it anymore." Janat pressed the point. "You hardly pray. You don't believe the Gods will help us. You think men need to fight men. You think—"

"Five of the prayer stones have been smashed, Janat!" Meg slammed her quill onto the table and stood. "The king has killed the magiels of the Great Houses and is persecuting the rest. How are the Gods helping us, hmm? It is we who must help the Gods. *Men* have to right the wrongs that men have done."

"And you encourage Sulwyn to fight. You champion war, and killing, and death—"

"I support the dream Sulwyn's chosen. Better than you. I'm not a burden, a millstone—"

"I am not!"

"No? You're afraid of your own shadow. You've always depended on everyone to care for you. Nanna. Me. That harebrained idea to go to the king's men—"

"That was a long time ago!"

"—Sulwyn. Did you ever love him?" Meg flared. "Or just trade comfort for security?"

"Meg!"

"Even Rennika had more pluck than you, pickpursing. She's the one who brought you work. Sewing. She's the one who brought you requests for spells. You sat and hid." Meg's words flew, as though a dam had burst and she did not stop until all the spite had poured out.

"Rennika's quiet-skinned!"

Meg blew out a breath in disgust.

Janat had to get out. Piss on the dangers beyond her walls. Piss on the cold. She marched to the hooks beside the pallets and, finding her sack, tore her clothing from the pegs, rolled up her blankets and pallet, and stuffed everything into the sack.

"You're leaving?" Meg's voice betrayed astonishment and satisfaction. "Janat?"

The blasted candle created more shadows than light. Janat had to find all her things. She was not coming back.

Meg said nothing, but Janat could feel her watching in disbelief.

Food. She went to the sideboard and found half a loaf left from supper. A sack of oats. An onion. Apples.

"Go, then," Meg said from the table.

The chetra in the pot. They were all hers. She had earned them.

"We don't need you."

We.

Janat pulled her cloak from its peg by the door and slung her sack over her shoulder. "You know." She stopped at the door, her hand on the knob, still shivering, and turned. "The stupid thing is. I'll always love you." She shot Meg a glare, and escaped.

CHAPTER 25

Huwen Delarcan consulted his figures. "Twenty-first ratchet mark," he commanded with a confidence that belied his perpetual uncertainty. Since his gangly frame had put on muscle, hardening with his time at the siege camp, and his voice had ceased to flip out of its rather pleasing baritone, he felt more like a king-to-be than a mere prince. But Father still treated him like a child. Told him nothing of war strategy.

The soldiers operating the trebuchet loaded the leather pocket with the requisite stone and began winding the winch. Huwen wished he'd paid more attention when his tutor was explaining the mathematics of triangles—particularly, how to compensate for a whistling winter wind.

Above them, the stone ramparts of Archwood bound cliff to cliff across a high valley. When the city hadn't fallen within the first weeks, it'd become clear it would only fall once the Amber no longer protected it. Eventually, the prayer stone's magiel or its royal would die of starvation, disease, or accident. But as long as Talanda's three magiel daughters and King Ean's daughter lived, the siege could continue for years. The continual bombardment of the city via trebuchet was more military exercise to keep the men occupied, with the outside chance of a damaging hit.

"A hit," the captain reported.

Father clapped a hand on Huwen's shoulder in encouragement, but it was clear the stone had fallen just below the crenels, and had left no mark on the wall.

"Reposition. Twenty seventh ratchet mark." Huwen wished he

could learn about command in one of the other skirmishes. Father had been training him in the current political situation and its roots. Arcan had made alliances among the seven kingdoms—well, six, until Archwood's walls fell—and created a single political unit under the guidance of one king, his father. And, it was true, the creation of an empire had required the centralization of prayer to the One God, the only true God, and this had necessitated the destruction of the obsolete prayer stones. All the stones, that was, except the Ruby, the stone used by Father and his magiel, Wenid Col. At least, that's what Wenid had said.

As a consequence, small rebellions cropped up, as not all peasants understood the necessity of unification. Rebellions led to the death of honest empire-supporting civilians. Rebels were cowards, ignoring the rules of engagement, wearing no uniforms, so they could hide among innocent villagers. Often, they used weak but cleverly cast spells against their king. Such uprisings were absurd, but Huwen had to admit, probably more exciting than this endless siege. Over a year, now.

"Majesty." A foot soldier made a brief bow to Huwen's father and indicated an approaching figure some distance down the snow-covered ridge.

The trebuchet released and the stone arced gracefully into the air and landed squarely on the corner of a crenel. Huwen thought he could see the faintest mark where a splinter of stone had chipped. The men cheered, and a small bloom of pride suffused Huwen. He smiled, accepting his father's nod of approval and Wenid's faint smile. "Reposition," he ordered.

The courier was getting closer; Uther, by his gait, climbing quickly. He'd arrived yesterday from Holderford, having delivered Father's instructions for supplies, and returning with mundane communications from Prince Avin, and some gossip from the capital. Saffen's family had returned to Summerbluff, which meant Anwen went with her. More importantly, he brought news about recent altercations between rebels and soldiers. A group of lesser nobles in Teshe renounced their pledges and sided with a group of rebels. Their deceit culminated with King Larin's death, leaving Father with no king in Teshe. Each revolt had been quelled, but cities, towns, villages—all—were   strained with apprehension.

And the uprisers' powerful new magic, treacherously unleashed at the failed surrender in the fall—which Huwen had seen firsthand at Father's side—had been confirmed by a second unexplained sorcery.

Father eyed the row of trebuchets and the soldiers plodding back and forth to reset them. "Come," he said to Huwen. "Interruptions are part of leadership." He crunched on the hardened path through the snow, Wenid hobbling along behind. Huwen shoved his paper in his purse and, turning his back on the mountain wind, made his way down the ridge behind them.

They met out of the earshot of the men. Uther nodded to Father. "Eamon is hurt," he said without preamble, his breath puffing white in the cold. "He appears to have cut his own wrists. You're wanted in the high camp."

No! Eamon had promised—

Father paled, his eyes riveted on Uther. "Gods," he muttered, and Wenid shot him a piercing glance.

"Physicians attend him," Uther continued in his urgently neutral tone. "They believe they will stop the bleeding, but the prince is not conscious. He may yet die. The Holder of Histories is by his side and will administer his death token if he feels the time is near."

By the One—

Father glared at Wenid. "This war," he growled. "This entire war, this upheaval in the country. So many dead. And he throws it away!"

Wenid grabbed Father's shoulders and gave him a shake. "Your end of the bargain. Until it is completed, the contract is not sealed."

Bargain?

Father shoved Wenid's hands away and marched at a reckless pace down the icy path.

What did Wenid mean?

Wenid's face reddened with fury. "Everything!" he fumed under his breath. "Everything we've fought for!" He glared at Uther, who shrank from him. "Your father would let the fate of the souls of his people rest on a boy's whim." He tromped down the ridge after Father, the wind whipping his cloak.

Huwen stood stock-still in shock. How could a man touch Father that way?

Uther lowered his head in sorrow and gestured for Huwen to precede him.

And . . . the war was about *broken trade alliances* . . .

Huwen took a step, followed by another.

Eamon, like to die?

And what had father meant, the war . . . this war was for . . . Eamon?

It was the next morning when Huwen was allowed to enter his brother's tent. He waited until Father had gone. Eamon lay on a cot on his back, one bandaged arm flung over his pale forehead, staring with glassy eyes at the canvas overhead. The Holder of Histories sat beside him, a bowl of cold soup congealing on the table.

Eamon glanced at him, then looked away. His eyes were filled with the pain Huwen had seen there ever since his illness, over a year ago. The Holder stood and bowed, and Huwen dismissed him.

Huwen brought the camp stool close to his brother's cot. "You promised," he said in a fierce whisper.

He expected Eamon to dismiss him with a curt, "I lied," but instead, he pressed his lips together, tears brightening his eyes. "You don't know," he rasped, "how I tried."

The words blunted Huwen's rage. Pity and bafflement took its place. "What . . ." He shrugged.

Eamon closed his eyes. "Uther brought a letter."

Huwen cast about, saw a folded paper near the soup. He unfolded it and read. He crumpled the paper. "Saffen's family went back to Summerbluff?" This information had dampened Huwen's spirits when he'd heard it; Anwen had been forced to go, too. "Mother's Lady-in-Waiting married?"

"Milanda."

Huwen puzzled. Milanda. The name was familiar.

"Milanda married."

And the pieces tumbled together. "The girl you loved. The one you never spoke to."

Eamon shot him a scathing look.

"Sorry." But, by the One God, Eamon was inexplicable. Nothing made sense. "Eamon . . ."

His brother rolled away from him.

It had something to do with what Father said. The war. Father had left Holderford—a year and a half ago, to settle a dispute in the hinterlands, *he'd said.* This was only days after Eamon had suddenly—miraculously—recovered from the illness everyone thought would kill him.

But it hadn't turned out to be a simple dispute. The Azurite and the Chrysocolla had been destroyed with no conflict. Their kings had simply handed the prayer stones over to Father. The kings wielding the Emerald and Amethyst were defeated shortly thereafter, after brief skirmishes. Then Father had laid siege to Theurgy to capture the Citrine, and somehow, the war was no longer about disputes in the distant parts of Shangril, but about worship of the One God.

Or was it? What had Father meant, this war was for Eamon? Huwen had a sinking feeling. Father had not told him the truth. At least, not the whole truth.

"Eamon."

Silence was his answer.

"What happened, the night you recovered from your illness?"

Eamon stilled.

"Eamon—"

"I don't know."

But he did.

"Eamon."

"I forget." He turned, and cast those too-adult eyes on him. Eyes that knew.

"I don't understand."

Eamon rolled over. "Go away."

Huwen knew Eamon well enough to know nothing he could do would make his brother speak.

"By your leave, Your Highnesses." The voice from beyond the tent door belonged to Uther. "I have a message from the king."

"Enter." Huwen sat back, defeated, and Eamon rolled over to glare at him.

Uther entered, nodding a bow to Huwen, and then to Eamon. He spoke to the latter. "Your father would speak with you."

Eamon turned back to the tent wall. "I'm ill."

Uther opened the chest by the bed and began to fill it with clothing that had been strewn about the tent. "Father has commanded you to go to Coldridge and would bid you farewell."

"Coldridge?" The boy turned, his eyes flashing with anger. "Where there are minders to tend me?"

"King Larin was assassinated by rebels, and your father would have a Delarcan at the keep. You leave immediately with myself and Wenid Col. You'll be taken by travois down to the main camp, where a courier has been dispatched to tell them to prepare a cart." He closed the chest and fastened it.

Eamon rolled over and sought out Huwen, his face drawn and defeated. "So. Pushed out of the way." His voice was barely a whisper. "Once more, I fail."

Uther raised the unresisting boy to a sitting position and knelt to put his boot on. "Odd way to look at it."

Eamon frowned querulously at the obscure reference.

Uther helped with his second boot. "I overheard Father talking to Magiel Col. You are to be the royal of the Ruby. At least for now."

"What?" Huwen cried.

Eamon stared at him in bewilderment.

Uther fastened a fur cloak around Eamon's shoulders. "I'm only a messenger."

Nothing made sense. The only royal to travel to the Heavens with the magiel of the Ruby was the *king*—

Uther clasped Eamon's arm about his neck and shoved his shoulder firmly under his half-brother's armpit. He nodded at Huwen. "Pages will be here momentarily to bring his chest." He and Eamon disappeared through the tent flap.

What was going on? Huwen did not for one minute believe that Eamon's melancholy was related to Milanda's marriage. Eamon had tried to hurt himself before he'd even met Milanda.

No, this had something to do with the night Eamon was made well.

A war. And now, control of the Ruby. It would make Eamon the most powerful person in Shangril. Disquiet sank through Huwen's stomach. *He* would be king, not *Eamon*.

Huwen had to untangle what was going on. What was really going on.

It was possible Eamon had been too ill to know what had happened. But Eamon wasn't the only one in his room that night. Father had been there, and Wenid Col.

And Uther Tangel.

CHAPTER 26

The constellation of Ranuat's seven murderers westered in a paling pre-dawn sky. A hint of wind skimming across the snow crust bore the scent of glacier. Sulwyn peed by a tree, a steaming hole in the snow. He buttoned his pants and, gazing up the valley toward the ghostly peaks, crunched back toward the group of yak hide tents. He was thirsty. A dipperful of ice water before breakfast would be welcome.

Eight weeks, they'd been on this campaign. His passion to broker a place for the wisdom of men at the kings' councils, and to do so, *peacefully* had failed. Artem had betrayed them. Beorn . . . Beorn had been a good man, and the soldier had died on Artem's spike. The soldier's death had sealed the uprisers' resolve, but now they talked of war. Sulwyn had wanted nothing more than to return to Wildbrook, then, to Janat, and leave such bitterness behind. Heal. Live. Let others carry on the work of freeing Shangril's people.

And yet, returning to Janat had gone wrong, too.

Janat'd been unhappy for some time. Sulwyn knew that. He'd intended to stay with her and make things right, but the distance between them had grown too great. Uncharacteristically, she'd left.

Hunt as he might, he could find no trace of her. At first, Meg took this news with angry denial, grilling him about his search and launching out to undertake her own. He accompanied her. But once realization that Janat was gone—actually gone—crept home, there was no reason, for either of them, to stay in Wildbrook. Meg had a commitment to Dwyn, and Sulwyn, too, was drawn back into the conflict.

They'd followed Dwyn from battle to battle, harrying Artem's troops, directing rebellions, recruiting men, refining Orville's steam machines, working out a plan to end what had become a civil war, but the glamour was gone. Cold and mud and death was all there was.

And for his hurt and guilt, there was whiskey.

Snow crystals crunched unevenly under his limp now as Sulwyn followed the path along the ridge. A movement, black against the gray of the valley, caught his eye.

In a gap in the trees, Meg, swathed in thin furs and silhouetted against the growing dawn, gazed out over the snow-filled Orumon valley. She turned at his footsteps. "Sulwyn."

She was not beautiful the way Janat was, but she had grown, under Dwyn's trust, into a confident, intense young woman. Sulwyn nodded his respect. Since they'd rejoined Dwyn's camp, he'd tried to keep his distance from her. He should get back to camp.

"Four thousand of King Artem's men." She indicated the valley.

Her words arrested his steps.

"But only two hundred, up on the shoulder where King Artem camps below the city gates." She turned back to her study of the siege's defenses. "Our spies are good."

"Fearghus is in charge of this campaign." Dwyn's guard, promoted now to his right-hand man. Dwyn had ridden, light and swift with only a handful of men, to Big Hill just north of Coldridge, to meet with a delegation of Teshe uprisers.

Her voice became edged. "How can he not see how vulnerable the king is?"

"You were at the council last night." Had she even slept? Or had she stayed up all night on a waft of Heartspeed, thinking? To be fair, he'd seen Meg try to voice her objections—good ones—at the council, only to be shut down. Fearghus was old-fashioned, and she was a woman. Without Dwyn at the council to listen, her words fell on deaf ears. Finn, Orville—even Colm—had not opposed Fearghus's plan.

"Harry their flanks in the lower valley? Nothing more?" she asked derisively. "If Dwyn does not express a certain course of action to take, Fearghus only repeats the same tactics over and over."

He had a headache from last night's beer and no stomach to rehash the arguments. "We don't have the manpower, training, or weapons to confront them, army to army."

"We need to attack the heart of their power. The king."

"We attack from safety, then melt into the woods. Deplete their ranks and lose as few of our own as possible." He wasn't sure why he was defending Fearghus. "Draw Artem's attention and resources from the siege."

"Flies about a horse's head." She snorted. "How many battles have you and Fearghus and the others fought? On and on and on, this civil war limps. A year! Artem's beheaded or imprisoned every aristocrat or magiel who's threatened to oppose him—any man who would lead us. He's cut off our head. We must do the same to him. Can't Fearghus see? Our assassins killed King Larin."

Despite himself, Sulwyn crunched through the snow to where she stood at the edge of the ridge and looked up the valley. "It's a fine idea, Meg. But Larin is not Artem."

"No." She drew her threadbare furs more tightly around her throat and he was conscious of their closeness. "The Many Gods won't permit Archwood to fall as long as the Amber remains in my mother's hand. We go in while the king is absorbed by his hopeless siege."

"Can you imagine the complexity of such a strike?"

She grasped his hand with hers in supplication. "Listen! I've lain awake. I've gone through the contingencies. The king's not in a fortress. He's in a flimsy pavilion, or at best, a stone house. No city wall. No castle wall."

He tried to pull back, her touch too warm, too inviting.

Her grip tightened. "I can deliver a curse under the dark of night. *Especially* if our men draw attention in the valley. I've climbed these hills."

A stealthy strike. "You didn't say all of that last night."

"Fearghus wouldn't hear me. Listen, Sulwyn. I could—"

"No. Not you. You're a Falkyn, for the sake of the Many!" He disengaged her hold.

"Fearghus has to let me use my magic for more than a curse on a horse's legs or a cloud of confusion in battle, instead of hiding me back here in the woods!"

"—which makes you too valuable to risk." Sulwyn could not lose her, as well as Janat. "Act as though you understand your importance."

She snapped her jaw closed. "The king thinks my sisters and I are trapped in Archwood. His men wouldn't be looking for me."

"He's not sure. Your sister was seen."

"That was over a year ago, and unconfirmed."

"*If* we have no royal spies in our own camps!" Sometimes, Sulwyn wanted to wring her neck. Sometimes . . . "We can't risk Artem becoming certain. Now, pretend you've heard and understood that."

She breathed contempt from her nostrils.

"I know your tricks, Meg. You take decisions into your own hands. I'm saying, don't do it this time. You took an oath to follow Dwyn. That means following his captains."

"You agree with Fearghus?" Her whisper was incredulous. She looked away in exasperation.

"Come on." He had to get out of her presence. "I'll start the fire. Sun'll be up soon."

However, her idea was good enough for Sulwyn to run it past Colm.

"You don't have to deliver the curse," Colm told Meg. "Have Sulwyn deliver it." Colm shoveled gruel into his mouth. "I don't see how Fearghus can object to that."

"Sulwyn?" That wasn't the response she wanted.

"Sure. He's too lame to fight."

Sulwyn pushed the stump he sat on back from the smoke that wafted his way from the fire. "Meaning, I'm expendable. You should talk." He nodded at Colm's arm—workable, but not strong enough for a sword.

Colm shrugged. "We're all expendable. Except our magiel." He pointed his biscuit at Meg.

"I have to be the one to go," Meg argued. "There are spell words."

"Teach him." Colm pushed a shank of hair out of his eyes and kept eating. "You infuse your curses with magiel magic when you create them, don't you? Not at the time they're used."

It was true. And she paid for her use of magiel magic at the time of creating the spell, too, which meant she could use them later without fear of suddenly finding herself in another fragment of her life. But— "Sulwyn couldn't get close enough," she insisted. She wanted to *do* something, not hide in the woods. "He'd have to administer the curse to the king directly."

"And you could?" Colm washed his breakfast down from a steaming cup.

She pressed her lips closed, frustrated.

"Your skin is erratic," Colm said. "Not only is it impossible for you to blend in, there are no women in those camps. You'd be spotted before you got ten feet inside their perimeter." He waved his cup at Sulwyn. "Send him. He can say he's a—I don't know. Messenger."

"They'd watch for spies." Sulwyn touched the death token in the band at his neck.

He was right. Talking his way into the king's tent would be next to impossible.

"Yes. But this siege has been going on for over a year. They won't be as vigilant as they should. That's one of the strengths of Meg's plan. We harry them, pick off a few soldiers, drive them back, and steal a uniform from the battlefield." Colm filled his bowl with gruel from the pot by the fire. "There. Messenger."

"King Artem uses his bastard son, Uther Tangel, as his messenger—and for personal communication, his *only* messenger." Meg shook her head. "Sulwyn can't impersonate the boy, and if he poses as another messenger, he'd have to pass the potion on to Uther. *He* couldn't deliver it directly to the king."

"All right," Colm said slowly, considering. "But with a uniform, Sulwyn could at least get into the camp." He turned to Sulwyn. "You know the high-born accent already. You used it for the merchant trade. What other duties could bring a man in uniform into the king's presence?"

"Servants," Meg said. "If we can steal a soldier's uniform, maybe we can steal a servant's livery."

"Good," Colm said. "That idea, at least, could work."

Sulwyn cradled a cup of water in his lap. "We don't often recover the bodies of servants on the battlefield."

"Livery can be the mission of one of our harrying raids." Gods. They could do this.

Sulwyn tilted his head thoughtfully. "Appearance is important, but I won't get far without knowing the protocols."

Meg nodded sharply with decision. "I can teach you royal protocols, and I can create a subtle spell that will only kill the king over days or weeks. So you have time to escape."

"Talk to Fearghus." Colm wiped the last of his porridge from his plate with a crust and put it in his mouth.

Meg had discovered that curses often exacted more of her than other spells; a curse that killed, especially so. She knew of none that left no trace, though perhaps some existed—she hadn't been practicing long enough to know any. And a curse that showed no effects for a period of days or weeks . . . each requirement added to the complexity of her work. This, on top of finding ingredients in winter, far from an apothecary or even a trade center, and with limited celestial alignments. For days, she wracked her brain, visiting and revisiting her same dozen death spells, delayed magic spells, and concealment spells simple enough for a worldling to administer. But she'd boasted to Fearghus that she could do this. And Sulwyn's safety depended on her.

In the end, she'd had to rely more deeply on magiel magic than her combination of spells would normally have warranted, reaching through time to find the day her dried spider web had been fresh, to find the drops of bat venom that had been collected under Sashcarnala's single star, to age the owl tears gathered under a noonday sun to increase their potency. She had to hold all the strands in balance and combine them in a far future when Kyaju's Arrow and the wandering star of the Blue Orum were aligned on either side of the One God's star.

She had done it.

Then crawled into the sleeping furs in her tent, dreading the payment.

Morning. Bright sunlight streamed through a glassed window, and the air was soft with summer heat. Meg knew this room. King Ean's castle in Archwood. Oh, Gods, she was home.

"When are you?" Mama's voice was sharp.

Meg turned her head. Mama sat on a couch beside her, holding her hands.

She was clean and dressed in a brocade robe, dainty shoes pinching her toes. The room smelled of sweet summer air and far away she caught a whiff of roasting meat.

The day Mama had called her to her room, and given her a spell to perform. A week before she and her sisters had fled the castle, running for their lives. She saw for the first time Mama's worried frown and hollow eyes. Her mother's strain. Oh, what a different world Meg had lived in. Blind.

"Meg. We only have few moments."

"When—"

"When are you?"

She snapped to attention. "The equinox will be in twelve weeks. I know to go to the tarn."

Mama's eyes closed briefly in relief. "Good." Mama gripped her hands. "You will meet a prince there."

This would change everything. "How can you know—"

"Nothing is certain, but I have—will have—" A look of confusion flicked across her face. "I have put the pieces in place. The importance of this is far greater than you can know, Meg. Do not be the link in this chain that fails."

Time could snap any instant. "I won't, Mama. But—"

Mama took her hands. "Train Rennika. I bore her to have the most power. She might—she might—even have the ability to reach the seventh Heaven, the Heaven of the Ruby and the One God. I pray she will."

"Rennika?" Shock rippled through her. "I thought—"

"Any of the three of you can use the Amber. If Rennika can't do it, do it yourself or call on Janat, but go beyond the sixth level. Do you understand? You must go all the way to the seventh Heaven. Pray to the One, not to Kyaju. You must—"

Wind slammed into the tent, shaking it.

Meg sat up in the dark, her heart thumping as if she'd just run a great distance, sweating beneath her woollen cloak. She was back in the uprisers' camp.

One discontinuity? Only one?

Rennika . . .

Mama had found a prince . . .

Huwen? No. Huwen was training at his father's side, doing everything he could to destroy Orumon. To destroy magiels. To destroy the prayer stones. He would never bring her the Amber.

Eamon?

She knew little or nothing about the king's second son. He was a recluse, and had been ever since he'd almost died, just before King Artem began his mad attack on his neighbors. Meg could not believe he would find his way to a hidden lake in some distant hinterland, a mere twelve weeks from now.

That left Jace. What did she know of him? He was younger than her, Rennika's age. Meg had only seen him a few times and paid little attention. He'd run around after his older brothers, stick in hand, brandishing it like a sword. So, he would be about twelve now. Again, how would he get away from Holderford to come to Coldridge without a retinue? Perhaps, Mama meant one of the deposed kings? They were dead or in hiding, except Dwyn Gramaret.

But King Gramaret was no prince, and hadn't been, when the war began.

And Rennika. Mama had borne her, gifted her with the most power. This fact held no surprise for Meg. Mama had gifted their youngest sister with stable skin, and she could easily disguise herself among the worldlings. Mama had foreseen a day when the beautiful complexion of a magiel would become a liability.

Rennika.

CHAPTER 27

A lesser darkness dimmed the stars. Sulwyn stuffed his white cloak behind a tree, and tugging his newly-fitted tunic into place, followed the outhouse path from the low scrub forest onto the open, snow-covered hilltop below the cliffs of Archwood, that was Artem's advance camp. Though nothing moved, his surveillance yesterday with Colm told him the men—particularly the servants—would soon be active.

A messenger had ridden up the valley late last evening, and Fearghus had withdrawn the uprisers to let him pass, urging Sulwyn to hurry, that he might overhear the message. Of course, the king's man was on horseback traveling on a beaten trail by a direct route and would clearly reach the king's encampment many candlemarks before Sulwyn could make the journey. It was disappointing but could not be helped.

Sulwyn hobbled to the tent he and Colm had identified as most likely the wash tent. It was unguarded. Within, a boy dozed by the fire. His timing was good. The servants had not yet begun their daily preparations. Sulwyn pilfered a set of matched, soft linen towels monogrammed in the colors of House Delarcan, before his movements woke the boy.

The child jumped to his feet. "Wash water, Sieur?"

"Yes."

"A bag of soap powder?" The unquestioning boy was sleepy and filled the linen bag from a bin, before Sulwyn could answer.

"And a shaving cup."

"Yes, Sieur."

He turned to leave, but the door flap opened. Another servant in livery identical to his stopped short when he saw Sulwyn.

The man took in Sulwyn's supplies. "Bit early, today?" he asked querulously. "The commander has asked not to be disturbed before the candlemark past sunup."

After a year of siege, the necessity of rising early was undoubtedly long gone. "I was summoned by Magiel Col," Sulwyn answered, grateful for Meg's information. He scanned the other's uniform for a sigil marking his position in the king's household. "—Sieur," he said, spotting the metal piece on the man's collar.

"Where's Fallon?"

Fallon. Must be Wenid Col's man. Sulwyn tucked the fact away. "Unwell, Sieur. I'm sure he will be better with another candlemark's sleep."

"Why haven't I seen you here before?"

"I just came up from the lower camp, Sieur."

The man eyed him askance, then nodded, and Sulwyn stepped into the predawn cold, his mouth suddenly dry and his armpits damp. He blew out to steady his breathing, then crunched purposefully if unevenly with his stiff leg and steaming pail up the hill. The sooner he was done his business and gone, the better.

Two soldiers guarding a large stone building with a proper thatched roof watched him approach. "No one requested a barber," one said.

Sulwyn frowned in perplexity. "I was told the king rises early today."

"No," said the other. "Who told you that?"

"Fallon," Sulwyn said in surprise.

"Fallon serves Magiel Col," the first one said. Confirmation.

"And why are you here? Where's Ioan?" the other asked.

"I'm up from the camp in the lower valley. Ioan is ill."

"This is irregular." The first one looked at the second. "Run down to check with the quartermaster."

Sulwyn shifted with his bucket. "The water's getting cold. Can I at least take it inside until this is sorted out?"

The first guard waved him in. "Don't wake the king," he warned.

An attendant dozed by an interior door, the embers in the hearth were choked with ashes. Heavy tapestries insulated the room, though the cold still penetrated the chinks in the stone. A map-strewn table stood in the center of the carpet, and the messenger—wrapped in furs and blankets—slept on a cot.

Sulwyn snatched a glance at the uppermost map. Memorized lines and symbols on familiar landmarks. He hoped he could remember.

But he had only minutes before the guards sorted out that he was not one of their men.

Without waking the attendant or the messenger, Sulwyn pushed the interior door with his shoulder and entered the king's bedchamber.

King Artem stood in a fur-lined robe by a tiny window, its drapes slightly parted, the pale light falling on his face.

Piss.

The king turned, his eyes abstracted; he resumed his contemplation of whatever lay beyond the window. Sulwyn flicked his gaze to the floor to cover his surprise and forced himself to breathe evenly. Servants were invisible.

He nodded a bow to the king's back and moved soundlessly over the carpets to the side table, where he poured steaming water into a basin and laid out the king's washing and shaving tools.

Sulwyn had counted on waking the king by bringing his bedside washtowel. Casting Meg's spell—and chanting the spell words—with the king awake would be more than just a little tricky. His fingers trembled as he laid the razor on the towel. He needed to do this deed and leave before dawn lightened the sky and the camp woke.

"Boy!" The king pitched his command loudly enough that Sulwyn assumed he was not being addressed, but he readied himself for instructions, even so.

The shaving mug. In his hand. Meg had created a curse the king could wash in; Sulwyn was not to let it touch his skin. He emptied Meg's powder into the shaving mug.

The servant from the outer chamber appeared.

Sulwyn covered the charm with soap powder.

"Send Uther in."

Uther Tangel. The messenger.

The servant bowed. "Yes, Majesty." He disappeared, returning momentarily to place candles about the room and stoke the fire.

Sulwyn added half a ladle of hot water to the cup.

The messenger, hair standing at all angles and livery rumpled, entered, closing the door behind the retreating servant.

"Uther."

"Father." The young man bowed his head, a quick nod. The king's eldest son bore him a resemblance, but only if one knew to look.

"I have a reply for you to take back to Lord Innes, Regent of Midell." King Artem waved at the desk across from the bed. "Get paper and ink."

"Yes, Sire." Uther did as he was bid and sat at the desk.

Sulwyn mixed the ingredients, an aroma of bitter herbs rising from the cup. The Gods must be on his side.

"Honorifics. And then: the three towns taken by the uprisers in the last few weeks must be regained at all costs," the king dictated. "Track down witnesses to the uprisers' reported new magic."

Uther wrote. Thank the Gods. Sulwyn hadn't missed the entire debriefing.

"Within two weeks I will send you a thousand troops." The king cast a glance at Uther, who wrote diligently. "Regarding your request for support from the treasury, I am obliged to inform you that you must raise the necessary funds yourself. You have my blessing to raise taxes on the farmlands of Midell."

Sulwyn swallowed, so as not to choke. The villain raised the revenues to fight his own people by taxing the people he would tyrannize. He repeated the king's words silently, fixing them in his memory.

He'd stopped stirring the shaving brush.

"I will visit Theurgy within four weeks. I trust you will have the military situation under control by that time."

Weeks. He resumed lathering the brush. Would Meg's curse have had time to work by then?

The king turned to Uther. "Read it."

Uther read back the king's words. Sulwyn turned his back, digesting all he heard. He bent over the soap cup and whispered the spell words.

"Good," the king said. "Take another letter." He eyed Sulwyn irritably. "Where is Ioan?" Sulwyn opened his mouth to reply, but the king waved his words aside and sat in a chair near the sideboard. "Shave me. Be quick."

The curse. Now.

Sulwyn propelled himself into action, pushing the king's hair back and draping him with a towel, hoping the spell words had taken.

Uther waited with paper and pen.

"This one is for Edrick of Storm River. Begin with the honorifics."

Sulwyn soaked a towel in the warm water of the basin.

"Is Edrick duke or regent?" Uther asked.

"Steward." The king composed himself. "In these times of civic strife, a levy is imposed on the mines of Storm River. It is required that three cut emeralds of royal quality and with the dimensions of a coin, be sent, with a dispatch, to Cataract Crag." He laid back and closed his eyes, and Sulwyn applied the warm towel.

By the Many, the guards must have discovered Sulwyn's lies by now.

Uther added the flourishes required by protocol and read the letter back to the king. Light seeped into the room through closed drapes. Piss.

Sulwyn removed the towel and applied the charmed soap to the king's cheeks and jaw.

"By the One, what kind of stinking soap is that?" the king snapped.

"Healing herbs have been added to protect against curses—"

"They stink. Don't bring them again."

"Yes, Majesty."

"Father?" Uther said.

The king waved a hand and Sulwyn stilled his razor as the monarch spoke. "Compose a letter to Jace's regent in Cataract Crag. I want the gems sold—bartered to Aadi, mind—and not for a pittance. By the One, we are scraping the barrels of the treasury to pay for all these uprisings."

"Very well, Sire," Uther said, and he bent diligently over his paper.

Sulwyn shaved the stubble from the king's chin, holding his breath to keep from trembling at this latest news.

The room brightened as Uther read his letter aloud and Sulwyn wiped the dregs of soap from the royal face.

"Took long enough," the king complained, glaring at Sulwyn. "Deliver the letters," he said to his son, rising from his chair. He bellowed for the boy in the other room to bring his clothes.

Uther left, and Sulwyn cleaned his station, taking his tools to the anteroom.

One of the guards awaited him, a liveried servant at his side. Hmm. Ioan, would be Sulwyn's guess.

"Ioan!" He piled the man with towels, soap and razor, vacating the antechamber as though he expected the surprised man to follow. "Fie on that Fallon. I'm just up from the valley. He told me to be here early for the king's shave, but clearly he didn't tell anyone." Sulwyn led the way, cursing his distinctive limp, to the wash tent, the suspicious guard remaining at his post by the king's hut in the growing light of dawn.

"Fallon knows nothing about this!" Ioan spluttered, trotting to keep up with Sulwyn. "You've entered the king's presence without authority!"

Two or three soldiers were making their way toward the mess tent and half a dozen servants now scurried through the compound. It was getting trickier and trickier to make his escape.

"Fallon said that?" Sulwyn reached the wash tent. "It's all a big mistake. Here. Let me dump this water and I'll meet you inside to explain. I need to take a piss, anyway." He stepped toward the edge of camp.

A glance over his shoulder confirmed that Ioan, shaking his head, had stepped into the wash tent.

Sulwyn limped as quickly as he could up the outhouse path, hoping no one in the waking camp would cast a glance his way. Or if they did, would not question his bucket. Ha.

The woods, low scrawny things, were an eternity away.

Sulwyn hobbled, the icy path treacherous beneath his stiff leg and stolen boots. He heard no sounds of pursuit, but did not turn to look.

Don't look up, he willed. *Don't look up. Do your duties without noticing anything unusual.*

The trees loomed closer.

Sulwyn stepped behind the outlier scrubs, still perfectly visible from the camp.

A shout went up in the distance behind him.

Piss! Did they have dogs? He hadn't seen any.

He hitched more quickly into the larger trees, slipping on a root.

A figure rose before him —

Meg.

She blew a powder in his face and chanted words of magic. "Walk fast," she said.

He dropped the pail, increased his gait, almost to a stumbling jog, and she kept pace with him. "I'm betting Fearghus doesn't know you're here," he said under his breath. "What's the powder?"

"A spell of concealment, but it won't work long and it won't cover our tracks."

Better than nothing. He took her hand and, limping, he ran.

CHAPTER 28

Meg raced, hand in hand with Sulwyn, through bright strips of cold sunshine and cool shadow, running, limping, dancing down among the hillside's sparse trees. Snow sparkled beneath their feet and the panorama of the Orumon valley spread below them. After a half candlemark of descent, the trees thickened and they panted along an animal trail paralleling the valley. "I can't believe it," Sulwyn kept muttering as she led the way back.

She smiled.

His voice, full of wonder, wafted behind her. "Everything, every color is brighter—"

This was how she felt.

"The air smells sweeter . . ."

She could not erase the foolish grin that had come over her in the grip of his euphoria. He was *alive*.

"Better than . . . better than whiskey."

There was no sign of pursuit. "Tell me. Everything."

He recounted each breath of the nerve-sharpening moments. She squealed with fright at his story, slowing to walk beside him and hold his hand when there was space, or prance at the significance of the information he had gathered. "And the curse!" she prompted. "You applied the curse." A subtle spell, the curse would strengthen over the next days and weeks, awaiting chance. Some event would prove fatal, a fall from a horse, a morsel of choking food, a bee sting.

"We're wearing away at the king's treasury," he said vehemently. "Artem can't maintain this level of spending. He can't. We're having an effect."

"And you're alive! You've escaped!" She took his two hands in hers and skipped a jig before him.

"But I wouldn't have. Not without your instructions." He grinned with giddiness at the audacity of their gamble.

"*You* had the stones to do it," she boasted. "To walk into the king's tent in broad daylight, and curse him, and steal his secrets, and then—walk out! He'll be dead within weeks. We've turned the tide of battle!"

Sulwyn stopped, panting with excitement. "But you saved me in the end, with your spell of concealment. You're brilliant!"

"Me?" She grinned, looking up into his face.

"Yes. You. You did it."

She flung her arms around his neck and fastened her lips to his.

And he kissed her back. A beautiful kiss. A passionate kiss. Stopped on the hillside, in the snow. Urgent, yet silken . . . tender and fiery all at once . . .

But—

She pushed back, her entire body suddenly aware of his. This was wrong. And . . . out of place.

He blinked, face flushed, confused.

"I . . ." She shook her head, unsure. "Can't."

Frowning puzzlement, he lifted a fingertip to caress her cheek, and his touch sent a tingle though her body.

She stepped back from him, as though from the edge of a precipice. What was wrong with her? Hadn't she wanted this to happen? Yes . . . she had. From the beginning, she had.

But things had changed. The image of Janat, framed in the doorway, sack in hand, blotted her vision.

A look of faint surprise and hurt touched Sulwyn's features. "It's Janat."

"No." Yes. No. It *should* have been Janat; it should have been Meg's loyalty to her sister. But . . . it wasn't that at all. "I thought . . ." What had she thought? She thought she could love him. Yes. But . . .

She didn't.

"I'm sorry," he apologized. "You must think I'm . . . " He shook his head. "A scoundrel."

"No. No . . ." He was glorious. Brave. Strong. Gentle. A rush of remorse overtook her at causing him pain.

"Janat and I . . ." He shrugged, and his expression grew distant, sad.

"I know." She did. It'd been clear to anyone with eyes. He had left her sister long ago. But . . . "I don't love you."

He frowned again, looked down, shuffling in the snow. Nodded without conviction.

She tried to take his hand, and he didn't resist, but did not grip her back. "I like you, Sulwyn. I admire you."

"We should go." He limped slowly down the track.

"It's the war." She felt a need to explain.

"You don't have to—"

"I want to. Sulwyn, I want . . . I want so many things." She followed him, spoke to his back. "I want to please my mother. Become magiel of the Amber." Though Mama had planned for Rennika to assume this mantle. "I want to serve my people. I want to serve my king. I want to see the work we've all put into this uprising succeed—"

He stopped in the snow. "You will."

She stopped behind him, still facing only his broad back.

He turned. "You have power." He held his jaw tight, and the lines of silver on his cheeks broke her heart. "You will. Do all those things."

He shook his head at her one more time, then turned and stalked down the hill in the snow.

Sulwyn had left as part of a small contingent to report his findings to Dwyn. Meg stayed with the camp, continuing to make potions to support the harry-and-run strategy.

She was writing out the curse Sulwyn used on Artem, on an unused corner of a page in her book, when Fearghus lifted the flap on her tent.

She finished a line. "I'm packed," she said without looking up. "I'll put this book in my saddle bag."

"It's not that."

She turned.

The upriser captain's stance was uncomfortable, silhouetted against the gray day. "I just came to tell you. You did a good job."

She blinked.

"You were right."

She opened her mouth to thank him but had no words.

"Keep up the good work." He nodded and left, letting the flap drop.

She sat back in her camp chair. Fearghus. Fearghus who thought she was nothing. A tool for creating potions and perhaps someday for magical prayer. To be kept in the background.

A warm glow spread through her. She could contribute. Her power was respected. She was one of them.

Coldridge.

Janat descended the dark stairs from the street to the tavern beneath the potter's shop. The door had been propped open; this, and a crack of a window, allowed smoke from the fire to escape when the stopped-up chimney would not. In spite of the smoke and chill draft in the tavern, however, locals, strumpets, refugees, and the occasional traveler crowded in for the cheer of good company and strong ale.

Sulwyn had told Janat to stay away from the cities.

Piss on Sulwyn.

After leaving Wildbrook, Janat had traveled at night from village to village, hiding during the day, unable to find work or respite from stares and whispers. When she reached Coldridge, she realized what she hadn't when she'd first come here with her sisters over a year ago: that cities were riddled with holes where misfits— including magiels—could hide. Even thrive.

Janat slipped into a dark corner of the ale house. She'd made an arrangement with the owner to sell charms for a share in the fee. There were those who didn't like the persecution of magiels which created a barrier to accessing spells. The harsher the soldiers became, the more willing taverners and landlords were—some of them—to shelter her. Knitting by the feel of her needles in the dim flicker of candlelight, she waited.

After a time, the proprietor's serving boy brought a girl to her corner. The girl, homely by any standards, stood self-consciously behind him.

Janat smiled at the girl—not much older than herself—as the serving boy disappeared.

The girl looked uncomfortably at the tables close by.

"Please, sit." Janat moved over on her bench.

Looking about, the girl slid beside her and bent her head low. "The innkeeper says you know a magiel?"

�֍

Janat undressed and hurried under her covers. The butcher's garret was chill and drafty in winter. Her stomach was full and she'd dropped five chetra into the mug on the table under the window. In the faint starlight shining through the attic window, Janat counted the coins in her mind. Five more, and she could stay another week. Another week closer to Mama's promise.

That was, if she didn't spend three on a bottle of whiskey, which she was sorely tempted to do. A nip after breathing in the smoke of the ganja she'd brought from Elsen floated her away from hunger and filth and loneliness. It took away bitter memories of her losses. Her mistakes. The disappointment she'd become.

Mama's promise.

So far away.

Or not so far away, perhaps. Eight weeks. Janat would follow Mama's plan: go to the tarn above the king's posting house on the road from Coldridge to Archwood. Mama had been interrupted before she could say why, but it must be to meet someone. Why else might she send them there? There could be no other reason. And who would they meet? A prince. It could only be a prince, with the prayer stone. Of course. But which royal could it be? Janat couldn't think how the Amber could come to a tiny mountain lake, but Mama had arranged it, so it must be. And then everything would go back to the way it was supposed to be. Janat only needed to survive until then.

And, tonight, she'd struck a bargain with that girl.

Women usually wanted love philters, or remedies, or potions to ensure the health of a child. Men sometimes wanted love potions, too—particularly the young men—and curses, or protections for their businesses. Janat played guessing games, trying to determine what each customer wanted. Wondered, too, if one young man or another looked at her with interest. But none of them was handsome. None was clever, or quietly honorable. None of them was Sulwyn.

Janat shook away the thought. She could not imagine lying with any man but Sulwyn.

This young girl. She wanted a curse.

Janat had been taken by surprise but not for long. The curse had been to kill a baby in the girl's belly before her father found out.

Janat had wondered what led to the girl wanting to kill her baby. Did she have a lover her father didn't approve of? Or had she been attacked, like so many Janat had known?

A curse to kill a baby without harming the mother was a delicate thing. It could be made of simple ingredients, but the best ones used magiel magic, which would mean Janat would be unable to work for a time as she recovered from disturbing her time stream.

Such a curse should bring in at least five chetra, maybe more.

Janat huddled under her covers, trying to stay warm.

Five chetra. To live a week longer. To subsist through the winter, until spring.

CHAPTER 29

The night had been cold and temperamental, but the morning's half-light crept onto the mountain, clear and still. It was King Artem's forward sentries, used to long stretches of watching a dead wall, who saw the refugees first, staggering through the snow.

In the stone hut that Father had reserved for his captains in the advance camp, Huwen Delarcan tossed aside his blankets, waking in the dark before sunrise with an inexplicable sense of foreboding. When the sentry came to him, he was already awake. He dressed and plunged into the crystal dawn, still fastening his yak skin coat.

He hurried forward with the sentries to help the skeletal people, dressed in rags, blue with cold. For a city the size of Archwood, the straggle seemed pitifully thin. This was it? After a year and a half, the carn had been defeated—without a battle? "I'll inform His Majesty," Huwen told the sentries, and hastened back to wake his father and his generals.

"Assemble a forward company. Archers, infantry, and war machines," Father ordered his commander. They stood, silent, in the mountain's shadow under a brightening sky. "Bring up the troops from the lower valley."

"King or magiel must be dead, then," the commander said into the pristine quiet, "with no one to wield the Amber."

"I'll secure the prisoners," a captain suggested. At Father's nod, he turned to his lieutenant. "Fetch me a scribe and I will interrogate them."

In short order, a company was assembled with Father at its head. Huwen marched at his side, and Uther came behind. They trudged through snow and disquiet, along the narrow treacherous road, and gathered before the city gates as the sky sharpened to a profound cerulean.

The parapets were empty, the tall stone walls, silent and still. The gate stood open, and no sentry challenged them. The main road through the city was devoid of people. Even starved dogs or rats still lurking in the shadows had become wary.

Father waited as companies of men fanned through the city to engage any resistance, but the messengers returned to report no movement in the city. No soldiers in the streets, no archers in the windows. As the sun rose, Huwen followed his father into Archwood.

The city was dead.

Buildings stood intact, signs above shop doors rattling in a faint breeze, but no movement, no sound could be heard above the crunch of their own boots in the snow. A rat skittered along a wall, the click of its claws unnaturally loud; a crow watched silently from a rooftop. The stench of unburied dead drifted on the air, but their search turned up few corpses, and most of them frozen; the citizens must have died in stages, while those who could dig graves remained.

Huwen looked over his shoulder. Nothing.

The king's company marched to the castle, and the fortress's gates swung on unoiled hinges, their screech reverberating in the eerie quiet. The chill of death settled on all of them, and no one spoke as they entered the great hall's large double doors. A nameless uneasiness crept into Huwen's bones. The walls echoed as they moved from room to room.

It had been a long time since Huwen had been here. He might have been eight or nine. He'd played in the garden with Uther and Eamon, and with those girls—Faris Olivin, and Meghra Falkyn, and the pretty one, Janatelle. Uncle Ean's cooks had fed them strips of seared goat, a local food, hot and dripping with juices—

Their silent inspection stilled at the sound of shouts and ringing steel. Their soldiers must have met someone still living. They waited, listening, but the clash was over within minutes. A messenger reported that a final guard had attacked them in the throne room, but these had been dispatched without delay.

Father and the others mounted the steps to the family's private suites. Huwen followed, heavy reluctance filling his legs as they covered their noses and inspected personal rooms. Some of the courtiers and children lay in their beds; others, no doubt, lay in graves.

King Ean, his queen, and his magiel were in the banquet room. Huwen's uncle, handsome and jovial, always fair-minded. He sat on a chair, cradling his daughter. Faris. Huwen's cousin, not yet a young woman—so thin. So thin. Though not an expert in such matters, he thought she might have died first, his uncle grieved to see his daughter taken from him. The queen, Huwen's aunt, her indulgent smiles gone, was draped over her husband and child, a slash and gout of dried blood beneath her chin, knife in her hand.

Talanda Falkyn, separated a little from the other two, sat on a chair, wan and stiff, only candlemarks beyond life, blood on her arms and dress not yet faded to brown. She'd always frightened him, with eyes that seemed to see nothing on this sphere. Eyes that remained open. But where were Meghra and Janatelle, and that little girl magiel? They must be dead, too. Huwen wondered if they'd been buried, or if he would see them laid out on their beds. Or worse.

Huwen's eyes burned, and he looked up at his father. *Leave this place.*

"King Ean must have died of the curse of disease." The commander's words grated, harsh against the silence. "With no person of the blood of the Line of Kings, Talanda could no longer use the Amber. She and the queen took their own lives rather than surrender."

Tears shone on Father's cheeks. "They will be buried. Properly. With all the mourning and ceremony befitting their rank," he said in a husky voice. "And then we leave this place."

The commander nodded.

Get out! Get out! Through force of will, Huwen kept his feet from running away.

"One more thing." Father indicated the bodies of King Ean and Magiel Falkyn. "The Amber."

The final prayer stone. To be sacrificed to the One God.

"It is our sole purpose for being here."

Huwen watched in horror as his father bent over the dead king. Father reached out a hand, hesitated, then touched the cold flesh of his youngest brother.

A wail rose up. The despoilers startled, hands to hilts. Huwen peered uneasily around the gilded room, gloomy within thick stone walls. Nothing stirred. The paintings hung on the walls, silent. The furniture sat on the intricate parquet, unmoving.

"Only the wind." Father's voice, harsh.

But a chill had entered the room; a cold deeper than the wintry weather, that penetrated Huwen's bones and lodged in him a fear he could not name.

His father's face pinched. The commander's gaze swept the room, his complexion pale. The soldiers shifted nervously.

Father resumed his search, feeling for the chain about the king's neck from which the prayer stone would hang.

Nothing.

He patted the corpse's pockets, reached inside the clothing.

It was all Huwen could do to remain in the room, keep from shrieking out in madness.

His father stepped back. "The prayer stone is not here," he said emphatically, his voice shaking.

The commander, though a brave man, looked sick. He nodded at Talanda Falkyn.

Visibly steeling himself, Father moved to the place where Talanda, the shimmer of her skin absent in death, slumped to one side in her chair.

The cold deepened, an agonizing ache in the bones. Frost appeared on Huwen's breath. On his father's breath; Uther's; the others'.

Again, Father hesitated. Then, deliberately, he felt for the prayer stone's chain at Talanda's neck.

Was it a trick of the shadows, or did the magiel grimace? No, that was not possible. She was dead. Huwen knew she was dead.

Father startled.

His gaze snapped to Talanda's open eyes, and he looked momentarily as if he were about to speak. Then he blinked rapidly, the muscles of his face spasming as if in pain. And still, Talanda's frozen face seemed to smile.

"Father?" Huwen's throat was tight, his voice a croak.

"It's nothing." Father released his touch, but his stare clung, bewitched.

Leave this place!

There was no chain.

Father shook himself and withdrew.

For a moment no one moved, and it seemed to Huwen the room took a breath of relief.

Then Father felt beneath the magiel's white robes for the treasure. Huwen turned away, sickness rising from his stomach.

But the prayer stone was not there.

The men shifted. *Get out!* Huwen's mind screamed.

Father straightened and turned briskly toward the banquet room door, and with audible relief, the rest followed at his heels. "Commander," he ordered. "Dispatch men to search the city for spies or soldiers. Turn the castle upside down. Find the Amber."

The chill of fear lessened when they left the keep, but it did not dissipate. They waited in the bailey, the shuffle of feet echoing from the castle walls. A page brought Father some water. He removed his helm to drink, then turned to thank the boy.

With a sigh, a feathered shaft appeared in Father's neck.

He frowned, surprised, raised a hand as if to pluck it from the dribble of red sprouting from the spot. Then he crumpled and fell.

A cry sprang up and men whirled, those nearest crouching to attend him, archers nocking arrows and aiming at the walls and windows above, swordsmen springing to hunt, others taking cover.

Huwen dropped to his knees and took up his father's hand, disbelief blooming in his chest. Blood welled from the wound.

His father blinked rapidly as a double line of men pushed Huwen back and, linking arms beneath his father, lifted him as a unit to carry him into the shelter of the great hall, a young soldier— no, *Uther*—pressing on the wound. A guard of his best men led the way, pushing through the opulent chambers and up to a royal suite with a generous canopy bed. Huwen scrambled after them, fear's grip hardening in his stomach.

The Holder of Histories hurried ahead and found linens to bind the gash around the arrow.

Then the men backed away, and his father, bewildered and pinched with pain, the pillow beneath him red, took Huwen's hand. "Huw . . ." He struggled to focus.

No—

The Holder stepped forward and unfastened the collar at his father's throat. His death token.

Dread turned Huwen's bowels to water.

The Holder laid the death token on his father's tongue.

Huwen wanted to leap up, cry out, shake his father, shake the Holder, turn back the sand glass—

A gentle breeze, scented with snow, wafted through the open windows. Father's eyes turned glassy, his mouth slack.

This . . . could not be. Only a moment ago, when? Only . . .

The Holder laid his fingers on Father's neck, just above the offending shaft. He waited.

No one in the room moved.

"The king is dead," he said quietly. "Long live the king."

CHAPTER 30

Janat rubbed her eyes. The stitches in the small clothes she was sewing for the wine merchant's wife two streets over had begun to blur. Her tallow candle was burning low, and bed beckoned. She put her sewing away, corked the whiskey bottle, stretched, used the chamber pot, and removed her robe. She crawled between the frigid sheets.

But her ruse to entice sleep by overtiring herself came to naught.

The moment she pinched the candle out, the image of the girl—the one she'd given the curse to, to kill her baby—came to her, the way Janat had seen her that afternoon. Beaten. A black eye, swollen closed. A bruise on her jaw. Holding one arm tight to her body.

Who would beat a young girl? Janat knew.

It'd been tricky to create a curse to protect the mother while killing the child. But the girl looked well when Janat had seen her outside the chandler's shop yesterday. The girl wouldn't stop to speak where she could be seen talking to a magiel, of course. But she'd thanked Janat with her eyes and with a nod of gratitude.

Something had happened between yesterday and today.

A small sound—the door flew open.

Janat scrambled up, blankets wrapped to cover her.

Soldiers sprang into the room, a chaos of shouts and footfalls. "That's her." Behind the soldiers, a plainly-dressed farmer or tradesman pointed at her.

A scream caught in her throat. The farmer looked fleetingly familiar—

The soldiers surrounded Janat's bed and two gripped her arms.

The man disappeared through the door.

Roughly they jostled her through the door and down the dark staircase. She squealed, her heart racing. The stink of the soldiers filled her nostrils. Fingers of iron gripped her biceps, her feet barely touching the steps.

And then she was out of the butcher's home and tossed in nothing more than her chemise and small clothes onto the icy boards of a cart. She yelped as one of the soldiers yanked her arm, rolling her onto her face, and catching her other flailing wrist, tied her hands with rough rope behind her back. Splinters and straw scratched her face.

The wagon creaked under the soldier's weight as he ensconced himself behind her. The others mounted their horses and the cart jerked into motion. Janat screamed, trying to sit up.

A mailed glove cuffed the side of her head, a disorienting blow, and the cart rattled over the ice.

�֎

Janat woke to the stinging touch of a cloth gently dabbing at her forehead. She tried to rise.

"Shh." Someone leaned over her in the barely perceptible light that filtered through a small window in the door of a large cold room. She could make out the forms of a few huddled bodies in the straw. Two others—women—sat near her, looking on.

"It's nothing. Only a scrape," the woman with the bit of damp cloth said, as much to calm Janat as to inform the other two.

"Where am I?" But she knew. The interminable journey last night had not taken her far from the butcher's attic. The cart had climbed a maze of streets, passed through castle gates, and stopped in a small bailey. She'd been forced down several flights of steps in wild torchlight and shoved into this dirt-floored cellar. The ropes around her wrists had been removed, and she'd shivered in the straw as one of the soldiers tossed a blanket over her. The door clanged shut, and the light beyond the peephole gradually faded to inky dark.

In the silence of skittering rats and the wheeze of its human occupants, Janat searched her memory to try to discover what her crime had been. And . . . where she'd seen the farmer whose pointing finger had accused her.

She'd never seen him before. But he had the look of the young girl who'd bought the curse. The one who'd been beaten.

Which was the answer. Of course. It had been only a matter of time before Janat sold a spell to the wrong customer.

"Artem's castle in Coldridge," the woman nursing Janat responded. She sat back and exchanged glances with the other two. "You slept late. You've missed the first meal."

Janat hadn't known she was hungry until the woman mentioned food. She struggled to sit up. She could guess why she was here, but why the others? "What was your crime?" she asked the woman who'd tended her.

"Being magiel." There was a pause. "And a woman."

Janat looked around the cell again. It was too dark to see if everyone had the inconstant skin of a magic wielder.

The equinox.

Gods—she could not miss the equinox—

Survive, Mama had said. The one thing—the *one* thing—Janat lived for, the end to all of Shangril's disputes and inequities—

She had to get out.

A scrape of footsteps on cobbles made them turn. The ruddy glow of firelight grew in the small rectangle looking out onto the corridor.

The footsteps stopped as keys jangled against metal and the door swung open. Janat shielded her eyes and crouched. The woman beside her put a hand on her arm. Two soldiers planted themselves on either side of the door as a third ordered them to form a line against one wall. He carried a beating stick.

Janat moved. Once they had emerged from the straw, Janat was surprised to discover there were more individuals—magiel women—than she'd thought: eight or ten. The soldier walked down the line, pulling each woman's face, one at a time, into the light of his torch. Janat eyed the guarded doorway. So close.

Three of them were shoved away from the wall, all with the most volatile of complexions. These, the soldier viewed a second time and selected one—a comely woman—to take from the cell. The other soldiers closed the door behind them.

Janat slumped back to the straw. She hadn't been brave enough to run. Foolish enough.

One of the women muttered under her breath, "And not one has come back."

Wenid jerked out of his doze in the anteroom of the women's chamber. The squall of a baby.

The candle on the table beside him had burned away to a nub and the excited chatter of women's voices percolated through the far door. The drapes had not been drawn over the glassed windows and a spray of stars glinted in the blackness. Perhaps one chime, by the shrine bells, not later. He straightened in his chair and rubbed the sleep from his eyes. It had been only four days since he'd accompanied young Prince Eamon to Heaven with the Ruby, praying for death tokens, and he was not yet fully recovered.

He did not have long to wait for one of the midwives to bustle from the room and curtsey before him.

"Boy or girl?" Wenid asked. A girl would be preferable: more powerful, at least in female things such as whelping the next generation of magiels.

"A fine, healthy boy," the woman beamed.

Well. Five more women were with child. And Gweddien Barcley could provide his talents again.

"He is a good size," she reported, "and he has all his fingers and toes. He nursed immediately, which is a good sign that he will thrive."

Better and better. "How does the mother?"

"She's tired but gave the full afterbirth and is not bleeding too much."

"Then the mother will live?" A healthy mother was more likely to raise a healthy child.

"She should be just fine."

Wenid climbed to his feet. "Good. I'll send a messenger to the king." Artem would be relieved—as was Wenid. Another step toward solidifying the one God's supremacy on this lowest sphere of earth. And, to confirm Wenid's place as the king's chancellor.

"Come to me immediately, if there should be any problem with child or mother."

The midwife hesitated. "Sire. The mother asked me to plead with you."

He turned, his hand on the door knob, cautious.

"She wants to know . . ." The woman wiped her hands on her bloodstained apron. "She wants to know how long she will have with the child."

Women were apt to become difficult when it came to separating them from their children, to the detriment of both. It was best she be calm in these critical few days and weeks. "You may tell her I have no heart to take her child from her."

The midwife's relief was evident. "Thank you, My Lord. The woman will—"

"But much depends on her." He would have to have this conversation with the woman, but not now.

The midwife's apprehension returned. "Upon what shall I tell her this privilege depends? She is distressed, My Lord."

Wenid rubbed his forehead. Piss. This conversation should come later. Or, perhaps he should have had it with her before. "Simply her compliance."

"She will want to know—"

"The child's power. She was instructed to endow him with magical strength." Though, there would be no way to ascertain this for some time, likely years. The youngest magiel in history—a magiel of the Amethyst almost two hundred years ago—had taken his position at the age of eight, though his king had refrained from allowing him to use the prayer stone until he was fourteen. Even so, the child had died before his twentieth birthday. Taking on magiel duties later rather than earlier was undoubtedly wiser. The child would have much to learn.

The midwife curtseyed.

"And she is not to instruct him on politics, religion, history . . . nothing." By the One, he would have to make a list. And have the mother watched. "No children's tales or songs or games that have not been approved." Sooner or later, though, they would have to be separated.

The midwife's tiny frown and nod gave him to understand that she comprehended his meaning. "I will inform the mother. I have no doubt but that she will agree." She curtseyed again. "Do you wish to name the child, Your Grace?"

Wenid considered. "Call him Dannle." His father's name.

"And a surname?"

"Lock." No reason. Or, perhaps, a wish to finalize his grand work.

Meg's fingers stilled on the pot of mushrooms, and she counted them for the third time. Thirty-four. She dipped her quill in the tiny pot of ink and got the number down on her precious sheet of paper before she drifted off again. By Kyaju, she was tired. The smoky candle flickered in the gusts of wind and rain that slapped her tent, making the bins and jars of ingredients she had collected jump and dance. Harder to count.

There were five hundred uprisers already camped here in the woods, a day's ride south of Coldridge, and more arriving daily. She needed to make scores of charms—mostly worldling potions— but some would need to be more powerful and magical. Dwyn Gramaret was rumored to be bringing a thousand men from Canyondell, and who knew how many Sulwyn would bring. She was to arm a special cadre of light infantry with curses to be delivered at close range, and all the troops would need Heartspeed, likely for many days running.

Sulwyn had left the upriser camp in the Orumon valley the same day he'd uncovered the priceless information in King Artem's high camp. The details he'd discovered were critical to the uprisers' mission, and Dwyn Gramaret needed to hear them directly from him as soon as possible.

Meg hadn't seen him since. A messenger came from Dwyn Gramaret two weeks later. An attack. On Coldridge. A big one, but no details about why Coldridge, or why now. Fearghus led them out of the Orumon valley, and she'd been here ever since, doing what she did best, and waiting for her king to call for her.

But winter softened and days lengthened, and the tarn haunted Meg's thoughts. She'd have to let Fearghus know she was leaving, but the timing was bad: the equinox fell just about the time the upriser armies were to be assembled. He wouldn't be happy. And Dwyn. She didn't want to fail him. But her first loyalty had to be to Mama.

Then, the news came.

Archwood had fallen. And, therefore, Orumon had fallen.

Mama. King Ean. Everyone she knew there was dead. The Amber, like all the other prayer stones, had been crushed. A public ceremony. No question, the messenger said.

Her rage, oddly, filled her with fire and hate but did not escape to energize her muscles or flinch her expression. Even the report of Artem's inevitable death, from a single well-placed arrow, gave her no joy. She'd sat after listening to the messenger, listening to the questions and debate and speeches. Numb on the outside. Hopeless inside.

Everything. Everything she'd worked for, believed in. Gone.

Except her work with the uprisers.

Meg crouched, shivering, in a doorway next to a cobbled lane as the sun rose. A few early risers brought carts up the street to what might have been a market square. What city, Meg didn't know, though something about the place seemed familiar. She was too tired to try to work it out. No one approached her. She must look like one of the many homeless refugees sleeping in corners, now so common.

Then—

She was running down a muddy street beneath overhanging buildings, almost out of breath, in a rainstorm. Janat, dressed in rags, ran ahead of her, slipping in the mud, dodging around a corner. Gods, she was usually careful to hide herself away after using magic, some place safe. She willed her flagging body to sprint, round the corner behind her sister. A jog, and the alley opened out into a wider street. No place to hide, here—

And she jerked awake among sheepskins on a pallet in a canvas tent. Winter sunshine glimmered through canvas joins, and someone sat nearby, a silhouette. Her tent in Fearghus's camp, though whether she was back in her own time or not, she had no idea.

"Meg?" The voice was Sulwyn's. She must be close to her own time. She'd heard he'd joined the camp late yesterday afternoon. She let her eyes slip closed. Gods, she was exhausted.

"Are you here?"

Sleep. If only she could sleep. "Yes." She tried to speak, but the word came out, faint, even in her own ears.

He lifted her head and she smelled the beer on his breath, felt the cold metal of a cup at her lips. She brought up a hand to guide it. She was thirsty, and the icy water was sweet. She lay back. "Thank you."

"Dwyn was worried about you."

Dwyn? "He's away."

"He's here. Arrived two days ago."

Two days . . .

"I've been here three."

She rubbed her face with her hands. "How long . . . until we attack?" She had spells to make. Dozens, perhaps hundreds.

He pushed her back onto her pallet with a gentle hand. "You're not to worry about that. You've been working too hard." He turned and spoke to someone outside the tent. When he returned, it was with a small wooden tripod and pillows to create a back rest for her. "By all reports, you haven't left this tent for near a week."

She looked at the chamber pot in the corner. She smelled no waste in the close confines, so it must be clean.

A boy arrived with a steaming bowl, filling the space with a savory aroma. She was famished. She sat up and took the trencher, spooning delicious gravy and turnips into her mouth.

"Good." Sulwyn sat back. "King Gramaret's armies need potions, but not every one must be made with magic. He needs you to be alert and awake when the attack comes."

She flicked her gaze up at him and stuffed a bit of flat bread into her mouth. He looked good. Thin and unshaven, but everyone in the upriser camp was all thin. He sat back at the foot of her pallet, and spoke as though the moment in the woods had never happened.

"Actually, I'm surprised . . . you're here." He gave her a curious look, the statement almost a question.

She gave him a small frown of puzzlement and washed her meal back with water.

"The equinox is only three weeks away."

Mama's plan. The defeat she'd shoved from her mind, the shock she'd worked so hard to repress, flooded back. "The Amber was smashed," she said bitterly.

"Was it?" His words in the gloom were not a query but a challenge. "How do you know?"

She shot him a black look. "Don't mock me, Sulwyn." Again, she saw the Amethyst. On the granite stone before the castle in Coldridge. Shattered under a sledgehammer.

"And . . . if Artem, or his advisors, didn't find the Amber in Archwood, do you think they would admit it?" he asked. "Or might they find another gem close enough to the Amber to be mistaken at a distance?"

She stared at him.

He shrugged. "I don't know."

Could this be true?

"But I wouldn't fail to meet your obligations to your mother based on a rumor. Especially one announced by Artem. Or Huwen."

CHAPTER 31

Rennika had roamed no more than a few days' travel from Colin's hut all winter, but when he twisted his ankle and they had exhausted their winter's supply of flour, Colin had no choice but to fit his snowshoes to her feet and send her to Highglen with her winter's weaving to sell.

Though the sun shone fitfully between flying clouds, and the gurgle of melt water ran beneath the snow down sun-freed rock, spring had not yet laid claim to this high valley. It was past noon when she entered through the upper gate used by highlanders bringing wool and milk and meat for trade, a sack of fabric heavy on her shoulders.

Within the gate, close to the castle, stood the largest, richest houses. The occasional grocer or butcher carried sacks or guided flocks or carts pulled by sturdy mountain ponies through the trampled snow, supplying the cooks of the petty aristocracy. Rennika's gaze climbed the castle walls, lingering on the turrets within. Once, she'd stood at windows of glass like these and looked out over the jumble of rooftops, and down on workers in the street. Not once had she been curious about them.

Now, she wondered if Hada Delarcan stood at one of those windows and looked down on her, or if the princess was far away in Holderford with her mother. Rennika'd only met Hada once. She remembered King Artem's youngest daughter as a spoiled child. Hada had only been nine when the war started.

No matter. Rennika bore her bundle down the icy cobbles in pig fat–coated boots, through softening snow, heading toward the lower town where artisans, tradesmen, and pedlars bought and sold their goods. A street branching from the main road opened onto a square where a gaggle of townspeople gossiped by a well. Here, amongst the signs for cobblers, butchers, chandlers, fletchers, and furriers, Rennika found a shop that sold dyed fabric.

"Hello," a friendly voice greeted her. "I've seen you before." A man—or a boy a few years older than Rennika—stood in the door to the shop, his smiling face freckled and curious. Over his loose pants he wore a bleached linen shirt, open at the collar, sleeves rolled up despite the cold. His hair, a wiry copper red, was neatly tied with a ribbon at his neck.

Rennika searched her memory. "I—don't think so."

"Sure! I remember you. You came here with Colin Cutter when he bartered his yearlings last fall." He leaned on the jamb. "And in the summer, too. I've seen you." He grinned, and his eyes flicked briefly to the crowd by the well, then returned to her.

His smile made her laugh.

"You're a summer girl." He crossed his arms over his chest. "Why don't I see you in the winter? Colin comes down sometimes."

"I tend his place."

"Aha. You smell like a yak herder." His eyes glinted. "Yak dung cook fire?"

She blushed.

"My name is Yon."

She smiled. "Rennika."

He tilted his head. "Unusual name."

She shrugged, but before she could think of anything to reply, he lifted the weight of her bundle from her shoulders.

"Here, that's heavy." He set it on the doorstep. "You're a weaver?"

"Yes."

He lifted a corner of the bundle and flipped through the upper layers with a practiced eye. "You must be looking for my master. You've come to sell your wares?"

"Yes. You're an apprentice—textile trader?"

"Sure am." He brought the bundle into the shop and Rennika followed. "Almost a journeyman."

Her eyes adjusted to the low light.

"Stay here. I'll fetch my master."

Before she could respond, Yon disappeared back into the common.

The shop was narrow, its walls lined with shelves stacked haphazardly with a scattering of fabrics, mostly undyed yak wool, but bleached and dyed wool, too, and linen, and a few swatches of rare fabrics that looked as though they might've been cotton and silk. It was a long time since she'd seen and worn—such rare fabrics. A door led to a back room with vats for bleaching and dying, and a staircase, likely to the master's living quarters and his apprentice's attic.

"So, what have we got?" A burly, balding man strode into the shop, Yon trotting behind him. Without looking at Rennika, the master opened her bundle. He flicked through the stack of folded fabrics, stopping to point to one. "Knots," he said. He nudged his apprentice. "Here. And here. Look."

Yon nodded.

The trader flipped down the stack and setting the top several pieces aside, pulled a length of fabric from the rest and looked closely at the weave. "Threads of different thicknesses. See? Here?" He opened the piece out and held it up. "Weave is uneven." He lowered the fabric. "You're lucky," he said to Rennika. "It's early yet. Not many yak herders down from the hills. How many pieces?"

"Twenty-four."

He thrust his tongue into his cheek. "I always pay the women too much. Twenty-four chetra."

"Twenty-four—"

The trader took a purse from his belt and gave it to Yon. "Put the bundle in back with the others. We may be able to do something with the best pieces." He nodded at Rennika. "Yak wool. Very common." He strode back out into the square.

"For the whole—"

Yon took her hand, palm up, and counted the chetra from his master's purse. "There you are." He smiled.

Her stomach churned. "It was my whole winter," she managed. "My whole . . ." Her throat closed off and her eyes prickled.

Yon's smile faltered. "The yaks are shedding. You'll strip good under wool before summer. Come back in a few weeks. Maybe you can get a better price."

She shook her head, unable to speak. In Seedmarket, she'd heard that good Gramarye wool was worth a fortune. She turned and gripped her money, not wanting him to see how her face burned. She had to find her way out of the shop, out where she could breathe.

She stumbled into the snow.

Too many people hovered about the well, gossiping. She turned back the way she'd come, toward the main road. There was no question of staying the night in an inn, and Ide was ill and Rennika couldn't impose. She must return to Colin's hut before the sun sank lower. As it was, she would arrive long after dark. It would be a cold night, and one with no supper.

She stopped where the lane met the road and wiping her nose, took a deep breath. What would she say to Colin?

"Wait! Rennika!" Yon's voice, behind her.

She turned in confusion. Had she left something behind?

He caught up to her, his steps slowing.

She swallowed back the tears and tried to look presentable.

"Do you need work?"

She looked at him. "What?"

"My master needs a job doing. I can do it—"

"I have to get back."

He held up his master's purse. "Five chetra."

Five—

"It won't take long. And it's easy."

"Doing what?" she asked suspiciously.

He smiled and turned back down the lane. "Trader work. Buying and selling. The work I do."

She caught up to him. "Why don't you do it, then?"

He pushed his thumbs into the top of his pants. "I can. I will, in fact. But I think you could be good at it. I can show you how."

She walked beside him. Five chetra. That would take the sting out of her loss, a little. "Why? Why would you do that for me?"

He stopped in the street. He looked toward the crowd at the well. Night would come on too quickly. She needed to go. "I should—"

He put a hand on her arm. "My master wasn't fair."

She felt her nostrils widen. Heat flashed in her chest. The master stood amongst the other craftsmen, arguing.

Yon's hand stayed her from marching over to the well. "Listen. It wasn't fair, but you agreed to it. I think he expected you to barter. Most yak men barter pretty fiercely. You took the money, so the contract's sealed. He'd call it . . ." He shrugged. "A lesson."

Ranuat.

"He'll get more than what he paid you on his first trade, even without bleaching or dying. In fact, if I make the trade, right now, without bothering him, he'll give me half the profit. If you do the work—make the trade—I'll give it to you. Five chetra, I swear."

"But—you could have the money. Why . . ."

"Come on. Before I change my mind." He led her back into the shop.

The fabric lay on the table where she'd left it. Yon bundled it up again and lifted it onto her back. "This way." He led her though the back into an alley and by a circuitous route to the main road. "First of all," he said as they walked down the hill, "our shop is the first one you came to."

"I was looking for others when you—"

"Never mind that. The best traders know which shops to go to. I'll bring you to one I know, where the old man will give you a good price. Second, you start the trading. Tell him you're offering him a bargain at four chetra apiece."

"Four!"

"And when he offers you one, act insulted and close up your bundle. I know other shops if this one doesn't work out. Leave."

Four chetra! How could—but she nodded, stumbling to keep up to his quick pace. "Leave. Yes."

"But don't leave too soon. He'll come around, make another offer. Tell him your mother is sick and you have to care for the twin babies—"

"That's a lie."

He stopped in amazement. "You want your money?"

She blinked. This was pickpursing. Only with words.

"Then tell him you haven't eaten more than a crust since the last blizzard." He eyed her. "That's true enough, isn't it?"

She laughed in puzzlement. "You're funny."

He grinned and led the way into a side street. "Remember, if you're to get the five chetra I promised, you can't settle for less than thirty-four for the bundle."

Rennika shook her head and followed him to a row of shops.

Yon stopped her. He looked her over with a practiced eye, pulled a bit of her hair over one eye to give her a more bedraggled look and pointed her toward a shop with a weaver's sign over the door. "Remember. None of the other yak men have come down from the meadow yet. Too much snow. The shops have only the dregs of last year's fabric to sell. And Highglen is known all over Shangril for its wool." He gave her a nudge. "Do it."

So she went.

He was waiting in the street, jerkin pulled tightly around him against the coming chill of night, when she returned with five gultra and twenty-two chetra.

She stopped in front of him. "You were right. On every point. He paid *three* chetra apiece."

His freckled face lit up. "I told you. I'm almost a journeyman."

"And what will make you a journeyman?"

He ran his tongue across his teeth. "The money to prove my worth to one of the lords." He held out his hand.

She lifted a finger. "Twenty-four chetra for the bundle." She placed the two gultra and four chetra in his hand. "Half the profit for your master—" She counted out another two gultra and four chetra. "If I take five, you get nineteen."

His lips moved and his thumb touched each finger on his left hand. He nodded. "You've a head for numbers. You'd make a good trader, with a little training."

"But I did the work. I should get more than five."

He stepped back, a wary smile on his lips. "But you agreed to five. One thing a trader does, whatever else he may do. Honor the contract."

"But you knew I could get more than ten chetra profit. I look pitiable and the old man knows you."

He held out his hand, brow raised in expectation. "If you wish to join a band of thieves, I can direct you there as well."

She wilted. She gave him the money.

He put the money in his purse. "I need my journeymanship."

She let out a deep breath. Still, she had five more chetra than she had before.

But twilight had descended around them. She didn't relish returning to Colin's hut in the dark, followed, perhaps, by the thieves so recently referenced.

Yon looked down at the snow. "I'll tell you what."

She tilted her head.

"A bard's come up from Zellora. He's at the inn near my master's shop. From *my* nineteen chetra I'll buy you a bowl of soup." He peered at her roguishly from beneath an eyebrow.

She laughed. She liked him. He was like a good-natured fox.

"Hungry?"

"Starving!"

He held out his elbow with great exaggeration, as though he were a king, and she were a lady. She took his arm and walked with him, the warmth of his shoulder driving away the cold of winter's final blast.

❖

The tavern Yon took Rennika to was a good one, with glass windows, several tables, and chairs with backs. The only taverns Rennika had been to were dark, low-ceiled, smoky places with trestle tables and benches.

But today, the room was exceedingly crowded with locals, gaffers and tradesmen, mothers with babies, and children chasing one another underfoot. With the bard about to make his appearance any time, she and Yon had to eat their rice and lentils standing up, their mugs resting on a recessed shelf along one wall. The food was tasty and filling, and the dumplings stuffed with sausage—by far the best meal Rennika could remember having since coming to Gramarye. And it didn't hurt that Yon entertained her throughout by pointing out each trader and imitating his voice or identifying him with a tidbit or scandal. And Yon told Rennika the gossip at the well: the high king was dead.

King Artem Delarcan. She remembered him, a little.

Dead. This was the day Meg had been waiting for.

"Here he comes," someone shouted, and the buzz rose. Some of the onlookers cheered.

Above the heads of the gossipers, a raised hand holding a lute made its way across the room. It sank behind the crush, and the chatter subsided. The sound of strings being plucked and tuned filtered through the room. "If Highglen and Zellora ever decide to compete for the most snow, Highglen will win without contest," the bard announced, and a ripple of laughter ran about the room.

"In Theurgy, the roads that aren't cobbled are mud, and in Arcan, farmers are planting." The bard strummed his lute. "Listen well, my friends," he said, and the chatter in the room fell away. "You may have heard rumors."

"The king's dead!" someone shouted out and there was a general cheer.

"I'm here to bring you tidings," the bard called out over the commotion, and the audience settled. "The significance in Gramarye and all throughout Shangril is far-reaching."

He sang.

Artem Delarcan, Arcan's lord
Fell to the One God's last reward
Huwen, grieving by his side
Took up the crown with valiant stride.

Born a prince in Holderford—

"I'll bet Huwen wasn't at his father's side." A young man squeezed in by Yon's elbow. "I'd wager my winter's earnings he was plotting with his chancellors to raise taxes."

"Like father, like son," Yon whispered.

"How do you know? The bard said Prince Huwen was there," Rennika said.

The apple-cheeked boy looked curiously at her. "Who's your friend?"

Yon grinned and put his arm around her shoulder, drawing her into the crook of his armpit. "Rennika, Miach," he introduced them. "Miach's an apprentice tanner. That's why he stinks."

"Don't listen to him. Tanning's a good profession." He touched her ale mug with his, by way of greeting.

"Shh!" A black-bearded man scowled at them.

"Shh, yourself," Miach said under his breath—low enough for his words to travel no farther than Rennika—and turned back to the bard.

Yon left his arm about her shoulder, and the effect on her was at once thrilling and frightening.

Long he sieged the traitor's hold
Till Archwood fell, as he foretold.
Pierced by final rebel's shaft,
He gave his life—

"Archwood!" a voice rang out. "Orumon!"

The word fell like a hammer on Rennika's heart, and the dark surrounding her closed in, a vibrating blackness. *Fallen.*

Mama. Home.

As if it had been a command, the bard's song fell to nothing in the resounding silence.

Archwood, breached by the siege. Mama was dead.

It was not a question. Mama would have died, rather than give up the citadel to Artem. Even if by some chance she was not dead before the royal troops arrived, no magiel of the line was allowed to live.

So.

Mama was dead. Tears knotted in Rennika's throat.

Rennika's home, the home of her childhood, was gone. King Ean. Faris. The children she'd played with. The maids and the cooks and the stable boys.

Yon's arm around her shoulder was the only solid thing in the world.

And Nanna. Nanna was dead, too. Nanna, who'd sung to her and rocked her as a baby, told her stories, taught her to read.

Meg and Janat. Taken from her. Somewhere in the seven countries of Shangril. If they were still alive.

After a time, the bard's lute began again to softly strum, and his voice was clear in the stunned silence.

. . . Amber, the final stone
Was brought before the good king's throne.

An undercurrent of voices began to murmur.

Crushed beneath the hammer's weight,

The swell of grumbling rose.

It joined the other pray'r stones' fate.

The din drowned out the bard's song.
"The last one!"
"Smashed—"
"Our Gods are stolen!"

All around them, people began to shift and gesticulate, angrily throwing down complaints, incidents and insults perpetrated by the imposition of a single God.

"Why can't we worship the Gods we choose!" The black-bearded man pushed his way through the rumbling crowd to get closer to the bard.

"Well, that's it, then." Miach snatched a jug of ale from the tavern wench and tucked a coin in her bosom. He held up his mug with a sneer. "To King Huwen. The *Beloved*."

Rennika lifted her mug automatically, then lowered it without drinking. Was the tanner serious?

"May the new king see the error of his father's ways and give us back our Heavens," Yon toasted.

"And while he's at it, how about returning our stolen lands, and end imprisonment without trial?" Miach and four or five others nearby drank to this.

But the Amber was gone. "All of the prayer stones are smashed except for the Ruby. Huwen *can't* give us back our prayers."

"Surely, he must see how his father's torn the countries apart." Miach's words spat like acid on water as he filled their mugs.

"Hush," an older man with a broken nose cautioned. "A change of kings. You do not know how the land lays. A day ago—a candlemark ago—you could be dragged to Princess Hada's dungeon for such talk."

"Huwen's as big a fool as his father if he doesn't know how the people feel about having their access to the Gods cut off," Miach said.

"The prayer stones are gone," the old man reminded him. "Nothing will be the way it was."

"Not the Amber." Yon quaffed his ale. "The magiel's daughter escaped before the king's army sealed the walls. She has it."

Rennika's attention flicked up.

"Gossip," the old man sneered.

"No." Yon put his mug on the shelf. "She's been seen in Theurgy — and Holderford, by the Gods — even as far away as Cataract Crag."

Rennika squinted at him. Did he mean Meg? She'd never been to Cataract Crag. Unless . . . she'd gone there after they separated. But Meg didn't have the Amber.

"You're a bloody fool," the broken-nosed man said. "The Amber was in Archwood during the siege. Only the magic of the prayer stone could've kept those walls from falling to the king's ladders and catapults. It's smashed now, boy. You're an ass if you think otherwise."

The room was oppressively warm and the stink of bodies made Rennika feel ill. She wanted to sit down.

War. The plan. She and her sisters were to be at a tarn above Coldridge at the equinox, almost two weeks hence. But if the Amber was destroyed, what was the point? Did Meg or Janat know more about Mama's plan?

Yon leaned forward to make a point to someone in the discussion. He was handsome, in a devilish fashion, and he liked her. Meg and Janat would go to the tarn, if there was any reason to go. Did Rennika truly have to go?

Her strength drained away, and she felt only despair and exhaustion. She slid out from under Yon's arm. Miach filled the mugs around the circle, and Rennika let the ring of jostling debaters close.

She put her mug on the shelf. In a corner of the room, a group crowded around a table, some sitting on chairs, others on a bench nailed to the wall. Rennika wormed her way over, and slid under the bench, her back to the heels that might nudge her, and drowsed in the warmth and mesh of voices.

Mama was dead.

With her boot as a pillow and her cloak as a blanket, she fought troubling thoughts until deep night.

CHAPTER 32

The shadow of the mountain had crept across the high valley beneath a golden sky by the time Meg crested the wide windswept snowfield. The yak herder's hut was barely visible in the dusk, made of gray slates and nestled against a copse of stunted spruce. A wisp of smoke drifted from its chimney.

Meg rapped on the door with frozen knuckles. She'd journeyed a long way from the melting valley to this wintry mountain, hope battling despair in her mind the entire time, and still she wasn't certain she wanted to be here.

The door opened to a waft of warmth and the fragrance of roasting sausage. Rennika stood before her, a puzzled frown melting into astonished delight. "Meg!"

Before Meg could speak, Rennika whirled her in and closed the door, wrapping her in a fervent hug. "You're—here!" she squealed. "How—? How—"

Meg dropped her sack and held her sister close for a long moment, a rush of joy engulfing her, hardly daring to believe she'd found her. Rennika had . . . grown. Tall. Her hair, a tangle, was the color of honey and her cheeks bloomed like roses. Her voice—lower, modulated with the highlander vowels. She was, what, thirteen? But the promise of great beauty blessed her features. "I didn't think I'd ever get through all that snow."

"Where's Janat? Tell me everything. It's been so long! What have you been doing?"

"Janat . . ." Meg faltered.

Rennika's face went white.

"Nothing like that," Meg hastened to reassure her. "Last I saw her she was—fine."

Rennika stared at her for a long moment, as if still not believing her eyes. "Last you saw her?"

"We parted ways. I don't . . . know where she is." Saying the words tightened her throat.

Rennika looked puzzled. "I thought—"

"We're fighting for Shangril," Meg said as brightly as she could, unwrapping herself from a layer of woolen swaddling.

"With the uprisers." Rennika took Meg's cloak. She produced a thick yak hide from somewhere and threw it on the hard dirt floor before the hearth. "We haven't much, but we have butter and a bit of honey for the bread. Are you hungry?"

"Starving!" Meg took in the single room of the hut. The walls were well-chinked and cemented with some sort of mortar that kept most of the drafts at bay. The hearth, though not large, dominated the small space with a bright turf fire and a large iron cooking pot. A loft made a small sleeping space over a table with two wooden chairs and a tidy set of shelves and bins. A spinning wheel and small loom dominated one corner, surrounded by skeins of wool. Meg pressed her lips together, all at once filled with inexplicable sadness and joy. "I met a woman in Highglen who told me how to find you," she said by way of explanation. "She said you're working as a maid?"

Rennika gave her a puzzled grin, and turning to a shelf, produced two mugs. "Come. Sit." She disappeared through the door and returned in a moment with a jug of cream. "Colin will be home soon. This is his hut, but he'll welcome you. He's a good man."

Meg sat slowly, reappraising the hut and her sister. Rennika had grown taller, and her body, from what Meg could tell beneath the girl's layers of skirts and shawls, was developing the shape of a woman. "And Colin is . . .?"

"My master. He feeds me and lets me sleep on his hearth." She knelt before the fire on the yak hide.

Ah. Not a lover, then.

Rennika's smile was still naive. "I cook and keep the hut and make *very good* worlding potions for him and his yaks." She pinched dried herbs from a small sack into a pot with a lid and a spout. She poured in hot water from a kettle by the fire. "And for the neighbors, for trade." She poured a bit of the thick cream into each mug. "Once summer's here, though, I'll be able to do a lot more to pay for my keep."

"This spring equinox will be the second since we left Mama," Meg cut in.

Rennika poured the tea into Meg's mug, then looked up at her questioningly before pouring her own. *She didn't remember.*

"We need to be in Coldridge before then," Meg reminded her. The Gods had done nothing to help the uprisers; if Mama had found a way to spirit the Amber out of Archwood, Meg and Rennika had to carry out their charge and be prepared to use it.

Rennika poured the second cup of tea.

"Rennika."

She set the tea pot down.

Her sister's silence was unsettling. "Rennika, before we left Archwood, Mama—"

"I know what Mama said."

Meg was confused. "We have a duty."

Rennika licked her lips and gave Meg her cup. "I thought it was only you who had to go."

"Mama said . . ." Said Rennika was strongest. Meg took her tea, then rested the mug in her lap. Rennika had changed. Since they'd run from Archwood, she'd always done what was required of her. Beg. Steal. Run. Always been their sister. A Falkyn. "Any of us can go, but it should be all three of us. You don't want to go?"

The girl took her own mug and brought it to her lips, but she did not drink. "It's a long way. Can't you just go with Janat?"

"I told you, I don't know where Janat is." Heat tightened Meg's chest. She hadn't expected Rennika to argue. "Do you have somewhere else you need to be?"

Rennika tilted her head, dismissively. "No."

"Then?"

She shrugged a little. "This war is about big people. King Artem— King Huwen, I mean. Uprisers like Sulwyn and King Gramaret."

"And you. And me."

Again, Rennika tilted her head in dismissal.

"Are you wed to this man? Colin?"

Rennika's head shot up, and Meg knew by her sister's shock that she'd missed the mark. "Colin's an old man."

Meg didn't speak, but she held her sister's gaze.

Rennika let out a sharp breath. "Look at this place, Meg," she said, relenting. "It has everything a person could want. It's warm. It's comfortable. It's away from the war. There's food. There are people in this valley who need me."

"This place?" Meg scoffed. Meg and Janat's attic in Wildbrook was more comfortable than this hovel.

Rennika frowned in frustration.

"It's people who make a home," Meg said. "A family."

"Colin's people. He's like . . . like a father. And there are the people of the valley."

"The yak herders?" Meg couldn't believe what she was hearing. "You grew up in a castle!"

"A long time ago."

"And once the world is restored, you'll be a magiel princess."

"I don't want to be a princess."

Meg stared at her. This wasn't about what she *wanted*. "Well," she said at last, "what do you want?"

Rennika fingered her mug. "I met a boy. A man, I mean. A weaver, in Highglen. An apprentice, but he is working on his journeymanship—"

"A weaver!"

"He's saving his money. Soon he'll be able to open his own shop, and one day, he'll be a master—"

"A weaver!"

Rennika shot her a black look. "You say that like it's a bad word."

"Rennika, I spoke with Mama. Four weeks ago."

This caught the girl's attention.

"I was flickering through moments of my life after doing a spell. I found myself in her room before we escaped. Mama told me something. Why we need to go to the tarn above Coldridge. She's arranged for us to meet a prince."

Rennika stared at Meg. "A prince?"

"He'll have the Amber." This, Mama hadn't said, but it had to be what she meant.

Slowly, Rennika's head began to shake back and forth. "It's

gone."

Meg pushed the lie. "Mama smuggled it out of Archwood."

"A bard was here. Three days ago. He said King Artem was dead. The prayer stone was smashed—"

Meg set the two mugs on the hearth and took her sister's hands, her pulse thumping. "The prince, Rennika. And the Amber. We have to go." They were so close. So *close*. "It's our duty to the people of Shangril to give them access to their Gods."

The girl paled, as if she were trapped. "*Your* duty, Meg. You're the oldest—" Rennika blinked about the room, as if looking for an escape. "It was to be you all along. You know that."

"I can. Yes." Meg gripped her sister's hands harder. "But the Amber might only take me to the sixth Heaven, Rennika. Mama thinks . . . Mama thinks you could go to the seventh. To the One God. End this war."

Rennika's nostrils widened, as if she sucked in air.

"Return Shangril to peace. Return the people to their Gods. Ending the war is more important than one person. More important than marrying a weaver."

Rennika's face was white and pinched in the firelight.

Gods, let Rennika see.

Rennika's eyes became bright and her throat worked, forcing out a whisper. "I'll go."

CHAPTER 33

The trip from Highglen to the tarn took eight days walking, pushing hard. There were towns—Zellora, Kandenton, Ubica—to avoid along the road, and once they passed Coldridge, soldiers from Archwood would be on the road, returning to Holderford.

But soldiers could be anywhere. It was best, Meg told her, when they were this close to the equinox, not to tempt fate and not to lose all because of a blurred hand seen at an inopportune moment. So they were alert to other travelers, few though there were, and hid in the woods at the first sound of footsteps or hooves. They carried potions and twice had to use a Confusion spell when strangers they'd failed to avoid became too curious. Once, they hid, breathless in a copse of trees, as the troops marching back to Holderford from the siege passed by. Likely under two hundred men, but was this the first company to return home, or the last? They didn't know.

As she walked, the likeness of Yon danced in Rennika's head. Red hair and freckles. His linen shirt hung so gracefully on him, sleeves casually rolled up. When he'd stepped into the sunshine his eyes had glinted with pleasure at seeing her. Only twice they'd met, but she was sure he'd been as eager to spend time with her as she'd been to see him.

But soon, she'd become magiel to a prince. Life would take her down different paths; paths that did not lead back to Highglen. But who was her prince to be? And how could this prince bring them the Amber?

She hoped it would all come to naught.

At last, they climbed through a steep pathless forest, over rock and deadfall, to an icy lake within the dubious protection of a high valley. Above, cliffy peaks looked impassively down on a few wind-whipped trees surrounded by spills of talus and scree, and the cold tongue of a glacier. By their calculation, the equinox would be that night, or the next.

No one was camping by the tarn. They built a scrawny lean-to with poles and branches, hauled up from the slopes below, that barely cut the wind. Meg hunted for firewood and brought more spruce boughs up from the forest to chink their shelter, scanning for movement on the King's Road below, while Rennika stood by the lake, watching cold mist swirl in the blustery sky.

She didn't want to be a princess.

Why couldn't she do something *she* wanted to do, marry and settle down? Become the wife of an apprentice weaver? She was thirteen. She should be making her own choices.

This was Mama's plan. To serve the people. But what was Mama's plan to ensure her safety and happiness?

None.

�֎

Huwen's horse picked its way through mud churned by the hooves of a year's armies. The road from Archwood to Holderford was long.

A number of messengers had raced ahead, of course, with letters announcing the king's death and Huwen's own ascension, but still, Huwen pushed his party long days. As they descended, winter gave way to mud and wet weather. Huwen's intuition, reinforced by his advisors, told him the transition from one monarch to another would be perceived by the restless in Shangril as a point of weakness, a window for attack. He needed to be seen, present, in Holderford as soon as possible. The armies would follow at their best speed.

And Eamon still had the Ruby. It was Huwen's now that he was king. He would have to speak to Eamon about that as soon as it could be arranged.

A steady drizzle chilled his bones, and the monotonous sound of horses' hooves in the mud gave his thoughts a restless rhythm.

And, the long journey gave his advisors time to brief Huwen on ongoing business. Details of villages captured by rebels and repatriated over the past year and a half; maps and histories scrutinized to reveal the thinking of uprisers; whisperings of spies and edicts against magiels; a growing wealth and too much education among the merchant and craft classes leading them to demand too much power, destabilizing their concept of their place in the world—all of this made Huwen wonder again, why his father had crushed the other kings' prayer stones; why he'd declared death to all the magiels of the Great Houses. What had prompted him to ride out that first day, a year and a half ago?

Watching the measured rise and fall of the haunches of the horse before him, Huwen mulled what he knew.

His advisors were uncomfortable at the question. They didn't know, other than the explanation that had been given all along: the country should be united under one God; the Goddesses of the first six spheres of Heaven were not holy at all, but demons. And . . . under questioning, his advisors admitted they had raised objections, which Father had overruled.

It all came back to what had happened the night Eamon recovered from his illness.

Eamon didn't remember, or wouldn't say. Father was dead. Wenid was in Coldridge with Eamon, and in any case, there was no point in talking to him. If Huwen was honest, the old magiel frightened him. Which left Uther. But Uther had gone to Holderford, bearing messages.

Or . . .

"Jovan."

Jovan drew his mount up beside Huwen's.

"The messengers that were sent across Shangril to announce my father's passing. Was one of them Uther?"

"I would think so," the courtier replied.

"To which city was he sent?"

Jovan frowned and took his gelding forward to consult with the captain, and presently fell back to Huwen's side. "Coldridge."

Coldridge? So close? "Not Holderford?" The capital city.

"Lason was sent to Holderford. Both Wenid and Eamon are in Coldridge, and this message was thought to be . . . particularly delicate."

Huwen snorted. As if it wasn't a delicate message for Mother.

But . . . Coldridge. Only another two days' ride.

And Uther would have answers.

The prince did not come.

They waited. Perhaps something had happened. He was delayed. The roads were difficult. Rebels were warring.

Rennika suppressed the part of her that skipped a beat, thinking of her return to Highglen. But another part of her was deeply saddened. So many—so many—had pinned their hopes on this slim chance. Meg, certainly. And . . . Rennika had, too. Part of her.

The equinox was long past.

Morning of the fourth day broke and lengthened. Watery sunlight ghosted in and out of cloud above the mountain's shoulder. The rock Rennika sat on was bone-numbingly cold, and the breeze from the tarn carried a glacial chill. She huddled in her cloak, mittened hands close to the dying fire. She should hike down to the valley for more firewood. Her empty belly complained.

A cold gusting rain crept down the mountains.

Meg poked at the fire with a stick, stirring up ash and smoke.

Rennika stood. She hadn't planned to, she just did.

Meg watched her idly, unwilling to move, as Rennika stepped to the back of the lean-to. She pulled a spruce bough from its slanting roof and flung it into the scrubby willows.

Meg frowned but said nothing.

But it was time. Rennika heaved a second branch from the lean-to and tossed it into the bracken. A third. A fourth. The breeze poked fingers through the gap.

"Stop." Meg trembled, irate.

Rennika took her knife to the rope that bound the ridge pole to a tree. "No prince came, Meg." She threw the pole away, and the rest of lean-to collapsed. "Mama never arranged it."

"Don't you say that!" Meg growled, her hair plastered to her face by the rain. "Don't you ever think that!"

"She might have tried. She might have thought she did it."

Rennika scattered the boughs of their bed. Then she stopped and let her arms fall to her sides, desolate with the grief of understanding. "She was raving, Meg."

"She was not! She—"

"The Amber took her wits a long time ago."

Meg stood, trembling, choking on her fury.

Tiredly, Rennika took their goat bladder to the lake and filled it with water, and, returning, poured the water onto the fire. "There's no more prayer stones. No more magiels. No Gods or Heavens or death tokens."

Meg stood by the doused fire, wreathed in smoke, anger puffing in small breaths from her nose. "Mama was the most powerful magiel in Shangril. If she said she took care of us—took care of her people—then she did. She spoke to the Gods!"

The rain driven horizontally by the wind cut between them.

Rennika rolled up her pallet, tying the cord around it. She stood and kicked gravel into the embers, then took her pallet to her pack frame.

"Over a year," Meg said, and a pleading tone entered her voice. "It's a long time. Something happened. Maybe the prince was hurt. Delayed. Maybe just delayed . . ."

Rennika tied her pallet, sack of clothes, and camp gear to the wooden frame she carried on her back. "I'm sorry." She didn't know what to say. "I know you wanted . . . *really* wanted . . . to change the world."

"No!" Meg grasped her arm. "Wait. Stay. Faith is believing, even . . ."

Rennika shrugged the pack frame onto her back, then straightened. "We haven't eaten for two days." She turned and trudged down the rocky slope.

"You'd ignore Mama? The hopes of our people?" Meg shrilled. "Give up the rest of your life in luxury? Because you're *hungry*?"

"The siege at Archwood's over." Rennika stopped and turned. "The roads'll be filled with soldiers going to Holderford. We have to find a place to hide, Meg. We have to go."

Meg's lips parted as though she would argue; then with a sudden frown, she turned and gazed out over the icy lake. "Gods," she whispered to the Heavens. "How . . . how can you abandon your people?" She lifted her thin arms to the wind, a pitilessly small figure beneath the swirling gray sky. "We've done everything . . . everything you demanded . . ."

Rennika's grief turned to lead in her limbs.

The wind rushed over them, buffeting them with rain and spearing their faces with icy needles, its endless lonely breath in their ears.

Then, as though she were an old woman, Meg shuffled to her feet, bent to the rocky earth, and rolled up her pallet.

CHAPTER 34

Huwen's party reached Coldridge as the sun was sinking behind the mountains. The weather had grown wetter and the track muddier, and they finally dismounted stiffly in the castle courtyard under a somber, freezing rain. Eamon and Wenid and all the courtiers the fortress town could muster met him with proper words about Father. Huwen closeted himself with Eamon—and without Wenid—as soon as could be managed, so they might grieve alone. But he did not raise the issue of the transfer of the Ruby. This was not the time. And, Huwen needed to understand the underpinnings of his father's crusade before he decided how to broach the issue.

It was not until midnight when Huwen, exhausted beyond sensibility, bathed and ate his mutton in his room. He sank into a pillowed chair before a bright fire as rain splattered against the castle's glassed windows, and called for Uther to attend upon him. Despite the candlemark, his elder half-brother appeared in breeches, woolen stockings and doublet, all of black: clean but plain.

"Sit. Please. Brother."

Uther did so, somewhat reluctantly, Huwen thought. He'd probably never called Uther "brother" before. Huwen instructed the page to pour them both wine and to leave the bottle before departing.

He leaned back in his padded chair, grateful for the heat of the crackling hearth pushing back the spring damp. It was not easy to be in Uther's presence; Uther, who would've been king now, if his mother hadn't been a mere serving woman. Uther, who had spent more time with Father in the past year and a half, by far more than

Huwen had.

Uther had left Archwood as soon as Father died—barely shedding a tear, as far as Huwen could remember—with letters to deliver. He'd not stayed in the fallen city to search for the Amber.

Huwen, himself, had barely managed three days in the captured city. Three days was all any of them could endure—and that, sleeping outside the city walls. A curse, or so the rumor had sprung up among the men, had descended on the whole valley: Talanda's curse. The magiel of the Amber and her king had not given up the fortress in life, and neither would she do so after death.

Huwen believed in the curse; but even without mystical justification, the devastation the day they entered the city had repulsed him. His stomach he was able to purge. His dreams he could not.

Uther set his glass down. "How may I serve you, Your Majesty?"

Huwen cradled his wine in his lap. It would take time to get used to being addressed so formally. This was Father's title, not his. And Father had left him, far too soon. The weight of grief, of war and reparation, of rebels and empty coffers, weighed like a mountain on his shoulders.

"Your Majesty?"

"I am king now," he whispered, lifting his gaze from the fire and looking around the small but comfortably-appointed room. Beeswax candles scented the air, and a tray of honeyed nuts and jam cakes lay on a plain table between them. Funny how he noticed these small comforts. The end of the war would be welcome: landed gentry could get on with promoting trade and making themselves, and the country, wealthier.

"Yes, Sire."

Sire. This, from his older brother.

"I was told . . ." Huwen found the words surprisingly difficult to say. "I was told you were in our brother Eamon's room, the night . . ."

Uther did not move, did not prompt.

". . . the night Eamon recovered from his illness." He masked his unease with a sip of wine.

The fire crackled. "I . . . was," Uther said tentatively.

Huwen lowered the goblet to his lap. "Tell me."

Uther's response was a long time coming. "What would you like to know?"

He frowned into his goblet, irritated. "You know what I mean."

Above the snap of the fire, sheets of rain whipped the windows.

"Piss on it." Huwen turned on the bastard. "I am the king. I have just inherited a war that has divided the country, emptied its coffers, and impelled rebels to organize against me. My father's war was not about trade, or disputes, or religion. I would end it if I could. What is it about, for the sake of all that's Holy!"

Uther fidgeted with his goblet, ran his tongue around his teeth. "I don't—"

"Don't tell me you don't remember!" He had no patience. "I am your king. I command it."

"I wasn't going to say I didn't remember." Uther looked him squarely in the eye. "I remember perfectly well. Every detail."

"Then tell me. That night. The night of Eamon's miracle. It precipitated—" Huwen searched for words. "—everything."

"I was about to say, I should not pass on what I have not leave from my betters to reveal," Uther said. "I am a bastard. A servant. Surely you can see that. If Father and Wenid Col would not tell you, it is not my place."

"Father's dead."

Uther's jaw flexed, and his face turned away.

"I have a right to know." How could he explain this to Uther? "Do you know? Can you know? How Eamon has wanted to die since that night? By the One God, Uther, if you have any compassion—"

"I'll tell you," he said into the dark.

Huwen breathed, calming himself.

"But you must promise to be satisfied." Uther leaned forward, staring into the flames, his face painted with firelight in the dark room. "I did not go to Heaven. I know nothing but what I saw—in those rooms—that night."

Huwen breathed again. "Tell me," he whispered.

❈

What is the station of a beloved bastard in the king's court?

Even after the birth of his brother Huwen, the legitimate heir, the king of Arcan came to his mother's chambers. Uther's mother was no longer a serving maid, but what title can be given to the king's mistress? None; nor position, out of political sensitivity to the queen's powerful family. Instead, his mother was given quarters in a distant part of the castle with a bit of walled garden and a friend to pass the time. A prisoner, really; a woman shunned by servants as much as by court. Yet loved, in stolen moments, by a king.

But Uther was given the title of page, and useful work to do, and the freedom of the castle. He played and learned with the children of kings and ladies, and with each of his royal siblings as they came along. Father was tolerant and let all the children play together, all who lived in the castle or the great houses of the dukes; it was the servants who called their children back, forbade them to associate with their betters, forbade them to think themselves equal when they were not. And, in the evening, the children had all to be sorted out; royal children dining at the high table, magiel's children to one side, revered and a little distanced from the others. Those with wealthy parents sat at the long tables, and the rest, like Uther, now stood in stiff livery behind the lords, holding flasks of wine or bearing silver plates with paper and ink, ready to run a message. Some of these were certainly bastards.

The spring Uther turned seventeen, an illness swept the land. The keening of grieving mothers could be heard throughout the stinking city of Holderford, and it was Uther, not his arrogant younger brother Huwen, the crown prince, who stood by Father at Prince Eamon's side as he tossed with fever. But Eamon worsened and slipped into a dreamless sleep.

It was Uther who was dispatched to bring healers with herbs and magic spells. And when the curse of the disease could not be lifted, it was Uther who was sent to bring the castle magiel. His father and the magiel prayed over the prince's wasted body for candlemarks on end, petitioning the Gods, their hands joined and frozen to the Ruby. Eamon's pulse continued to beat and his breath continued to flow. But he did not wake.

When the Ruby slipped from the king's fingers, he and his magiel returned from their prayers in the spheres of the Gods, both collapsed with exhaustion.

But still his brother worsened.

Uther was privy to his father's anguish as, one by one, the high magiels of Midell, Pagoras, and Gramarye, summoned to Holderford, delivered the same verdict: nothing could be done. The boy lived, but his ghost no longer inhabited his body. Then the magiels of Teshe and Elsen, and even the magiel of distant Orumon were sent for. The boy was a golem, they said, living on without mind, without will, without sense.

The Many Gods were weak, or their magiels too frightened to act.

Uther stood by the door as his father paced the floor, knelt by the bed, stood at the window searching the stars for answers. Uther brought his father food in the night and took it again in the morning, untouched. Uther watched as his father grew thin; as he turned away his advisors; as whispers filled the halls and meaningful glances were exchanged among the nobles; as his father's younger brother, Avin, took on more and more of the duties of state; as the queen retired to her chambers and the solace of her personal magiels and their potions of forgetting.

Uther was summoned. To bring secret visitors up back stairways. Other magiels—lesser, not high magiels of the Great Houses—to plead with this God or that. They came in silks or in rags, to confer with the king and administer other remedies; more questionable; more futile. As long as the boy breathed, his father would not give up.

The night came when Eamon lay wasted in his golden chamber, his skin so translucent in the candlelight, the veins, and even bones, seemed to shine through. The king, as though bent under a great weight, turned from his vigil. Calling for Uther, he sat at his desk and wrote a note, affixing his seal. He wrote an address on its outer wrapping.

"Come, boy," he said in a voice that rasped like his quill on the parchment. His eyes shone, dark and liquid, as he placed his big hand on Uther's head and drew a finger down to lift his chin. "Call the coachman. Go to this house. Wake the magiel you find there. Wenid Col, his name is; a magiel devoted to the worship of only the One God. Bring my summons to him."

The cult of the One God. Even Uther had heard of it.

His father pressed trembling lips together. "Your brother is dying, Uther. Be swift."

Uther was frightened, and looking at Eamon, wondered, *Is this the last time he breathes?*

His brother lay motionless. No lash fluttered. His blue-tinged lips were parted as if suspended in mid-gasp. *Did* he breathe? Or did the flicker of the candle flame mimic the rise and fall of his chest? Uther glanced at his father and held his breath. Eamon was like a figure of wax.

Father hastened to the bedside. He bent low, a cheek to feel the faint sigh of breath. His head plunged to the narrow chest, listening.

A moment.

His father growled or moaned and lifted his brother by the shoulders. He shook him, once; let him drop to the pillow. He listened, watched, shook again.

"No!" The growl was louder this time. He whirled and caught Uther by the arms, his grip crushing. "Go!" he cried, shoving him toward the door. "I've delayed too long—"

Uther bolted out the door, clattered down the stone steps, and flew into the midnight rain, screaming at the coachman to *wake! Wake! Whip the horses for all they're worth!*

Empty streets flew past in a lifetime of bruising corners and jouncing ruts. Cobbles gave way to streets of clay transformed by sheets of rain to grease beneath the wheels. The nightmare journey ended in a plunging halt before a building sandwiched between a silent tavern and a glazier's.

Uther tore from his seat and pounded on the door. A spring storm—cold and full of power—slapped his shoulders and drenched his hair. "Answer in the name of the king! Answer—"

The door opened and a servant looked Uther up and down.

"Please, Sieur!" Uther held out his father's letter in the driving rain.

"Who is it?" A wheedling voice rattled from the interior.

"A messenger." The servant took the letter and scrutinized the seal in the dim light of a single gusting candle ensconced in the entryway. "He says he's from the king."

Above the pounding of the rain, Uther heard an interior door flung open. A stooped old man came to the entryway, his face a web of wrinkles, his eyes round and hungry. He snatched the letter and held it up to the candle. "Let him in. Shut the door." He tore the outer velum away and scanned the contents of the letter. "This is it," he breathed.

"The king has capitulated?" the servant asked.

The magiel turned to Uther. "You've seen the boy? How bad is he?"

"I—I don't think he'll live, Sieur."

"Don't think? Or is he dead already?"

"I don't know—"

The magiel struck a table with his fist and shot his servant a penetrating look. "Why did he wait?"

"The price is high," his servant answered.

"Now the cost to the boy will be high as well."

"And to you," the servant said.

The magiel swiped the air in denial. "I don't care about myself."

"If you do this thing, magiels of the Great Houses will band together to cast you out."

"Please, Sieur!" Uther begged.

The magiel pulled a hooded cloak from a peg. "We've been through all that. It's got to be done."

"For the glory of the One."

"For the glory of the One." The magiel threw the cloak over his shoulders and, pulling up the hood, plunged into the rain.

And then the magiel was in the coach, and Uther was in his place clinging to the handholds on the back, listening to the crack of the whip above the gusts of rain as the horses labored up the hill, hooves clattering on cobbles.

Get on! The king awaits!

The beasts blew and steamed and the guards stood aside as they flew into the castle bailey, coming to a halt at the side entrance. Uther jumped from the coach and ran up the tower steps to lead the magiel to his father.

Wenid Col strode through the dimly lit corridors and, glowering at the guards, flung open the royal chamber door himself.

Uther's father lay in the light of a single candle, prostrate across the bed, across Eamon, shuddering with sobs, and Uther understood then, the words of the magiel.

His brother was dead.

"Stand!" the magiel cried in a voice so used to whispering that his croak barely pierced the howl of the gale.

Uther eased the door into its jamb, cutting off the knowing whispers of the servants.

Dead. Like the son of the scullery girl who carried her infant about the kitchen, moaning. Like the yeoman, lying on his pallet with flies nipping at his eyes until the Holder's men took him away. Like the noisome corpses piled on the hauler's wagon, bumping over ruts through the city gates.

His father moaned with an anguish that swathed Uther in an urge to run to him as he had as a child. "No, no . . ."

In three strides, Sieur Col crossed the room and put his hand on Father's shoulder, pushing him onto his back with a force that belied the magiel's thin stature. "Do you wish your son to live?"

Father slithered from the bed to wallow in grief on the floor. "He's dead! Dead! You're too late!"

Uther's throat tightened at the knowledge. The guilt.

The magiel crouched before him, still obscenely clutching his shoulder. "Nothing is beyond the power of the One God."

The king shook his head in bewilderment, raised his hands, trembling and useless, to pull at his hair. "My son! My son . . ."

"Swear. Swear fealty to the One God, and *only* the One God." The magiel shook Father by the shoulders. "Swear you will denounce all others as demons, and your son shall be returned to you."

The old man's words made no sense. Eamon was dead.

But his father lifted eyes full of confusion and hope.

"You know the cost," the magiel said.

The king—the king!—bowed his head. "I do." He pushed his lank hair back with his hands.

"All the prayer stones," the magiel commanded. "The Amber. The Citrine. The Emerald—all six must be sacrificed to the One God. Do you swear? No one will have access to Heaven. Only the Ruby will remain."

Uther's father sat up straighter. He searched the magiel's face with disbelief. "I can," he gasped. "I will. The kingdoms will be taken by surprise. I can secure them all."

"Because the Many Gods are *false* Gods. Demons. You know this to be true."

"False Gods," the king repeated. Streaks glistened on his cheeks. "Only the One has the power to save your son. Say it!"

"Only the One." A choking voice. A whisper.

"You believe?"

"I believe." His father's shoulders crumpled and tears coursed again.

"I will endure the ordeal for you, My Liege," the magiel said softly. "For the boy, and for the glory of the One God."

Wordlessly, his father scrambled to his knees and kissed the magiel's hand.

The magiel shed his cloak. "Bring the Ruby."

Uther shrank into the shadows of the velvet drapes.

The king took the prayer stone from its locked box on the pedestal and knelt beside Eamon as Uther had seen him do so many times before. He held it out: a glinting crystal sparkling red fire in the candlelight. Golden rays snaked from its center.

The magiel stood at the head of the bed and laid his hand on the king's wrist.

And that was all. The magiel and the king became abruptly motionless.

Through the night Uther watched. His father and the magiel prayed, their spirits lifted from this lowest sphere of earth, to traverse through the first sphere, the Heaven of thieves and murderers, through the second, the third, and so on, to the very highest sphere of the One God. Silent and motionless were their bodies, as their spirits pleaded for the life of a boy.

The storm raged and waned and raged again, beyond the glassed windows.

Uther stoked the fire and relit the candles.

Morning drew near.

The rain lessened and the howl of the wind diminished. Dawn filtered through blustery clouds to cast pale streaks across the parquet floor and the snowy coverlet on the bed. Uther opened the east window and a cool zephyr lifted the filmy drapes, scenting the room with promise.

His brother sighed, and turned his head.

His brother. Eamon.

The magiel crumpled and fell to the floor. Father's eyes fluttered and he collapsed against the side of the bed. The Ruby rolled onto his lap.

Within days, the king sent his best cadres to each kingdom's strongholds, traveling light and swift, racing rumor. *Relinquish your prayer stone and swear allegiance to the One God,* his message read.

Or give up your lands in bloody battle to be redistributed to ambitious royals, loyal to their king, was unsaid.

Teshe capitulated and in due course its prayer stone, the Amethyst, was destroyed. Elsen, Gramarye, and Pagoras fell within the first weeks, and the Azurite, Chrysocolla, and Emerald were smashed. The king of Midell fought for a bloody eight months, but the Citrine was shattered. Far south on the edge of the wilds, Orumon—protected by the Amber, second in strength only to the Ruby—resisted.

"You know the rest," Uther said.

Huwen took a deep breath and shook his head slowly. "Yes," he said. "I know the rest."

CHAPTER 35

The trip east from Postinghouse was made in silence, punctuated only by practical necessities. Meg's fatigue was no longer the sharp exhaustion of lack of sleep from overuse of magic. It was the dead kind of weariness that came from having no purpose. Yes, there was the rebel camp. The cause. But what was she now? A common village magiel, working for a politics that had no way to succeed. Gods, how much had changed since she'd left her childhood in Archwood.

Where the Orumon River met an unnamed creek, they came to a crossroad. A post driven into the ground, bright in the rays of the westering sun, bore arms pointing down each track. Coldridge, Cascade Creek, Big Hill, and behind them, Archwood. She and Rennika had to choose a direction.

It was too late to travel further. A short distance into the woods they found a place flat enough to camp. As Meg collected spruce boughs and suitable poles from the deadfall to make a quick lean-to, Rennika gathered a few early fiddleheads and onions for a thin soup.

When they were settled in their robes, radiance of a small fire reflecting into the sloping roof of their lean-to, Meg raised the question of their destination. "We need to find Janat." Dwyn expected her. Of course. But what was the point of the uprisers' cause now? The new king, Huwen, would bring the Ruby back from Archwood, and they could not fight the magic of Heaven.

"And Sulwyn?" Rennika asked.

"Janat. Family." Meg would mend things with Janat, if she could.

Rennika was silent for a long moment, head resting on a bent arm, face bright-lit in the firelight. "I'm going back to Highglen. To Yon, if he'll have me."

Meg had dreaded this response. Rennika was thirteen and had pinned her hopes on the first boy who'd charmed her. "And if not?"

"I have a home with Colin."

"Less than a year?" Meg asked bitterly. "And you've already abandoned your family for a new life?"

Rennika scowled without responding, and Meg wasn't sure if her sister was avoiding a quarrel, or if she had no grounds for argument. Then Rennika shrugged. "You could come."

The pain stabbed. Come to Highglen? And what?

"Why don't—"

—a crunch.

Meg listened. An animal?

Rennika tugged awkwardly at the branches beneath her, freeing a spruce bough and slapping it on the fire. With a gout of white smoke, the flames abruptly died back.

They laid still and listened.

Definitely. A crunch behind Meg.

And a crunch on the far side of Rennika.

Meg tied the throat of her cloak closed, preparing to run, and in the gloom she saw Rennika silently do the same.

A weapon. Her spells were in vials in a sack, tucked down by her feet. How could she be so stupid? So distracted? Her boots were there as well.

Slowly, trying to be silent, Meg brought herself to a sitting position and picked up her boots.

"Stay where you are!" A handful of men leapt from the woods around them, steel reflecting dull red in the gloom.

Meg and Rennika both scrambled to their feet.

But Rennika was better prepared. She gave a quick nod and Meg took in a lungful of air, and, ducking, ran into the woods. A cloud of confusion rose behind them as Rennika uncorked her vial and ran.

Meg and Rennika, bereft of all their travel gear but the cloaks on their backs, rode into the rebel camp in the hills south of Coldridge the next morning on cavalry horses stolen in the confusion of their attack. It was the only place Meg could think of to go where they might find safety and welcome.

The encampment was a quagmire of chaos. Each day since Meg left must have seen the addition of new troops. Runners with messages had proliferated, and squads of armed men moved purposefully on tense assignments. The camp had bloomed into a large, disorganized town. Meg guided her mount between cobblers and smiths, armorers and cooks, asking the way to Dwyn's tent.

They dismounted, letting the tired horses muzzle fresh sprigs of grass springing up among the dry stalks from last fall, and Meg told Dwyn's page she'd returned. After a short wait, they were admitted.

Dwyn perched on a stool at one end of a campaign table spread with a large and detailed map of Coldridge and its surrounding fields and forests, one hand over his mouth, listening to his counsellors. Sulwyn was there, Orville and Finn, and Fearghus. Sulwyn's eyes softened in relief at her entrance, then flicked away.

As soon as Rennika saw Sulwyn, she ran to him, and he gave her a warm but brief hug.

Dwyn held up a hand to stop Finn's words and nodded to Meg. "It's good to see you returned safely," he said with iron in his voice. "We will talk later about why you were not at your assigned post."

His entire demeanor changed as his gaze landed on Rennika. He turned back to Meg. "Your sister? The little one? Whom I hid in Gramarye?"

The keenness in the king's response unsettled Meg. She should not have brought Rennika here. Though—where could she have taken her? "She is."

Calculation flitted through his eyes. ". . . Rennika." He smiled at the girl. "Welcome."

Rennika drew back from Sulwyn and returned the king's look with one of guarded suspicion. She nodded, a hint of a bow.

Dwyn summoned his page. "Bring Meg what food can be found." He nodded at Rennika. "Take this one to Meg's tent. Bring her food and whatever else she needs."

The page bowed and led Rennika from the tent.

Meg drew in a breath and curtseyed. There was no point in telling him about Mama and the Amber. It was of no consequence now.

"You have missed much that is important for you to know. You can go to your tent later."

"Yes, Sire."

Dwyn waved to Finn and he continued his briefing. "Orville and I will assemble our machines here." He placed his finger on the map showing the woods on the south side of the river. "We have fifteen teams, and we'll use the bridge to bring the trebuchets forward after the archers and infantry are in place. Before dawn, Gods willing."

"And what do we know of these weapons' secrecy?"

Finn exchanged glances with Orville. "The steam trebuchets and *bombs* have been used in three campaigns. We have to assume the royal forces have heard stories, though it's our experience the magnitude of the weapons' effectiveness is poorly grasped. This battle will be our first use of the *cannon*."

The king frowned a nod at the map. "Huwen Delarcan's armies have already been marching out of the Orumon valley, heading east toward Arcan. We see no indication that they know we intend to attack Coldridge." He lifted his head. "Sulwyn. How long until the six hundred from Fairdell arrive?"

The page nudged Meg's elbow. He'd returned with a mug of ale and some dried yak strips.

". . . then we attack in four days," Dwyn was saying. "There's no advantage to waiting longer." The king straightened. "Fairdell's men can rest one night and prepare to support us in reserve." He adjusted his position to scrutinize the map of the interior of the town. "Meg."

She swallowed her bite. "Sire?"

"You've been inside Coldridge castle."

"Yes, Sire." She set her food on a stool and stepped forward. "Twice."

"I have not. How accurate is this map?"

She studied the castle outlines inked on the linen, the thoroughfares and warren of smaller streets outside the castle wall, the courtyard before the castle gates, and various buildings within. "I've never seen a map of Coldridge, but from my memory of walking its halls and bailey, I would say you have a good drawing."

"Some of our maps have been found to be less than reliable." He placed his finger on a building within the grounds.

"The shrine to the Many Gods," she said. "Or, likely it's now been converted into a shrine for the One."

"And this?" He pointed to an identical tower at the far end of the great hall.

"The king's keep."

"Is this where King Larin's apartments were located?"

"It is," she said cautiously.

"You've been missing for three weeks," he said testily, "so you would perhaps be unaware, but we have learned that the Ruby is in Coldridge."

The Ruby—King Artem's—*King Huwen's* prayer stone. "In Coldridge?"

He turned to Fearghus. "We'll have to assume the Ruby is in the shrine." He returned to Meg. "A tower rising above the castle wall on the southwest corner is clearly visible from the road. Is that this keep?"

She'd been in that tower. Overheard Artem and Wenid plan death to magiels. Its windows overlooked the castle wall, the city wall, to the fields, road and river. "Yes, sire." But—

"Well, Sieur Haye?" Dwyn turned to Orville. "You say your *cannon* have destructive power at range. Can you destroy this tower?"

If the rebels killed whichever royal ruled Teshe now that King Larin had been assassinated—would there be anyone in the castle to use the Ruby against them? She didn't know. But . . . the keep was deep in the castle behind not only the fortress wall, but the town wall as well. No trebuchet could destroy it from the fields below the town.

"It is definitely possible," Orville said.

"Possible?" The king turned.

"Coldridge is a small borderland fort that has seen little conflict until this war began," Orville said in his thick accent. "Its walls were not in good repair when Artem took it, which is one of the reasons it was vulnerable, and he has not yet restored them. Nevertheless, their original construction was sturdy, and they are thick. Assuming we have the time to get the range of the keep and land a dozen good shots, then . . . yes." He pointed to the field on the map. "From this distance, there should be no problem."

"We need to destroy the tower while Eamon is asleep," Fearghus said. "He can't have time to get to the Ruby, and we can't damage the shrine. That is critical. There are no guarantees we'll have time to land even six or seven balls."

The advisors studied the map.

Meg held herself back from interrupting. Eamon was in Coldridge? And the Ruby? But the Ruby had to have been at the siege. Absenting herself from Dwyn's councils had been a mistake.

"Bring the *cannon* across the bridge before the infantry," Fearghus suggested. "Set it up overnight. Attack before dawn."

Dwyn shook his head. "If the keep doesn't fall immediately, Eamon will have time to flee. He'll go to the shrine and use the Ruby."

Three were needed to pray to the Gods. Prayer Stone, magiel, and royal. Three potential weak points. A possibility nudged Meg.

"Can our armies infiltrate the town?" Finn asked. "Before dawn? So far, we believe they know nothing of our presence here. Surprise is on our side, and if Eamon can't cross his bailey from the keep to the shrine . . ."

Infiltrate—

Fearghus bit his lip. "Our spies were able to enter, but they were searched. You'd never infiltrate with weapons or armored men. And if you try to break the gates—" He shrugged. "—we're back where we were. We'd never reach the keep on time to prevent Eamon from getting to the Ruby."

"An assassin," Meg whispered. It was obvious.

Dwyn looked up from the map.

"Sulwyn was able to get close to King Artem at his siege headquarters at Archwood," she argued. "Our men assassinated King Larin on his hunt. Why not send a man into the castle now, before we attack? If—Prince Eamon—is too heavily protected, target Wenid Col."

Fearghus looked as though he was about to object.

"But this time, no slow poison." It could work. "A proper killing attack."

"Coldridge is no tent camp in the woods," Fearghus snorted.

"We have three days before the Fairdell contingent arrives," she pressed. "You just said you were able to get spies through the gate."

"Through the *city* gate. Unarmed." Fearghus let out a deep breath. "Do I need to outline the barriers to getting an assassin anywhere near a magiel?"

"No," Meg said curtly. "You perhaps forget, I grew up in a castle."

"Then you should understand better than any of us," Fearghus snapped. "It would be impossible."

"I do understand better than any of you," Meg retorted.

"Enough," Dwyn charged.

But Meg could not hold back. Her pulse quickened with the possibilities. "What harm can be done by sending in a man, or a small cadre, to at least try?"

"Harm?" Fearghus spun to face her. "If our man is captured, he could be tortured to give up our plans. Destroy the critical element of surprise."

"Select a man—a volunteer from among your infantry—who's not privy to this council. How many thousands do we have? One must have the skills of an assassin."

"Any soldier in our camps has an estimate of our numbers—"

Dwyn Gramaret lifted a hand to stop Fearghus's words. "You've been inside the great hall?" He looked up at Meg from beneath his brows. "Getting a man in is possible?"

"I've been inside the *royal apartments*," Meg confirmed, all fatigue from her long night's ride gone. "That tower. I advised Sulwyn when he infiltrated King Artem's camp, and I can advise your assassin. I could sketch most of the rooms inside the keep and the great hall."

Dwyn shifted, his gaze landing on each of his advisors, gauging the leaning of each.

"A cadre, I think," the exiled king said, and a flush of triumph fluttered through her. "Three. Two assassins, to increase our odds. One can provide cover or lead a distraction, if necessary; or courier news back."

The king had the attention of everyone in the room.

"And for route finding, disguises and poisons," he said, looking at Meg. "A magiel."

A thrill shot through her blood.

"No!" Sulwyn stood. "She'll be spotted—"

"Wait . . ." Finn spoke uneasily. "Our only magiel . . ."

"Her curses have been cast. She can use a magic disguise. Besides," Dwyn went on, "as of today, we have a second magiel."

Rennika.

"Your grace," she stammered. Rennika had no place on a battlefield.

Dwyn straightened to look at Sulwyn. "And what are we saving her for, if not for this push on Coldridge? Hmm? This is our one attack. If we do not succeed, there will be no other." He turned to Meg. "Do you accept?"

She blinked. It had been her idea. And . . .

The thought of it made her feel alive.

"Sire, I do."

Dwyn gave a short nod. "Fearghus, find two volunteers." He turned to Meg. "Prepare. You leave before dawn."

CHAPTER 36

Too soon, Rennika's sleep, so deliciously luxurious on a pallet of new straw in the warmth of a tent, was broken. Someone moving. A candle flame. She brought herself to her elbow in her sheepskins and peered at Meg's silhouette. "It's the middle of the night."

"I'm going to Coldridge." Meg sat at her feet, wrestling her foot into a boot.

Rennika rubbed her eyes. "Why?"

She flashed a grin at Rennika and her words, though hushed, vibrated with excitement. "We attack tomorrow. I'm aiding an assassination on the royal magiel. So he can't use the Ruby in battle."

Rennika tilted her head. "Ruby?" Why would the Ruby be in Coldridge?

Meg tightened her bootlace and leaned over to kiss Rennika on her forehead. "Stay here." She gave her a long look in the dark. "I'll be back before you know it."

Rennika squinted at her. Meg's face was in shadow, but her voice had changed. It frightened her. "Meg—"

"I have to go. They're waiting." And the canvas flap lifted and fell, and she was gone.

"Meg!" Rennika scrambled to the door of the tent. A cold rain fell, and the black forest hemmed in the encampment. A figure swathed against the sleet was helping Meg into the back of a laden wagon. A second man clucked at the horse and a handful of uprisers watching the departure turned back toward their beds. The wagon rattled away between the army's tents.

Rennika, drenched and shivering, crawled back under her

covers, but sleep had abandoned her. Not two days ago, she'd sat at a campfire with Meg, planning her return to Highglen, to Colin and, maybe, Yon. Now she was on the edge of a battle with nothing more than the clothes she wore.

Meg had disappeared into King Dwyn's council as soon as they'd arrived and Rennika, dead tired, had slept and later wandered alone through the camp. The camp was full of troops sorting out where each was from, how to negotiate space and resources, sharing rumors, waylaying runners with messages. Men sang songs of exhortation around their campfires, and some talked in low voices about sleeplessness in the night, offering to take sentry duty rather than toss on the ground, wrestling with fear.

A handful of soldiers at a campfire had given Rennika a bit of supper, and Sulwyn showed up there at dusk. "There you are. I've been looking for you since dusk." He lowered himself to the log beside her, his bad leg extended. "I don't mind your wandering off, but maybe you could let me know where you go."

She stared at him. "Meg and I went from Gramarye to Orumon on roads full of thieves and enemy troops. We did all right."

Sulwyn lifted a brow in surprise. "Yes. Well. I guess you did." He reached into a small sack and withdrew a corked bottle. "But soldiers can be rough." He nodded at men on the far side of the fire, who just then burst into laughter. "I'll find a minder to stay by you and keep you safe."

"Am I a prisoner?" Colm had wanted to hold them, the first time they met, and Dwyn had sent her to Highglen with no recourse for appeal.

"No," Sulwyn said, and then blinked at the idea, as if he was not fully certain.

"Where's Meg?"

He turned back to the fire and uncorked his bottle. It smelled of whiskey. "Busy. She's Dwyn's royal magiel."

Meg had told her this on their travels, but it didn't explain where she was now. "When do the uprisers attack?"

He cast her a querulous glance. "You ask a lot of questions."

She wasn't surprised he avoided her. No one ever answered her questions. The men at the fire poured into their cups from a small cask. Beer, by the foam. "Well, what am I supposed to do? I want to go back to Highglen."

He sipped from his whiskey and eyed her. "By yourself?"

"I'm not afraid."

"I'm sure you're not." He turned back to the fire.

"Well?"

"Just at present, we can't spare a horse. Or a tent, or food. Or money."

He had her there. She was stuck. "So, what am I supposed to do?"

"Do you want to help?" He looked back over his shoulder at her.

Help. With the war? "Doing what?"

He shrugged. "Meg will be busy for a few days. Make us some potions, if we need them."

Magic. She was good at that, forever making spells to increase the supply of yak milk or encourage yak fertility, or heal a sick child or a cut finger; but to make a curse, or a spell of Confusion or Shape Changing, that would be interesting. And Meg had likely collected a curious array of ingredients, and maybe had a book of spells. She agreed.

But now, lying in her skins in the dark before dawn, Sulwyn's words returned. Meg would be "busy" for a few days. In Coldridge. Assassinating the king's magiel. And the uprisers wanted Rennika to be their magic wielder.

In case Meg didn't come back.

Kilovan Kynton and Xanther Jameson were the uprisers selected to the team to assassinate the king's magiel. Xanther had spied in the guise of a king's guard until too many suspicions surrounded him. Then, audaciously, he'd shaved his head and beard, and returned to Coldridge to work as a milkman's assistant, watching the castle's pedlars' gate, identifying patterns of the craftsmen's comings and goings and striking friendships where he could. He knew the layout of the castle and carried a face-altering potion Meg had devised, in case of need. Kilovan was a potter from Pagoras who'd watched his farm burnt by royals, and who'd developed a taste for murder.

At first light, the three drove a cart to the city with a load of vegetables for market. The morning was dull with cold rain, the ruts in the road frozen. Meg, tight with apprehension, huddled on the jolting wooden boards in the back of the cart under her cloak. Sacks of the previous fall's parsnips, carrots and turnips jostled uncomfortably on top of her, heavy. The pony slowed at the gate, and Meg held her breath, trying not to shiver from the penetrating rain, listening to the guard's muffled voice, waiting for him to poke a sword through the vegetable sacks.

But no. Xanther answered his questions and there was a riffling of the sacks over her, then they passed beneath the portcullis.

They halted, finally, in a lane off a winding mud street of stables and chickens coops. Xanther helped Meg out from beneath the vegetables. In an alcove, screened by Kilovan, Meg spread an illusion spell on her hands and face, Kilovan pointing out any place she missed. Xanther watched the comings and goings in the road. At length he indicated a grizzled man driving a wagon full of clay pots up the hill.

Now. Her turn. A tickle of anticipation washed through her.

Xanther and Kilovan kept watch out of sight in the lane as Meg, mouth dry, stepped into the dull drizzle to waylay the man who delivered the king's milk. Hoping her accent was convincing, she drew him into the alley with a story of needing help reattaching the pony's harness to the tongue of her cart. Once he was out of sight, away from the street, Xanther and Kilovan leapt on him. Meg pressed herself against the wall, flinching at the man's cries, as her companions silently trussed, gagged, and stowed him in a corner of the lane behind the vegetable cart.

Meg scoured the doors of the lane, the windows above and the street beyond, but the scuffle was finished in the blink of an eye, and no one seemed to have alerted.

She breathed, and Kilovan gave Xanther a half smile of congratulation. They took their supplies and bundled onto the seat of the milk wagon while Meg emptied the vials of Well-Being and Confusion into a handful of mugs in the back of the wagon.

This time, she huddled, swathed in her cloak, on the back of wagon bed, legs dangling over the road. They'd done it. The first step, just as they'd rehearsed. A breathlessness energized her at their audacity.

Morning lightened the cloud cover as their pony brought the wagon, rattling on the cobbles of the upper city streets, to the castle's rear gate.

"You're late," the guard grumbled. "And where's Gwynne?"

Meg huddled in her cloak against the cold drizzle, listening to the exchange at the gate. The next barrier. She'd used an illusion spell more and more often as the world grew colder toward magiels, but never without the apprehension that this time, the soldier would somehow see through it.

"Sick," Xanther said. "Took a bit of bad pork last night."

The guard's voice was unsympathetic. "Kitchen's having conniptions. Who's them?"

"Gwynne's cousin, come to help."

"And her?"

Meg swallowed, trying not to shake, forcing herself to turn her head to watch. Averting her eyes would be suspicious. She wondered if Cook was inside, and Bess, the scullion, who'd helped her the day—over a year ago now?—Uncle Chirles had been executed.

"His wife. They just come up from Grassy Bluff." Xanther's words were smooth as glass. "Here. Gwynne just got a new cow." Xanther jumped down from the seat, and Meg smiled, watching as he splashed through puddles around to the back of the wagon. He pulled one of her mugs from between the crocks and poured milk into it. "This milk is some good."

The guard looked skeptical. Beyond him, inside the castle gate, a scullery maid hovered.

"Still warm." Xanther's voice overflowed with good cheer.

Nothing from the guard. And then, "I don't rightly know as you should be bringing the milk without Gwynne giving leave. You only started with him a week ago."

"He's pukin'. Ain't fit to come."

Meg bit her lip, trying to keep her breathing regular, trying to keep her smile from congealing on her face, gawking at the castle courtyard like a rube. Her life might depend on its geography later. They'd looked at a sketch Xanther made and compared it to hers, as they came down from the hills. It showed Wenid Col's suite, and it was consistent with, and refreshed, her memory. Had she played on these cobbles, on her visit with Mama? Nothing—and everything—looked familiar. The door to the kitchen, the scullery maid approaching. The kitchen garden, not yet planted. The smithy, stables. Familiar.

"Do you want the milk?" Xanther sounded impatient. "We can unload and be gone. Or we can take it to market and sell it."

The guard grunted. Assent?

Xanther took it as such. "All right, then. Kilovan—"

Kilovan clucked and the wagon jerked as the pony clopped toward the kitchen door.

Meg allowed herself to breathe. By the Many Gods, she was sweating despite the cold.

But they were only in the bailey, not the great hall.

She and Kilovan climbed down from the wagon and unloaded the crocks as Xanther gave mugs of the wonderful spell-laced milk to the scullery maids and cooks. She and Kilovan put yesterday's empty jugs back onto the cart. A job to focus on. It steadied her.

Kilovan touched her arm.

The maids and cooks were chatting jovially, mugs in their hands.

The two of them slipped through the kitchen into the servants' wing as Xanther drove away.

✠

Meg and Kilovan stepped into a smaller eating area for servants, separate from the room bustling with cooks and scullery maids that they had just left. It was empty, an organized chaos of tables, work benches, chests, cupboards, and the like, with a fire glowing beneath a soup cauldron on the hearth. Besides the door to the castle kitchen, there was a landing leading to a servants' stairs and a corridor at the end of the room that might lead to servants' chambers. Meg hadn't been in this room before.

"Who are you, then?"

Meg whirled, panic in her throat.

A grizzled man in the dress of a laborer stood behind Kilovan in the opening to the garden, brushing soil from his hands. He held no mug of charmed milk.

Meg's knife with the poisoned blade was in her purse. She had no wish to hurt a gardener.

"Ah!" Kilovan said in relief. "Maybe you can help us. We're looking for Jory."

"Who?" the old man frowned, stepping inside.

"You know, Jory." Kilovan fumbled with his handkerchief, approaching the man.

Meg understood and pulled out a phial. Gods, they'd barely started, and they were using more potions than enough.

Kilovan's gaze darted to her closed hand. He lifted his head to the old man, his wrapped knuckles smashing the gardener's face. With a grunt, the man crumpled to the ground.

Before he could regain his feet, Kilovan and Meg rolled him onto his back, and Meg poured a sleeping potion into the man's sputtering mouth. They held his struggles, muffling his shouts, for interminable moments, until he relaxed beneath them. Then Meg pocketed the empty container, and the two of them pulled the man back from the entry before any of the charmed scullery maids or cooks thought to wonder about the masked scuffling sounds. Kilovan closed the garden door.

Meg waited by the gardener's side as Kilovan silently ran to the bedroom corridor. He returned after an agonizing several minutes to squat by her side. "Four rooms," he breathed. "Two might be occupied, not sure. We'll put him in the first one on the left."

She nodded, and they each grasped an arm and dragged the sleeping man—surprisingly heavy—into the chamber. Meg found a towel and swiped as best she could at the streak of mud his legs had left on the floor. Kilovan shut the door, screening them from observation.

Meg's heart pounded against her ribs, and she clamped back on the sudden need to jump, dance, laugh. She forced her focus to the task.

The room was simple. A window, admitting cold air and early morning light; a pallet with a chest at its foot; a brazier, cold now; a rickety table with a pitcher and a basin, a knife, and a brass mirror; a chair; several pegs on one wall with clothing.

Meg opened the chest, found small clothes and stockings; from the pegs on the wall, she pulled pants, a shirt and a doublet in Delarcan livery and threw them on the pallet. No boots. Their own would have to do.

Kilovan stripped out of his wet jerkin. "No good."

She glanced at him. He'd squeezed himself into the shirt, but the pants were clearly too small for his tall frame. Whoever used this room was small.

"We might not find anything for me, and we might not find women's clothing." The sounds of undressing underlay his voice. "Can you disguise yourself as a man? With your magics?"

"Yes." One thing Meg had not stinted on was spells. As he flung the clothes at her, she pulled them on, stockings and pants, shirt and vest, keeping her own underclothes with the pouches of vials. She ripped a hole in the pockets of the pants, so she could reach the magics beneath. The fit was surprisingly acceptable.

A knife on the table by the basin. Sharp, used for shaving. "Cut my hair."

Kilovan wasted no time hacking it short, stuffing handfuls of long strands into the chest with Meg's clothing. She squeezed her wet hair to flatten the unkempt locks into something resembling a proper man's coif, wishing she had a bit of kitchen grease. As she cleaned her boots, Kilovan crept from the room to find clothing to fit him.

She swallowed a potion to age her already calmed skin and hair. From the silence, Kilovan must have found what he was looking for. Next, they'd need to find something, a tray of meats or a jug of water, to give them purpose to go to the royal suite. Meg had never been in the servants' quarters, but Uther Tangel had chased her into the large kitchen once, playing a game of Catch Thief. And, she'd been there the day she tried to ask King Larin for refuge. She knew the way to the royal apartments.

Kilovan hadn't returned.

The morning was lengthening. Tonight in the dark, the upriser troops would march onto the field of battle. They must do what needed to be done and be gone.

Where was Kilovan?

She picked up the brass mirror. Her skin had eased to the waxen color of age, drooping about her rough chin and sprayed with a web of wrinkles. Her hair was flecked, gray and black, and her arms were corded with stringy muscles. She tested the voice, and it came out low, with a bit of a croak. She would do, for several candlemarks.

"Hey! You!" The voice came from the corridor.

Meg flattened herself behind the door.

The sound of scuffling broke out, and feet—may sets—running into the servants' area.

A cry, and then an instant of silence.

". . . get in here?"

Voices.

"Better see if there are any more."

CHAPTER 37

Nowhere to hide in the servant's quarters. Reflexively, Meg squeezed through the window, thankful she was small about the hips and shoulders. The escape left her clothing dusty, with a tear on the hip of her pants. It was mostly covered by her vest.

The garden before her provided no cover. She flattened herself into a niche in the castle wall, blinking in the cold mist, heart pounding.

Kilovan. That cry had to have been his. By Kyaju. *Kilovan* had volunteered to be the assassin, not her. Xanther was a soldier. He had killed. But she was the only one left.

And she looked stupid and obvious, huddled against the castle wall. She needed to look busy, purposeful. She pulled the knife from her purse and scanned the garden.

Daffodils. She blinked. Early spring daffodils.

She sliced their stalks and shook off the raindrops. There. Busy.

A gardener's work. She was not dressed as a gardener, and though the drizzle now lightened to a soggy mist, she was getting wet.

What was she to do, walk out through the tradesman's gate, dressed as a servant for the great hall? What questions would be raised, then? By the Many, she had not got very far.

Flowers. She cut more flowers.

She could use one of her spells of Confusion or Memory Loss, perhaps—she still had several hidden in the quilting of her small clothes. But then what?

Someone over by the kitchen door was calling a name. The voice came closer.

The gardener—asleep on the floor in the servant's chambers she'd just vacated. Was someone looking for him?

And the soldiers who'd—presumably—caught Kilovan. They might be satisfied their captive explained the sleeping gardener, but she would be a fool to operate on that assumption. All men broke under questioning.

She shoved her knife in her pocket and gripping the daffodils like a lifeline, skirted the outside of the castle along a gravel path, away from the voices. It would be some time until her earlier spells of Confusion and Well-Being wore off and the cooks and scullery maids began to piece together that Xanther had not taken his passengers, but those questioning them might deduce the facts earlier.

The stone wall was long and unbroken, and the garden disappeared in favor of storage sheds and outbuildings. Smithy, butchery. Luck was with her, and no one was about. Yet.

A door. Into the back of the great hall.

She tried it. A simple thing to open with magic, but no need. It was unlocked. She stomped the muck from her boots.

The bakery, full of bakers and their helpers. Piss.

She turned—

A servant's stairs. Yes!

Someone called to her.

"I've been summoned to Lord Wenid's suite," she responded in her new voice, and ran up the stairs. This body, however, did not run three flights of stairs as Meg would have wished. She'd slowed considerably—and was panting—by the time she reached the top. She wiped her boots on a carpet and shook off the dampness clinging to her clothes.

A corridor. A vase on a table. She shoved the daffodils into it.

Kill the magiel? The thought made her mouth go dry.

Kill.

How she had wanted to. Kill the magiel who'd stolen her life. Kill the king who'd permitted it. Kill the soldiers who'd followed such foul orders without question.

She had wanted to, when she was safe in her hovel, when she was in a tent on the mountainside. When there was no chance of her being able to do it.

But now, the castle crawled with those who would imprison her. Behead her.

Her mission would fail.

Meg picked up the vase with the flowers. Her feet moved with false confidence down the wide corridor.

A maid servant came out of a room carrying a chamber pot and closed the door behind her, turning purposefully the other way.

Meg walked, taking in everything before her, around her.

A guard, bored, stood before another door.

The corridor echoed with the scuff of her boots on marble. A voice carried from some distant room.

There was nothing to do but find Wenid's chambers. What came after . . . she would face when she got there. If she got there.

She remembered this corridor. But somehow, it didn't seem to align with Xanther's sketch. Gods, why? A finding spell would only work with—

And then, the magiel was in front of her.

Emerging from the top of the wide stone steps, slowly, leaning on a cane, two attendants by his side.

Why did he look so frail?

When she saw him a year ago, he had no cane. But he walked— toward her—as if he were in pain.

Oh, how could she kill a helpless old man?

He stopped at a double door, and she set the vase on a ledge in front of a glassed window. She pretended to arrange the haphazard stalks, one eye following the magiel's movements.

Guards opened double doors, and he and his attendants entered. The doors closed.

She'd found his chamber. Yes! *If* that was his chamber.

She took a deep breath, biting back her grin, her insides vibrating.

One step at a time. Don't think.

Meg turned back to the flowers. She had no idea what to do. All the plans she'd come up with. All the eventualities she'd discussed with Kilovan and Xanther. None had come close to the situation she was facing now. She was not Kilovan, strong enough to throw a curse into the guard's face and drag him inside a door. She had . . . daffodils.

Taking a breath to calm herself, she squared her shoulders and lifted the vase. She strode up to the guards at Wenid's door. "Fresh flowers for the chancellor." The voice she used was pleasingly gruff.

One of the guards put his hand on the knob. The other frowned. "Now?"

Hurry. What to say? "They are fresh now, Sieur." Although, to be truthful, they were beginning to wilt. Her poisoned knife.

Another spell of Confusion? She had one left.

At the far end of the corridor, near the servant's stairs she'd run up, the baker, covered in flour, pointed to her. "That's the one."

Weeks. Weeks, Janat had lingered in the cell. Like the others, she'd tried her hand at manipulating the door's locks, but a magiel of some power had warded them. Artem's magiel, Wenid Col, no doubt; reinforcing his spells, knowing he was detaining magic wielders. Without knowing the magiel's work, Janat could not guess how to go about breaking it.

She'd missed the equinox. Lost her opportunity to learn what Mama had wanted for them. The opportunity to right the wrongs that had turned her world upside down.

Had Meg or Rennika kept the rendezvous? It seemed unlikely. How could they? Two women in a world of thievery and war. And . . . nothing, as far as she could tell, had changed. No great magic had been wrought.

Now, it was hard to convince herself that anything mattered.

She and the other women were not treated badly, only confined. Their food was meagre but healthy and varied, they were not left in manacles, and they were allowed a few minutes of well-guarded exercise above ground each day. Their captors told them nothing but appeared to want them able-bodied. At random times, one was taken, and that one did not return. The women speculated on the fate of the selected ones, but that's all it was. Speculation. New captives were brought; always, the one with the most capricious skin was taken.

Today, though, in Janat's case, they appeared to make an exception, perhaps because she'd been here, now, longer than any of the others.

Her hands were bound and the door behind her clanged shut.

A soldier on either side grasped her upper arms. She swallowed back her apprehension and schooled herself to observe their route, to orient herself to the geography. She'd been in Larin's castle before, the summer Mama toured the seven countries. She took note of where they were taking her, of hiding places and ways out.

They climbed from the underground cells and crossed the bailey in the rain to the great hall, going in through a servants' entrance by the kitchen garden. They climbed servants' stairs and came to a plain but comfortable suite, such as she had not been in since leaving Archwood. The room was dominated by a canopy bed which, she guessed, held a feather mattress. A sitting area, with table, chairs, and a couch before a fireplace, was warmed by a fresh blaze. Glass-paned windows overlooked the stables. In an attached room, a handful of maids poured hot water into a bath.

A bath. How Janat had longed, this past year and more, for a bath.

The soldiers unbound her and were gone, locking the door.

※

The decanter was metal, as were the goblets. There was no poker or candlestick or plate of sufficient heft to use as a weapon.

Janat wasn't daft. She hadn't refused the bath or the scents or the supple robe, nor had she refused the hot and tempting meal. She had declined the wine in favor of water. But now, beneath the watchful eyes of the maids—who, she had no doubt, would intervene if she chose to do something to alarm them—she roamed the suite hunting, hunting for anything to use in her escape. Part of her wanted to pour a goblet of wine to calm her nerves, but yet, she held back.

Doubtless all the magiel women brought here before her had done the same. There was not even a whiff of any herb that could be manipulated into a charm.

But unlike the lesser magiels, Janat could likely make her way to the great halls' doors; and as a daughter of one of the Great Houses, she could, with an effort, call forth magic without the use of ingredients. Even throw spell words a short distance. All she needed was a chance.

The sun had long set and the room was dark but for the glow of a few soft candles and the flicker of the fire, when the door to the corridor opened.

Soldiers, again. This time, they stood aside as a hazy-skinned man, dressed in a clean, decent shirt and pants, entered.

"Gweddien?" The name escaped Janat's lips before she questioned the wisdom of revealing herself.

It took him only a moment. "Janat?"

She blinked.

"Leave us." He flicked a finger and the soldiers withdrew. "All of you," he barked, and the maids scurried away. The lock snicked behind them.

How it was possible, she didn't know, but the unexpected sight of someone she knew released a surge of grief. Without warning, tears streamed down her cheeks.

"Shh, shh." He rushed to her and gathered her into his arms.

"Oh, Gweddien—" She wept on his chest. How long had she known him, on the road, and in Silvermeadow? Maybe half a year, at most? She'd had eyes only for Sulwyn then and couldn't remember . . . had Gweddien and his mother left Silvermeadow before she and her sisters went to Kandenton, or after? And what had brought him here?

No . . . he'd gone missing. She remembered. His mother had been beside herself.

"Hush," he murmured into her hair. "What are you doing here?"

"Captured." And all the events since Archwood inundated her and overwhelmed her.

Gweddien led her to the bed and sat beside her until her sobs quieted. "I am so, so sorry."

"But . . ." This made no sense. She gestured to the room. "Why . . . why has King Artem—Huwen, I mean—seized us, only to give us these luxuries?"

Gweddien's face became subtly darker. "It's exactly what it looks like."

A crawling sensation crept over her skin. "I . . . don't understand." But she did.

"It's not Huwen." A sheen broke out on Gweddien's skin and his eyes darted, restless. "It's Wenid. He wants magiel babies."

She jerked back.

His mouth curled as though he tasted something bitter. "I don't know why."

Her gorge rose. "And . . ."

The bed.

She stood, backing away.

Those women. One each night. "You . . ."

He straightened ever so slightly. "There's no hope, Janat."

She gave him a sharp look. Something was wrong with him. He was ill.

"The soldiers will be on guard outside the door all night. If we don't perform, we'll be punished." The words were almost perfunctory. He'd said them before. Many times.

"Then they can punish us."

"I've seen what he can do." He looked away. These whispered words came out hoarse, agonized. Honest.

She couldn't help herself. She felt a sneer crawl up her lip. "You're in on this?" she asked. "For the sake of regular meals and a gilt cage to live in?"

His eyes flashed, black. "No!"

"No?"

He spoke vehemently. "There are rebels, Janat. Maybe you don't know. Revolutionaries fighting Artem's madness."

She remained silent. She knew. But this masquerade might be intended to draw her out.

"I was *one* of them," he spat. "Don't accuse me of treason for my own gain."

She lifted a brow. The evidence of his treachery was right before her.

He let out a helpless breath, seeming to lose all the bones in his body. "I'm ensorcelled. Can't you see?"

"No. You look to be in full possession of your body, your mind, and your will." Or . . . no. There was something wrong with him. There was. A . . . palsy. "Would you force yourself on me?"

"Don't!"

She paced, abruptly filled with the need to move, to distance herself from him, to strike out. "We're magiels! There must be some way we can escape."

Coldness settled on Gweddien and his eyes lidded. "Not for me." He looked up impotently. "We will do as Wenid wishes. Gently, or forcefully."

Gweddien was an enemy.

"I'm sorry, Janat. But I can't . . ."

Sorry? She wanted to spit on him.

A peculiar change came over his expression. "Janat. Falconer." He stood. Watched her. Wiped the sweat from his brow and rubbed one eye, shivering. "My God. Janatelle. Falkyn. From Archwood," he whispered.

That name. She'd never told him.

He marched to the door and knocked. A soldier opened it. "Summon Chancellor Wenid."

No! *Gods*, no!

"He must come immediately."

CHAPTER 38

Huwen slumped in his chair, staring at a supper he no longer had a stomach to eat. The dull light of the rainy evening gave a gray cast to the opulent chamber, robbing its carpets and tapestries of color. It was not the fatigue of travel or even grief for his father that dragged down his shoulders, so much as the words of Uther's story turning over and over in his head. The uncertainty he'd felt all day, observing his advisors, seeing his entire life, his entire world, with new eyes. Uther's tale had confirmed nothing but implied much.

Eamon had died. Almost two years ago. The child had seen Heaven, not as a king caring for his magiel saw it, gray and stripped of rapture, but in all its radiant glory. Return to this earthly sphere was a torment the boy could not endure.

The page announced his magiel, and Huwen straightened. "Wenid."

"Your Majesty." The old man bowed, steadied by his cane.

Huwen indicated the seat at the table opposite him. "Please. Sit. Eat."

"I've dined, Your Majesty, but thank you." Nevertheless, the old man, dressed in rich vestments of silk brocade, accepted the seat. Interesting. He didn't wear the unbleached linen of a magic wielder. And within the lined face, the eyes were sharp and . . . curious? . . . predatory?

"I spoke with Uther last night."

If the news was significant to Wenid, he made no sign, but his countenance veiled with caution. He avoided Huwen's eyes by perusing the jam cakes.

Huwen tapped his fingers on the tablecloth. "I asked Uther about the night my brother died."

This stopped Wenid's hand, only fractionally, as he reached for a small cake. "Praise the One God for His mercy," he murmured.

"I am the king. You are my magiel. There should be no secrets between us."

This caught the old man's attention. "Certainly not."

"From Uther's story, I'm led to understand that you brought my brother back from death."

The eyes calculated. "It was a near thing, Majesty."

He shook his head, once, sharply. "Not near death. *Death*."

His magiel studied him, judging. "When you attend me in Heaven, Your Majesty, your . . . comprehension . . . of the circumstances will clarify."

Not an answer. A carefully worded insult. But Huwen had more pressing matters than to rise to the bait. "And in payment for violating the death taboo, for dragging Eamon back to earth, all Gods other than the One must be stripped of their followers. Do I comprehend that?"

Wenid licked his lips. "Yes." He looked Huwen directly in the eye as he spoke, yet something in his manner made Huwen think there was a hidden complexity in this response, too.

"My father's war is not about trade, or politics, or even religion. It is about his debt to the One God."

For a long moment, he thought the inscrutable man would not answer, but he spoke. "It is about all of these matters. Sire."

Huwen's heat rose. "You are aware that since that time Eamon has been tormented. That he has wished to take his own life."

"I am aware." His face was flat. Dangerous.

And understanding crystalized. Not to *end* this life, but— "To return to Heaven."

Wenid made no response.

"Is that why Father sent him here with you? With the Ruby? So you might travel with him to Heaven for brief moments, to *feed his illness*?"

"You are asking—"

"Father's *dead*!"

The magiel's mouth snapped shut.

His brother. Touched by the realm beyond death, the realm of perfect beauty. And with Wenid and the Ruby, he could dissipate his life in its pursuit.

And waste Wenid, too. Which was perhaps why the old man seemed so much more frail. Wenid no longer had the power to object. They fed each other.

Disgust turned Huwen's stomach.

What was he going to do? Demand the Ruby, for one thing. Eamon would not touch it again.

A loud rap sounded on the door. "Your Majesty!"

He pierced Wenid's face with his gaze.

"Your Majesty!" Another sharp knock.

"Enter."

The page stood aside and a handful of his guards strode into the room. His general entered, and a mud-spattered young soldier knelt on one knee. "Sire, rebels have gathered an army south of the Coldridge River."

"What?" Huwen pivoted in his chair.

His general nudged the young man to stand.

"At dawn today, my platoon returning from Archwood discovered an upriser encampment six miles from here," the soldier reported. "We surprised them but were grossly outnumbered. They slaughtered many of us before we could escape."

Huwen was on his feet. "Details."

"I was unable to see the extent of their numbers but there are several thousand, at least, with horses and dressed in common clothing in the fashion of Teshe, Midell, Gramarye, and Elsen. The scouts who routed us were armed with a variety of weapons, including good steel."

"General."

"I have called a war council in the Blue Room with your ranking officers. However, the majority of Arcan's armies are en route from Archwood or on their way to Holderford. I have sent scouts to recall them."

The transition between kings. A small borderland fort. And the new king, his magiel, and his brother. And . . . the Ruby. All, together. The rebels' strategy—and information?—was staggering.

His own position was far too overconfident.

Huwen bit his lip. He had no experience of war, other than the endless siege at Archwood, and little training. He nodded to the general. "Assemble your maps and whatever else will aid in our planning. I will be there directly."

His general saluted.

"And, to you . . ." he said to the soldier. Older than him.

". . . Grayson."

"Grayson. Good work."

The soldier saluted, and the contingent departed.

Wenid had risen.

Huwen turned to his inner chamber. He must dress. "We will continue this discussion later."

"And Archwood?"

Wenid's change in subject came from nowhere.

"Sire, I have a great desire to know." Wenid leaned forward on his cane, and the facade over his hunger faltered. "Your courier brought the news. Archwood has fallen. But . . . the Amber?"

"What of it?" Huwen shoved away the sudden image of the uncanny stillness and silence. The stink of death.

Wenid closed his eyes, trembling with self-restraint. "Is the Amber destroyed?"

Huwen shook himself. He had no time for this. "The Amber was smashed publicly, as were all the other prayer stones." He could withhold some complexities as well. "We can discuss details later. Now." He had to show strength. "Prepare yourself. I will be at the war council directly. I expect you there."

"Sire."

"What!"

"Such a battle as we face here is nothing to the One God. If unopposed by any prayer stone."

Huwen hesitated, a hand on his chair.

"A prayer." Wenid leaned a fist on the table. "Is all it takes."

The suggestion gave him pause. Of course, he was the royal of the Ruby, now. Huwen had known, part of him had known, this day would come, yet it took him by surprise. And . . . something cautioned him. Such a solution, calling on the One God for intervention, was too easy. "Praying would absent me from my troops. Both at prayer, and then in recovery."

"Your generals, by your leave Sire, are more experienced in directing a battle on the ground."

"A king must be seen to lead."

Wenid straightened slowly. "Your brother could take your place."

"At the head of the army?" The idea was preposterous. Eamon was fifteen.

"In Heaven."

Huwen knew the answer before he allowed himself to speak. "No."

Again, Wenid knew better than to argue. He drilled Huwen with his eyes.

Huwen shook head slowly. "He can't." The days, weeks Eamon had spent. Sleeping, hiding in darkened rooms. Disinterest in food. In friends, in family, in self-pride. His brother was too young to disappear into a dark void of dependence. Then— "Where is the Ruby?"

Wenid's eyes lidded. "In the shrine. Of course."

A wash of relief eased through him. "Eamon must not—"

"Your Majesty!" A pounding sounded on his door.

Huwen whirled. "I am coming!"

The door flew open and a member of the household guard entered in sudden confusion.

"What!"

The boy blinked and bowed. "A—an urgent message for Milord Chancellor."

Gods, was his private chamber a crossroads for every messenger in the kingdoms?

"Speak," Wenid said.

"Your servant, Gweddien." The guard licked his lips. "He urges your immediate presence."

"Your Majesty." Wenid bowed. "I request leave to depart."

Huwen stared at the two. Stranger and stranger. But his generals waited. "Granted. Do *not* be late to the war council."

✼

Rennika peered into the camp from the door of her tent. Twilight was gone. After a tedious, rainy day of being in everyone's way as soldiers finalized preparations for their dawn attack—and at the same time, spotted the instant she drifted near the horses or supply tents—Rennika found herself edgy with worry and frustration. Meg had not returned. And there was nothing, absolutely nothing, Rennika could do.

Now, though, the upriser camp was deserted. Well, not quite. A handful of cooks and old men, farriers and such, and a minimal crew of sentries, mostly boys about Rennika's age, remained. In one corner of the camp, a company of soldiers that only arrived last night were preparing to leave for battle as replacements. But the thousands of men, who had been here until dusk, were gone.

At sunset, the camp had sprung to sudden life. Something happened—Rennika never did determine what—and the rebels' entire strategy changed. They mounted and left before the last light had gone from the sky.

And now . . . nothing. The rain had stopped, and the constellation of Faolan's Crown rose behind scattered cloud. Rennika knew she should sleep, but until Meg returned, sleep would not be possible.

Now, though, no one was inordinately concerned with watching the horses. Or the supplies. Or—since her minder had become distracted gossiping with the cook about the change in plans—her.

Sulwyn's breath puffed white in the cold air as he sat his horse on a slight rise, overlooking the last hundred yards that separated the upriser army from the city wall, gates closed, beyond the river. Twilight had faded from the sky, and the shot of battle whiskey had faded from his blood.

He fumed. Meg's horses. Two nights ago, she and Rennika had been surprised by a party of Arcan soldiers on the road from their rendezvous and escaped by stealing two mares. The soldiers had tracked them.

Their sentries had been solid, given a good fight, killed or captured the enemies. All but two, and that was enough. Their men gave chase, right to the walls of Coldridge, and managed to kill one with a fortuitous arrow. The other gained the safety of the fortress.

Piss!

Meg, Kilovan, and Xanther had gone to Coldridge in the early candlemarks, to return before nightfall—if they could—and the rebel army was to have departed at midnight for a predawn attack. Not now. Dwyn ordered an immediate mobilization, and now they waited while Orville moved his cumbersome machines into place. Not an auspicious beginning.

Surprise attack, the uprisers' weapon, had evaporated.

Dwyn arrayed his archers in a long line, many ranks deep on the battlefield, pike and swordsmen ready with shields and ladders. The rain had stopped but the ground was soft, and Orville's machines were heavy. They crawled along the field through mud churned by draft horses, pushed by straining men. Sulwyn hoped Orville's promise that they could function from a distance was true; and that their troops could hold out against the royal forces long enough for the machines to prove their worth.

The good news was a courier had arrived in the night, reporting a successful surprise infiltration of Storm River and a surrender parley at Farfalls. Umber had fallen to upriser forces.

Now, if only Xanther and Kilovan—and Meg—would report back. To attack Coldridge in the face of the power of the Ruby was folly. And he did not want to attack while the assassination party was inside the city walls. While Meg was inside the city walls. The murder, if it were successful, should have been accomplished by now.

The horse next to him nuzzled the stubble, lips questing for a bit of green. Sulwyn glared at his lieutenant, and the man brought his mount's head up.

But the men had been standing, tense, waiting Dwyn's command for more than a candlemark. They were not mercenaries, not professionals. They were bakers and smiths and farmers. Each was prepared to die for what was right. For their mothers and daughters and lovers. For the sake of an ideal and a toast of whiskey among brothers.

By Kanden's goodness, why was there no sign of Meg? Sulwyn pulled out his wine skin, filled now with whiskey, and took a mouthful to push the worries back.

The city was on alert. Meg and the others were not going to come running from the front gate. And if they did, they'd be shot from the parapets.

No, Meg Falkyn would come by some hidden route. Or not at all.

✤

Wenid did not leap to obey the summons' of servants, but just now, the request to go to Gweddien had come at an opportune moment. The boy king would be a handful, he could see. He needed to rethink his strategy with the youth. The Amber, crushed. Yet . . . the young lion cub had not told all. He would need to be coached in better dissembling.

Wenid followed the guard to Gweddien's appointment chamber.

A girl stood in the corner, balanced on the balls of her feet like a cat about to dart. Her skin barely shimmered, and Wenid would have dismissed her as a half-blood unworthy of his Marigold plan.

Gweddien, sitting on the unused bed, ashen and clammy, jumped up as soon as Wenid arrived. "I didn't want to send information with a messenger in case you wanted this quiet." He eyed the guards.

Wenid nodded and they left. The girl watched them, calculating escape.

"Janatelle Falkyn."

Wenid whipped around. "Falkyn!"

The boy nodded, clammy with his need for glim, but earnest.

Wenid re-evaluated the girl. "You're sure."

Rage and fright widened her eyes and she had frozen, staring.

"I traveled with her for a season—more! A year ago." Gweddien would not lie. Wenid had established that early on.

There was no purer bloodline. Her skin, only faintly blurred, was a testament to her mother's power over her own biology. In fact, this girl was likely a stronger magiel than Wenid was.

She also—potentially—knew about the Amber. Huwen had been evasive. Neither had he reported that Talanda's daughters' bodies had been found in the city. Something had frightened that boy, badly, saying that Talanda had cursed Archwood—Orumon— from beyond death.

Such a thing . . . could not be possible.

He studied the girl, her expression hooded now, wary. She would divulge nothing about the existence of her sisters. The Amber. Her mother's power.

But the debauched magiel fawning at his side would tell him anything.

Well. That decided it. Wenid rapped on the door to the corridor and his sentries returned. "Bring her."

"Sire?" Panic sent Gweddien's voice a register higher.

The girl paled in fear.

A crack like thunder exploded somewhere beyond the walls, and the floor convulsed.

He gave the boy a faint smile and nod. "You may come as well."

CHAPTER 39

When the door rumbled shut and clanged against its stone sill, the depth of lightlessness in the dungeon had been absolute. The emptiness of the silence had been absolute. Meg sank against the rough wall and slid to the floor, hugging her shoulders for courage.

She'd been only superficially searched. Her knives were taken, her male body patted down. It mystified her. The quilting in her small clothes still concealed her four undiscovered potions. But someone had shouted an order, and the soldiers shoved her here, not taking time to make her strip.

She shivered with the penetrating cold.

By Kyaju, this was not supposed to happen. *Kilovan* was to have assassinated Wenid. Meg was only supposed to be along to find their way through the castle and if need be, to toss a spell of Confusion into the air to mask them as they escaped.

She touched the outlines of the vials she still carried, encased in thick padding. A Heartspeed, a Confusion, a Memory Loss, and a Poison—the last to be taken only under the worst conditions, before she could betray secrets.

The poison was swift but not instantaneous. She'd seen a rat die of the stuff once. It stiffened and shuddered, trying to crawl as it convulsed—

Her bowels loosened. She would not have the courage to put the vial to her lips.

But, would she have the courage to face— She had no idea what her captors might do. Rape. Torture. Magiels were burned.

The plan to assassinate Wenid Col had been hers. Why had

she been so angry, so confident, so—so stupid? Every other time, Sulwyn had stepped in, forbidden her to act on her wild plans. Protected her. She should've listened.

She shifted her position, fingers exploring the time-smoothed oak of the door, the moss-furred stone of the wall. The air in the cell was close, stale, and it stank of piss, and worse.

Hunger came, then faded.

The silence of the tiny space was broken only by her own breaths, the sound of her clothing moving against her skin and the rough stone as she adjusted her stiff limbs.

So.

She waited in the dark. The cell door did not hold her; she could open it when she wanted. Something had happened to Kilovan. He'd been caught. She knew he'd been caught. He was imprisoned elsewhere, or dead. She hoped he wasn't dead.

Something touched her and she screamed, her shriek dying almost immediately in the small space. A spider on her neck, that was all.

She hadn't found a chamber pot, so she dampened the earth a few paces away, then returned to her stony seat.

She slept, and woke with a start. How long had she been here? She was no longer certain of the time. Not long, though. A few candlemarks. She was barely refreshed.

She peed again, then rasped her tongue around her mouth, searching for moisture. A headache throbbed against the back of her neck. No food or water. They'd forgotten her, and there would be no sentry beyond the door. It might, by now, be deep night.

She climbed to her feet, too anxious and restless to sit longer. She couldn't stay here. To remain, guilty with spells and flickering skin, was to invite discovery. She was a magiel. She would be put to death. She was a rebel. She would be tortured. She was a woman. She would be raped.

Deep night—if it was—or the chaos of the battle, which should start at dawn, would give her the best opportunity to escape.

Or . . .

To commit murder. Meg was—almost certainly—the only one left to do it. The thought made her stomach twist.

How could she? She had no weapon.

Four spells.

Heartspeed, for her own endurance.

A Confusion. No good for killing. Besides, she needed it to escape the castle.

A Poison. To take if she was captured. It would kill Wenid, though.

A Memory Loss. Why had she brought such a silly spell? She should've brought another Disguise instead. She touched her cheek. The stubble of her old man camouflage was mostly gone and she could now feel her own youthful hair and supple skin. So. Fifteen candlemarks, at most, could have passed since she'd swallowed the elixir. It might now be past midnight.

She touched the door, the handle, the lock. The door was thick and the iron strong, but it was meant to withstand force, not tricks. The interior of the lock was simple, and she readily found a time when the position of the tumblers was open. To use magic was a poor strategy when she needed her wits about her, but this was a small magic, its costs most likely fleeting.

The door eased in its jamb. She pulled with all her strength on its massive bulk and it grated away from its stone sill. She wet her lips, a fluttery, empty feeling in her stomach.

The opening on the far side was as inky as her prison. There was no guard.

But the air moved slightly. She oriented herself. She'd come from the left, she was sure of it.

She pulled the door closed behind her with an ear-shattering clang, announcing to all that she had gone. Reaching into her small clothes for the triangular vial, she removed it from her clothing, and shook it. Small crystals clinked against the glass; the Memory Loss. She poured a single crystal into her palm and pocketed the container.

❈

The uprisers had swallowed Meg's spells of fearlessness and strength. They shuffled now, with restless energy, and grumbled with focused aggression. On King Gramaret's order, they took the battle to the walls. Their missiles, though less skillfully loosed than their counterparts', found their marks.

And, wonder of wonders, Orville's machines flung fire and iron into the city, toppling crenels, cracking stone, burning timber. The king's men could not hold against their fury.

�֍

Janat's wrists were tied behind her.

"My Lord Magiel!" Gweddien scurried to his master's side fawning, panicking. "I didn't mean for you to do this *to her*. Don't do it! I'll do what you want. I'll hold her down—"

The magiel turned on him. "Do you wish to come?"

Gweddien's mouth closed and he swallowed, wildness flitting through his eyes.

Gods, what had alarmed Gweddien? And where was the old magiel taking them?

Janat crumpled to the floor. But the soldiers lifted her by her upper arms and dragged her, wriggling and screaming, toward the door until the pain in her twisted shoulders was too great. She walked.

And when Gweddien tried to catch her eye, a guard shoved him. He stumbled forward. A second crack of thunder reverberated overhead, rocking the floor. It was too early for spring thunderstorms.

The corridors of the great hall had taken on a different character. Pages, serving girls, soldiers and courtiers, tense and pale, hurried this way and that. Panic?

The magiel pushed his way, hobbling on his cane, down a spiral stair.

Gweddien had tried to signal her.

Traitor. He'd given her up to Artem's magiel. Given her *name*.

They descended into darkness, stopping briefly at a niche where one of the guards took a handful of candles from a box. Wenid lit them with a word. A small magic with little cost.

They came to a deep basement and at the end of a short roughhewn tunnel, a door. They entered a chill, dank cell. At a nod from Wenid, the guards released her and stationed themselves just within. "Unbind her," Wenid told Gweddien.

Gweddien slipped behind her and worried vigorously at her

knots. "Don't drink it," he whispered. "On your death token, swear—"

Wenid's head snapped around. "You are dutiful?" he asked. "You would not wish me to deny your need."

Gweddien pulled the ropes from her and hurried to where Wenid placed his hands on a warded closet by a table. Oddly, there was a bed beside the table.

Janat calculated. She would not bypass the soldiers guarding the room's solitary egress. She would not be able to wrest a blade from them. There might be spells here . . . Wenid's spells. And he would know where they were and what they could do.

She could cast without ingredients. Weakly. Not powerfully enough to stop a magiel.

Gweddien watched hungrily as Wenid poured a small measure of some powder into two goblets and added a mouthful of wine to each. As soon as the older magiel gave him a mug, Gweddien gulped its contents greedily.

Don't drink it.

He shot Janat a look of shame, then lay on the bed, curling himself away from her.

On your death token. Swear.

What was in the wine? Wenid turned, holding out the second goblet.

She could not run, could not fight.

She took the goblet. Yes. There was wine, and something else. Wolf tears, strong. Lotus. Black moly root. And . . . a plant she didn't know. Only a little of this, but collected under the rising Warrior Star.

"You have no choice," the magiel said.

She pulled the unknown plant back to a time when it was fresh-sprouted. Gods, she hoped this weakened its potency.

She smelled the wine. "Is it a love charm?" Wolf tears. She found a time when the wolf smelled smoke, and the tears were more water than magic. The black moly root. She brought it forward in time, wizened it, dried it to flakes to precipitate out of the wine.

Wenid put a hand on the back of her neck, more strongly than she would have thought possible, and pushed the cup to her lips. "No more delay." The wine splashed against her throat and she swallowed reflexively, stumbling to her knees.

He bent and tipped the glass hard against her lips. She choked, gulping most of its contents before shoving the cup away. He let it fall, dribbling only dregs into the packed earth floor.

And then . . .

She stood *beside* Janat and Wenid.

She watched as he took her elbow, and felt no touch.

She blinked. Curious.

There should be sounds of voices as the guard's and Wenid's lips moved, but, no. She heard only the sound of wind on a glacier.

Then she was looking down on the three of them from far above the low ceiling. Wenid led the Janat in the cell to lie on the pallet beside the unmoving Gweddien.

She lifted through stone and wood and glass, now looking down on the city from a great height. The forest. The . . .

A gray mist engulfed her, swirling, neither light nor dark, damp nor dry, warm nor cool. A limitless expanse that shifted restlessly, sorrowfully, touching her with vast anguish.

Ghosts. Clear now, and visible. Untold numbers of them, wailing in despair.

She . . . was not a ghost, not dead, but surrounded by, filled by, translucent, colorless grievers. The dead. Worldlings and magiels with no death token when they passed. Never to attain even the lowest sphere of Heaven.

Still she rose, floating above the sea of spirits, hoping she had in some small way, blunted Wenid's magic. Somewhere far off, Gweddien, like her, rose.

As she ascended, formless, she lightened, buoyed, filled with joy. She had no ears to hear sound, no eyes to perceive color, no nose to scent freshness, yet her nonexistent senses burst with vibrancy within peace and wonder. Her nonexistent body thrummed on the edge of an intense pleasure just out of reach.

She came to a barrier.

And beyond lay . . .

Euphoria.

❋

Huwen paced the parapets of the castle wall in the capricious flicker of the torches, touching a man's shoulder here, giving an encouraging word there, playing the king. The ultimate father, younger than most of them. Oh yes. That was him. The one in command. He schooled his face to keep from betraying his sickness at the carnage. Shame at his hand in this slaughter. His terror of Wenid's grip on his brother.

By the One, he'd never commanded an army—not one up to its neck in blood and death. His generals shouldered most of the work and the details of deployment, but the ultimate responsibility was Huwen's, alone.

Three men jostled past, darting toward a ladder cresting the wall, adding their strength to the swordsmen hacking at men clambering up. Archers shouted about a runner below, and three of them loosed missiles at the hapless man.

It was heartbreaking. Brother hewing brother.

By all reports, the attackers were possessed. They had charged fearlessly through a rain of arrows and climbed the slopes below the town walls, and Huwen's own men, professional soldiers, faltered in the face of the magic that drove them. Despite lack of training and inferior weapons, the uprisers were on the brink of victory.

With earth-rocking explosions, demon machines had flashed brilliant light, and the stones of the town wall, and of *the keep*, leapt into the air and fell in a rain of destruction. They flattened a section of the city wall—ten feet thick—sending the people of the town streaming into the castle, refugees. Now, these machines—from the distance of almost *a mile*—threatened the walls of Coldridge castle.

The streets below the castle walls, and as far as Huwen could see, were filled with sparks of torchlight glinting on a sea of seething bodies and gleaming blades. The smell of sweat and crap and vomit and blood filled the air, amid the grunts and screams of men.

The ladder was repulsed, but one of his men lay against a crenel, an ax wound in his neck. There was no one to carry him away—all were engaged, running to the next ladder, nocking arrows—

Was this better? Better than using the Ruby against his own people?

The bargain his father had made with the One God for Eamon's life bound Huwen to his father's debt. It was not possible, under divine curse, to give in to upriser demands for a prayer stone.

How could he cut short this bloodshed? Talk with the commoners? His first act as king, to reveal his weakness as a leader? And how effective would such talks be when he had no olive branch to offer them?

Perhaps Wenid was right. Using the Ruby to quell the rebellion must be more merciful than this brutality.

A roar went up, and below the castle gate the uprisers pulled back from one of the coughing, fire-and-steam-spouting trebuchets.

The royal general's men were quick to use the distraction to push their struggle with renewed shouts and clanking of swords, but the uprisers held their ground.

Most of the uprisers' machines remained in the field, but a cadre of fanatical warriors had brought this inferno snarling within an iron cage before the main castle gates. Only now had it begun to hiss clouds of hot steam, its fires flaring in the dark, its hideous growling and rattling rising to crescendo. The uprisers defended it fiercely, and Huwen's men had not been able to get near it. Sooner or later, it would begin flinging chunks of stone at the castle.

A man shrieked, shoved onto the side of the machine, branded.

The soldiers Huwen commanded were good. The men below and on the parapets fought with discipline. But they were too few, and too exhausted from weeks of siege. They needed more men.

Huwen spotted his general a short distance down the wall shouting incoherently in the din. Uther was at his side. There was no use calling to either of them.

Huwen shouldered his way among the men until he reached the commander. "More men!" he said into his ear.

The general gave him a look that showed he comprehended the order, and equally, failed to comprehend where they were to find them.

"The household guards," Huwen yelled.

The general took only a moment to nod. He took Uther aside and bawled instructions into his ear.

CHAPTER 40 ───────

The horse Rennika had stolen from the Arcan soldiers the night she and Meg escaped capture was no rebel horse, so she felt no compunction about leading it quietly from the upriser camp, laden with a filched tent and a bit of misappropriated food. Supplies would be helpful, no matter what she decided.

Once out of earshot, she mounted and guided the beast through the woods in the direction of the King's Road. To reach Highglen, if she were to follow the road, she must go through Coldridge. *If* Highglen was her destination. She wanted to return to Yon and Colin and Ide. Yet . . . she wanted to know what had happened to Meg. So there was no decision to make until she reached Coldridge.

She emerged from the forest near the bridge. The wide plains below the hill where Coldridge sprawled were filled with upriser armies. Little was visible in the dark except patterns of torchlight, but the armies had engaged. Archers flung darts from both sides of the conflict.

—something bizarre had happened to the town wall.

It was as though a careless giant had stepped on one of the battlements, for a chunk of it had dissolved into a pile of rubble, crawling with men like a disturbed ant hill. Platoons of attackers wormed forward under a canopy of shields, bringing their ladders into the deserted streets outside the town wall; and fiery, smoking trebuchets, such as Rennika had never heard of before, lofted rocks or flaming balls of pitch over the walls.

Rennika could leave the road, stay on the south side of the river, and make her way through the forest to Grassy Bluff. But the horse would be difficult to take through the dense trackless woods, especially if there were waterfalls or cliffs, and particularly at night. And walking to Grassy Bluff, carrying her tent and food on her back, would take a week. Besides she didn't want to lose the horse she'd so carefully stolen.

And still. Meg was in Coldridge.

Thunder cracked—from the battlefield?—and impossibly far away, a shower of stone sprayed from the king's keep.

Curious.

There was nothing for it. Rennika took the horse across the bridge and, leaving the road, skirted between the river and the milling chaos. Perhaps she could slip past the distracted men in the dark.

"And where are you going?"

Or, perhaps, not.

An upriser detached himself from a knot of men bending over a casualty, running forward to catch her horse's halter. He peered up at her face. "Sulwyn left you back at the camp."

"I wanted to come. Help. I can make healing potions." She looked up at the town, its walls a pale smudge against the dark sky. Meg was inside.

The sentry eyed the saddlebags and rolled pallet behind her saddle. "Get down. We don't have a man to spare to take you back."

She sighed and lowered herself from the horse.

A roar of shouts went up and the sentry turned. "Ranuat."

The town gates had opened, and a river of soldiers poured out.

"Stay in the healer's tent, then," he shouted, mounting the horse. "Make yourself useful."

Wenid brushed past the page announcing him into Eamon's outer chamber and closed the door on the child. "What is it? I was busy."

"They're shooting." Eamon paced, his complexion pale with fright. "We're under attack. And there's something—huge. It's shaking the keep."

The thunder. Not thunder. Wenid had ignored the first rumble, and the second, fixating on the Falkyn magiel. But since Eamon's page had pleaded for him to come, there had been two more explosions, and it was true: the blasts shook the very stones of the tower.

"We have to go to Heaven. We have to pray for our lives."

The boy was overreacting. "Such prayers are best done before a battle begins."

Eamon stopped pacing and stared at him. "Well, we didn't, did we?" He shoved his hands through his hair. "And when it started, no one could find you," he accused.

"Huwen has forbidden us to use the Ruby."

"What?" Eamon whirled. "He's mad."

"He says professional soldiers and a strong keep can repel peasants."

Eamon returned to pacing. Wenid had rarely seen the boy show more than indifference in almost any circumstance. This agitation was unlike him. "Do you believe him?"

"Actually, I do, in this instance. They have no magiel." He had Janatelle Falkyn, though her presence raised the question of what had happened to her sisters. "No prayer stone."

A blast resounded overhead, and again, the candlesticks rattled. "What's that, then?"

"Noise."

This seemed to calm the boy a little. "I still think we should pray. I'm going to the shrine."

"I want to be alert over the next few days. As should you."

"Why?"

Because. He didn't trust Huwen. The lion cub had discovered he had teeth. Small needles, to be sure, but Wenid was not just sure how sharp his nip could be. "It's late. You should sleep."

Eamon's brows lifted. "In this?"

"It won't affect us here." He considered. "Do you need a sleep draft?"

Eamon sat abruptly on a chair before the fire, tapping on its arm. "No."

"A dram of whiskey to calm your nerves?"

He gave a short, sharp shake of his head. "No."

"Well, with your leave, Your Highness, I believe I will retire to my chambers."

The boy's head turned. "Now?"

"Yes." The girl in the cell did not need Wenid to watch her; the guards would be sufficient as she slept. And it would be morning before she woke and gave him what he wanted. Besides, the cell was cold. Huwen had commanded Wenid to follow him like some kind of puppy, but Wenid was disinclined to cooperate. A nip of whiskey would help a natural sleep to find him. And the ungodly trebuchets the peasants were using *were* loud.

✤

Stay in the healer's tent? Rennika had to smile. In what world did he expect her to do that?

Meg.

Was she still in the town, or had she escaped? Where would she go if she'd freed herself?

Report to the king. Unless she was hurt.

Uprisers surged up the hill, pushing with spell-fueled daring into the maze of buildings that clustered outside the town wall, to engage the new forces streaming from the gates. Only a few clusters of defending uprisers remained on the churned muck of the farmers' fields near the healers' tents, the command tent, and the war machines.

Rennika flitted into a healers' tent. Meg was not there. She left before she could be called upon, and ran to the next. She had to think like Meg.

The Ruby. In Coldridge. A magiel and royal could use it to defeat the army with little or no fighting. Meg had gone to kill the magiel. Had she succeeded?

How long had the battle been waging? Rennika looked up at the stars. Not long, but victory for the rebels had to be fast and decisive, or everything, the people's stolen lands, their death tokens, everything, would be lost. Meg would be lost.

But the prayer stone had not been used yet, or the battle would not still be engaged.

Why had the king not used it?

An explosion boomed almost beside her. Rennika dove to the earth, ears ringing, as a cart bearing a smooth iron log leapt on its wheels. Far behind the town wall—behind *the castle wall*—a shower of stones sprayed from the keep.

The weapon she'd heard of in the camp. From Aadi.

A strange-looking fat man directed a crew to reposition the machine.

But if this little man could crush the keep—the king's personal apartments—he might kill the city's sovereign. The Ruby would be useless but safe. As long as it was elsewhere.

How many more missiles could he launch before whichever royal governed Coldridge used the Ruby? Not many. The keep walls needed to come down on his next ball, or perhaps the one after, or the royals would use the prayer stone.

"Sieur." She scrambled forward.

"Out of here." Two heavy hands landed on her shoulders and she was lifted and shoved away from the machine. She stumbled over her heels into the mud. A soldier glowered down at her.

The fat man had not heard her but continued to direct his men.

"I can help," Rennika cried. "I'm a magiel. I can—"

The soldier snorted his disbelief. "Get away, urchin. We haven't time to give you a proper beating right now." He lifted a foot to kick her.

She scooted back, out of range.

But she didn't need to tell this man she was a magiel. And she didn't need permission.

Tracing the wall lightly with her fingertips, Meg felt her way, one step at a time on the uneven stones, down the passage. Six doors identical to her own might have led to other cells or storage rooms. Then her foot bumped a stone step and she began to climb. She was wide awake and alert with a deep inhalation of Heartspeed. She played through her memory to construct her hasty descent.

As she climbed, the stairs became more regular in height, and a gray light seeped around her when she reached a landing. Narrow corridors extended in two directions, one faintly illuminated from some distant light source—possibly a torch ensconced on the wall. Far off sounds of fighting reverberated off the stone. She must be in a servants' stair. And the servants? Gone, called to their masters' sides.

The stairs continued upward into darkness. She followed them.

A second landing, then a third, both similar to the first, all echoing with boots and shouts and the clash of swords. Following her memory of Wenid's apartments, she felt her way along a passage, hoping she was traveling in the correct direction. At an intersection she recognized the corridor where she'd been arrested. Here, the sounds of fighting echoed only faintly from far below.

In one direction, the hallway ended at a double door. She turned in the opposite direction. Several closed doors stood between her and the central sweeping staircase, but no guards stood watch. Odd—she would have expected soldiers.

A thunderclap boomed overhead, and the floor shivered, rattling statuary. Had the morning's cold drizzle changed so radically to the violence of thunder and hail?

Wenid's door was the last one before the central staircase. She could not waste time creeping. Heart thumping, she walked as quickly and silently as possible along the tiled floor.

The magiel's double door. She'd been here—this morning?— with a vase of wilted flowers. Mouth dry, headache pounding, she reached for the door handle.

Panicky voices from the floor below were more distinct, a soldier giving instructions, sending men to various points on the castle wall. Sulwyn's army must be drawing the royal guards from their posts. A stroke of luck. So . . . the battle had begun. Those thunderclaps— trebuchet strikes? No, not from this distance.

No matter. She had no time. She opened the door to Wenid's suite.

Within, a candle burned, its light glittering on gold leaf and marble, mahogany, and porcelain. A page dozed on a chair next to a door in the far wall. A fire burned low on a grate.

She entered, easing the latch into its seat behind her.

The candle flickered. Did the boy move?

No.

She barred the door to the corridor, wondering if doing so would protect her from interruption or trap her.

She still held the Memory Loss crystal in her hand. Not an easy spell to administer: the boy would have to swallow it.

But he slept on. Maybe there would be no need.

Meg crept across the carpeted floor to the door by his slumped shoulder.

The handle turned soundlessly beneath the soft pressure of her fingers.

The boy started, eyes and mouth wide with surprise.

She shoved the crystal onto his tongue, and he sputtered. Had he spit it out? She rammed her hand over his mouth and leaned on him, pushing him back in his chair.

The page struggled under her weight, breathing sharply through his nose, trying to bite her hand and cry out. He wriggled down the chair, loosening her grip. "Help! Magiel!"

No!

She shoved him with both hands and he stumbled, knocking his head against the wall.

She flung an arm out, catching his elbow as he scrambled past her, knocking over a small table, trying to reach the door to the corridor. She gripped his arm. He stumbled, and she fell on him.

She rolled him onto his back, sat on his stomach and pinned his arms beneath her knees as he screamed and tried to kick her. "Stop screaming," she whispered, and covered his mouth. He bit her.

She pressed her thumbs onto the soft spot of his throat where his death token collar sat.

His eyes bulged, tongue extended, and he redoubled his struggles, almost knocking her away.

She held on, elbows locked, her full weight on his arms and throat.

A clap of thunder blasted her ears and the room shuddered. No, not thunder. Something demonic.

Gradually, his kicking weakened. His eyes lost focus. He stilled. She pulled away, panting, watching for him to twitch, but he lay still, staring at nothing.

There was a long, narrow cloth on the table. She flicked her gaze at the door to the corridor. No sound. She pulled the cloth from the table and wrapped it as tightly as she could around his mouth. Any sounds he made would at least be inarticulate. She tied his hands behind his back with his decorative sash. The trussing might slow him down.

The boy lay disheveled and inert when she was done. The smudge of ghostly interest fluttered near him.

Had . . .

Had she killed him? Her pulse sped.

No. She wasn't strong enough for that. She hadn't held his throat closed long enough. She couldn't have.

Time. No time. Someone would hear, send reinforcements. Her magic would catch up with her. She left the boy, hastening to her feet. Still no pounding from the corridor, no sound from the bedroom.

She entered Wenid's chamber.

By midnight, the uprisers had breached the city wall, gains far beyond Sulwyn's imagination.

Then Coldridge's gates opened and spewed forth a stream of royal infantry. Now the folly of night warfare surrounded him, a melee of bodies impossible to distinguish in the dark. Still mounted, he urged his mare forward into the fray, dispatching two men with disabling cuts, his horse turning in the chaos. His man-at-arms fell and was trampled trying to free his death token. Sulwyn was too far engaged to intervene. The stink of horses and blood and excrement and mud stained the air.

A lull in his immediate vicinity.

He drew back to survey the battlefield —

Someone in the middle of the field, sprinting. Toward the broken battlement.

A girl?

In the faint starlight, she ran across the field from Orville's *cannon*, ducking past the odd skirmish that still raged there.

Sulwyn had the sickening feeling . . .

Gods. It was Rennika.

An explosion sounded from the *cannon*, and the horses screamed, his own mare dodging sideways.

An Arcan horseman bore down on him with his sword. Sulwyn parried, turned in his saddle, his horse bumping up close to the man. He shoved his dirk into the man's gut. Warmth gushed over his knee.

He whirled, trying to see the girl again. "Waymond!" It was no use. None of the men could hear him in the din. None could extract himself.

She was a child. A magiel, a *Falkyn*.

An upriser foot soldier took a blade to the neck, and blood fountained into the air, spurting over Sulwyn's boot and jacket.

There was a gap. Ahead. He spurred his horse.

A horseman—a royal?—charged him from the side. Sulwyn pulled his mare short and he took a stinging cut to his arm. Someone sliced the man, shoulder to gut.

Again, Sulwyn spurred his horse toward the gap, through the city gate, now remarkably free of fighting. He turned his beast into the lane, skirting clashes. Flames crackled from the upper windows of a shop, and his mount shied.

Rennika, if it was her, must have entered the town west of him, where the wall had been breached. Why? By all the Gods in Heaven—

. . . she'd come to find Meg. Of course.

Where would she search?

He urged his horse along the interior of the city wall, slashing at any who engaged him.

There. The mound of rubble that had once been the town wall. Rennika could enter . . . but she wasn't here. He turned his horse in a circle. Where . . .

The castle. She'd deduce Meg had gone to the castle.

Rennika and her sisters had lived in Coldridge a year ago. She would know the streets. He turned his mount up hill.

CHAPTER 41

The upriser cavalry and infantry surged toward the city gates, where royal reinforcements spewed from the city. Rennika darted across the almost-deserted field and up the bushy hillside to the first houses at the edge of the town. A blast behind her and a high whine overhead preceded an explosion somewhere in the city. Reflexively she ducked, and staying low, kept running. She reached the shops on the crooked streets of Coldridge's outer town. As she dashed from corner to doorway to step, swordsmen seemed to take her for a frightened child in the dark, and ignored her.

She climbed the mound of broken stone that had once been a battlement and scrambled up among the legs of the clashing warriors, ducking their blades. More than once she used her talent to find a moment in time when a passage between two scuffles opened briefly, through which she could scurry. She made her way, stumbling on fallen stones, through the inner town, from the wall toward the castle. A weird ruddy light painted the streets as buildings crackled with flame. Despite living here for weeks or more after leaving Orumon, twice she became disoriented in the flickering dark and found herself in dead end alleys.

But the keep, thick-walled as it was, was built into the castle curtain wall. She flattened herself against its fitted stones just as a barrage burst overhead. A spray of rock and pebbles flung themselves into space, raining down on the cobbles.

She closed her eyes, pressing as much of her body against the frigid wall as she could, reaching in, feeling for times when ill-fitted niches, crumbled corners, and shifts of restless foundations sent cracks up through its structure. Found them, multiplied them, held one time against another, against another, against another . . .

Held the cracks, held them, waited . . .

Until an iron ball overhead struck the crenel.

※

Meg slipped through Wenid's door, closing it behind her and willing her trembling to stop. She scanned the lavishly-appointed room in the ruddy light from the hearth. The bed was massive, enclosed by heavy velvet curtains. Four tall windows admitted no light, and the chill spring night was kept at bay by embers on the hearth.

There. On a table stood the remains of a meal. A goblet.

She fished the poison from its hiding place in her small clothes, uncorked the vial, wafted the sickly scent to confirm its identity, and poured the contents into the goblet. She added a few drops of whiskey to the cup to mask its smell and crept across the thick carpets. Opened the bed curtains.

In the gloom within, a figure snored softly beneath a down duvet.

"Your Grace," she said in a low voice.

The magiel slept on. How could anyone sleep in this clamor?

She touched his shoulder, a gentle rousing. "Chancellor Col."

He shifted, snorted, started to rise and fell back onto his pillow.

"Sire. Your medicine." She slid an arm under his shoulders, prompting him to raise himself, and touched the cup to his lips.

He grunted and opened his lips, frowning.

She tilted the goblet and he swallowed, gagging on the whiskey.

"A bit more," she soothed, tilting the cup higher.

He gulped, choking, and she upended the cup.

"There." She pulled the cup away. That was surprisingly easy.

The magiel thrashed in his tangled bedcovers, choking. "I have no medicine!" he managed, furiously extracting himself from the snarl.

She backed away toward the fire.

He flung back the bed curtains and thrust his feet over the side of the bed, reaching for the bed post as though he were suddenly dizzy. "Who are you?"

"The Holder's apprentice," she said. He had drunk all, or most,

of the potion, she was sure. Would it be enough? Or would he
merely sicken and recover?

A sinking regret churned her stomach. She'd done it. *Ranuat,
Goddess of Murderers and Theives, forgive me.*

Had she?

He glared at her, and she saw his face clearly in the dim firelight.
His complexion was inconstant, like hers. He was a magiel. The
old man she'd seen this morning entering the apartment with his
retainers.

"I don't know you!" Then—abruptly—his anger vanished,
replaced by internal preoccupation.

"You are Chancellor Wenid Col," she confirmed.

He gagged. A watery smudge interposed itself in her vision. A
ghost, drawn by death.

It had worked. The poison had worked. "My name is Meghra
Falkyn." Though her face was no longer disguised, he would
not recognize her. They had never met, except the one time she'd
dressed as a maid and overheard his talk with King Artem.

His eyes narrowed. "Meghra . . ." He shook his head. "All of
you? Here?"

What did he— "All of who?"

He closed his eyes, paled, brought a hand to his stomach. "You've
come . . . for your sister?" His words slurred.

Rennika? Ice flooded Meg's stomach. She'd left her in the rebel
camp—

He lurched forward, spraying vomit over the carpet and his
night shirt. No! He mustn't vomit it up—

But— "What do you know about my sister?"

He slid from the bed to let himself onto all fours, staring in
surprise at the stink before him.

Come for— "Is she in Coldridge?"

Again, he heaved, and again. "The One God will sweep aside all
obstacles . . ."

If Rennika was here, Meg had to—

No. The magiel could not be left alive. Meg would find Rennika,
bring her out. But first, she must finish with Wenid.

Gods, would enough of the poison reach his blood? She cast
about the room for a weapon.

Candlestick. Table.

—a plate, and the remnants of food. A knife thrown carelessly across bones and unfinished turnip.

She edged toward the table. Picked up the knife in a trembling hand, palm slick with sweat.

Wenid stared at the vomit. "It doesn't matter." Blurs gathered near him. The spirits sensed he would cross the portal. Soon.

But Meg had seen ghosts denied as well.

She took a tentative step toward him. He was still strong. If she came close, he would grab her arm.

She waited, but he did not move, did not vomit.

"There is only one God." His voice rasped. He lifted a hand to his collar.

Then, unbidden, his stomach heaved.

She darted in, stuck him below his ribs with the knife, and darted out.

He crumpled, the side of his face in the lumpy puddle, grasping his ribs. "Rut you," he wheezed, voice tight with pain, fingers scrabbling at his throat.

She'd done it. She'd stuck him. Her heart beat wildly. She stood well back, watching him.

She glanced at the door. Still no sound from the outer room.

The coals flickered a moment with flame, then dulled.

Was the wound mortal? Too low . . .

He raised himself weakly from the reek, holding his reddening nightshirt to his side. He panted, then spewed again, a massive heave for a bit of spittle. Again, she darted in and stuck him, closer to his gut.

He grabbed her ankle, his grip hard.

She tripped backward, yanking her leg from his grasp, fear screaming through her.

But he moaned and crumpled over the fresh hurt, and his stomach convulsed again. "My . . . death . . ."

A shudder ran through the magiel's torso. His body stiffened, and he rolled on his side, his face a rigid grimace. He retched again, convulsed.

From somewhere came a distant whine, akin to the sound of a mosquito. Then, with a clap—the ceiling overhead cracked.

Meg flinched as a handful of pebbles and a shower of choking dust clattered to the floor. She scrambled to her feet and crouched with her knife, slick with blood, in her hand.

He wasn't yet dead. She could see his side rising and falling as he panted.

She circled around behind his head. The light in the room brightened. Flames, beyond the windows.

He tried to roll toward her, but feebly.

She sliced the artery beneath his ear. A spurt of blood arced into the air. Another, spurt, weaker. A third, a burble. She stood watching, panting.

The ghosts gathered.

A jolt of accomplishment coursed through her.

The magiel shuddered then stilled, staring blankly at the dim ceiling where hearthlight and firelight from a burning city played on a painting of the One God in his Heaven.

Ranuat, absolve me. Meg dropped her knife and fell to her knees beside him. She fumbled at his collar. She pulled out the flat round disc and held it to his lips.

To give him Heaven.

Heaven. An eternity of bliss. When he had robbed so many of their eternal rest. Her hand pulled back a fraction.

She'd killed a man. What would she pay for this act of murder?

To deny him eternity . . .

The token fell from her fingers to the floor.

The magiel lay still. Meg sat back on her heels. *Rennika.*

Thunder cracked, and more rubble fell from the ceiling.

✤

Sulwyn pulled his mare to a halt.

There. At the corner of the castle wall, the base of the keep. In the snap and dancing glow of the burning city.

Rennika pressed herself against the wall as though she held it up with her outstretched arms.

What did she—

It didn't matter.

Two soldiers, one bloody and limping, emerged from a lane,

their breath puffing white into the night air. Sulwyn's shoulder bled freely and he'd taken a slice to his leg, above the boot. The power of his adrenaline and whiskey was fading, and he saw the men through a haze of fatigue. He pushed his horse toward them, reaching out with his sword.

The stroke was weak, and he would have touched only air, but the men approaching him were as exhausted as he was. He drew blood across the arm of the uninjured one. The man staggered, stabbed the mare's ankle.

Sulwyn's horse screamed and reared, stumbling to the cobbles, momentarily pinning his leg until she rolled in her agony and hobbled away.

The men floundered toward him as, with an effort, Sulwyn climbed to his feet.

Overhead. The whine of a *cannon* ball.

The soldiers cast a single frightened glance to the smoking sky, dropped their weapons, and staggered away.

Sulwyn faltered toward the wall, toward Rennika, his arms outspread to cover her from the blast.

Stone splintered overhead.

❁

A crack skittered across the plastered ceiling and the overhead beams groaned as they twisted. Meg had to get out.

She kept the knife, washed it furiously, scrubbed at her hands and face in Wenid's basin. The old man's body stared at her the whole time, the grimace frozen on its face.

Murderer.

"You killed more," she told it and in her own ears, her voice was high and thin.

The crack split between two stones in the wall.

What have you done? it accused. *You've condemned me to torment on this earth forever.*

"You took the people's Gods from them!" she cried. Yet, in the act of withholding his death token, she'd damned herself. Hadn't she?

But did that excuse her?

She wanted to scream at it, kick it, beat it into disregarding her, into leaving her alone, into closing its penetrating eyes. But the keep was disintegrating and Rennika was somewhere in the castle—

A chill touched her shoulder. She whirled, slapping at nonexistent fingers. "You can't touch me!" she cried.

But a tale was told of her mother when Archwood fell. That Talanda Falkyn had cursed the carn and its valley, haunting all who'd lain in siege. Could Wenid haunt her?

By Kyaju, she'd done the right thing. She had.

But . . . killing Wenid hadn't reinstated the people's access to Heaven.

What had she got? Revenge for Mama's death. The satisfaction of holding power over the high king's magiel; of letting him know before he died that it was a *Falkyn* who'd killed him. But she hadn't obtained access to Heaven.

There was no time for regrets. Time would rebound on her, from her use of magic. She could not be caught inside the castle when that happened.

And the crack in the ceiling. The wall. Hovered, waiting to devour the keep. Red light from beyond the windows flickered. Like Archwood, that night so long ago, the city burned.

She poured another Memory Loss into her palm, and stared at the clear crystal. She could swallow this, and the last moments would disappear from her awareness.

Free her from imagined haunting.

Free her from memory.

Free her from what she had done. From the pleasure it had given her.

It was so small in the palm of her hand. So innocent.

But she had committed murder. She had.

She closed her fist on the spell, and removing the vial of Confusion from its concealment, hastened from the room.

She would not erase memory of what she had done.

Rennika sat in a padded chair in a plain but comfortable bedroom with stone walls and rich tapestries and carpets. The canopy bed was raised

from the floor, and its matress was undoubtedly made of wool and feathers. Through a glass-paned window, a brilliant sunset faded over distant mountains. There was no sound but the distant sigh of the wind and a stream nearby.

She wore a simple but thick robe of good Highglen wool, stained, like her hands, with blue and red and yellow. A stink of tannery clung to her and to the room.

A future . . . her future.

Highglen.

CHAPTER 42

A ladder toppled, crushing a score of attackers.

Huwen made his way along the parapet amid cheers from his men. Finally, a gain. Encouraged, his men renewed their ferocity.

Another ladder fell, and another. His archers rained arrows down on the peasant fighters before they could raise their shields. A wind sprang up, and the shafts of the attackers were blown back, failing their marks, while royal bolts flew on guided wings. The soldiers cheered.

The rebels' fiery machine exploded, killing dozens of their own. The battle, as by a miracle, had turned.

And Huwen knew what his brother had done.

He clamped his mouth closed. Wenid was supposed to have joined him, here on the ramparts. But the battle had called Huwen away, kept him occupied—

Wenid and Eamon had defied him.

Huwen caught an archer by the shoulder and the man dropped to one knee. "Majesty."

"Send a page to fetch Prince Eamon to my apartment. Tell the page to instruct my brother that I will brook *no* excuses." Exhausted by Heaven or not, Huwen would see him. He considered sending for Wenid as well, but he had no stomach for another confrontation like this evening's. Huwen would send soldiers to arrest him.

The archer hurried away, brushing past a courier rushing in the opposite direction. Uther.

"What news?" Huwen asked.

Uther handed him a paper, his face grim.

The seal of the Holder of Histories. Huwen broke the wax and read.

Wenid Col was dead.

�֎

Colm could not believe what was happening. Or . . . he could, and it sent dread into the pit of his stomach.

A candlemark after midnight, the tide of battle reversed.

They'd breached the outer walls and entered the city, but now, against the castle wall, their ladders were repulsed. Capricious winds deflected missiles from their marks. Royal weapons struck true.

Magic.

Behind the castle walls, a mighty prayer had been granted. Meg must have failed in her mission. Which meant she was imprisoned or dead.

Colm, directing replacements to take up the ranks of the fallen, looked to Orville's machine, moved now to the middle of the street before the castle's main gates. If only this monster, though made of metal by mere men, could defeat their enemy. It was their one hope.

Another ladder was repulsed. No matter the heart and skill of the uprising attackers, it was they who found uneven ground to trip them, blows missed or squandered. Imperial ranks pushed them back, forcing hand-to-hand combat against the city wall.

Then word came from the troops attacking the castle on the east. Dwyn Gramaret had taken an arrow to the chest. Fearghus, just visible, mounted, consulted a courier. Did he know?

Colm roared at the stars to drive away the image of his rebel king toppling from his horse, lost to sight beneath the melee. Sulwyn was nowhere to be seen.

Swinging his blade, Colm spurred his beast. Touching the death token at his neck, he urged his men forward. But the result was a weak gain followed by a deeper loss as men fell back to a rain of bolts, buoyed by the wind to unprecedented range.

Magic.

The steam trebuchet coughed, spouted fire and clouds, and

exploded in a deafening burst of flying metal brands. A crater appeared where it had once stood, surrounded by a writhing mass of bloody bodies.

The gates opened. Swordsmen poured out, flooding the square. The uprisers' cheer fell to silence.

Then, defying the Gods, Orville's *cannon*, standing almost alone in the far battlefield, landed a true shot on Coldridge's keep.

The ancient structure crumpled as though built of sand.

❋

The boy lay on the floor, working at the belt holding his wrists behind his back, his breath a ragged rasp, his throat beneath his death token collar, bruised. He stared up at Meg.

Thank the Many, he lived. Had he swallowed her charm of forgetting? Meg knelt by him and showed him the knife. "Cry out and I'll stop your voice with this." Her hands were trembling and she wasn't sure she could carry out the threat. But then, she hadn't thought she could stick a knife into Wenid.

The boy, eyes huge, nodded.

She pulled back his gag. "The magiel has my sister. Where is she?"

Terror of a different caliber flicked across the boy's face. "I don't know," he whispered. "I swear—" He was sensible, at least. Perhaps she hadn't managed to administer the Memory Loss.

An explosion burst overhead and a beam in the ceiling cracked, angling down into the chamber. Stones smashed to the floor, bouncing, shattering. Meg ducked and shielded her face from the spray of shards and pebbles.

The boy's brows shot up. "He has cells. Dungeons."

Yes. Of course.

"I can show you."

She rolled him over and, untying the sash, hauled him to his feet. She fastened her fingers on the back of his collar. "Go."

❋

A crack shuddered through the keep. The floor beneath Meg's feet lurched. She and the boy stumbled before they could catch their balance. The corridor was eerily empty, several doors standing open. She gave him a shove, and he scrambled for the stairs.

Holding the smooth railing, she raced down the sloping marble steps behind him. The livery she wore was blood-soaked, but blood would not make her stand out. Her skin and gender would, though. If need be, she had a spell of Confusion. She didn't know how long she'd spent in the dungeon, or in Wenid's apartments, but through the window the blazing city was still swathed in deep night.

An ear-shattering boom shuddered through the keep. The stairs sighed, and leaned further, rubble raining on them. Meg and the boy bolted down the next flight of stairs.

A massive block of stone dropped silently from a great height above them. Meg yanked the boy back, throwing him to the wall and covering him with her body. The block smashed onto the steps below, shattering into a spray of cutting shards. A fragment of marble struck her back as shooting splinters of stinging rock splashed across them.

"Go." She hauled him to his feet and propelled him around the broken steps as another block landed behind them.

They reached the main corridor. Servants and courtiers ran toward the entrance.

"This way." He dodged left through a door and down a spiral into the dark. "Here." He stopped by a niche and grabbed a handful of candles. "Can you light them?" This was no time to question use of magic. She did.

At the bottom of the stairs, he pointed to a short tunnel. "There's a door. At the end." He took a step back. "Please, my ma—"

She registered the boy for the first time. Only a boy. "Yes. Go."

He turned and sprinted up the stairs.

She stepped to the end of the tunnel. The door was locked, but it yielded to her touch.

Within, a single candle stub guttered in a tiny cell. A man knelt over someone lying on a low bed. He wept.

There was no time for his grief. "Is this my sister?"

The man rocked back and forth against the bed, moaning softly.

Meg came closer. A woman in a fine dress curled into a ball on the bed under the man's protective arm. The woman wept as well.

Not Rennika.

—Janat?

Meg fell to her knees beside the man. "Janat?" She shook her. The woman's face was buried in her hands, but her form, her hair . . .

The woman's body tightened and her keening deepened.

"What's wrong with her?" How had *Janat* come to be confined in Coldridge? And where was Rennika?

The man did not reply. The man . . . *Gweddien?* How—

The keep had collapsed under Orville's cannon. They couldn't wait on whatever grieved them. "Can she walk?" Meg demanded.

Neither the man nor the woman responded.

Meg fixed her candle to the table and pushing Gweddien aside, pulled the woman to her feet. In the flickering light, she saw her tear-swollen features. It was Janat.

Huwen stood back from Wenid's body, laid out on the floor of the throne room in the pale light of dawn. In the city, fighting continued but had shifted to hunting out those final nests of uprisers who had not died or fled.

"A stab wound." The Holder of Histories pointed to a gash just below his rib cage, congealed, now. Much of the blood had been wiped away from the magiel's skin and the dark wounds looked like incongruous mouths. "Here. And a second, here," the Holder went on. "Likely, these disabled him, and then the assassin cut his throat, to be certain he was dead." He pointed to the gash beneath the magiel's ear.

The commander spoke. "I interrogated Wenid's guard. He left his post just after one chime, when a call came from the wall for reinforcements. The assassin could have entered his apartments then."

Huwen's order. Piss.

But the Ruby had only just been used, maybe a candlemark ago. Had the magiel been attacked while insensible in Heaven? And if so, why was Eamon not taken with him? And where was Eamon? "Where's the Ruby?"

The holder lifted his head. "In . . . the shrine," he said uncertainly.
"It wasn't on Wenid's body?"

"No."

"But it was just used."

The holder frowned.

Something . . . "Go check. Be sure the Ruby is safe."

The events did not add up. If Wenid was dead, who had prayed to the One God for victory in battle? Eamon could have done so, but Eamon could not go to Heaven without a magiel.

The page he'd sent earlier to summon Eamon appeared and bowed.

"Speak."

"Prince Eamon is not in his apartment."

Meg pushed Janat over a tumble of stones clogging the stairs to the cells. Her sister stumbled stupidly as though she cared nothing for the destruction of the keep. The war. Life. Gweddien had not even roused himself to leave the cell.

Gods, to be able to find the solice of a shrine. The listening ear of a Holder.

Meg and Janat emerged into the bailey. A crowd of townspeople milled or sat, exhausted. The smell of smoke lingered. Ghosts, too.

In the light of the paling sky, the back gate where Meg and Kilovan and Xanther had entered with their milk jugs—only yesterday morning—was closed.

Piss.

She propped Janat's arm over her shoulder to keep her from sinking to the earth in helpless despair, and they made their way with the other refugees toward the main gate.

And the bailey vanished.

Meg lay on the sharp scree of a cliffy, windblown mountainside. Night. Early fall, with the smell of snow in the air.

She shifted, lifted her head from the shale. Janat. Her sister was so young—and Rennika, only a child. They lay snuggled close to her, sleeping. Nanna's eyes were closed, her mouth open, an arm thrown over Rennika. Far below, faint shouts rose from Archwood's walls.

The night they'd run from King Artem's men.

She, too, had been young, then. Not so much in years—what was seventeen compared with nineteen?—but in naiveté. She'd wanted gowns from Aadi. She'd wanted to be a celebrated magiel taking her people's wishes to their Gods. Now . . . she wanted only to survive.

No, she did want something. She wanted her sisters.

By the Many Gods, Meg hoped her seventeen-year-old self inhabiting her body could escape Coldridge castle.

CHAPTER 43

The rebounds in Meg's time stream had settled. Whichever version of herself had lived the past few moments of her escape from Coldridge castle had hidden in a shadowed corner of the compound, and she and Janat were still here, still alive—and still caged within the castle walls. The situation was bad, but it could have been worse.

"Janat?"

Her sister stared at some other world.

"Did you do magic? Are you traveling?"

"No." Janat blinked as though her thoughts moved slowly. "I did. I'm back."

Meg had too many questions. What was Janat doing in Coldridge? In a dress? In prison? But there was no time.

Tears again leaked down her sister's abstracted face. Whatever happened, it had shaken her badly.

"Can you walk?"

Janat's face rotated toward her as though she forced herself to stay in this world. "Why?"

"To escape!"

Again, her sister seemed unable to comprehend. She stared off distractedly, as though trying to fix on the ghosts.

A wave of exhaustion came over Meg. She'd not yet recovered from her own magic. She wanted nothing more than to lie down here and sleep. But the archers were descending from the parapets now, several carrying stretchers or supporting the wounded.

Meg shook herself. She couldn't let her fatigue or Janat's . . .

melancholy interfere.

The portcullis rose and the archers, unstringing their bows, drew swords and ran into the city streets. A handful of soldiers and uprisers clashed in small scuffles, but the reistance was feeble. Where were the rebels who, when the night was young, had scaled the fortress walls?

Meg tugged Janat's hand, and they shuffled with the other refugees, following the sounds of rout.

Ranuat. She'd killed the magiel. The king's chancellor.

Meg pulled Janat's unresisting arm, and they tripped down the cobbled streets, unhindered, toward the main road to the city gate. A few citizens looked out their windows or came onto balconies, or even into the street in wonderment. Dead and dying—both rebels and soldiers—lay on the cobbles in a fine layer of ash, and a few kind souls tended to those in pain.

Magic.

The battle had turned on magic. A complete reversal.

Meg bit her lip as they walked, her breath coming ragged, her face streaming with tears.

How? Only the Ruby had this power. And it took a royal *and a magiel* to wield it.

Piss!

Piss! Piss! Piss! Piss!

She'd killed Wenid Col, by the Gods! He was the only magiel—

Unless—

Could some captured magiel, one destined to be burned for his Gods, have betrayed their cause? So near to the rebels' victory?

No.

It was not possible. Any magiel whose hand touched the Ruby in the presence of a royal, who found himself face-to-face with the One God in Heaven—*any* magiel—would plead for the denouncement of the king who'd taken the people's Gods from them, taken the people's lands. Such a prayer could not be blackmailed by threats of reprisal.

A sudden, magical turn of battle should have had the castle doors open to uprisers pouring *in.*

Meg took numb steps, her feet crunching the gravel of the road. She'd killed Wenid Col. Her mind could not get past this simple fact. His image superimposed itself on her vision. His pale face, staring eyes, gasping lips, body shuddering with convulsions.

She had murdered. And, for what?

She felt dirty, soiled, damaged.

For nothing.

A man before her tried blindly to crawl.

She knelt beside him and Janat stopped, too. Meg cast about for a bandage, a— No. He would be dead soon. Ghosts surrounded him. There was nothing she could do for him.

Nothing.

She had a Memory Loss. She placed a crystal in the man's mouth, and in a moment the pain in his eyes gave way to confusion, and then to sightlessness. She removed his death token from his collar and placed it on his tongue. His face relaxed in the peace of Heaven, and his body across her lap became limp.

She lifted her eyes to look at the street. So many. So many who would become ghosts, wandering in torment on this earth forever. How many had been able to place their death tokens on their tongues before death? How many, after almost two years of war, even *had* death tokens?

A woman wailed in the distance. She'd found a father, a son, a lover, or someone she loved.

Another man groaned.

Meg moved from soldier to rebel to soldier to rebel, tying tourniquets, improvising bandages, expending the last of her Memory Loss crystals, and administering death tokens. Janat followed mechanically, helping listlessly when directed, silent, tears streaming down her face.

Mourners, mothers, kin. Soldiers now moved from fallen to fallen, carrying some to wagons, giving the kindness of death and death tokens to others.

And—

—a silhouette.

No.

A form she never wanted to recognize.

Heartbeat choking her, Meg crawled over stones and gravel and dirt. A mound of rocks, the blocks fallen from the king's keep. Soldiers, and others, were moving chunks, stacking them. But there was a form buried beneath.

Janat, following numbly behind her, stood over the body as if cast in marble. Then she crumpled, fell to her knees and lifted that precious head to her lap, releasing a rage of tears.

Sulwyn.

Oh, Gods, Sulwyn, not Sulwyn.

A deep wound from his scalp above his forehead and across his cheek. Crusted.

A soldier pulled away another block and helped Janat roll him over.

There was another form beneath him.

—Rennika?

But Rennika *moved.*

"Rennika!" Meg breathed.

The man helped Janat hold Sulwyn's protecting body away from the girl's, and Meg felt her sister's head, her neck, her back. "Can you move?"

She blinked. "Meg?" she whispered. The fingers of one hand wriggled.

"Rennika!" Janat wept.

The soldiers working on the pile shifted the remainder of the rocks to free Sulwyn's legs and reposition him to unburden her.

"I was . . . trying—"

"Hush," Meg said.

Rennika pushed herself up, cried out and fell back. Blood smeared her clothes and bruises bloomed on her face and arms. "I think my wrist is hurt." She winced in pain as she rolled over and Meg cushioned her head in her lap.

"Lie still," Janat murmured, and she did.

"Sulwyn?" Rennika asked. A comprehension furrowed her brow. "Is he . . ."

Meg's throat closed. She nodded. Touched his cheek.

Skin, cold as the ground on which he lay.

Pulse, chest, still.

Janat touched the collar at his neck. Her face softened, just a little, and Meg knew. His death token was gone.

The day was cool and capricious, sun hidden by low cloud. Huwen Delarcan was beyond tired, but he rode out with a contingent of men nevertheless to view the results of battle. Vultures wheeled overhead and rats skittered from the corpses on their approach.

He directed his men to take rebels and soldiers alike to the healers, if there was hope of recovery; directed them to let the women bear their husbands' bodies away for burial if there was not. As much as it tore at him to do so, he needed to see the destruction that had been wrought in his name.

Couriers had begun to arrive from the nearest cities, all with the same message. Just before dawn, the tide of each rebel skirmish had turned. Every garrison—at least, those reporting so far—had won. Royal arrows flew true while rebel darts suddenly began to miss their marks. Royal swordsmen became energized while their opposites quailed.

A powerful magic had been called.

And Eamon had not been located, anywhere in the castle.

Nor had the Ruby.

But how had his brother petitioned the One God with no magiel?

Huwen had ordered the castle scoured for any anomaly, anything to explain what had happened.

Nothing. No clue.

Rain began to patter on the stinking field. There was no more Huwen could do here. He called his men to return to the carn. Work aplenty awaited him there.

As he turned toward the gate, a group of horsemen left the city, riding in his direction. Uther was at their head. Huwen rode to meet them.

"Sire," his half-brother reported. "I may have the answer to your question."

"Yes?"

Uther indicated they should ride a few paces away. Huwen directed his guard to retreat, and followed Uther to a deserted part of the battlefield.

The courier spoke in a low voice. "We've been scouring the castle to account for all courtiers and servants. Wenid had rooms set aside in the women's wing for five women and their babies. More women in a cell in the basement."

"What?"

"They are guarded and not permitted to leave their quarters and their garden."

"What does this have to do—"

Uther's features settled into a frown of disgust. "The women are all magiels and half-borns. The babies are capricious-skinned." He grimaced. "Bred to ensure the Ruby is never without a magiel."

Huwen's stomach sickened.

"There's more."

God.

"One of the mothers and her child are missing. The oldest child, three weeks old. Dannle, the child's name is." Uther's nostrils flared. "The night of the battle, just before dawn. Servants say Eamon took both."

Huwen's mind leapt to the obvious, and he recoiled. "Eamon used the Ruby to petition the One God to turn the battle—using a *baby*? Or the mother?"

Uther took a deep breath and raised one brow. "He dared not use the mother. Once in Heaven, he would have no way to control her prayer. Magiels have no love for Eamon. But the baby . . ." He shrugged. "All I can think is that if Eamon experiences Heaven like a magiel rather than a royal, he might also communicate with the Gods."

"That's—that's—"

Uther nodded.

"Beyond disgusting."

Huwen considered the implications. "If both Eamon and his magiel are subject to the wonder of Heaven, how can they return? It's the royal's place to bring the magiel back."

Uther shook his head. "A servant, perhaps? To break their grip on the prayer stone. Or . . ." He looked away momentarily.

"Or?"

"Exhaustion. Inability of their bodies to withstand so much . . . pleasure."

Huwen had seen how both Eamon and Wenid had changed, became reclusive, crippled.

"I'm assuming Eamon cloaked the mother and child. Likely, took some money and slipped out of the castle during the turn of battle. Maybe in a cart with a driver, if he was stricken by the madness of prayer."

"Was that possible?"

"Our men would let Eamon pass," Uther reasoned. "The field was confusion. The rebels were a chaos of undisciplined peasants. But such men, farmers and the like, might well have let—what they saw to be—an apparently injured man, wife, and child pass them by, particularly if they were dressed as peasants. If he could survive a stray arrow, perhaps with hidden armor, he might have done it. With money, he could buy horses and protection in Big Hill."

"And go to Midell." The country Father had given him. Only a few days' ride.

Uther let out a long breath. "One can only surmise."

"He's stolen the Ruby." Fear stabbed Huwen's gut. "It's treason."

His half-brother gave him a peculiar look. "Father gave him the Ruby. Last winter."

"Not to keep!"

Uther made no comment.

With the Ruby, and behind the ramparts of a keep, Eamon would be invulnerable. "He must not take sanctuary behind Theurgy's walls."

Uther gave a sharp nod.

"Send men. Immediately. By the One God, Uther, deliver him to me."

"He has a full day's start—"

"He's traveling with a baby and a woman. Catch him!"

The courier bowed his assent. "I will inform your general, and men will be dispatched with all haste," he said. "But Sire. With the magic of the Ruby at his disposal, do not expect your brother's return."

❀

Meg thanked the wind for slapping her face. It gave her opposition to push against as she marched back and forth with her sisters to the edge of the woods, collecting brittle branches and hauling them into the field. Yet, even this foul weather could not distract her from the visions that played again and again in her mind.

The uprisers' utter defeat.

Wenid's accusing body. Death token, fallen to the floor.

Sulwyn.

Oh, Sulwyn. Lying here as she piled the wood higher. She'd used her Confusion spell to steal a hand cart. She and her sisters brought his body here, to the far edge of the battlefield, near the woods.

Oddly clear light stretched over the land as the watery sun dipped below the cloud, approaching the mountains. Women searching for lost brothers and husbands and sons still wandered the fields, but the soldiers had gone. A few groups of gravediggers swung pickaxes and shovels at the icebound earth. A scatter of funeral pyres already burned.

Rennika would not stay put as she'd been told, but she carried what branches she could, one-handed. Janat, moving like an old woman, returned to the copse along the riverbank, snapping dead branches from the undersides of evergreen boughs. The overwhelming despair that had crippled her when Meg found her had lessened, but she would not speak of what had happened to her in the dungeon. Wenid was an evil man, was all she would say.

Meg had failed, and now she paid for her sin. Her hubris.

The men and women she had fought beside for the past year or more, her friends and brethren and family, were gone: dead or captured. Scattered to the four winds. Not through her doing, perhaps, yet the punishment was justified.

She wrapped her arms around a bundle of sticks and trudged back to the field. She lit the pyre, and Janat and Rennika joined her. Flames crackled, eating their way into the mound of sticks and logs around Sulwyn.

Meg put an arm around Janat's shoulder. "Janat, I'm so sorry, I'm so—" By Kyaju, if she could take back what she had done to her sister . . .

Janat turned and buried her head in Meg's neck, sudden sobs rising in convulsive waves to crash over her, into her, through her. And the anguish of Sulwyn's death bloomed in her again, and Rennika was beside them, holding them, weeping with them.

The wind blew, and the sun disappeared behind the hills. Flames snapped in the wind.

"You're alive," Janat whispered, lifting her head, laughing through her tears. "You're alive and Rennika's alive and we're here." She wiped her nose, and Meg laughed and Rennika laughed.

"Janat, I am so, so—"

Janat put her fingers across Meg's lips. "Don't. I'm sorry, too. I . . ."

Meg looked down at the man who had been Sulwyn. The man who once had helped three girls running for their lives. Who had loved them, each differently. Who had loved this land, even more. A man of peace in a world of war.

Janat pressed her lips together and shook her head, unable to speak, and Meg touched her forehead to hers.

"I . . ." Janat said. "I loved him. But I didn't . . . know . . . how to love him." She shrugged her inability to articulate her thought. "I was never the right . . . woman. I think . . ." She shrugged again. "You were."

Meg shook her head. "No." She reflected. "I thought I could be, but I was wrong."

They added wood from the vast pile. Rennika joined them in the warmth of the pyre.

"Did you . . ." Janat asked Rennika, and the quiet melancholy that had lingered with her all day returned. "Did you go to the tarn? At the equinox?"

"Meg and I did. There's no Amber," Rennika said.

"Dwyn and the uprisers have done what they could," Meg said. "With all the prayer stones but the Ruby destroyed, there can be no revolution."

Janat gazed into the flames. "What will we do?"

"Dwyn—King Gramaret," Meg clarified, "has a farm in Canyondell. Colm told me, with time, the king might heal from the arrow he took. We can stay with him. Work there."

"Then there's no going back," Janat said softly. "No soft beds. No balls or fine dresses." She gave a soft laugh. "You know, I've never seen any future but rags and running."

"No going back," Meg confirmed. "But there might be soft beds. Somewhere."

Rennika watched the enchantment of the flames. "We have to

live like worldlings now. And that's all right."

Janat peered at her as if not understanding.

"Rennika is sweet on a boy," Meg grinned, bumping her sister's shoulder with her own. "But she's right. It's up to us, and our own hard work."

Janat shrugged wistfully.

And when at long last the funeral fires had done their job, they walked together back to the rebel camp.

ACKNOWLEDGMENTS

I will always owe unending thanks to the members of the Imaginative Fiction Writers' Association and all those who helped me along the way with discussion and critiques, but particularly to my Shadow Ascension Workshop partners. More personally, I learned a great deal about the subject matter of this book from close friends, lovers, and family members. The topic has led me to plunge into research, including books (*The Anatomy of Addiction*, Mohammad, Akikur, 2016), films (*Risky Drinking*, HBO) and podcasts (*On Drugs*, CBC, Geoff Turner). I thank Lucas K. Law for his faith in me and his amazing support of this series. Finally and always, Don.

ABOUT THE AUTHOR

SUSAN FOREST is an award-winning author and editor of science fiction, fantasy, and horror. She has published over 25 short stories in Canadian and international publications. *Bursts of Fire*, the first in her seven-book series Addicted to Heaven, is not only a tale of rollicking adventure, but also an opportunity—one she appreciates—for an examination of the complex world of addictions. There is no family today that has not been touched by the heartache, stigma, struggles—and the often-unrecognized courage and hope— that underpin the illness of addiction. This motif is one Susan is humbled to explore with the aspiration of provoking dialogue, and the recognition of—and respect for—those whose battles are ongoing. Visit her online at www.speculative-fiction.ca. Follow the Addicted to Heaven series online at www.addictedtoheaven.com.

READER'S
GROUP GUIDE

Questions and Topics for Discussion

1. The central character of *Bursts of Fire*, Meg Falkyn, is only seventeen when she suddenly becomes responsible for her two younger sisters. In what ways does she make life easier for Janat and Rennika, and in what ways does she fail at this responsibility? What dreams do you think Meg had to give up? How was she able to deal with her own grief at the loss of her mother, and of everything she knew?

2. At times, Janat comes across as selfish. In what ways does her selfishness suggest she is caught in a cycle of grief that she can't get past? In what ways is she simply a spoiled "princess"? In what ways does she act generously?

3. As the youngest sister, Rennika adapts more easily to the changes in their circumstances than her sisters. What external factors, such as her relationship with her mother, her age, the way she is sheltered, and so forth, and what internal factors, such as her personality and her appearance, help her to embrace the life of a peasant?

4. Huwen moves from being certain of his world and his role within it, to very uncertain. What circumstances cause him to question the morality of unfolding events? How does his relationship with his father change as Huwen ages?

5. Eamon behaves in ways that are counter intuitive for a child: he engages in suicidal acts, sabotages his attempts at love, and withdraws from his family and friends. Why?

6. Wenid can be seen as a narrow, controlling individual, but how are his actions driven by what he considers to be the good of Shangril?

7. Uther occupies an unusual role in his family. How does his position as eldest bastard son to the High King give him more freedom to move in different social circles than other characters in the book? In what ways does his personality limit him in exploiting this niche? How was his personality shaped by his birthright and rearing? How important is his mother in his life?

8. Magic can be a powerful tool in Shangril. In what ways is it used for good, and in what ways is it misused? Why is suppression of magic difficult for royal forces to control? How is steam technology similar to magic?

9. Central to the political conflict in Shangril is power over who has access to death tokens. What are these, where do they come from, how are they used, and what is their significance? How is the afterlife more important to people of Shangril than their present lives?

10. Sulwyn describes a world in which a rising middle class of artisans and merchants are called upon by local kings for advice. How does this changing political and economic structure threaten Ormond? How much of this threat motivates Wenid in his advice to the High King?

11. Ormond precipitates the events of *Bursts of Fire* through bringing his son (his *second* legitimate son, not his heir) back from the dead. Is this an act of love, an act of love gone wrong, or an act of selfishness? How is his commitment to Eamon a misuse of power and a betrayal of his positon as king of Arcan? Should he have let his son die?

12. Ormond's armies are never large enough to take on the combined might of the six other nations of Shangril, and yet he is surprisingly successful. How is he able to accomplish this feat? What modern world events mirror this military action?

How does fear of war in today's world allow governments to force their will on others (neighboring countries; their own citizens)? How much of this condition is related to denial, lack of foresight, desire to maintain the status-quo or other factors? Does this mean we should stop seeking peaceful solutions?

13. Because Wenid, and by extension Ormond, fear the power of magiels, magic-users are persecuted. How is it possible for people with no magical power to suppress those who are able to use magic? What modern parallels do you see to this process? How are people muzzled by using their own psyches against them?

14. The story ends with the three sisters' reunion. With this comes a change in their relationships with one another, and their understandings of their world and their place within it. At the same time, neither they nor the rebels have achieved a defeat of the High King. In what ways would more closure be satisfying? In what ways is the open-endedness of this book realistic?

15. *Bursts of Fire* is Book 1 of the Addicted to Heaven series, and as such, deals with some aspects of addictions. Wenid's use of glim on Gweddien and Janat are obvious examples, but what other addictive substances and behaviors are evident in the book?

16. In what ways do the characters in the book take a moral view substance use? For instance, in what ways is substance use celebratory, accepted and encouraged, and in what ways is it condemned? How closely does this reflect the modern world?

17. In Shangril, there is no law against the use of substances (alcohol, glim, magical herbs, etc.). They are used for cooking, healing, recreation, and magic. How is this system functional, and what reasons might there be to regulate it? Does the answer to this question change when substances can be concentrated and intensified, as magiels do in Shangril, and as chemists do in our world?

Why Mental Health & Anti-Discrimination Resources?

There is nothing better than cracking open an epic fantasy. Swords. Sorcery. Adventure! That was my inspiration when I sat down to write this series: to create a joyous, terrifying escape from everyday life. But . . . deeper ideas crept in. Why? Well first, in the best adventure stories, characters must care deeply about things: political situations, societal conditions, personal troubles. If a character is going to fight *and possibly die* for something, that "something" must be worthwhile. But there was another process operating. As I learned when working with youth at risk, counselling does not need to prod people, precisely because whatever is on a person's mind will rise to the surface. So, too, with writing: ideas, not always fully conscious, were making their way into my fiction.

So it was, when I was discussing the Addicted to Heaven series with Laksa Media's publisher, Lucas K. Law, he asked me a very important question: what is your book about? *Really* about? Not three girls running for their lives, but underneath? What were the political, societal, and personal issues at the core of the story? And it took one blink for me to respond. Addictions.

Addictions are one type of mental illness, which is present in every family. Mine is no exception.

Alcohol is complex. Although it has taken the lives, life savings, and personal relations of family members and lovers, it has also been at the center of celebrations, good times, and significant rites of passage in my life. Our society and history (political and cultural) are steeped in this substance, for both good and ill. Scientists and the medical system still have no definitive answers about how to manage alcoholism and other substance use problems, though recent research has made steps toward better understanding.

And addictions cannot be viewed in isolation from the spectrum of mental and emotional functioning. My world, too, has been affected by multiple forms of discrimination, including bullying, discrimination based on sexual orientation, discrimination based on disabilities, and the stigma of suicide. Society attempts to function in a mechanistic manner, with expectations around time, reliability, and social norms, that are taboo to break. Square pegs struggle mightily to fit into round holes, and as a society we often view those square pegs as morally deficient. That hurts. Not only emotionally, but it hurts the individual's ability to live a fulfilling life.

Hence the importance of opening conversation. Recognition that we are not alone, that all individuals, families, and societies face these issues, provides relief and support in itself; but further, it allows dialogue to begin. Talking about issues can lead to the political will to support governments that fund research and programs. It can provide creative solutions to people struggling with their own health concerns and recognize the daily courage of those facing the uphill battle of addictions. Or, in the case of Laksa Media books, it can provide specific resources, such as the following Appendix to Mental Health and Anti-Discrimination Resources. But responsibility does not end with one half of the conversation. Look through the Appendix following. If you have any doubts about a situation in your life, if you are wondering, *Is this normal, or is it a problem?* don't wait for it to progress. Prevention is easier than recovery. Check out the resources, either here, or through your community, your doctor, or your pastor. A dialogue is not a dialogue without a response.

And—what better way to begin this dialogue than through epic fantasy?

—Susan Forest, Calgary, Canada, 2019

LEARN HOW TO MANAGE YOUR STRESS . . .
LEARN DAILY MINDFULNESS.

APPENDIX:
MENTAL HEALTH RESOURCES
AND
ANTI-DISCRIMINATION
RESOURCES

Because of the dynamic nature of the internet, any telephone numbers, web addresses or links provided in this section may have changed since the publication of this book and may no longer be valid.

A listing in the Appendix doesn't mean it is an endorsement from Laksa Media Groups Inc., publisher, editors, authors and/or those involved in this series project. Its listing here is a means to disseminate information to the readers to get additional materials for further investigation or knowledge.

RESPITE IS KEY TO YOUR WELLBEING.
GIVE YOURSELF A BREAK . . .

How is your Mental Health? Do you think you have experienced one or more of the following recently?

- More Stress than Before
- Grief
- Separation and Divorce
- Feelings of Violence
- Suicidal Thoughts
- Self Injury
- Excessive or Unexplained Anxiety
- Obsession or Compulsion
- Paranoia, Phobias or Panics
- Post-Traumatic Stress
- Depression
- Bi-polar
- Postpartum Depression
- Eating Disorders
- Schizophrenia
- Addictions
- Mood Disorders
- Personality Disorders
- Learning Disabilities

MENTAL HEALTH SCREENING TOOLS

More information:
https://screening.mentalhealthamerica.net/screening-tools

- The Depression Screen is most appropriate for individuals who are feeling overwhelming sadness.
- The Anxiety Screen will help if you feel that worry and fear affect your day to day life.
- The Bipolar Screen is intended to support individuals who have mood swings - or unusual shifts in mood and energy.
- The PTSD (Post Traumatic Stress Disorder) Screen is best taken by those who are bothered by a traumatic life event.
- The Alcohol or Substance Use Screen will help determine if your use of alcohol or drugs is an area to address.
- The Youth Screen is for young people (age 11-17) who are concerned that their emotions, attention, or behaviours might be signs of a problem.
- The Parent Screen is for parents of young people to determine if their child's emotions, attention, or behaviours might be signs of a problem.
- The Psychosis Screen is for young people (age 12-35) who feel like their brain is playing tricks on them (seeing, hearing or believing things that don't seem real or quite right).
- Eating Disorder Test is to explore eating-related concerns which may impact your physical health and overall well-being.
- Work Health Survey is for exploring how healthy or unhealthy your work environment is.
- Worried about Your Child--Symptom Checker: **https://childmind.org/symptomchecker/**

10 Ways to Look after Your Mental Health
(source: www.mentalhealthamerica.net/live-your-life-well)

1. Connect with Others
2. Stay Positive
3. Get Physically Active
4. Help Others
5. Get Enough Sleep
6. Create Joy and Satisfaction
7. Eat Well
8. Take Care of Your Spirit
9. Deal Better with Hard Times
10. Get Professional Help if You Need It

MENTAL HEALTH RESOURCES & INFORMATION

If you or someone you know is struggling with mental illness, please consult a doctor or a healthcare professional in your community.

Below is not a comprehensive information listing, but it is a good start to get more information on mental health/illness.

Emergency Phone Number

If you or someone is in crisis or may be at risk of harming himself/herself or someone else, please call your national Emergency Phone Number immediately.

Canada	911
United States	911
United Kingdom	999 or 112
Ireland	999 or 112
EU	112
Australia	000
New Zealand	111

Canada

- To locate your local Canadian Mental Health Association: **www.cmha.ca**
- Specifically for children and young people (aged 5-20), call Kids Help Phone's 24-hour confidential phone line at **1-800-668-6868** English or French. More information online: **kidshelpphone.ca**
- There are a number of resource materials and list of organizations that you can reach out to on the Bell Let's Talk website: **http://letstalk.bell.ca/en/get-help/**
- Mental Health & Addiction Information A-Z (Centre for Addiction and Mental Health): **https://www.camh.ca/en/ health-info/mental-illness-and-addiction-index**
- Canadian Coalition for Seniors' Mental Health: **http://ccsmh.ca**
- List of local crisis centres (Canadian Centre for Suicide Prevention): **http://suicideprevention.ca/need-help**
- The Alex—Changing Health, Changing Lives: **www.thealex.ca**

United States

- National Suicide Prevention Hotline: **1-800-273-TALK** or **1-800-273-8255**
- For more mental health information: **www.mentalhealthamerica.net/mental-health-information**

United Kingdom

- The Samaritans (**www.samaritans.org**) offers emotional support 24 hours a day--get in touch with them: **116-123**.
- A to Z of Mental Health: **http://www.mentalhealth.org.uk/a-to-z**
- Free Mental Health Podcasts: **https://www.mentalhealth.org.uk/podcasts-and-videos**

Ireland

- The Samaritans (**www.samaritans.org**) offers emotional support 24 hours a day--get in touch with them: **116-123**.
- Childline Helpline (**https://www.childline.ie**): Confidential for young people (under 18). Phone: **1-800-66-66-66**
- For more mental health information: **www.mentalhealthireland.ie**

Australia

- Helplines, websites and government mental health services for Australia: **mhaustralia.org/need-help**
- Kids Helpline: Confidential and anonymous, telephone and online counselling service specifically for young people aged between 5 and 25. Phone: **1800-55-1800** or visit **www.kidshelp.com.au**
- Lifeline: 24 hour telephone counselling service. Phone: **13-11-14** or visit **www.lifeline.org.au**

New Zealand

- Helplines, websites and government mental health services for New Zealand: **www.mentalhealth.org.nz/get-help/in-crisis/helplines**
- Youthline (for young people under 25): **0800-376-633**. More information online: **http://www.youthline.co.nz**
- Lifeline: **0800-543-354** or **(09) 5222-999** within Auckland
- Suicide Crisis Helpline: **0508-828-865** (0508-TAUTOKO)

International

- Mental Health & Psychosocial Support: International Medical Corps (**https://internationalmedicalcorps.org/program/mental-health-psychosocial-support/**)
- International Association for Youth Mental Health (**https://www.iaymh.org/need-help/**)

- Crisis Helpline for Various Countries: **https://yourlifecounts. org/find-help/**
- Emergency Number for Various Countries: **http://www. suicidestop.com/worldwide_emergency_numbers.html**
- Suicide Crisis Helpline for Various Countries: **https:// en.wikipedia.org/wiki/List_of_suicide_crisis_lines http://www.suicidestop.com/call_a_hotline.html**

ANTI-DISCRIMINATION RESOURCES

Discrimination is an action or a decision that treats a person or a group negatively for reasons such as:

- national or ethnic origin
- colour
- religion
- age
- sex
- sexual orientation
- marital status
- family status
- disability

What is Discrimination? For more information (Canadian Human Rights Commission): **https://www.chrc-ccdp.gc.ca/eng/content/ what-discrimination**

Canada

- Promoting Relationship & Eliminating Violence Network (Prevnet): Information on bullying, resources on bullying and prevention at **http://www.prevnet.ca**
- List of Crisis Centres in Canada: **http://suicideprevention.ca/ need-help**
- Free LifeLine App (Apple & Android): **http://thelifelinecanada. ca/lifeline-canada-foundation/lifeline-app**

United States

- Cyberbullying Research Center: Facts, Information, Blogs, and Resources at **http://cyberbullying.org/resources**
- The **Crisis Text Line** is a not-for-profit organization providing free crisis intervention via SMS message. The organization's services are available 24 hours a day every day, throughout the US by texting **741741**.

United Kingdom

- Bullying UK Helpline: confidential and free helpline service (Phone: **0808-800-2222**). Information, advices and resources at **http://www.bullying.co.uk**
- Anti-Bullying Alliances: Resources and advices at **https://www. anti-bullyingalliance.org.uk/tools-information**

Australia

- Bullying. No Way! **https://bullyingnoway.gov.au**

Books:

The Bullying Workbook for Teens: Activities to Help You Deal with Social Aggression and Cyberbullying (by Raychelle Cassada Lohmann and Julia V. Taylor) - Instant Help; Workbook edition – ISBN: 978-1608824502

Violence against Queer People: Race, Class, Gender, and the Persistence of Anti-LGBT Discrimination (by Doug Meyer) - Rutgers University Press – ISBN: 978-0813573151

The Mindfulness Workbook for Addiction: A Guide to Coping with the Grief, Stress and Anger that Trigger Addictive Behaviors (by Rebecca E. Williams and Julie S. Kraft) - New Harbinger Publications; Csm Wkb edition – ISBN: 978-1608823406

PAYING FORWARD, GIVING BACK

READ FOR A CAUSE
WRITE FOR A CAUSE
HELP A CAUSE

MISSION:

Laksa Media Groups Inc. publishes issues-related general audience and literary experimental fiction and narrative non-fiction books. Our mission is to create opportunities to 'pay forward' and 'give back' through our publishing program. Our tag line is Read for a Cause, Write for a Cause, Help a Cause.

A portion of our net revenue from each book project goes to support a charitable organization, project or event. We do not deal with any charity that promotes politics, religions, discrimination, crime, hate and inequality.

The charitable causes dear to our hearts are literacy, education, public libraries, elder care, mental health, affordable housing, and prevention of abuse or bullying.

HELP US CHANGE THE WORLD, ONE BOOK AT A TIME

laksamedia.com

Laksa Anthology Series:
Speculative Fiction

The anthologies in this series have been recommended by *Publishers Weekly, Booklist, Kirkus Reviews, Library Journal, School Library Journal, Locus, Foreword Reviews,* and *Quill & Quire.*

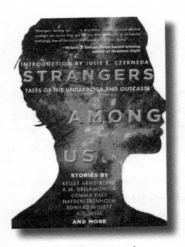

Benefit: Canadian Mental Health Association

STRANGERS AMONG US
Tales of the Underdogs and Outcasts
Edited by Susan Forest and Lucas K. Law

2017 (Canadian SF&F) Aurora Award winner, 2017 Alberta Book Publishing Award winner

There's a delicate balance between mental health and mental illness.

Original Stories by Kelley Armstrong, Suzanne Church, A.M. Dellamonica, Gemma Files, James Alan Gardner, Bev Geddes, Erika Holt, Tyler Keevil, Rich Larson, Derwin Mak, Mahtab Narsimhan, Sherry Peters, Ursula Pflug, Robert Runté, Lorina Stephens, Amanda Sun, Hayden Trenholm, Edward Willett , A.C. Wise, and Julie E. Czerneda (Introduction)

Benefit: Canadian Mental Health Association

THE SUM OF US
Tales of the Bonded and Bound
Edited by Susan Forest and Lucas K. Law

2018 (Canadian SF&F) Aurora Award winner, 2018 Alberta Book Publishing Award finalist

The greatest gift to us is caring. What would the world be like without someone to care for or to care with?

Original stories by Colleen Anderson, Charlotte Ashley, Brenda Cooper, Ian Creasey, A.M. Dellamonica, Bev Geddes, Claire Humphrey, Sandra Kasturi, Tyler Keevil, Juliet Marillier, Matt Moore, Heather Osborne, Nisi Shawl, Alex Shvartsman, Kate Story, Karina Sumner-Smith, Amanda Sun, Hayden Trenholm, James Van Pelt, Liz Westbrook-Trenholm, Edward Willett , Christie Yant, Caroline M. Yoachim, and Dominik Parisien (Introduction)

Laksa Anthology Series:
Speculative Fiction

The anthologies in this series have been recommended by *Publishers Weekly, Booklist, Kirkus Reviews, Library Journal, School Library Journal, Locus, Foreword Reviews,* and *Quill & Quire.*

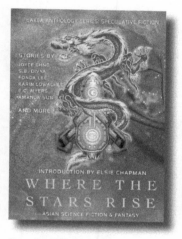

Benefit: Kids Help Phone

WHERE THE STARS RISE
Asian Science Fiction & Fantasy
Edited by Lucas K. Law and Derwin Mak

2018 (Canadian SF&F) Aurora Award finalist, 2018 Alberta Book Publishing Award winner

Take a journey through Asia and beyond to explore identities, belonging, and choices.

Original stories by Anne Carly Abad, Deepak Bharathan, Joyce Chng, Miki Dare, S.B. Divya, Pamela Q. Fernandes, Calvin D. Jim, Minsoo Kang, Fonda Lee, Gabriela Lee, Karin Lowachee, Rati Mehrotra, E.C. Myers, Tony Pi, Angela Yuriko Smith, Priya Sridhar, Amanda Sun, Naru Dames Sundar, Jeremy Szal, Regina Kanyu Wang (translated by Shaoyan Hu), Diana Xin, Melissa Yuan-Innes, Ruhan Zhao, and Elsie Chapman (Introduction)

Benefit: Mood Disorders Association & Alex Community Food Centre

SHADES WITHIN US
Tales of Migrations and Fractured Borders
Edited by Susan Forest and Lucas K. Law

Come and discover the fractured borders of human migration to examine the dreams, struggles, and triumphs of those who choose or are forced to leave home and familiar places.

Original stories by Vanessa Cardui, Elsie Chapman, Kate Heartfield, S.L. Huang, Tyler Keevil, Matthew Kressel, Rich Larson, Tonya Liburd, Karin Lowachee, Seanan McGuire, Brent Nichols, Julie Nováková, Heather Osborne, Sarah Raughley, Alex Shvartsman, Amanda Sun, Jeremy Szal, Hayden Trenholm, Liz Westbrook-Trenholm, Christie Yant & Alvaro Zinos-Amaro, and Eric Choi & Gillian Clinton (Introduction)

If you like *Bursts of Fire* or any of Laksa's anthologies, please write a review or recommend the book to your public and school libraries.

Thank you for supporting our projects, Canadian Mental Health Association, Kids Help Phone, Mood Disorders Association, and The Alex: Changing Health, Changing Lives.

**HELP US TO CHANGE THE WORLD,
ONE BOOK AT A TIME**

IT'S A DELICATE BALANCE BETWEEN MENTAL HEALTH
AND MENTAL ILLNESS . . .

BE ALERT!

Want to know more about *Bursts of Fire* and Addicted to Heaven?
www.addictedtoheaven.com

Want to know more about our projects?
Sign up for our newsletters at **laksamedia.com**

LAKSA MEDIA GROUPS INC.
www.laksamedia.com

CPSIA information can be obtained
at www.ICGtesting.com
Printed in the USA
LVHW111423250719
625327LV00002B/300/P